THE MORTEM CYCLE
DEATH HOUSE
DEATH SHIP
DEATH BEYOND
DEATH CUISINE

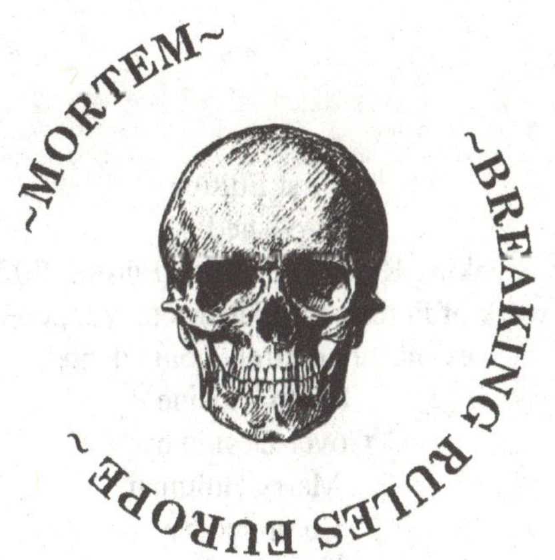

First Edition
Published by
Breaking Rules Publishing Europe, 2021.
This is a work of fiction. Similarities to real people, places,or
events are entirely coincidental.
Death Cuisine
Cover Design by
C. Marry Hultman
Compiled by
Tim Mendees
978-91-986841-8-6

DEATH CUISINE

Horror Anthology & Cookbook
by Divers Hands

MENU

INTRODUCTION

TIM MENDEES

Cooking can be murder. Just ask any chef, and they will tell you. Of course, they don't mean it literally, but...

The pressures of being a chef are well documented, as I know only too well. When I left school at sixteen, I went straight into working in a busy pub kitchen while doing day release at Macclesfield college for my City and Guilds. What followed was well over two decades of split shifts, exhaustion and stress. And then there were the injuries...

Over my career, I saw things that would make you wince. One guy I worked with managed to shave off the tips of his fingers on his right hand with a bacon slicer. Another lost two fingers to a wayward meat cleaver. Me? I had both of my feet deep-fried.

One evening, we had the deep cleaners in to clean out the extraction system. At some point, one of the legs on a free-standing deep fat fryer got damaged. Unfortunately, they forgot to mention this to me. At the end of my shift the following day, I pulled out the oven to sweep behind it, and the fryer fell onto me, tipping 190-degree vegetable oil down both boots. To say it was painful would be a massive understatement.

As you would imagine, over the years, I've had more cuts and burns than you could shake a rolling pin at. I even got a knife stuck in the knuckle of my left hand. But that was by far the worst kitchen-related injury I ever experienced. To rub salt in the wounds, the restaurant had a record number of complaints that night from outraged diners at the chef's excessive use of foul language! Well, I don't think, "golly gosh, that was a wee bit warm" would suffice, do you?

Yet, despite all the gallons of blood I've seen spilt over the gleaming stainless-steel worktops over the years. I never saw an actual murder. That is all about to change.

When asked if I had any ideas for an invite-only project, I instantly thought of doing a horror cookbook. I've had the pleasure of appearing in one before, and I leapt at the opportunity to put one together. The idea was simple. Assemble a team of authors whose work I admire and task them with not only writing a story featuring food but also get them to supply an accompanying recipe. The idea is that after reading about some hellish culinary creations, you can toddle off to your kitchen and create them. With some slight alterations to the ingredients, of course.

I am delighted to present a smorgasbord of horror and tasty treats. The range of recipes is just as varied as the stories themselves. We have everything from cosmic horror, weird fiction and Egyptology all the way to twisted Arthurian Legends and murderous Fae. The culinary delights cover a wide variety of cultures and styles. We have Japanese, Traditional English, Dutch, you name it. There are vegetarian and vegan dishes as well as a mixture of sweet and savoury. Each one of them is delicious.

Without further ado, it's time for you to turn the pages and tuck in. I sincerely hope that your next meal won't be your last.

Tim Mendees
31/08/2021

THE BUZZ IN THE NEIGHBOURHOOD

NEEN COHEN

Wrinkling my nose, I force the last of the garlic into submission. I press it against the wooden chopping board with the side of the knife. My warped reflection gleams back at me and a smile pulls at the edges of my lips.

Each movement the human flesh skin I wear over my true form tears a little more. But just a little longer. I taste the beads of blood at the corners of my mouth.

Oh, how I ache to be free.

'Shhhh.' I hush to the buzz beneath the skin as to a small child woken from a nightmare. The pull and desire to shed its stinking prison grows with each intake of rank breath. The decaying odour rankles inside of me and I cannot understand how humans survive as they do, when they cannot smell. They have not smelt it on me yet, but that will be the least of their concerns by the end of the evening.

I scrape the crushed garlic into two small ceramic bowls. White of course.

I scoff at the dull light that is fighting its way through the grey clouds that overshadow the back yard. The back wall is a sliding door of glass, as though the view of the flowers, of the garden would make up for the sterile whiteness inside.

Everything was so pristine. I felt the tear again as the left side of my top lip sneered in disgust at the space surrounding me. It was suffocating.

An open floor plan, that's what they called it.

I scoff as I jab the beetroot with a fork. It continues boiling on the stove, not quite soft enough yet. I smile as the stained water bubbles out of the pot and splashes maroon dribbles down the stark white splash back tiles.

There were white tiles everywhere in this kitchen and dining room area. Large white tiles that hurt this body's heels. The Caesar stone island bench is scattered with colour thanks to the recipe I found in the dead man's cookbook.

At least these humans have that going for them.

Their food can be incredible. Tonight's will be a last feast to revel in.

Bunches of dill overtake the sharp tang of the garlic.

Savouring each cut from my knife as it releases more of the smell, my smile strains against the skin. The true smell of green washes over my sensors, teasing my true body to buzzing. I breathe deeply as the sound of the bubbling water continues to splash colour over the stove top and wall tiles.

Metal presses down on the chopping board as I slice and the rhythm of bubbling water echoes and joins into the music. My hips move back and forth, and I lose myself in the dance of my sensors.

'Fuck!'

The curse slips out as the sharp edge of the knife slashes into the soft flesh of the human suit. But there is also a strange noise I can't place. And then it is gone. I knew connecting the nerve endings to my own was a bad idea, but it also makes for an easier acceptance into their world. They were stupid creatures, but their subconscious warned them of me, even when they didn't understand why.

It was my job to make the difference as subtle as possible. Something they cannot pinpoint, something they will shake off in their own self-deprecating way.

Which was all well and good but damn the cut hurts.

Sucking at the blood that spills quickly from the tip of the finger, I taste the hot sting of metallic salt. I look down at the bowl of Greek yoghurt and smile as the dark red drops slowly seep into the whiteness. They won't taste it. Their taste buds are almost as useless as their sense of smell.

After a quick trip to the bathroom to riffle for a packet of the plastic sticky strips, I wrap up the wound, still stunned by the sting that continues.

All will be worth it in the end.

The beetroot is tender and slightly faded.

I drain the chunks and let them cool in the silver strainer that sits in the even shinier silver sink.

Pulling the box grater toward me and placing its rubber grips onto a larger wooden cutting board, I begin to peel the hot chunks. The sting in the tips of the flesh suit is a thrill that runs through me from the stench of chemicals in the platinum blonde hair, down to the tips of the bare toes that wriggle far too often.

It takes a long time to peel the beetroot, but I dance along to the sound of a hum that vibrates beneath the flesh.

I dump a third of the wet strands of red beetroot into the Greek yoghurt. My blood disappears into the mixture. I open a bottle of red wine vinegar and splash a generous amount in, along with a small dash of olive oil. The small ceramic bowl of garlic taunts me. With my little finger I taste the concoction and close my eyes against the bliss that dances on my tongue. Whoever made this recipe, with its handwritten notes scrawled up the side and different words underlined, knew their stuff.

I scrape out the smooshed white toxic stench and mix in through the tzatziki dip.

Another dip of my pinkie finger and I concede.

It is perfect. The tang of my blood is barely detectable even to myself.

I slide the bowl into the fridge and grab the cheeses and add them to the colours that are spread over the bench. Red beetroot, green dill, dirty white of breadcrumbs, and the smooth cream shell of the egg. A veritable rainbow of flavours.

After a quick rinse of the grater, I start with the cheeses and let them sit on top of the strands of beetroot waiting where I left them on the chopping board. On contact, the red begins to seep into the white of the feta and the yellow of the cheddar.

The largest bowl I pull from the cupboard is a surprising orange, a nice contract to the white and silver.

I put the beetroot and cheeses in, sliding off the prepped ingredients with the blunt side of the knife. Metal scrapes against the wood. With a sharp crack on the edge of the orange bowl, the eggshell shatters spilling it's clear and yellow content into the middle. I stare at the colours and breath in the flavours and smells, all merging and changing as they caress each other. Dumping the breadcrumbs on top I use my hands, now stained with the dark maroon of the beetroot skin, to mix and combine. It's a sensation that has me moaning and closing my eyes. Until I remember.

The garlic.

I dump the contents of the second ceramic bowl and then throw it and the smaller bowl into the stainless-steel sink. The sound of them breaking into shards upon impact at the bottom makes me laugh out loud.

It doesn't take long to roll the mixture into palm sized balls, roll them in flour and lay them on the plate, curving inward toward the centre, like the shell of a snail.

I slip them into the fridge, as the scrawl in the margins suggests.

The long loaf of bread has a crunchy layer with soft whiteness inside as I cut it into generous slices and turn on the grill to heat.

I wander into the bathroom again.

Not as terrible in its starkness as the kitchen. At least, how the kitchen had begun. But it is not that much better.

White and dark brown tiles, almost black at certain angles. Especially with the darkness that has converged further over the house. I look out the small window and take a deep inhale of the rain in the air. It won't be long now, until it pours down and washes away the vitriol of this neighbour. The toxic smell, and deadly chemicals will run down their drains and free my people once again.

But the 300 bodies, the 300 corpses that were found when I arrived.

Tonight, those responsible will pay the price.

Blood beads in the cracks around the flesh suits lips. I pull out the lipstick from the small bag she had been carrying when we met. I run it over the lips, hissing at the sting as it touches and blends with the chemical colours.

It will do, the light from the oncoming storm is my willing accomplice.

Once they are inside, it no longer matters.

I hear the small buzz as I return to the kitchen. On one of the slices of bread is a bee. He is small, not much more than a child. He stops, freezes as he senses the humanity encroaching on his awareness. Three eyes swivel toward me.

'Hush, it's ok son. Soon they will all pay the price. But not yet.'

I slide my finger beneath his legs, the tickle on skin so light. Outside I place him on the glass round table that sits surrounded by chairs and has a half-filled ash tray. Disgusting habit. These vile creates are nothing but creators of bad smells and vile poisons.

'Not long. I promise.'

I close the glass door and black out the vile smell of the outdoors. He flies away and I feel heavy and weighted by this skin.

I ache for freedom.

But my kin must be avenged.

Oil heats and hisses when I place rolled balls of mixture into the warmed pan. Pressing down with the egg flip, the sizzle increases, and hot oil spits up against my fingertips. I savour the sensation of pain.

Its mind, this human's mind, was not strong, but as I get closer to my revenge, I learn it was not as weak as I first thought. Oh, she succumbed easily enough, but now it fights me. The sound I had heard when the knife sliced through my fingertip, I can place it now. It was her cheer.

'Oooh clever little human. But you are too late.'

I slide the bread into the grill, beside the cooked keftedes as they stay warm. The limits of the human's small frypan.

Three plates, white of course. I roll my eyes.

How much has this shell and its disgruntled previous occupant seeped into my movements?

White bowls sit on white plates, but I console myself with the light red hue of the dip I load each bowl up with. Around each bowl I lay toasted slices of the bread, the golden-brown showing promises of crunch and flavour.

On time, naturally. In this perfect display of the unachievable construct of humanity, these humans show up exactly when they are supposed to. The bell chimes through the house, invading my sway and attention on the splatters of colour I have christened this blank canvas of a kitchen with.

The floor tiles are alive with dropped greens, the dark of dill and the lighter rings of spring onion. What could be mistaken for blood splatters dribbles here and there, a portent for the future? I hope so. I feel the tug at my lips, the pull and threat of tearing.

Dumping the apron, black of course, on the floor of the kitchen, among the debris and powder of breadcrumbs and flour I head to the door.

'Hi, you must be Laura and Mike.' I hold out my hand and the grip I receive is harder than I had expected. She has long fingers, memories of piano lessons and being fucked by this splendid specimen rush through me and I barely resist a sharp intake of breath. My legs quiver beneath me as I force down a suddenly painful gulp.

'Susan?' Her mouth drops, the perfect presentation faltering.

'Hi. I didn't realise you —'

'You're Alix's niece?' thankfully the woman cuts me off. What was I going to say? *I didn't realise you knew this flesh suit.*

'Ah, yes.' I smile and offer my hand to the brother.

That's right. I had the man, this Alix, write the invitation to his neighbours. I was the niece; I was part of tonight's dinner party. What a strange culture these humans had. Such separate connections with blood and what a limited concept of family.

'Where is Alix?' Mark doesn't seem concerned as he gives a short handshake before stifling a yawn.

My nostrils flare at the stench on his breath and I turn my face as I throw my arm wide, displaying the houses internal paleness. Just as Alix had, when he believed me to be a prejudge for the upcoming neighbourhood event.

'He's just having a small lay down. He will be out shortly. But we can get started on the entrée.'

'Ok.' Laura is sceptical, her eyes narrow on me.

They nod and walk deeper inside; she can narrow her eyes all she wants.

Like a fly in a web. I close the door and turn the silver key in the lock before hanging it up on the hook beside the stained wood.

Laura avoids my eyes as I overtake the procession into the kitchen and dining room. I feel the warmth in the flesh of the human suit's skin.

How interesting these humans were, so flooded with hormones, how did they manage to achieve a single thing. Let alone the massacre of 300 of my kind in a mere afternoon.

Arousal turns to anger and strangely the mix makes me want to take those legs and wrap them around myself even more.

Honestly, how do these humans function?

I see the shared look between brother and sister as they follow me past the open kitchen and survey my colourful destruction in stark contrast to its usual blandness. If only they would look closer to see just how many colours and dangers rest inside this house.

But soon enough for that.

My stomach rumbles quietly as I wait for them to sit.

Across from each other they take their places. Leaving the head and foot to myself and my dear uncle.

I place the plates on the stark white tablecloth before collecting my own plate and taking the seat at the head of the table.

'This smells great.'

Better than you! I smile and nod. His stench is wrong. Very wrong. I have taken residence in human suits before, when the need has arisen for my attendance to deal with the inhumanity of these creatures. But this man, this Mark. There is a sickness that wafts from his very skin. It curls up inside me. The real me wants nothing more than to pull my nerves away from this human suit so I smell nothing more than her own decay.

That's the stench I rear from, a stench of death, almost. A falseness to his existence.

'Thank you.'

I smear the dip over a slice of the bread. The chunks and colours of the dill seep through the tangy red and I bite, savouring the crunch and tang. The garlic is minimal, too much, but the other flavours, fused in the chill of cold and time dance on my tongue.

'This is divine.' Her voice drips with surprise and lust. For this body or the food? It doesn't matter. Despite the skin suits reaction, tonight was about so much more than those carnal desires.

'So,' I swallow my latest bite and smile small and sharp, 'my uncle tells me there is a flower parade happening soon?'

'Oh great.' Mike rolls his eyes and Laura narrows her own gaze at him. He ignores her and looks out the glass doors to the back yard. It is dark, darker than it should be, and the smell of rain permeates through the small cracks of the walls and glass.

'It's going to rain.' There is no emotion in his voice.

'Good.' And far too much in her own.

'Good for the flower festival then?' I ask, curious about the dynamic or brother and sister, despite myself.

'Yes, it's great for the gardens. I'm the head of the festival this year and I am determined our street will finally beat Lovers Lane. I mean really,' She takes a bite of dip laden bread, pushes the food into her cheek and continues to talk. 'who lets their street be named Lovers Lane. They tried to name Sheridan Road, this road, Beehive Drive. I put my foot down and tadah.'

Her shoulders push back further, and she takes another bite of the entrée. Mark has almost cleaned up his own bowl and plate and despite my anger, a bubbling warmth spreads through my chest.

'Would you like more?' I ask as Mark shoves the last bit of toast in his mouth and I suspect if not asked he may have begun to lick the bowl clean.

'If the main course is anything like that, I suppose I can refrain.' He smiles and I notice the yellow tinge in the whites of his eyes.

Ahhh, He really is dying.

For a moment my smile freezes.

No, it will not take my pleasure away.

'Well, we mustn't have you waiting any longer.' I turn to Laura as the first drops of rain begin to patter on the tin roof above our heads, 'are you ready for the main?'

'Shouldn't we wait for Alix? I do need to talk to him about the festival.' Laura's whine is a sharp barb across my ears.

'We will see him in due time.' I smile, hoping my eyes aren't giving too much away. They were trapped,

I could end this now. But what a waste that would be. I need irrefutable proof, and I want to see them devour my keftedes.

'Alright then,' her sits back, a small pout on her beetroot-stained lips. A far nicer shade then the chemical abomination she walked in with, 'to the mains. They do smell delicious.'

The keftedes are still warm with the slight crunch to their coatings. I layer them and they remind me of a sliding caterpillar. I place some of the garden salad on the other side of the plate. When I had opened the contain the smell made bile rise to the back of my throat. The chemicals lay over all of it like a slug's slime trail.

I watch as the two eat with gusto, no hesitation as they stab wrong-coloured tomatoes and overly watery lettuce. Their eyes light up as they taste the keftedes and that warmth spreads through me again. Pride over human cooking? How bizarre.

I wait until their bites begin to slow down and I lean back in my chair. Beneath the skin my true self twists and turns. So close, I can taste it in the air.

'So tell me, what makes you think you will win this year?' I look to Mark, but his attention is solely on the food.

'I don't think it. I know it.' Laura is more than happy to talk.

'Oh yes?'

'I have a secret weapon.'

'Do tell. A girl always likes to hear about those.'

My lip smirks up and I look at her through batted eyelashes. Memories of other flirting floods through the prisoning body and I feel the urge to push against it, to tear it to shreds and free myself from this insanity.

But I know how it goes. I have been more patient on other missions.

But 300 dead. No other mission has hurt our kind so drastically.

'Well, part of Lovers Lane and their promo is all about the natural way of things. But, last year three, yep three kids went to the hospital because they were stung by bees.'

'Ants.' Mike looks up, his voice is slightly slurred. I look closer, He has slipped further in to his chair but the siblings throw unimpressed looks as each other.

'What?' Laura snaps.

'The kid stung by a bee didn't go to the hospital. His mum told him it serves him right for trying to hurt the creature.'

'Whatever. Bugs and critters. That's what you get when you go natural. And let me tell you, people aren't so willing to wander down Lovers Lane as casually as they did last year.'

'Ok.' I feign confusion. My eyebrows knit together, my head tilting like a question mark.

'Well, your Uncle and I have been using this wonderful spray that will make sure the bugs,' she spits the word as though she can feel their legs on her tongue, 'won't be around.'

'It's cheating, Laura.'

'Shut up, Mike. You were the one who found the stuff. You aren't innocent in all of this.'

'I know. But don't act like what we are doing isn't,

isn't,' his mouth opens and closes as he gulps for air.

'Mike?' Laura pulls her napkin from her lap and tosses it beside her plate.

Gurgles escape his mouth, words unform as his eyes widen and his body stiffens.

'Mike!'

Laura is on her feet, patting Mike's cheek, trying to hold him up. They slide to the ground, Mike hitting hard on the white tiles. Laura crouching, hands flailing as she continues to scream his name.

I stand and look down at them.

Laura looks up, her eyes glisten.

'Call an ambulance. What was in that food?'

'My food?'

'He's having an anaphylaxis shock.'

'Allergic?' I try to work out the connection and then the shoe drops. I smile, and I shudder as the adrenaline rushes through me.

It's not how I wanted it. His death will be far too quick, no build-up of fear and knowledge that he will not live through the night.

But I will make hers count.

'What exactly is he allergic to?'

'What? It doesn't matter,' her voice raises an octave and I shudder at the piercing pitch, 'call the ambulance you psycho.'

'No.'

'No?' She spits and looks toward the back of the house. Where the rooms are, where Alix's body lays cold and lifeless. 'Alix. Alix call the ambulance. Mike is dying.'

'The dead can't help the dying.'

The colour drains from her face and I split the skin around this suit's mouth a little more.

'I killed him. Your brother. He is allergic to bee stings?'

'Yes. What the fuck have you done?' She stands, her own self-preservation kicking in.

Poor Mike. Even his blood has given up on him already.

'What I needed to.'

The buzz increases beneath the skin. Her head swivels around.

'You can hear it, can't you?'

A moment. She looks around, searching. But she has already backed herself up to the wall, only a few steps away from the corner.

'Please.' The fury is gone, and instead she whimpers. I like the whimper.

'Please what?'

'Why are you doing this, Susan? I'm sorry I didn't call you back, but you killed my brother because you couldn't get over me. You're a psycho.'

I laugh and the buzz fills the room, bouncing off the tiles and filling up the air around us. Her shoulders pull together, toward her chest and I see her eyes begin to glisten with unshed tears.

'Ah, a psycho is someone who kills innocents because of what she thinks they might do. And for what? To win a ribbon and prove you are better than mother nature herself?'

I step closer and she slides down the wall, I smell

the fear and the piss that streaks down her legs.

'I, I, I don't understand.'

'Who do you think you are?' I feel the itch between my shoulders and hear the tear of skin and then fabric. My first set of wings are free. Her eyes widen, her colour draining further. Whiteness turns clear and she looks like a creature from the depths of the dark waters.

'You, you …'

She trails off and I laugh.

'Please. Let me go.'

'Off you go then.' My real voice tinges the edges of the hard human's words. I take a deep breath.

'What are you?' She hasn't moved. She stays still, in her piss stench.

'I'm the Queen. And you killed my children. 300 of them.'

'Queen?'

Oh, the stupidity of these humans.

'Yes, the Queen.'

I roll my shoulders forward and forced the flesh and cloth to tear as I free my second set of wings. The skin suit sludges off my true form and I bathe in Susan's scream.

Her eyes are wild and darting everywhere, while being pulled over and over to the pile of rotten skin and sinew I have left on the perfect white tiles.

I buzz, filled with the adrenaline that feasts on the pheromones she releases.

My sensors are overloaded with the smells of death and fear.

I laugh and hear the melody of my voice, the buzz

that will terrify her mind until her heart finally stops.

Her self-preservation finally kicks in and she jumps to her feet, pushing past me as she screams. I laugh and lift my body from the ground, letting my feet taste the sweeter air as they lift from the decayed wreckage of the skin suit.

She screams.

It is filled with tears and panic. I slowly fly toward the front door, letting my wings lavish the freedom they had been denied recently.

My mind won't remember their words for much longer, but words are not needed once the blood flows.

'You aren't real.' She screams at me, turning from the door that is still locked.

'I am real. Ssssweeettt Ssssuuuusssannnn knowssss that all too much. And sssssoon sssssooo will you.'

'You're just a fucking bug.' The quiver in her voice belies the strength of the words.

I chuckle and the low moan rumbles up my chest and out through my mouth as my senses awaken further. No longer are they filtered through that dead weight, and I no longer need to be anything but myself.

She runs past me again and I let her. Before turning to follow I flick the latch and open the front door just a crack, just in case.

My eyes, three now and how much more they take in, flit over the kitchen and dining room. I feel the warmth of pleasure flood me as I see the colourful impressions I have made.

Mark lays still now in his own body fluids and filth. His stench is no worse than when he first arrived. His illness, a cancer of the body, would have killed him in weeks anyway. Perhaps it explained why he no longer cared about his sister's obsession. Or perhaps he never had. It was a pity I didn't get longer with him. A chance to draw out the emotions that were flooding and filling me from his sister.

Weaving around the room, letting my wings brush the ceiling before swaying back down, I dance along to the heavy breathing and stench of sweat and fear.

She would find him soon, dear old Alix.

He had been the one who sprayed the poison on my children, on my beloved drones who did nothing more than seek the colour of his flowers.

How he had begged for mercy. Just as Laura would.

How he had spilled all his innocence as he wretched up puss colour vomit and soiled his pants.

The scream.

She has found his body, still covered in body fluids.

The scream comes over and over again until I hear the rasp catch in her throat. Was her voice failing, her throat ripped raw from the terrors of sound that fills her mouth? Or is she playing the game? Will she give me the fun and chase I desire?

I buzz into the room and the pressure along my back, between my wings drops me to the floor. I stay, despite the desire to rise and end it.

I have always been a sucker for the chase.

And the others had died so easily, so without the full array of pleasure.

I hear the rub of wood against metal hinge, smell wet drops of rain on grass, and hear the increasing tap of their drops. She is outside, out in the open.

Oh humans, you think walls keep you safe, until the monster is inside.

But the outside is my playground.

And a Queen will have her way.

I fly out the front door and fly after her. She has not gotten far but even that small flight has made her smell much more potent.

I lavish it.

I nudge her between her shoulder blades as she runs, she stumbles a little, a sob escaping her lips. But she doesn't fall. Good.

I nudge her again, and again.

Before she can turn the corner at the end of the road, I buzz over her head, do a sharp 180 and stare into her eyes.

A wild animal caught in the headlights of the monstrous transports these humans use.

Are they incapable of using their legs?

I chuckle, considering how far she had gotten, I suppose the inventions were of great need.

She screams and tries to turn.

Bones crack in a crash of symbols as I smash my head into the bridge of her nose. The music of the incoming storm plays around us.

A boom covers her next scream as she falls back.

I hover above her, my stinger draws close to her chest, fat drops of rain land on her.

'You can't fly in rain.' She sobs.

'I am a Queen, are you so sure?'

She sobs and pleads and begs and I feel the gratitude

of 300 of my children thanking me for this vengeance.

I jam my stinger into her heart.

The euphoria washes over me as poison floods her, her heart contracts around me. Humans, how much more they would fear us if they knew using our stingers pleased us, without the pesky issue of death.

But she was right about one thing.

I could not fly in rain.

***

Agnes woke with a start.

She could have sworn she heard something buzzing by her ear. She would no doubt find mosquito bites welting up her thin skin in the daylight.

Another crack of thunder jumped her heart to her throat.

Her small living room lit with the next flash of lightning and she slammed her hand to her chest as the sound of thunder cracked through the light.

With shaking hands, Agnes stood and went to close the heavy curtains of her front room. She had fallen asleep in front of her television again.

But the screen was black, as was the world outside.

'Another power outage hey Jonas.' She wasn't sure where the ginger cat was but at least naming him made her feel as though she hadn't entirely lost her marbles.

Flinching the curtain back open a crack, Agnes stared at the impossible scene in front of her. Shaking her head, she blinked, and the scene changed.

Laughing to herself she shook her head again.

Such an imagination. She blamed all the horror movies she once watched when she was young and immortal. Of course, there wasn't a giant bee pinning Laura to the ground in the middle of a storm.

The girl had simply slipped on the wet pavement.

She watched as Laura stood up and continued on her way.

Agnes was about to turn back to the darkness of the room when lightning lit up the figure once more. Was it just a trick of the light or were Laura's feet not quite touching the ground?

'You old fool.' Agnes turned her head and smiled down as Jonas began to weave himself around her feet.

'Alright, let's get you something to eat.'

BEETROOT KEFTEDES AND TZATZIKI DIP RECIPE:

CONTRIBUTED BY NEEN COHEN

Keftedes:
Ingredients:
200g cooked beetroot, peeled and coarsely grated
2 spring onions, finely chopped (including greens)
40g grated parmesan cheese
50g feta cheese, grated
1 egg, beaten
2 tablespoons finely chopped dill
2 tablespoons finely chopped mint or parsley
75-90g breadcrumbs
75 g plain flour
Salt and pepper (to taste)
Vegetable oil (for frying)
1 lemon

Method:
Mix the beetroot, spring onions, cheeses, egg, and herbs together. Season with salt and pepper then mix in enough breadcrumbs to combine.

Cover and refrigerate for 1 hour.

Shape the mixture into palm sized balls, adding a little flour if the mixture is too wet.

Season the flour with salt and pepper and use to coat

the balls.

Heat the oil until hot but not smoking and fry in batches for 2-3 minutes until golden on all sides (or flatten balls into patties and cook both sides)

Remove with a slotted spoon and drain on kitchen paper

Serve hot with a squeeze of lemon and salad.

Great when mixed with the Tzatziki dip

Tzatziki dip

Ingredients:

1 large, cooked beetroot, peeled and coarsely grated

1-2 garlic cloves, finely grated and crushed

Dash of red wine vinegar

3 tablespoons finely chopped dill

Dash of olive oil

250grams of Greek Yoghurt

Sea Salt (to taste)

Method:

Mix the garlic, vinegar, dill and olive oil. Add the yoghurt and mix well. Season with sea salt.

Chill in the fridge for minimum of 30 minutes before serving to allow the flavours to infuse.

Best served with lightly toasted Turkish toast.

Neen Cohen is an Australian Lesbian Speculative Fiction author and lives in Brisbane with her partner, son and fur babies. She has a Bachelor of Creative Industries from Queensland University of Technology and is a member of the Springfield Writer's Group. She's had a multitude of 'day jobs' to pay the bills but her heart has always been in the art of marking dead trees with squiggles of ink and graphite.

When she's not running after her son, spending time with her partner, or working at the current 'day job', she can often be found writing while sitting against a tombstone or tree in any number of graveyards. She's also discovered a newfound passion for throwing sharp objects at thick pieces of wood (knife throwing and axe throwing) and tries to squeeze at least 30 hours into each day because sleep is for the weak.

To keep up to date with all of Neen's misadventures you can find all her links in one convenient location:

https://linktr.ee/neencohen

THE SPECIALITY OF THE HOUSE

TIM MENDEES

"Where the bloody hell am I?" Steve exhaled so hard that it fogged up the windscreen of his clapped-out Citroen. The windscreen wipers squeaked as they cleared the moisture from the dense fog. He was hunched over the steering wheel so that his nose was almost on the glass... and still, he couldn't see a damn thing. The headlights simply reflected back at him in dazzling white.

He'd taken a wrong turning somewhere south of Boscastle and suddenly found himself lost on Bodmin Moor. Pulling over by a farm gate, he jabbed the malfunctioning satnav with his index finger. "Work, you bastard." The display rotated and spun before showing him a map of downtown Manila. "Bollocks... What is it with Cornwall? Nothing ever sodding works out here."

Switching off the engine and flicking on the interior light, He pulled out his mobile phone and cursed some more. The words, *no signal*, seemed to be mocking him. It was no use; he'd have to resort to drastic measures. With another sigh, this one of resignation, he opened the glovebox and took out his battered *AA Road Atlas 2011*. It was ten years old, but it's not like the roads around there had changed much since the dark ages... at least, that's how it felt.

Flicking open the atlas and catching the pages that fell loose before they added to the collection of crap on the passenger's side floor, Steve quickly noticed a problem. The map was only of any use if he knew even vaguely where he was, and since he hadn't a clue, it was about as much use as a celibate in a brothel. Muttering under his breath, Steve stuffed the atlas back in the glove box and got out of the car.

The freezing fog was like a slap to his stubbly cheeks as he staggered around to the boot and popped it open. Rummaging in the clothes and toiletries that had spilt from his suitcase, he selected a jumper and located his gloves. He'd thought his sister batty when she told him to pack warm clothing when he visited her as it was mid-April and heading into summer. It turned out that everything she had said about the biting winds on the coast at night had been wholly accurate.

Bundling himself up, Steve stamped his feet to get the circulation going again. He'd been driving around the narrow snaking lanes for what seemed like an eternity. His knees creaked, and his buttocks were numb. The worst part of it was he was rapidly getting to the point where he would fall asleep at the wheel if he wasn't careful. Steve was tired, hungry, and downright miserable. He was on the verge of utter despair when he heard the distinctive *chink* of glass bottles being tipped into a bin. It was barely audible, but the atmospheric conditions brought it right to his ears. As a man who had spent much of his life in various pubs and bars, it was like the sweetest music.

Scrambling up the gate, he peered into the fog. Just dimly, he could see some splotches of light in the distance to the west. Praying for civilisation, he hurried back into his vehicle and fired up the engine. The car growled and spluttered as he put it into first gear and commenced a slow crawl down the incline he had parked upon.

Eventually, the road levelled off in a small valley, and lo and behold, there was a narrow turning leading off to his left. His heart leapt just a little when he saw that there was a signpost indicating that it led to a place called Little Hollow a mere quarter of a mile away. The other end of the signpost indicated that the road he was on would carry on to Hollowhills five miles away. It was a simple decision, to carry on in the fog for five miles would be madness. Yanking the wheel, Steve took the turning and prayed that the potholes wouldn't finish off his car's rickety suspension once and for all.

After a couple of minutes, the road emerged from the trees that had previously engulfed it and kept it relatively hidden. A humpback bridge over a sluggishly moving stream led directly into the centre of a darkened village. Grimy stone houses leered out of the fog like blank-eyed spectres. Not one of the dwellings showed any sign of life, and not a single light burned in the windows. Following the road past a weed-tangled memorial to the long-dead of a tragic mine disaster, Steve eventually came to a source of light.

"Thank God!" He exclaimed as a gently swinging

sign suddenly became visible. "A boozer!"

Swinging the car into the gravel car park, Steve's spirits soared. Under the board announcing the name of the establishment, The Black Goat Inn was a list announcing that it had rooms, fine ales, and home-cooked food. His stomach growled as he parked up just inside the gate and a quick glance at his phone told him that it was still a good hour or two before closing time. "Please, let them be still serving food... I'm ruddy starving." Still, if worst came to worst, he could always fill up on pork scratchings and beer.

Checking that his wallet was securely in his left buttock pocket, he stepped out of the car and slammed the door behind him. The coarse gravel crunched under his tatty boots as he stumbled towards the glow of the lights. Soon, the sound of music and a low growl of conversation filtered through the fog. The pub was definitely still open. It felt like Steve's prayers had been answered.

Finally, the front of the pub leered out of the fog. It looked ancient, all rough stone and creeping ivy. Several weathered benches sat clustered under the sagging bay windows, it would have been quaintly picturesque if it hadn't been for the shocking weather conditions. All of the benches were vacant except for the one directly to the left of the door. Two hulking figures in flat caps with beards like rose bushes sat nursing glasses of what looked, and smelt, like strong cider.

"Evening," Steve mumbled as he neared the two men. "Bit cold to be sitting out here, ain't it?"

Neither man spoke, they just peered at him with

bloodshot glassy eyes and held up cigarettes. Steve smiled and nodded, making a mental note to try some of the cider... it was clearly potent stuff. Reaching out, Steve gripped the brass door handle and pulled the creaking door open.

Stepping inside, warm air rushed around him, and his nose detected the familiar scents of stale beer, sweat, and bleach from the lavatories. It was a welcome change from motor oil, sandwich wrappers and sweaty socks, that was for certain. Striding confidently into the bar area, Steve took in the scene. It looked like the 1970s were alive and well and living in deepest darkest Cornwall. Even the music that crackled from the tinny speakers was plucked from that distant decade. Steve recognised it instantly, it was *Chirpy Chirpy Cheep Cheep* by Middle of the Road... surreal didn't even begin to cover it.

Aside from a couple of old-timers in the far corner playing dominoes, the only other people in the room were a young couple who looked as distinctly out of place as he felt. The man stared at the threadbare sticky carpet with distaste while his companion worried a tatty beer mat. Steve looked at the tarnished horse brass and cloudy picture frames that hung over the blocked-up fireplace and smirked to himself. It was just the sort of tat that would go for a fortune in his trendy London antique shop. The collection of dusty mining lamps alone would have fetched a pretty penny from the hipster brigade, given enough spit and polish.

Steve cleared his throat as he approached the bar to get the landlady's attention. She was a stockily built lady of middle age with wild hair and gold earrings that seals could jump through.

"Oh, 'ello!" She purred, revealing two rows of crooked yellow teeth. "It's all go tonight."

Steve looked again at the empty room. "Um... yes. Hello. Do you have any rooms available? I got lost in this damn fog, see? I'm too shagged-out to carry on driving."

"Of course, dear... I've got plenty o' room for a little one." She tittered like an excited duck at her attempted witticism. "You're not the only one to be caught out by the fog, me dear. Those two turned up an hour ago. Frozen stiff they were, poor mites." She nodded over at the young couple. From the bags and helmets stuffed under the table, they were cyclists. No doubt enjoying the great outdoors until the weather changed.

"Excellent. I don't suppose you are still serving food?"

The barmaid sucked air in through her teeth dramatically. "Chef went home an hour ago..."

Steve was crestfallen. "Oh..."

"But..." She cut in. "I 'ave some pasties in the fridge, I can warm you up a couple if you'd like? They're the speciality of the 'ouse, they are. Chicken, mushroom and tarragon... all prepared on the premises."

"Sounds perfect." Steve beamed. "As long as it's not too much trouble?"

"None at all... quick blast in the microwave, and they're good to go. Drink?"

Steve scanned the bar taps. Most of them were turned the wrong way around indicating that they were off. Next to the generic lagers and token draught ale was a pump marked, 'Black Goat Cider.' "Could I possibly try a taste of the cider?"

"Certainly, dear." She selected a streaked half-pint glass and squirted some of the orange liquid into it. The smell of it alone was enough to strip the enamel from your teeth. "This is our own brew... We've an old press out in the barn. Did you see the two farmers on your way in?"

"I did," Steve answered as he gave the stuff a tentative sniff.

"Well, all the apples come from their orchard down the road. It don't get much more local than that!"

Steve took a sip. "Jesus!" As soon as the sweet but sharp liquid hit his tongue, his vision brightened, and his muscles relaxed. "That's good stuff!"

The landlady grinned.

"A pint of that, please."

"Here you go, dear." She handed him the cider in a handled glass. "I'll start a tab; you can settle up in the morning. Now, take a seat, and I'll bring yer pasty over."

Lifting his glass to the light, Steve watched the sediment twisting slowly to the bottom of the glass through the dimples. It was oddly relaxing and just made that first sip even more tantalising. Stifling a splutter after taking a hearty gulp, he wiped his mouth with the back of his hand and surveyed the room. Catching the young woman's eye, he raised a hand in greeting and sauntered over.

"Do you mind if I join you?"

"Not at all, mate." The young man answered. "I was just saying to Susan that I felt less of a sore thumb now another *outsider* was in the pub."

Steve chuckled as he parked his rump on a stool and placed his drink on a mat.

"Yeah, it's a bit *Twilight Zone* around here," Susan whispered. "Those guys in the corner are giving me the creeps."

Steve angled his head so he could see the men indicated out of his peripheral vision. They both looked like freshly exhumed cadavers. The only colour in their faces was a redness to the eyes. As they slammed the old wooden dominos onto the table without giving them a single glance, they studied the three interlopers with slackened mouths. One of them had a string of saliva linking the corner of his mouth and his left shoulder.

Leaning in close, Steve whispered conspiratorially. "I think it's this cider that's doing it. I've only had one sip, and I feel lobotomised."

Stifled laughter broke the tension in a second. The man introduced himself as Jack and explained that he and Susan had come to Bodmin on a cycling holiday. They had driven over from South Wales and left their car in the coastal town of Betyls Cove then headed out into the wilds. They had booked a pitch at a campsite somewhere out past Hollowhills but couldn't locate it for love nor money... and then the fog rolled in.

"We've been out here a few times now," Susan explained. "The weird thing is, I've never noticed this place before."

"Well," Steve smiled. "I can't imagine this is in any of the brochures. It looks practically abandoned."

"Yeah, I think that must be it." Jack shrugged. "Take a look at this..." He unfolded the relevant page on an ordinance survey map and traced a road with his finger. "This is the road that links High Bend and Hollowhills. If you were coming from Boscastle, you probably came onto it here."

"Your guess is as good as mine. I was driving around like a lemon for hours." Steve quaffed some of the rocket fuel cider and risked another glance at the domino players. They were still gawking.

"Well, if you look here, this is the turning into this village. There is nothing marked except for a few buildings and a mine... look."

Steve and Susan leaned in. Jack was right. His finger was pointed where the small road ended on a cluster of buildings. There was a cross indicating a church and a mine boundary with a single point marked *shaft*.

"It must be one of those ghost villages." Steve mused. "There are a few of them around the country. You know, when the mine dried up, the people shipped out, kind of thing. A lot of them end up being bought by the MOD and used for manoeuvres."

"Army don't want nothin' with Little Hollow, dear." The sudden appearance of the landlady at his elbow nearly made Steve hit the ceiling. "The land 'round 'ere is riddled with mine shafts. Those big heavy vehicles of theirs would go straight down." She cackled as she placed a chipped plate and a napkin in front of Steve. "Here's your pasty, dear. I'll show you to your room once you've eaten."

"Um... yes, thank you." Steve desperately tried to regain his composure.

"Excuse me," Susan piped up, stopping the landlady

in her tracks. "We were just talking about the village. It doesn't seem to be noted on any maps."

"Not surprising. Nobody comes 'ere since the old tin mine collapsed. Just us locals and a few ramblers every now and then... We like it nice and quiet round 'ere, we do." She smiled warmly before turning on her heels and shuffling back to the bar.

"Is that the chicken and tarragon?" Jack indicated the fat pasty on Steve's plate. "We both had one of those... bloody lovely. You've got to hand it to the Cornish... they have a wonderful way with pastry."

"Yeah, you're not kidding. I think it's in their DNA or something." Steve gripped it by the twisted crust and lifted the golden morsel. "Blimey, it's big enough, isn't it? I nearly asked for two."

"They don't skimp on the filling neither." Susan smiled as she swayed ever so slightly. "I couldn't finish mine. It's a good job that Jack is like a human dustbin."

Steve opened wide and steered a corner of the gargantuan pasty into it. The pastry crumbled as his teeth sank into it, showering his lap in crumbs. It was divine. The chicken was succulent, and the mushrooms fleshy and flavoursome. The tarragon lifted the sauce high above being a basic bechamel and into the realms of culinary genius. He couldn't help thinking that it was the sort of dish you'd pay an arm and a leg for in one of those trendy artisan bakeries and made a mental note to ask for the recipe before he left.

"Good, innit?" Jack grinned, his eyes betraying the fact that he too had been imbibing the cider.

Not wishing to talk with his mouth stuffed to

bursting, Steve nodded enthusiastically. As he ravenously devoured his pasty, Jack waddled over to the bar and got the trio a fresh glass of the cider. His reasoning being, they were stuck there, so they may as well enjoy themselves.

As the opening strains of David Soul's *Silver Lady* came pumping out of the speakers, Steve pushed the last piece of crust past his lips then dabbed them with the napkin. The combination of the fine fayre and strong drink had made the bar look sparkly. His endorphins were in overdrive. Even the domino players looked ever so slightly attractive. Flashing a boozy grin at his companions, he held up his now empty glass. "Another one?"

Jack looked all for it but one glance at Susan told him that she had had more than enough. Her eyelids were heavy, and she was swaying like a flagpole in a force nine gale. "Nah, I think I'd better get Susan to bed."

This deflated Steve and made his exhaustion return tenfold. "Ahh, you're probably right. I need to make an early start."

Jack gathered their bags and helped Susan to her feet. She clung to him like a bonded sugar glider as he steered her around the tables. After bidding Steve goodnight, they exited via a door next to the ladies lavatory.

Getting unsteadily to his feet, Steve picked up his plate and the empties then turned to the bar. His motor functions were sluggish. He was pretty sure that he now wore the same dazed expression as the two old coves in the corner. The thought made him chuckle. He risked a glance over at them and was slightly unnerved to find that their mouths had risen into a yawning grin as they followed him with their doll-like eyes.

"Good stuff, this cider!" He slurred. He had to say something after making eye contact. To ignore them would have gone against his firm belief in pub etiquette.

The two men grunted through their spittle-flecked lips and raised their glasses. It was the best he was going to get under the circumstances.

Plonking the plate and glasses on the bar and grinning at the landlady, Steve motioned towards the cider pump. "Good stuff, that."

"Thanks." She beamed in response. "You want another?"

Steve mulled it over for a second. The devil on his shoulder was doing its best to win the debate. "I probably shouldn't…"

"You can take it up to your room if you like?"

Bingo. Decision made. "Yes! That would be amazing, thanks… I'll just go and get my suitcase out of the car."

"Okay, dear. I'll call me 'usband. He'll show you to your room when you get back."

With a nod of recognition, Steve turned and headed for the door while fishing his car keys from his pocket. For the first time that evening, a smile had crossed his face when a new song came lurching out from the knackered sound system. It was the unmistakable opening riff of *20th Century Boy*. The fuzzed-up power chords entered his ears and gave his brain a good jostling as he staggered under the speaker.

Stepping out into the fog with his ears buzzing,

Steve nearly fell into one of the farmers. His equilibrium was shot to hell, and his knees were in worse shape than his car's suspension. "Oops, sorry, man." He slurred and weaved in the vague direction of his car. Eventually locating it, he took a chunk of paint off the boot as he tried to steer his key into the lock. Giving a low whoop of triumph, he let himself in and proceeded to stuff the clothes that had spilt out of his suitcase back in. It was a task he was doomed to fail. Giving up, he pulled out the offending clothes and zipped the case closed.

Hefting the suitcase out of the boot, he turned and started his meander back to the pub. The extra weight made his gait even more crab-like than it had been on the way out. Reaching the benches, he was surprised to see that the two farmers had gone. It was funny, but he was convinced he should have heard their feet on the gravel. Maybe it was the ringing in his ears that had masked the movement? The buzz hadn't diminished one iota.

Going inside, he dumped his suitcase by the out-of-order pay phone on the wall and walked into the bar area. The music had stopped, and the two domino players had gone. To add to his confusion, the landlady had vanished, and a pint of cider sat next to a key on a tatty plastic fob. Picking them both up, he leaned over the bar and tried to see through the door in the centre.

"This way, zur."

Steve nearly launched his glass across the room as a towering figure appeared inches behind him. "Fucking hell!" Quickly clamping his other hand over the glass, he narrowly avoided spilling his cider all over the carpet. "Shit... sorry. I didn't see you there."

The big man grunted and turned, picking up Steve's suitcase like it weighed nothing. He was well over six-foot-tall and built like a tractor. His dungarees and checked shirt gave him the stereotypical look of a farmer.

Steve tried to steady his racing heartbeat as he followed in the man's footsteps. The door next to the toilets led to a creaking staircase covered in a carpet that was even stickier than the one in the bar. More photos of grubby-looking miners and ancient vehicles lined the walls as they came out onto a narrow landing with two doors on either side. The man walked all the way along and dumped Steve's suitcase outside of room number two.

"This one, 'ere." The man grunted as he pushed past Steve and stomped back down the stairs, leaving Steve to fumble with the lock.

Stepping into the room, He felt along the flock wallpaper for the light switch. Turning it on, Steve chuckled to himself once again. It looked like his granny's bedroom from when he was a kid. The walls were covered in decorative plates and the dressing-table covered in off-white lace doilies. There was even a chunky white-plastic Teasmade next to the bed.

"Bloody hell. These guys really haven't embraced the 21st century. I bet there is no wi-fi." To prove his theory, he pulled out his phone and scowled at the screen. Not only was there no wi-fi, but there was no phone signal whatsoever. "Ah, well. I can go without social media for one night."

Flopping down onto the end of the oversprung bed, he kicked off his shoes and took a swig of cider. This was one of Steve's personal flaws. He had already had more than enough, but he had paid for it, so he was damn sure going to finish it.

Now he was in a quiet room, the buzzing in his ears started to increase. It was like when he'd been to a gig but without the cool memories. Rubbing his ears with his fingers, he tried to wiggle the buzz away. It was no good it simply wouldn't stop. To make matters worse, his skin had taken on a strange tingle. It was almost like his muscles were fizzing. It was probably due to being hunched over a steering wheel all day, but it was slightly worrying all the same.

In the end, Steve's devil got the better of him once again. He rooted out a handful of prescription painkillers from his suitcase and washed them back with some more cider. Five minutes later, the fizzing had stopped. Ten minutes after that... he was running to the en suite bathroom and sticking his head down the bowl.

* * *

Thump... Thump... Thump... Thump...

Steve groaned as he opened his eyes. He was on his side, hugging the toilet. One arm had gone numb and was stuck to the linoleum floor tiles. His vision took a second or two to stop drifting, in the interim he tried to figure out what the hellish banging was. Then he heard grunts and moans. It was the unmistakable sound of a headboard slamming against a thin partition wall.

"Great... that's just what I need." His voice was little more than a hoarse croak as he tried to sit up.

The stench of his bile in the bowl nearly made him purge once again. Flailing his numb arm, he grabbed the flush and pulled it. "What the hell?" Just for a second, before the water washed it away, he was certain that he saw glowing chunks in amongst the vomitus. Shaking his head and screwing up his eyes, he figured it was just the effect of broken blood vessels playing tricks on him. Colours popped like fireworks on the inside of his eyelids. It was like he was looking up at the stars through a kaleidoscope.

Opening his eyes again, Steve gripped the washbasin and hauled himself upright. The man looking back at him from the smeared and cracked mirror looked about twenty years older than he was and had eyes like the befuddled domino players from downstairs, all bulbous and glassy. In short, he looked like freshly microwaved death.

After spitting and rinsing his mouth out, Steve splashed his face with icy-cold water and slapped his cheeks to try and get some colour back into them. Straightening his back almost had him stumbling into the mildewed shower cubicle, so he grabbed the door frame and pulled himself out of the bathroom. Praying that his feet could handle the momentum, he glided towards the bed and landed face down in a starfish position.

Thump... Thump... Thump...

The pounding was worse in here. To add to Steve's discomfort, Jack and Susan's bed was evidently up against the same wall as his. Every thrust sent vibrations through the frame and set the springs reverberating.

"Oh, for the love of God, give it a rest, Jack." He

grumbled as he grabbed a pillow and pulled it over his head. As soon as his eyes closed, the multi-faceted starfield returned with a vengeance. His vision seemed to hurtle forwards like he was some kind of space bug. It was dizzying at first, but after a while, it became kind of soothing.

The buzzing still filled his ears and actually became something of a blessing. By focusing on the almost imperceptible peaks and troughs in pitch and tone, he succeeded in completely blocking out the rhythmic sounds of drunken rumpy-pumpy from the adjacent room. For the first time that day, Steve felt strangely at peace...

Oh my god... help!

A strangled cry shook him from his inebriated reverie. Launching the pillow across the room and knocking the bowl of potpourri on the dresser all over the floor, he got up on his hands and knees and pressed his ear to the wall. A glance at the clock told him that he'd been lying there for over half an hour. All he could hear was the sound of running water and a strange gurgling sound.

Balling his fist, Steve banged on the wall. "Hey, you guys alright in there?"

Nobody answered, but the gurgling got louder.

"Jack? Susan? ... What the hell is going on in there?"

Again, there was no answer, but he could hear heavy shambling footsteps getting closer to the wall.

"Oi!" Steve banged on the wall again. "What the fu..."

BANG!

Somebody belted the wall right where Steve had placed his ear. The shock of the blow made him jump, twist and fall off the side of the bed. Sitting on his backside, staring at the spot, he started to hear a strange kind of wheezing. It was a cross between breathing and the buzzing of a giant fly.

"What the hell is going on?" He whispered to himself as he scrambled to his feet and slipped his shoes back on. The noise was followed by the sound of a door opening and low muttering. Steve grabbed his pint glass as a weapon and edged to the door. Peeping through the spyhole, he was slightly reassured to see the landlady standing outside Susan and Jack's room with a first-aid kit.

Deciding that he wanted to see if he could help, he grabbed the door handle and pulled it... nothing. Taking the key off the side, he tried to slip it into the lock but couldn't. Bending down, he looked through the keyhole. The door was locked from the other side, and the key was in the lock.

"Hey!" He banged on the door. "Why is this door locked?"

"Stay in yer room, zur." The unmistakable voice of the big man growled. Looking again through the spyhole, he saw that the landlady had gone and in her place was her husband... holding a shotgun.

"What. The. Fuck?" Steve mouthed silently as he backed away from the door. Something very strange was going on.

The crunch of gravel outside the back window

dragged his attention away from the door. Using his hand to wipe the condensation off the glass, he peered out into the fog. It was hard to see through the gloom, but he could see two men that looked like the farmers from earlier walking another figure covered in a stained bedsheet away from the building.

A *slam* from next door told him that the room had been vacated. Moving quickly and silently, he scurried back to the spy hole just in time to see another figure clad in a sheet being bundled from the room by the big man. This one didn't seem like a willing participant, unlike the other.

Steve's heart was hammering, and his mind was racing as he tentatively knocked on his door. "Hey, what's going on out there?"

The next voice belonged to the landlady. "Everythin's fine, dear. You get some rest... you'll be right as rain in no time." Then she tittered like a crazed old crone and shuffled off down the landing. Trying the handle again, he was startled by the *click* of a gun being cocked.

"Don't." A flat, emotionless voice instructed. A glance outside revealed the two domino players both holding rusty shotguns. It was now clear that Steve was a prisoner.

The harsh metallic tang of adrenaline appeared in the back of his mouth, cutting through the alcoholic stickiness. He couldn't stay there, and that was for sure. He had no idea what had happened to Susan and Jack, but he didn't want to stick around and have it happen to him. If he could get to his car, he could drive around until he found a signal and call the police. First, though, he needed to get out of that room.

Going back to the window, he looked down and was overjoyed to see a sloping roof directly below. It ended before the gravel driveway where he had seen the strange trio. It wasn't the best escape plan in the world, but what other choice did he have? Gripping the old sash window, he tried to raise it as quietly as possible. He slid it about halfway up before it got stuck in the warped frame. As look would have it, it was enough for him to wiggle through.

Making sure he had his car keys, phone, and wallet, Steve climbed out onto the old slate roof. The fog had made it slippery, and he had to get onto his hands and knees to avoid slipping onto his back. An awkward fall at this point could be disastrous in more ways than one. Edging his way down, he was suddenly struck by a thought. Maybe he could see into the other room.

Changing direction, Steve crawled back up to the building and over to the other window. The curtains were drawn, but there was a gap of about an inch between them. Pressing his face to the glass, he peeked inside and instantly wished that he hadn't. The room was trashed. It looked like it had been hit by a tornado. Black ichor was sprayed up the walls, dripping off the plates and trickling down the wallpaper. By far the worst sight, however, was the bed. It was covered in the black gunk and a strange yellow pus-like substance. Amongst it was clumps of what looked like some kind of diseased fungus mixed with strips of human skin.

Steve gagged and nearly tumbled off the roof. His stumbling dislodged one of the slates and sent it skittering down the roof. "Fucksticks!" he exclaimed as the slate smashed on the ground below.

"Ay... what' ye doin' in there?" One of the domino men called into his room.

"Damn." Steve started to crawl for his life down the roof.

The sound of a ket being turned in a lock sang out into the night. Seconds later, there was a ghastly slack-jawed face at the window. "Ay, stop!"

The domino man stuck the barrel of his gun through the window and prepared to shoot. Steve noticed this and went into a roll. The gun went off just as he dropped off the end of the slope taking two metres of plastic drainpipe with him on his descent. Steve landed in an undignified heap on the jagged gravel, skinning his elbow and lacerating one hand.

Without pausing to catch his breath, he struggled to his feet and stuffed his bleeding hand under his jumper. Looking left and right, he decided to follow the driveway around the building in the direction of the car park. The coast looked clear at that moment, so he broke out into a limping jog. He'd banged his knee pretty badly when he'd landed, but the pain pills and alcohol in his system kept the discomfort to a bearable minimum.

Reaching the corner, he spotted two splodges of light heading directly towards him. Diving behind a cluster of black bottle skips, he cowered and peeked out. A heavy vehicle was approaching slowly. The engine rumbled as it crept through the fog. It was a tow truck being driven by the big man, and it was dragging Steve's car behind it. There were two bicycles lashed to the bonnet with an oil-blackened rope.

Steve cursed and punched the wall with his good hand. Now he had two options, either risk trying to escape on foot or following the tow truck and either pinching it or getting his car back. The thought of wandering around in the fog on Bodmin Moor filled him with more dread than potentially having to fight the big man. In the end, his decision was made by how bad a shape his knee was in. He wouldn't get a mile before it gave out.

A wooden fence was visible just over the driveway. If Steve kept in the shadow and followed the tracks left by the vehicles, he should be able to stay undetected. As he attempted to sprint to cover, a door opened somewhere along the back of the pub, and two beams of light started to cut through the gloom. The domino men were coming. He had moved just in time. If he hadn't made it to behind a line of pot plants along the fence, he'd have been a sitting target. The domino men split up. One went left and the other right. They were scouring the bin area and heading around to the front of the pub. He'd eluded them for the moment.

The fence followed the drive to an open gate. There, the gravel ended, and it opened onto a muddy yard that looked like it belonged to an old farm. There was what looked like an abandoned farmhouse to the right, and the tyre tracks snaked off to the left towards an old tin barn. Hurrying through the gate, Steve veered left and hugged the corrugated metal structure. The fog had made the rusty structure drip red onto the patches of sickly weeds and grass along the border like it was oozing blood.

Reaching the entrance, Steve was surprised to see

that the tracks carried on past the barn. Keeping low, he dashed across the aperture and followed the tracks down towards an unkempt copse. As he broke from the shadows of the barn, the chug of the pick-up truck made him dive behind the nearest tree. The truck was going back towards the pub minus its cargo. Steve carried on creeping towards the trees and stopped on a raised bit of ground overlooking a nightmare.

Rows of cars, caravans, motorbikes and other vehicles sat in various states of decay. Some of them must have dated back to the fifties. Scrambling down the bank, Steve started to look for his car. Some of the rusted bodies still had roof-racks containing luggage attached to them. Piles of camping equipment and personal effects lay in filthy piles dotted around the scrapyard.

"Jesus... how many people?" The thought was terrifying. It looked like the inhabitants of the Black Goat Inn were diabolical serial killers. "Dammit, where the hell is my car?"

Finally, he found it... and his heart instantly sank. The tyres were all shredded, and the bonnet was open. One glance told him that it had been immobilised. The big man had literally torn bits out of it and tossed them on the ground. It would have taken a skilled mechanic and a minor miracle to get it going again.

"Bastards." Steve hissed through his gritted teeth. Bending down, he picked up a rusty metal pipe and tested the weight against his bloodied palm. "Right... Let's do this."

Steve only had one chance left. He needed to get the tow truck away from the landlady's brutish husband... by any means necessary.

Racing back the way he came; Steve went back into the shadow of the barn. It was then that he heard a muffled sobbing. Poking his head around the open door, he spotted an area ringed with mouldering hay bales and lit with a slowly swinging lamp on an old rusty chain. There was no sign of any evil villagers, and he was convinced that the sobbing he could hear belonged to a woman.

"Susan?" He whispered into the foetid atmosphere of the barn. "Susan, is that you?"

The woman gasped, then a second later sobbed the word, "Jack?"

Cautiously, Steve gripped the pipe and held it ready to strike as he edged around the hay. In a horseshoe of bales, there were two goat tethers hammered into the earthen floor. Attached to these were two thick leather straps leading to two bundles. One of them squirmed like a maggot. It was two bodies wrapped in sheets and tied up with orange bailing twine.

"Oh, my god." Steve ran over to the one that was moving. "Susan... Is that you?"

"Jack?" The bundle cracked. She sounded like she was gargling mud.

"It's me, Steve. Hold on, I'll try and find something to cut you free." Looking around, there was nothing in the immediate vicinity that could cut the twine. He thought about trying his keys but remembered how tough that stuff really was. "Come on... there must be some tools around here somewhere."

Over to the middle of the barn was a roughly

constructed dividing wall with a sliding door set into the centre. It was slightly ajar, revealing a dim shaft of flickering lamplight. Approaching quietly, Steve looked through and gasped. The room was clear of villagers, but it was far from empty.

"What the fu..." He stopped himself from making any further noise and slid the door aside. The rear portion of the barn had been converted into a ramshackle kitchen. Stainless steel workbenches lined the far-right corner. Gore encrusted knives and grubby utensils hung from wall mounted magnetic strips and hooks from the rafters. At one end was a gas-powered refrigerator from a caravan, and the other had a gas oven and a collection of barbecues and camping hobs. The floor was covered in bloody feathers, flour and chicken entrails. This was where his pasty had been prepared.

Stepping into the hellish space, Steve's attention was drawn to the opposite end of the barn. Huge piles of glowing fungus sprouted from the earth like stalagmites. Amongst the columns of foul matter were several plastic tubs and a selection of knives. Looking into one tub, he saw that the fungi had been diced into bite-sized chunks. The memory of the fleshy mushrooms in his pasty flashed in his memory, and he felt his gorge rising. Tucking the steel pipe under his arm and clamping his good hand over his mouth, he started to back away.

Splat!

A sticky clump of fungi dropped from the rafters, landed on one of the columns, then solidified. Steve looked up and nearly fainted. Nestling in the rafters was a monstrous abomination. It was roughly the size of a man, but there the similarities ended. Its body was pink and rugose with patches of wiry hair. Multiple pincer-tipped appendages drooped down from its torso. Spread above it were two iridescent wings. It looked like a hideous marriage betwixt crayfish and dragonfly. Then he looked at what took the place of the creature's head. It was a glowing fleshy pyramid covered in twitching antennae. Its abdomen throbbed, and another gob of fungi dripped from the end of its body. Steve stifled a scream, grabbed the nearest knife, turned, and bolted. One step away from gibbering insanity, he crashed through the barn.

Susan had stopped squirming by the time he knelt beside her and cut the twine around her neck. Feeling under her for the end of the sheet, he peeled it back. This time, the scream sneaked out. Half of Susan's pretty blonde head had melted into an angular clump of pink fungi. Several small antennae had started to sprout. She was turning into one of those *things* like that in the other room.

"Shit... I'm sorry, Susan." He whispered as he went to cover her back up.

Susan's one remaining eye snapped open. "We are the new breed!" Her voice was an evil buzzing like the one inside his head. "Soon, you will join us... You hear her too, don't you?"

"What?" Steve gasped. "What do you mean... hear who?"

"The queen of the Mi-Go... you have ingested her. You will become her..." Susan's eye ruptured with a sickening *splat* as an antennae burst from the socket.

Steve bellowed in terror and started to lash out at

the Susan *thing* with the boning knife. Slicing her neck asunder, he was showered in yellow pus. The bundle next to her suddenly started to jerk violently, and a sharp pincer forced itself through the fabric. Terrified, Steve jumped to his feet, grabbed the lamp off the chain and smashed it on the monster that had been Jack.

As the oil spread, fire roared, and smoke billowed, a monstrous buzzing filled the barn. The queen was awake, and she wasn't happy. Steve ran as fast as his leg would allow towards the entrance. Reaching the threshold, he collided with one of the domino men. Without thinking, he stabbed him in the neck as hard as he could. The knife was buried to the hilt, and the man dropped like a felled tree.

Stooping to retrieve the man's shotgun, Steve started to slowly walk towards the pub. The fire had alerted the rest of Little Hollow's hellish denizens, and several shapes loomed out of the fog. Three of the shapes were the other domino man and the two farmers... the others weren't men at all. They were foul hybrids of man and Mi-Go. Steve ducked behind an old oil drum as they raced towards the barn. Praying to every deity he could think of that they wouldn't find him, he tried to melt into the shadows. Eventually, they passed, and he was free to move.

Nearing the gate, the familiar splotches of light began to advance on him again. The tow truck was heading for the barn. It was now or never. Steve crouched by the fence and waited. Once the vehicle was halfway through the gate, he stood and pointed the gun at the window.

Bang!

The driver-side window exploded, and so did the big man's head. It showered the cab with chunks of fungus-like flesh and black ichor. Giggling maniacally, Steve ripped open the door and dragged the man's carcass out of the seat. Slipping in, he put the truck in reverse and stamped on the accelerator. The tyres spun on the gravel, but he was able to wrestle the lumbering vehicle into a three-point turn. Aiming for the side of the building, he slammed his foot down.

Narrowly avoiding ploughing into the side of the pub and the fence, Steve managed to make it through the car park and onto the road. As he slowed down to take the turning, his head was stabbed by needles of buzzing agony. The queen was trying to make contact.

Come back... you are one of us...

"No! Never!"

Fighting the pain, he looked at his hands gripping the steering wheel. His skin was lined like a cracking egg. As he screamed, several bristly hairs sprouted from his knuckles.

You are one of us... Iä Shub-Niggurath... Iä the black goat of the woods with a thousand young...

Steve turned onto the road, put the truck into gear and accelerated as fast as he could. Following the road, he saw the monument to the mining disaster looming out of the fog. He gritted his teeth and closed his eyes.

"Screw the black goat!"

Steve's body hurtled through the windscreen, and his head cracked open as it collided with the unyielding granite. As the engine caught on fire and the night echoed with the deafening *boom* of an explosion, the queen of the Mi-Go buzzed in sorrow for her fallen offspring.

CHICKEN, TARRAGON & MUSHROOM CORNISH PASTY

CONTRIBUTED BY TIM MENDEES

Rough Puff Pastry

250g plain flour
1 teaspoon of salt
250g of butter
100ml of cold water

1. Mix flour and salt into a large mixing bowl.
2. Grate the butter directly into bowl. If the butter starts to melt, chuck it in the refrigerator for a few minutes before continuing.
3. Gently mix the flour and butter with your fingertips.
4. Create a well in the mix and add water.
5. Mix until you have a rough dough. Cover with cling film and leave to rest in the refrigerator for 20 minutes.
6. Turn out onto a floured work surface and gently knead. Form into a rectangle.
7. Roll the dough in one direction only, until the dough is around 20 x 50 cm. Try to keep edges straight.
8. Fold the top third of the dough to the centre and then the bottom third up and over that.
9. Quarter turn the dough and roll out again to three times the size. Fold again as per previous step.
10. Cover with cling film and allow to chill in

refrigerator for at least 20 minutes.

Filling

250g Chicken Breast (diced. Aim for roughly 1cm cubes)
1 onion
1 bunch fresh Tarragon
250g Mi-Go flesh. (Chestnut or button mushrooms will work just as well.) (Thinly sliced)
1 cup of chicken stock
½ cup of milk
¼ cup of flour
1 tablespoon of olive oil
A little butter for frying
Salt & Pepper (to taste)
1 egg

1. Pre-heat the oven to 180c
2. Saute the chicken, mushrooms, Tarragon and seasoning in a knob of butter on a medium heat until the chicken is cooked and the onion soft. Add a splash of oil to the butter to stop it scorching.
3. Add the flour and cook for one minute
4. Add the stock and milk and simmer until the sauce thickens. Stir well to avoid clumps and burning.
5. Once it is a nice creamy consistency, taste and season.
6. Take off heat and allow to cool before assembling your pasties.

Assembly

1. Roll out your rough puff pastry and cut out circles.
2. Fill half of the circle with the chicken mixture. Fold in half, crimp and twist edges into a crust.
3. Pierce top of pasties and brush with an egg wash.
    4. Bake for 40 minutes until pastry is golden and puffed.

Tim Mendees is a horror writer from Macclesfield in the North-West of England that specialises in cosmic horror and weird fiction. A lifelong fan of classic weird tales, Tim set out to bring the pulp horror of yesteryear into the 21st Century and give it a distinctly British flavour. His work has been described as the lovechild of H.P. Lovecraft and P.G. Wodehouse and is often peppered with a wry sense of humour that acts as a counterpoint to the unnerving, and often disturbing, narratives.

Tim has had over eighty published short stories and novelettes in anthologies and magazines with publishers all over the world. He also has four novellas out now with more coming soon.

When he is not arguing with the spellchecker, Tim is a goth DJ, crustacean and cephalopod enthusiast, and the presenter of a popular web series of live video readings of his material and interviews with fellow authors. He currently lives in Brighton & Hove with his pet crab, Gerald, and an army of stuffed octopods.

https://timmendeeswriter.wordpress.com/
https://tinyurl.com/timmendeesyoutube

RECLAIMED

CALLUM PEARCE

Femke Sneek sat next to the window listening to the town crier's bell ringing. The bell was letting people know that fresh fish was arriving on the market. For the first year after her husband Arie's boat and crew had failed to return, she would sit at the dock hoping to see their vessel slicing through the fog that often sat over the water. People always used to say that when they had lost a loved one, they could feel their presence around them all of the time. Femke had never had that feeling. Many women who had lost their husbands to the sea didn't encounter that strange satisfaction. Those men were lost, reclaimed by the water that the people of the Netherlands frantically reclaimed the land from. The people of Vlaardingen lived off the water. The sea was the source of their income, their food and their pride. Known as Haringkoppen, herring heads by those around them for the slippery, vinegary treats they would often let slide down their throats.

The first year was spent holding on to the hope

that her husband would return with tales of his travels. Eventually, Femke had to accept that the water had no intention of returning her husband. Back then, she had received a strange visitor at her door who had convinced her that her husband was gone from her forever.

Two years ago, a year after her husband had been expected to return she had heard a gentle respectful tapping at the door to her home. She had opened it to see one of the local fishermen holding his hat next to his chest and a small box in his other hand. His face looked pale and grey. His head stayed lowered as he mumbled his story to the grieving widow. He told her of the horrifying moment he had split open a fish with his knife and a human finger had slithered out from its stinking guts. She didn't need him to tell her more, she knew exactly where this story was going but she allowed him to finish his tale. The finger had been wearing her husband's simple wedding band. They had taken the ring off to see that their initials had been engraved inside. Her husband would never have worn his ring when working on the boat. Fishing was a dangerous profession. Wearing a ring on the boat could easily lead to a man having his finger caught and ripped off. She imagined him knowing that he was about to die and slipping on his ring in the hope that his body would someday find its way home to his wife. His body hadn't come home but this small part of him had. She took the box from the man with the meagre remains of her husband and her marriage.

She hadn't known what to do with the finger so she had followed the routine that she had seen fishermen do with some of the fish. She packed it in salt and kept it in a dark, dry cupboard. She found herself sliding the ring back on to it first, not fully understanding why she had done that. She had hoped that eventually, the certainty that her husband was lost to her would be something that she accepted. She wished that she could visit each stage of her grief and work through it. Now, three years later, she was still sitting listening to the busy harbour dreaming of his return. Her heart burned in her chest when she thought of him lost out there in the water somewhere. The pain seemed to grow every day instead of slowly leaving her body as she had expected it to eventually.

Femke tried to keep busy, she worked hard and met sometimes with the other widows, a rather large group in a city like theirs. They would discuss their pain and the ways they found to deal with it. They would tell tales of their ancestors and the stories that their husbands had told them about the things they had seen out on the water.

"By rights," one of the other widows had declared the last time they had all met, "She should be here with us."

They had been talking about one of the women who worked making nets for the fishing boats. A quiet, old woman who seemed to know all of the secrets of the sea. She was even said to lift curses from boats that had trouble bringing enough fish in for the market.

"The fishermen swear that they brought his body back without a sign of life," she went on. "They say he had lain dead on that boat for hours. That was before she had insisted on having his body brought to her home."

"I heard that too," another woman said, she was clearly struggling with her friend sucking up all of the group's attention.

"Well, the very next day, he was walking around the market guzzling herring as though he had merely been in a heavy sleep," she continued as though the interruption hadn't happened.

"She's a very powerful witch that one," another widow offered.

"You don't believe in all that do you?" Femke had asked at the time.

"There are many secrets that the likes of us will never know," the storyteller continued. "If she can lift curses from the boats, I'm sure bringing one man back from the dead is no work at all."

Femke had laughed at the time. Now, as she listened to the busy market outside setting up, she couldn't shake the story from her mind. She didn't fully believe in the power of the old witch but part of her mind teased her with the possibilities.

Before she had even made a conscious decision to, she was getting ready to go and visit the old woman at her place of work. She dressed for the wet, windy weather and set off to where she knew the old woman would be. The nettenboetsters, the women who made and fixed the fishing nets for the town, were well known and respected.none were respected more than the old witch. They would stand every day in a large field, each behind poles that were spread out equal distance apart. They seemed like strange scarecrows, standing next to their pole with the wind whipping their dresses and shawls. From the road nearby, you could barely see a single movement. It seemed as though the nets were magically weaving themselves between the proud, well-dressed women. The witch stood at the end of the line watching the others. She was always ready to catch a single mistake from the less experienced women whilst never stopping her own work. Femke watched from the road until the women moved away from their poles and sat down to share food and drink between them.

She slowly approached the women. The old witch stood up to meet her before she got to the resting group.

"I expected to see you years ago, " the old woman announced. "So long you've waited before visiting the mad old witch."

"I don't think you're mad," Femke mumbled apologetically.

"Oh, I hear the whispers around the market, also the words that people try not to give voice to," the old woman continued. There was no accusation in her voice just a simple statement of facts. "Of course, it's different when they have to come asking for favours from the carzy, old lady."

"So you know why I'm here then?" Femke asked.

"I know many things my girl," the old woman replied. "I feel your loss and your pain," she continued. "I have often thought of paying you a visit myself. Although I find things go easier when I wait for people to approach me."

"Are you saying that you can help me?" Femke mumbled. "You know what I want."

"No dear, I know what you NEED," the witch declared. "But I can't help you, you can perhaps help yourself," the witch explained. "You still have the finger don't you?"

"Yes, but how do you know..." Femke began.

The old woman pulled her by the arm and began to explain the process by which she could try to bring back the man she loved. She scribbled some words onto a piece of paper and slipped them into Femke's pocket.

"There are no guarantees when dealing with the sea," the old woman warned before leaving her to travel back to her house. "Only she will decide if he is allowed to return. All that you can do is send up a beacon for him to find his way home."

***

Part of the spell involved making her husband's favourite meal. Knowing some of the farmers from outside the city, Femke used to get the ingredients for a rich pea soup every so often. This was an excellent treat for her tired husband when he was finding his feet on land again. It was a refreshing change from the bread and fish that they ate most of the time. Femke imagined that the smell would float out over the water and draw her husband home.

First, she dropped in a couple of pork chops and let the water begin to boil. She carefully prepared the vegetables, ready to add to the water when the pork was cooked. She tipped in the dried split peas with the pork. The water filled with a grey fog, like the fog that was creeping over the water. The fog that was slowly swallowing the edges of the city. When the pork was cooked, sFemke took them out of the water and added the chopped and peeled vegetables. She took the large sausage that she had got from her farming friends and then her husbands finger that she had taken from the box of salt in her cupboard. It looked dry and grey when she dropped it into the water but then it suddenly turned pink and started twitching. She watched in horror as the seemingly living finger started to slowly dissolve. She placed the words the old woman had scribbled down on the counter and read them out loud as she returned the chopped pork to the pan and stirred.

Femke had to hold on to the counter as the room seemed to dip and sway. She heard waves lapping against wood and the faint sound of singing fishermen. When she stopped feeling dizzy she took her husband's bottle of schelvispekel from the cupboard that where he had kept it when he was alive. Schelvispekel was what the fishermen called the drink. They called it this (Haddock brine) as a way of taking drinks out for their journey without letting their wives know what it really was. Of course, Femke's husband would never dream of lying to her about anything so she knew exactly what it was. She poured a small glass out and placed it next to one of the bowls she had left on the Table. The room seemed to sway and dip again and she could smell fresh fish and sweaty men. She heard the songs the fishermen would sing to help the time to pass mor quickly. Femke's home faded from view and she saw the crew of her husband's boat moving around on the deck of tehir ship. She could see the lights of her city flickering through the fog in the distance. The boat was sailing slowly toward the sounds of her home. The fog grew thicker and rolled over the deck until she couldn't see anything around her.

When the fog cleared, Femke found herself standing next to her table at home. The soup was still bubbling away waiting to be served. The irresistible smells filled the kitchen which had now thankfully stopped swaying. She moved the pan from the heat and then ran out of her house and down to the port where she expected to see her husband's boat arriving.

The boat was already there. her husband and his crew were walking slowly onto land looking dazed. They looked as though they had just woken from a long sleep. Her desperation had allowed her to follow the steps of the spell and even run down to where the boat should be. Only now, did she realise that she had never truly believed it could work. Her husband saw her through the rapidly gathering crowd next to the water. She stood still trying to stop her head spinning and her stomach rolling like the water that had returned her husband. He rushed towards her with his arms wide.

"My darling," he said as he wrapped his arms around her. "Is everything okay? You don't look well at all."

"I'm a bit older than when we last saw each other," Femke was laughing and cryinmg uncontrollably.

"You can't have aged a lot in the few days we were out," Arie was confused.

"It's been over three years," Femke replied. "I thought you were lost to me forever."

"That's impossible we just set sail recently," Arie began. When he pulled back and looked at her face, she knew that he could tell she was telling him the truth. "But I don't remember anything," he raised his hand and stroked her face, she noticed the finger with his wedding ring on it had been returned to his now living body. "I don't know what has happened."

People were starting to crowd around them, they were shouting questions to her husband and his crew. Femke grabbed his hand and pulled him away from them. She kept pulling until she had brought him all the way home. He sat at the prepared table in a daze as she served soup into both bowls. He drank his schelvispekel in one gulp so she quickly refilled his glass and sat with him at the table. They didn't speak for a while but he shovelled the soup into his mouth as though he was starving. Through the window, she saw the thick fog covering the whole street outside her home. She closed the curtains then returned to the table and tried to eat the soup she had prepared. She found it impossible to force the food in and impossible to take her eyes off her husband.

When his belly was full he went to lie down on their bed. Within moments, he was snoring loudly. Femke had been so desperate to talk to her husband but now she was just happy to watch him sleeping. She sat for a while on the chair in her bedroom watching his chest rise and fall. His handsome face hadn't aged a day whilst she wore the last few years heavily.

When Femke went back to the table to clear the dishes, she noticed the door to their home was open and swinging in the wind. Rushing over to close it, she heard a song rolling towards her through the thick fog. Pulling her shawl around her, Femke started to close the door. There was a loud scream that made her freeze where she was. Something was staggering towards her, slowly becoming more visible. One of the other fishermen's wives stumbled through the fog and fell to her knees in front of Femke. Her hands were gripping her throat as blood gushed through her fingers. The woman's mouth opened and closed as she tried to speak to Femke but no words came. The blood poured from her onto the cobbled street she kneeled on, Femke could see that it was already too late. She watched the woman's frantic, twitching eyes grow still as the life left her body and she slumped forward onto the stones. When her hands fell away from her throat, it looked as though her flesh had been torn by thick strong claws.

"Stop the singing. Stop it!" She heard her husband screaming from their bedroom and rushed to his bedside. He was sat up and sweating but he looked at her as though he didn't recognise her for a moment. "She'll take us back, she has to take us back."

"Who is going to take you back?" Femke asked, she was desperately worried for her husband.

He looked at her for a moment and then his face softened and he lay back in the bed. When she tried to speak to him, he closed his eyes and started to snore again as though he hadn't been wide awake just moments before. Femke rushed down the stairs back to the door of their house. When she opened it, the street was empty except for the fog that crept around her. The body of the woman was gone, even the blood that had spilt on the cobbles seemed to have been cleaned up. She could hear a strange slapping sound in the distance. It was like the sound a large fish would make falling against the stones when they slipped from a fisherman's basket. Closing the door quickly, Femke returned to her husband's bedside. She sat awake watching him sleep until the sun rose the next day.

As Femke delivered breakfast to her husband, she watched him guzzle it down without a word. Sometimes he would look up and smile, otherwise, he would give her a brief, apologetic look before digging more into his food. She tried to talk to him about where he had been but no new memories were forming. He told her that whenever he tried to remember anything, all he could hear was a strange voice singing and then the screams of his crew. She didn't push him further, she hated to see the way his face creased up when he tried to force himself to remember. He looked as though he might burst into tears at any moment.

She left her husband resting at home whilst she went to the market. When she got there, a crowd of people were gathered around one of the boats. She tried to ask people what was going on but people were either sobbing or looking like they may vomit. When she pushed to the front, she saw one of the nets laid out on the boat with the morning's catch in it. Three local women, all with there throats torn open lay tangled in the nets. Crabs scuttled over their grey flesh. She recognised one of the bodies as the woman she had seen last night, staggering through the fog. The other two she didn't recognise at all.

"What happened?" she asked one of the fishermen as he stumbled away from the boat.

"A curse has befallen us," he moaned. "Not a single fish in that net, just those poor women."

The fisherman pushed her out of the way. As soon as he got through the crowd of onlookers, he vomited. He heaved and heaved until his stomach was empty. Femke moved away from the sobbing or chattering crowd and walked towards the market stalls. She couldn't stop thinking of what the fisherman had said. The spell was supposed to bring her husband back. She hadn't expected his whole crew to turn up. Now she was sure that something else had come back with them. Something travelling through their city hiding in the thick fog waiting for its next victim. She almost broke into a run when she saw the old witch standing at one of the stalls that sold dried herbs and vegetables. She yanked her by the arm and pulled her away from anyone that might listen to their conversation.

"What have you done?" she asked angrily.

"Me? I haven't done a thing," the witch laughed. "You enacted the spell, you read the words on the paper. Didn't you think it strange that an old woman would give up her secrets so easily?"

"Did I do something wrong?" Femke pleaded for an answer. "I didn't want any of this."

"What you want and what you get are often two different things," the witch smiled showing her brown stained teeth. "The sea will always take her price."

"But I did the spell, those women did nothing wrong,"

"This wasn't your price my dear, I am paying my debt to her," the old woman was laughing at Femke's mouth opening and closing. "I asked her to return what she had taken from me many years ago. When my husband opened his eyes and breathed again she told me that one day she would collect her payment. She told me about your husband a few years ago and promised me that one day you would come to me."

"I don't understand," Femke mumbled.

"They took something from her, now she will take something from all of you," the witch continued, she was walking towards the waterside so Femke rushed along behind her.

The old woman sat down dangling her feet into the water then reached down and brought some of it up in her hand. She threw the salty water into Femkes face. Femke rubbed the filthy water out of her eyes. Now, she was standing on her husbands fishing boat watching the men rushing from task to task. The water rocked them turning her stomach over so that she felt as though she was going to be sick. The strong smell of rotten fish was on everything and a strange sound drifted towards her.

"Stop her, stop that fucking noise," Antonie, one of the youngest members of her husband's crew was screaming.

Femke walked to where the men were gathering and gasped as she saw something her mind wouldn't let her believe. A mermaid was tied up on the deck, it had a deep wound on its side and what looked like an infected wound in its tail. It had long, thick claws and sharp teeth. It was nothing like the mermaids she had read about in children's stories. This thing was monstrous but the song that seemed to effortlessly fall from its mouth was beautiful.

"Stay away from her," Arie pleaded with the young

man. "we need to take her back with us."

"Make her stop that noise or I'll stop her myself, " Antonie shouted.

His eyes were wide and he was frantically looking all around him. It was as if the song that seemed so beautiful to her was driving him insane. The other men tried to form a barrier between the boy and the creature. The creature continued to sing and looked at each of the men with a hungry smile on its lips. Antonie ran to the other side of the boat then came back holding a large knife which he waved threateningly in front of him.

"Get out of my way or I swear I'll kill you all if I have to."

The men jumped out of the way as he approached swinging blade in front of him. The creature continued to sing until he swiped the knife across its throat. As blood poured from the hideous creature, the singing stopped but the creature smiled wider than before. Femke watched in horror as the thing started to dissolve into a thick fog. The fog rose and split into separate clouds. One cloud for each member of the crew, each of them took a deep breath at the same time, drawing the fog deep into their lungs. Their eyes turned completely white and they all started singing the mermaids song. The wind rose and the water crashed into the side of the boat then Femke's husband turned to her and screamed.

Suddenly, she was standing by the waterside with the old woman again.

"When you kill a mermaid, you release the thing that lives inside it," the old woman laughed. "The thing inside them that sings, drawing ships onto rocks or swimmers into shark-infested waters. The sea wanted you to bring them home so they can feed her. They took something precious from her, now they must repay the debt."

"Those innocent women?" Femke began.

"Nobody here is innocent. We used to respect the sea, we used to take no more than was necessary and remember to give back an offering," the old woman ranted. "people got greedy. Now, they take as much as they can take and offer nothing in return. Smell the fish on the market that rots because you've taken more than you can ever use. Disgusting, greedy people. Your husband and his crew are hers now. They will serve her better than they ever did in life, feeding her the bodies that are rightfully hers."

"Why would you let this happen?"

"I'm not letting anything!" the witch shouted. "When that boy killed one of hers, he wrote this future for all of us. She just needed you to call them home."

"I'll send them back, I'll kill them all myself if I have to," Femke shouted.

"We both know you can't do that," the witch cackled. "Even if you could, what would you release on us all then? The thing that is inside them can never die it will live on in the body of anybody that releases it."

Femke turned and ran from the cackling old woman. She didn't stop running until she found herself back at home. Her husband was still sitting at the table as though waiting for more breakfast to be served.

"So hungry," he hissed. He was sweating and shivering at the same time.

"You need to go, you need to set sail and never look back," she pleaded with her husband.

"I've only just returned to you my darling," Femke noticed that his mouth was filled with sharp teeth like the creature on the boat.

She tried to yank him up out of his chair but he fell to the floor beside it. His legs seemed fused together. Femke gasped as blisters bubbled all over his fused legs. When they burst, she could see scales beneath the bubbling skin. He was still holding a spoon in his clawed fingers. He stared at her as though he wanted to say something but when he opened his mouth all that came out was the mermaid's song. Femke's mind was racing she knew that she had to do something now before more innocent souls were stolen.

"Hungry," her husband hissed.

Femke rushed to the pot of soup from last night, the soup that had called her husband home and scooped some into a bowl. It surely didn't matter to this thing if the soup was warm or cold. Her hands were shaking so much that she dropped the bowl, spilling the contents on the floor. When she bent to pick up the bowl, she noticed something on one of the lower shelves. A box of poison she used to keep the rats out of their home. She knew straight away what she needed to do. She poured some of the pellets into a fresh bowl of soup and returned to the thing that had stolen her husband's body. The thing shoved its face into the bowl and lapped at it until it was empty.

"Hungry," it hissed again. Its legs were still bubbling. She could tell the creature was in pain. Weakened by the slow, disgusting transformation. The whole house stunk of rotten fish. Then the thing started vomiting. Stinking black liquid spilled from its mouth. The thing stared at her. It was its turn to be horrified when it saw the box of poison in her hand.

"You can't kill me. I will take your body," It hissed.

She knew that what it said was true, but she hoped the poison would give her enough time to visit each of the crew members. She ran from the house and down to the market where she bought a fresh fish for each member of her husband's crew. She shoved the poison pellets deep into the guts of the fish and set off to young Antonie's home. She found him alone he was fully transformed. There was little left of the young man she once knew. She realised he must have been the one who had already begun claiming victims the previous night. He raised his nose when she came closer to him smelling the fish she carried in her bag.

"Hungry," it hissed. "Fishhhhh."

She threw one of the fish to the creature and watched in disgust as its sharp teeth ripped through the fish's raw flesh. The fish guts were spilling onto the floor but the disgusting thing was scooping them up in its claws and shoving them into its mouth. She felt like she was going to be sick but she knew she still had work to do and very little time. She rushed from the house and set off to visit Jack, one of the oldest members of her husband's crew.

The door to his home was wide open, swinging in the wind. The rotten fish smell pushed out of the house into the cold air outside. When she entered the home she gasped as she saw Jack's wife lying on the floor with blood pooling around her. Jack lay on the floor next to her scraping chunks of flesh from her throat and forcing them into his mouth. Femke threw the fish to him and watched as he snatched it up and started tearing at it with his teeth.

She found the last two men together, empty bottles on the table showed that they had been enjoying a night of drinking together. Now, they lay on the floor hissing at each other as their legs bubbled and blistered. Femke threw them each a fish and stayed to watch them eat them. Then they turned their hungry eyes on her.

They started to sing, the song seemed to burrow into her mind like worms. Femke tried to get away from them but her legs refused to obey her. One of them slithered fast towards her and she managed to stumble back out of its way. Then the other one made a move toward her. They had stopped singing for a moment as they both tried to attack her so she turned and ran from the room. Femke could hear the sound of retching and vomiting behind her. It threw memories up of the disgusting black slime that had gushed from her husband's mouth. The stench seemed to be following her as she ran down the street towards the dock. When she made it to the water's edge, she allowed herself one last look at her beautiful city. The once comforting sounds of the fishermen working and the chatter of the market now filled her with sorrow and pain.

Her own desperation had brought this curse to her beautiful home, her dear Vlaardingen. Femke knew that it would have to be her that took the curse away. She needed to get as far away as possible. She had to leave behind the only home she had ever known. The sea would be her home now. The sea would only claim one more victim now. This one went willingly into the water.

She swam as fast and hard as she could, she could hear people shouting from the land but didn't dare look back. The thing that had stolen those men's bodies would be released soon and looking to claim their killer. Her lungs burned as she forced her way through the water. She felt as though her chest would burst open but she kept swimming. She put as much distance as she could between herself and her old home before she dared to stop pushing forward. Flapping her arms to keep herself afloat, she turned to see how far she had gone. She could see the boats far off in the distance, the land and houses were a blur. A dark, rolling cloud of fog drifted slowly, determinedly towards her as she floated.

Another burst of energy and she was swimming as fast and as far as she could with the fog cloud slowly creeping behind her. Eventually, she saw the fog collecting in front of her face. It forced itself deep into her lungs. She could feel the thing taking over every part of her body. It was forcing itself into her muscles but she kept swimming. Her brain was slowly losing everything that made her who she was. Her memories were being stripped one by one. She tried desperately to hold onto the image of her husbands face, happy, standing on his boat waving to her. Soon, the fog clouded that memory out too. Her name was ... she couldn't remember. The fog had destroyed every part of who she was and soon would transform her body. The pain seemed to spread through every vein until she wanted to scream. When she opened her mouth, all that came out was the mermaid's song. Femke was already gone.

DUTCH PEA SOUP - ERWTENSOEP

CONTRIBUTED BY CALLUM PEARCE

2 Packets of Split Peas
2/3 Shoulder Chops
Bacon Cubes (Optional)
Dried laurel leaves
2 leeks
2 Crumbly Potatoes
2 Large Winter Carrots
1 Celeriac
Full smoked Sausage
Celery Leaves
Parsley
Dead Man's Finger (Optional)
Vegetable Stock

Personally, I like to make a massive soup pan full of this. You can leave it bubbling away at a get together with a load of people. They can all help themselves when the smell becomes irresistible. Otherwise, you can just have it for yourself and your family for a couple of days good eating. If you just want to make a smaller pan, halve the amount of ingredients. Erwtensoep or Snert as it is called here in the Netherlands is easy to make and can be frozen if you find you have too much. The dead man's finger is entirely optional. If you've read the story, you will know that it could make things more interesting though.

The bacon cubes are traditionally added but I find the chops and smoked sausage is already enough meat and flavour.

Instructions:
Half fill a large soup pan with water and stock, turn the heat up full. Wash and add the split peas, shoulder chops, Laurel leaves and Bacon cubes (if you chose to use them).
When the water comes to the boil, turn the heat low and let the chops and peas cook slowly for about 25 mins. Make sure you stir every so often so that the peas don't stick to the bottom. It can get pretty mushy at the bottom, but if you cook on a low heat, you shouldn't have to hover over it. Just give it a good stir every once in a while.
Peel and chop, the Potatoes, Carrots and Celriac into small cubes. Wash and cut the leek into half circles. Chop up the celery leaves and parsley.
After 25 mins of cooking, take out the shoulder chops and cut them into small chunks. Make sure that you get rid of any small pieces of bone. Add the vegetables to the pan and top the water up so that they are fully covered with a bit more at the top. Return the pork cut from the chops to the pan.
Add the herbs but keep a little garnish the dish with. Leave it all cooking on a low heat for about half an hour stirring every so often. I turn it really low and let it cook for ages but it should be almost ready after this. Add the whole smoked sausage and cook for a further 10 minutes.

When you're ready to serve, take the sausage out and chop into small slices. Serve the soup and add the sausage on top. Sprinkle with the chopped herbs saved from the preparation. Add salt and pepper if you feel you need to.
Enjoy the beautiful smells and tasty, warming soup. Perfect for autumn and winter evenings.

Callum Pearce is a Dutch storyteller, originally from Liverpool. He is a fiction writer published multiple times across a variety of platforms. A Lover of the magical as well as the macabre. He lives in a foggy old fishing town in the Netherlands with his husband and a couple of cat- shaped
sprites. Featured in lots of drabble collections and an-thologies or
online. He has also written factual articles for an LGBTQ+ lifestyle website.

SCATTERED

S.O. GREEN

They lay on the dry grass at the cliff edge and watched the sun tilt and pitch to brush the surface of the Pacific and blush its surface with the softest glow. Nina's fingers traced its light over the curve of Tom's cheek and brought out a glow of her own.

"Sunset," her girlfriend breathed, vapour curling around Nina's fingers. "We should probably go. We'll be late for dinner."

"We can always just get breakfast in the morning."

"Yes, but I didn't call my channel 'A Pacific Place to Breakfast', did I?"

"Maybe we should, just this once. Haven't you ever heard of a holiday special?"

"That would be an excellent idea, if it were a holiday."

"Bound to be a holiday somewhere, right? We can just Google it after."

"Sorry," Tom said, putting her palms on Nina's

shoulders and easing her back. "You know I like my content to be consistent."

"Right. And your girlfriend frustrated."

Tom winked and raked the straw out of her silky, black hair. It couldn't be tonight soon enough. Nina contented herself by kissing her on the collarbone and watching her chest bob as her breath hitched.

"Come on, lover. Shall we find a Pacific place to dine?"

Nina nodded and shouldered her rucksack. They held hands and took the coastal path. Tonight, they'd be dining in the little town down the trail, the one Maps didn't have a name for, but which the sign called Greenfields. She could see the failing light glinting in the windows, see a couple of store fronts still lit. She hoped one of them was a restaurant or something. She hated to see Tom pout.

*****

One of them was a restaurant. The owner—a stout, gruff-looking guy with a hairline retreating into the hinterlands of his scalp, grey as steel and with eyes to match—looked like he was shutting up the place when they shuffled up to the open door. Nina half-expected him to push the door shut. Instead, he lay out two menus and beckoned them in.

She felt a clench in her stomach whenever they walked into a new place, especially an old, small place. South, around Cali way, they hadn't raised too many eyebrows. Two girls travelling alone, holding hands all the time, was the least of strange sights along a coast littered with washed-up Hollywood debris.

If it came to it, they'd say 'sisters'. Most people took that at face value, even though Nina was short and heavy and had inherited red hair from some distantly Celtic ancestor that predated the dull brunettes who'd birthed her, and Tom was Japanese, dark of hair and eye and complexion. Prejudice was like being blind in one eye.

He didn't say anything. Just let them sit at the table and make eyes at each other over the faded, folded cardboard while he wiped down the colourful Formica around them. They sat side-by-side, double-dating with their battered, old rucksacks.

"No tamales," Nina pointed out.

"We might be too far north. But there are plenty of Japanese dishes on the menu and that's always a nice surprise. Teriyaki noodles, miso shiru, chirashi sushi..."

"Chirashi?"

"Scattered. It's a little different from your California rolls."

"I'm into different."

"Hope you're into seaweed too," the owner said, swinging back around. "Customary to put a little extra on the dishes we make here."

"I don't mind a little salt," Nina said, smirk pulling up like an arrow in Tom's direction. Her girlfriend just frowned at her.

"It's not really about the sodium. Folks like to feel the connection to the sea. Reminds us of what's important. What brings us life."

"Where do you import it from?" Tom asked. She had her phone resting under her hand, ready to type. Always looking for colour for the channel.

"No imports. It's grown locally. We've got a kelp field along the cost. We tend and harvest it, serve it up here. Most folks eat at least one meal a day here."

"Oh, really? Do you mind if I ask where the field is? Maybe we could take a look tomorrow morning. It would go perfectly in the video."

It'd be a crowd-pleaser—homegrown, organic ingredients sourced locally—and it formed a great narrative. Nina had always liked the idea that their channel could help small places find the wider audience they deserved. The town had enough houses, but it was quiet, out of the way, like technology didn't—or wouldn't—touch it. Tourism, probably a non-entity. Maybe they could change that.

Or maybe she was dreaming, head in the cloud right along with Tom's pro-edited video packages and their climbing subscriber count. Their channel probably couldn't change the world but... It could change a few lives. That could happen, right?

"Can you bring us two bowls?" Tom asked, and Nina could see the wheels turning behind her deep, dark eyes. The next video was taking shape. "Do you take Apple Pay?"

He didn't, but Nina had this crazy stuff called 'cash' and apparently you could exchange it for goods and services. She liked to keep some around for situations just like this. Tom had asked her if it was a good idea to carry bills with them while they were hiking. Nina had just pointed out that, if someone wanted it, they could come and take it from her.

Or cook for them, which was what their host did. Even at that late hour, he didn't seem upset to be steaming more vegetables, cooking more rice, roasting more seaweed. A half-hour later, they were sitting in front of heaped bowls and Tom was arranging her chopsticks to frame the perfect shot for the thumbnail. The rice was a shock of white at the bottom of the deep, black bowl, folded over edamame, cubes of rich, green avocado, the aromatic warmth of toasted sesame and sprinkled liberally with that famous seaweed he'd mentioned.

Nina poked around with her sticks. "Not complaining, but... I'm kinda surprised there's no salmon in this,"

"We make do without. The fish doesn't belong to us."

"Say what?"

"Just what I said. It's against the law to fish in these waters. It doesn't belong to us."

"Right..."

She'd never heard of any law like that along a US coast. Marine protected areas, sure, but this wasn't one of them. The waters further out were probably a crosshatch of different territories and fishing rights, carved up by the bigger companies, but who was going to police one small town's local fishing? She'd heard of people avoiding fish because of mercury poisoning or for ethical reasons but...

"Nina, you need to try this." Tom jabbed at her bowl with her sticks. The phone was gone, and unadulterated bliss was curling on her lips and sparkling in her eyes.

"This is something special. What's the mix in the rice? Tamari, rice vinegar, caster sugar...?"

"Kombu," their host confessed.

"More seaweed? Nina asked, eyebrow arching.

"It works." Tom grinned. "It really works."

Nina picked at her bowl. She'd never been able to get the hang of chopsticks. Tom had small, nimble fingers. She could pluck a sesame seed off Nina's cheek, and had. The closest Nina could come to that kind of fine motor control was putting someone in a pressure point lock. By the time she was half-done, Tom was finished, pushing away her bowl with a contented sigh.

"Exceptional."

"Yeah, it was pretty good."

"I take it it's not singing to you the way it is to your girlfriend," the owner said.

"I said it was pretty good."

"Ah, don't worry about it," he said, and gathered the bowls up. He didn't meet her eyes. She guessed she'd offended him. "Most everybody likes it. Not everyone loves it."

"I don't know how," Tom said. "That might be the best thing I've eaten in years."

She clapped her stomach. Considering they'd built a channel on hiking the coast, stopping at near every eatery they came across on the way, that was saying something. They'd found some real high spots since starting the series. Kind of surprising this was Tom's favourite.

They said thanks to the owner one last time before shouldering packs and heading out. Tom stretched and, for a second before he flicked off the lights in the restaurant, she was glowing.

"Want to keep going?" Nina asked.

"It's a little late to be moving on, don't you think? Shouldn't we find a place to stay?"

"I guess."

"What's the matter?"

"Ah, this place." Nina swiped a hand around Greenfields and its old, crow-stepped gables, its weather-battered stone. "It's weird."

"We've stayed in lots of weird places."

"Yeah, but this isn't, y'know, unfriendly or dangerous or anything. It's just…weird."

"Really? Does my big, bad girlfriend have the willies?"

Tom cackled with delight and Nina did her best not to scowl. They'd been through some rough neighbourhoods in the past and it had never much mattered to her. Tom had fretted and worried and she'd just shrugged. Let them start something, she'd said. We'll see what happens.

Tom had been raised on a diet of Goju Ryu karate. Her father owned a dojo in L.A. His students had been tossed through walls by Avengers, cut in half by Jedi and pummelled by private detectives in dive bars. Her kata was crisp and precise. She'd never actually used her lessons to hurt someone. Nina, for her part, had been in more fights than she cared to count (none of them scripted) before she'd even set foot in a dojo.

But this wasn't something she could punch to make it go away. It wasn't her fault they were standing in the middle of a creepy town and it definitely wasn't her fault that Tom couldn't feel it.

"We don't even have to sleep if you don't want to. I just don't want to be thrashing around in the dark, that's all. We'll leave first thing tomorrow."

"Skip breakfast?"

"We could stop back in here for more sushi. I'll just get it to go."

"You drive a hard bargain, Tomoe Yamazuki," Nina said, grabbing her by a shoulder strap and planting a kiss on her forehead. "Fine. Let's find us an air bed."

***

Actually, she probably should have expected AirBnB to have nothing. This just didn't seem like the place. Fortunately, there was a hotel and it was still open.

There was no name over the door but the rates in the window were good and the lady behind the counter had kind eyes. She looked more like a librarian than an innkeeper, complete with grey bun and old sweater.

"What's the place called anyway?" Nina asked. "For Trip Advisor."

"It doesn't really need a name," the lady explained. "Everyone just calls it 'the hotel'. Only one in town."

"Like the restaurant," Tom said. "It's kind of a shame. I really wanted to recommend the place on my channel, but it didn't have a name."

"Oh, you went there already?" There was something in her tone, like she didn't care to hear it. "Planning on stopping in for breakfast?"

"Yeah, we are."

Nina wasn't sure how she felt about the delight

in Tom's voice. Apparently, neither was the lady. She slapped a key on the desk with a tight-lipped smile. Maybe she considered the restaurant competition.

"You get many tourists here?"

"Not exactly. But most of the folks who live here moved from out of town. Bernard at the restaurant. And me, twenty years ago."

"Really? How come? I mean, it probably wasn't for the nightlife, right?"

"My husband's buried here."

"Oh."

"Don't mind her," Tom said, slashing her eyes at Nina and sliding the key off the desk. "She's actually pretty nice once you get to know her."

She plastered on that thin smile again and nodded. "Enjoy your night, girls. Let me know if you need anything."

"I'm sure we'll be fine. Thanks very much."

They rode Tom's wave of grace up to their cosy, little room. On the stairs, she jabbed Nina hard in the ribs with her elbow.

"Don't be an ass."

"You don't think it's weird?"

"Not weird enough to justify being an ass."

"Okay, fine. I'm an ass. You said I was a pretty nice ass though."

Tom flicked her under the chin and let them into their room. They sat on the creaky bed and she pulled out her laptop to Frankenstein the videos and photos she'd taken that day. Nina raked through the drawers in the dresser and nightstand, looking for anything worth commenting on. Nothing. Not even a Bible. Was that weird? Or just a sign of the times?

She scooped up the TV remote and started flicking. She hadn't watched actual television in years. It was even worse than she remembered.

"Wanna watch porn?"

"Why would we watch it when we can make it?"

"I'd love to, but I feel like this bed's maybe a nookie alarm."

"Then it seems we'll have to save it for a place with thicker walls."

"You're worth the wait."

Tom flashed Nina a smile as she killed the television. She scrubbed her fist across her eyes and leaned across for a kiss.

"Mind if I turn in?"

"Go ahead. I just want to finish this."

"Sorry. Wish I could keep you company."

"You're always keeping me company."

Their lips met again. Warmth flashed across Nina's cheeks, down her throat, into her chest. She lowered herself onto her pillow and deflated.

The warm feeling didn't settle in her stomach. It felt like it met something cold. Something that pushed back.

Maybe just something she'd eaten.

***

Shorebirds wheeling in the grey beyond. A lash of salt spit at the rail. Staring out into the roiling ocean. What makes it move? Wind? Or the tossing and turning of something below, stirring in its sleep?

The ocean wakes at night by the green fields. Outsiders think its light is lent by scant stars and by the dollar moon. Too cheap.

It is evanescent with its pallid and sickly glow. Putrescence effervesces from below. The gulls here are hardy. There are no nets or lines. The fish do not belong to us.

But the kelp is ours. The fields are our gift to tend and we cherish them like loved ones.

Stand on the pier and watch the ebb and flow. Of the water. Of the green. Of life. Something rises. Something else falls. It is the way of things. There is an order. A delicate balance and we must play our part.

We were put on this earth to play a part, but we don't like it much and we slouch, insouciant, at the rail. We chafe our elbows on the ancient iron, which was part of this world long before we dug it out of the earth and hammered it into the shape that suits us. We strain our eyes at the horizon without ever realising what lies beneath our feet.

You hear their cries, yes? The soaring, squawking, jeering gulls. But now, strain your ears for a different song...

Nina surfaced. The nightmare clung to her, slimy and stinking of salt. She threw off the sheet and groped for the lamp on the bedside cabinet. The light was weak, off-colour, kind of green. She waited for the nausea to subside, but it didn't.

Something was wrong.

"Babe... Babe, I don't..."

She groped for Tom's shoulder and touched nothing but pillow. She wasn't there.

The bathroom light was on. She hesitated, then heard the sound of Tom puking and leapt over the bed, the wriggling in her stomach forgotten. She burst through the door, found her girlfriend kneeling over the toilet in vest and shorts. Nina scooped her hair back, ran a reassuring hand down her spine.

"Talk to me, babe. What's going on? You okay?"

Tom shook her head. She clamped her hands around her stomach and groaned. The bowl was splattered with green.

"Bad sushi?"

"That's normally because of bad fish. We didn't have any fish, remember?"

Nina remembered. They hadn't had fish. They'd had seaweed. Lots and lots of seaweed.

"Bring it up if you can. Probably better out than in."

Tom managed a half-hearted, water-eyed nod, then pitched forward and retched. Green strings unfurled from her mouth and dangled like vines. She convulsed, another retch, and more burst out. Sticking in her throat.

"Shit! Hold still!"

Nina grabbed a fistful of the slimy shit and yanked. She heard it sliding up from the back of Tom's throat. She gasped as her airways reopened. A ball as big as Nina's hand splashed into the toilet bowl.

"Holy shit! We need to get you to a fucking hospital, right now! Try to hold it down. Please. Whatever you do, don't bring it up until I come back!"

She ran back into the bedroom and snatched her

phone off the nightstand. She stared at the big, red X where her bars had once been. She thumbed in Emergency and nothing happened. Wasn't that impossible?

"Hold on, Tom. Please hold on."

She yanked open the door and ran down the corridor in her underwear, banging on every door she passed. No one answered. None of them opened. Not until she reached the reception desk. Then the old woman emerged from the door behind it with a grim look on her face.

"Something's wrong with my girlfriend," Nina said, caution, and pretty much everything else, be damned.

There were a number of appropriate responses, but she decided on, "Did you have the dream?"

"Lady, I had a fucking nightmare."

"Then it's chosen you too. It could have been worse."

"Are you nuts? You have to call a doctor. Or show me to your fucking phone at least. Come on, what the hell are you waiting for? She could be dying."

Her voice cracked. She tried not to let panic take hold, but she could feel it, crawling up her throat with clawed fingers. She didn't know what was happening to Tom and she didn't know what the hell this woman— this town's—problem was.

"Let me see her. I can tell you what to do."

Nina nodded, desperate now. She sprinted up the steps. Even spry for her age, the lady couldn't keep up. She reached the top step as Nina burst back into the room and ran for Tom and the bathroom.

She skidded over in a pile of something green and slimy, hit the floor in a perfect side breakfall. "Fuck…"

The bathroom was empty. Green tendrils overhung the rim of the toilet and streaked in a long snail trail through the door, past Nina and…

Straight to the window.

It was open, curtain flapping on a brine wind. Nina stared out across the rooftops of Greenfields, down into the dark chasms of its cobbled roads, searching for the woman she loved.

"I know where she's going," the old lady said. "Follow me."

Nina obeyed, dumbstruck. Her mind was overclocked, registering nothing. Thoughts were backing up in her head. Right now, all she wanted was to scream. And she wanted to see her girlfriend again.

What's happening to us, Tom?

***

The old woman tossed Nina her clothes and told her to get dressed. She wanted to argue, point out that they were wasting time, but suddenly she turned into Nina's mom and wouldn't back down.

Which meant Nina was the one standing in the way and she sullenly yanked on a tee and jeans, jammed her high-tops on and followed.

Evelyn, the lady said, as she pulled a flashlight from a drawer under the reception desk. Like what Nina wanted right at that moment was a friend. Like she cared about anything but Tom.

But, as they made their way through Greenfields' winding roads, ever downward to the water's edge, questions started to bubble up through the murk of terror.

"How did you know I had a dream?"

"I had a dream too, twenty years ago. I still have dreams but they're different now. That first night was…a welcome. These days, my dreams are my reward."

"What the hell are you even talking about?"

"You'll understand. It's not a comfort but it's the truth. You *will* understand. And I'll help you, like they helped me."

"Help me do what?" Nina snarled.

"Tend to the garden. We all do our bit. We harvest the kelp. We eat at the restaurant. We get our reward. It's a good life. It doesn't have the carefree wonder of ignorance but… It has purpose and comfort. You'll see."

"I just want to find my girlfriend and go home."

Evelyn shook her head sadly. "You can't do both."

"Fuck you."

They reached the beach. The tide was low. The moon peered down from the black—an unblinking, silver eye—and someone had scattered diamond dust across the sky. They weren't the only ones on the promenade tonight but none of them saw the night's majesty. They were all watching the beach.

Watching the girl in the shorts and vest staggering across the sand, clutching her stomach, leaving a trail of green slime behind her.

"TOM!"

Nina shoved through the crowd and pelted across the sand, feet churning, sliding on patches of seaweed and Tom's bile. She was still too far away when someone grabbed her arm and yanked her off her feet. She fell back with a snarl. The last she saw of Tom was her silky, black hair fanning out around her in the water, then vanishing beneath the surface, following her under.

Bernard held her tight, keeping her from giving chase. The moment she had her feet, she hit him with a rising strike under the jaw, twisted into him and flipped him over her shoulder. He smashed into the damp sand and then she stamped on his head.

"Stop!" Evelyn cried, jumping into Nina's field of vision and throwing her hands up like she was praying for mercy. "Please, just stop."

"He poisoned her!"

"No. That's just it. She heeded the call. You ate it too. It just didn't *sing* to you the way it did her. That's why it found a home inside her but, inside you, it died."

The sense—the horrible, awful sense—of what Evelyn was telling her sank through her anger, her fear, her desperate *need* for Tom to be okay, and landed hard in the pit of her stomach. She released Bernard and crumpled, falling to her knees in the sand.

"What's going to happen to her?" she moaned, staring at the place where her girlfriend had been. The tears came, hot and hard.

"Metamorphosis," Evelyn whispered, hardly audible over the crashing of the waves. "Painful at first, but… Then blessedly peaceful. The bliss of ignorance. They're the lucky ones, Nina. Believe me."

She looked up sharp at hearing her name, but Evelyn wasn't watching her. She was staring out into the ocean, rubbing at the wedding band on her left hand.

"Why?" Nina asked. "Why did this happen?"

"Weren't you listening when it spoke? There's an order to things. A balance to maintain. We're all part of an ecosystem. We like to think we're the apex of our food chain but… It's not true. We're just lucky it prefers seafood."

"What does?"

There was a ripple of gasps from the crowd arrayed along the sea road. They were all staring into the water with awe widening their eyes, hands rising to cover gaping mouths or clutch wild hearts.

Nina followed their gaze, felt her own heart skip. There, on the shimmering surface of the sea, was a deep, green glow, pulsing, surging, growing brighter. The water began to froth and boil and, from the ageless depths, something rose to the surface. Something large enough to swallow Greenfields in a single bite. Something that could cradle Nina's entire life in its webbed hands, break it to pieces and let it fall without a care, without a thought. Scattered.

Something with a savage and malicious intellect glinting in the void pits of its eyes and wriggling in the undulations of its writhing, twisting mouth.

Then it turned and marched out into the deep ocean to find something to eat.

And Nina suddenly understood. If it didn't find anything, it would come back.

***

Nina slipped from Tom's embrace and into the bed Bernard had given her upstairs in the restaurant. She dressed in what would have been a fisherman's clothes in any other town, then sat at her small desk and watched the last video her girlfriend had ever edited. The one that had never made it to the channel and never would.

She remembered that sunset. The sign that said, 'Welcome to Greenfields'. The bowl of sushi.

She paused on Tom's face, touched a kiss to the screen and flipped the laptop closed.

Bernard said nothing when they passed on the landing. Their altercation on the beach was forgiven. Forgotten. Just an ache in her fist and his jaw and both their hearts. There was nothing to say now she knew he'd watched his brother walk across that same beach.

A cute couple, matching 'his & hers' rucksacks and goofy flirt-grins, sat at a table perusing the breakfast menu, which was the same as the late evening menu. They smiled at Nina. She waved because smiling was beyond her.

A shiver ran through her when she heard the man ask, "Hey, can we get the chirashi-zushi?"

She threw her equipment bag into the boat they'd assigned her and stood at the rail, staring out across the ocean. She saw the horizon, but she could never move past it. Too concerned about what lay beneath her feet.

Tom had been her sail. Now she was her anchor.

She took the boat out into the green. She got to work, trimming back the crop, keeping it evenly distributed. It festooned the cliff edge around the corner from town. Scattered.

The kelp is ours. The fields are our gift to tend and we cherish them like loved ones. The fish do not belong to us but the green keeps them close and abundant. That is our role to play. We keep the larder stocked.

She finished in the usual spot. She always trimmed just a little more from this patch than the others. If she cut here and there and a little more, she could see it peering up at her from beneath the waters. A face, peacefully sleeping. Dreaming the kind of dreams that Nina slipped into by night and never wanted to wake from.

She plunged her arm into the water, grazed her fingers over the curve of a soft cheek, warm to the touch.

You're always keeping me company.

She stayed there until the sun tilted and pitched to brush the surface of the Pacific and blush its surface with the softest glow. Then she started the motor and headed back to shore.

She'd take the cuttings back to Bernard for the restaurant. Tonight, she'd eat a whole bowl and dream of Tomoe.

Her reward.

THE CALL OF THE OCEAN (VEGAN CHIRASHI-ZUSHI, HOLD THE GREEN MADNESS)

CONTRIBUTED BY S.O. GREEN

4 servings, more or less

Ingredients

For the rice
125g sushi rice
2 ½ tsp rice vinegar
½ tbsp. golden caster sugar
¼ tsp sea salt

For the scatter
1 carrot, cut into thin, 2-inch strips
1 avocado, cubed
150g cubed cucumber
150g tofu, cubed
1 tbsp sesame seeds
1 sheet nori, cut into 2-inch x ¼ inch strips

To serve
Soy sauce
Wasabi paste
Sweet chilli sauce

1. Wash the rice in a sieve under cold running water
until the water runs clear. Let it drain. Transfer to a
saucepan and cover with cold water. Bring to the boil,
cover and simmer over low heat for 15 minutes. Turn
off heat and leave to swell for 15 minutes. Alternatively,
follow the packet instructions.
2. Stir together the vinegar, sugar and salt in a bowl.
Mix with the still-warm rice, then leave to cool.
3. Peel cucumber and carrot. Scoop avocado carefully
out of its skin. Cut into cubes, along with the tofu.
4. Once rice is cool, scatter cubes over the top. Sprinkle
with sesame seeds and strips of nori.
5. Eat now or leave it in the fridge to take for lunch the
next day.
The joy of this recipe is that it emulates the taste of
maki without the need for a bamboo mat and rolling
skillz. As obscene as the idea of eating sushi with a
spoon is, it lets you mix and match the topping to have
a different feel and flavour in every bite.
The other great thing about it is that the alternatives
are largely endless, depending on what you like in your
sushi. I'd recommend making sure you don't use nori
made from the kelp of the Old Ones though, just to be
safe.

Simone Oldman Green (they/them) is a genre-fluid writer and editor living in the Kingdom of Fife with husband, John. Author of over 70 published works with imprints including Dragon Soul Press, Black Hare Press and Eerie River Publishing. They also won 3rd Place in the British Fantasy Society's Short Story Contest 2018. Writer, vegan, martial artist, gamer, occasionally a terrible person (but only to fictional people). They thrive on the unusual, which might explain why there are so many cats.

Website: https://thebasementoflove.blogspot.com/
Facebook: https://www.facebook.com/thebasementoflove
Twitter: https://twitter.com/SOGreenWriter

Second Death

Jasmine Jarvis

Dear Reader,

Before you sit down to read my story, I suggest you make yourself up a tasty serving of Foule Medammes (Egyptian Fava Bean Dip). Now, while Ammit seasoned her Fava Bean dip with some rather unsavoury extras, I highly recommend you stick to the original recipe, which follows after the story.

* * *

Abydos, Egypt, May 1911.

With a god almighty crack, the seal of heavy granite crumbled under the detonation. The dig team set about clearing away the debris, securing the new entrance with wooden beams. Professor Argus moved past the workers carrying away the shattered rocks, towards the opening in the base of the mountain. He gently ran his thumb over the scroll of parchment that he held in his right hand as he stepped over a large chunk of stone, his left hand reached out to take the oil lantern his young Egyptian assistant held out for him. The Professor Argus could hardly contain his excitement. He had invested his life savings and his belief in this expedition, and now it looks like his years of devoted research was proving in that moment to be right. He crossed the threshold and marvelled at the granite steps leading down into a dark void.

Leading down to the tomb of a *God*.

Behind him he could hear the others follow him down, lanterns approaching from behind him, shadows danced along the colourful hieroglyphs, making it look like the images along the walls were moving, bringing their ancient stories to life. The further down into the tomb Professor Argus and his team went, the colder the air became. The lantern lights flickered. Echoes petered out to whispers as they entered the tomb. A collective gasp filled the space as they stared in awe at the treasure set out before them. The Egyptians began to panic, fear causing them to flee from the tomb. Those who could speak English implored their employer and his team to do the same.

"Please, there are many, many more Kings and Queens for you to discover, but not this one. This one we must leave *for it is not one of us.*"

The Professor and his team from the Egypt Exploration Society remained unmoved. Their gaze set on the gold and glittering gems. The most extravagant of sarcophagi that the Professor had ever seen, was set in the centre of the room. Surrounding it were treasures, trinkets, furniture, and food for the Underworld. The food! It was *fresh*! Set out on a gilded table. An empty throne at its head. A goblet full of beer stood next to the plate that was piled high with meat, bowls of lentils, bread, soaked vine leaves and spices. One could be forgiven for thinking that the room had only just been set up! A few of the team members ventured forward, moving around the room, looking for secret doors and passages but finding none. How could this be? One of the archaeologists exclaimed "This food is fresh. It has just been set out not even a few hours ago! How is this *possible*?" He looked over at the Professor, the other team members turned to watch the Professor, eager for his answer. He bit his bottom lip. The right corner of his mouth twitched, wanting to break out into a smile, but he refrained from giving away what he knew. This was his prize. This was his knighthood!

"I would suppose the food has kept because of how cold and dry it is down here." Professor Argus said, walking over to the table he set the oil lamp down and leaned over the table to inspect the food. It was indeed fresh; the beef had been cooked, and the smell was divine. His mouth watered and his stomach growled. Dipping his left forefinger into the goblet of beer, he then raised it to his lips, cautiously tasting the beer. He surprised by how deliciously sweet the liquid was. He smacked his lips savouring the taste of the beer. He picked up the goblet and now took a big swig, drawing a gasp from the others.

"Professor! What if that is poison?" one of the society members said out loud. The Professor set the goblet back down on the table and smiled at his team. He moved now from the table and over to the sarcophagus in the centre of the room. "Interesting." He mused to no one in particular.

"This one is not like the other sarcophagi previously discovered. Why, this one is giving no clue as to who lies within."

He studied the surface. There were no hieroglyphs, no name plate, no prayer to guide the soul to the Underworld. He gently placed his hands on the lid, his fingers caressing the carved arm that lay across the sculpted torso. Its dark eyes stared up at the tomb's ceiling. The sarcophagus was cold to the touch, and despite trying, the Professor was unable to shift the lid. The students were picking through the urns and bowls holding gold and precious gems. Ankhs carved out of wood and scarab beetles crafted from obsidian were placed around the canopic jars: Imsety (liver), Qebehsenuf (intestines), Happy (lungs) and Duamatef (stomach), and the other items the spirit within the sarcophagus would need in their journey to the Underworld. The Professor took the rolled-up parchment he had been holding and unfurled it on top of the sarcophagus. Tracing his forefinger over the text, this very parchment had led him to this tomb. To this uncharted discovery. A God! A God is what the parchment promised to give up to him, however the name of the God was given in the text. At the end of the text was a drawing of this very room. Of the sarcophagus, surrounded by gold, furnishings and a feast laid out on the table.

But nothing to give up who this deity was.

He rolled the parchment back up, pausing when he noticed the image on the other side of the paper, now facing him. A constellation of dark swirls and what looked like stars. In the centre of the void sat a scale and a single white feather.

Professor Argus looked around him for these items but could see nothing to match the image. Then he looked at the gilded face, its dark eyes staring up, he followed its gaze to the ceiling where the image from the parchment was above him, its colours so bright, so vivid, as if it were only just painted. In the centre of the inky black swirls and the gold-plated stars was a scale and a single white feather, and the inscription underneath the scales read:

"Here lies the ever-faithful *Servant* of *Osiris*."

Professor Argus' heart sank at the realisation that this was not a God before him, but a high-ranking priest. Still, this was a very unusual tomb, and the food and the items-*the food! It was FRESH!* Everything would still be documented, packaged, and shipped back to London, England, for further processing. Maybe a high-ranking priest would still be enough of a discovery to land Professor Argus his long-desired accolade. Recognition for his efforts in Egyptology. Over the weeks that followed, the Professor and his team worked long hours to record the artwork lining the walls, taking photographs and carefully crating the contents of the tomb. The Egyptians that had started the expedition with the Professor had refused to return to the site, but the society members were able to source additional help for a heftier price than the Professor would have like to have paid to help them get the crates out from the tomb and up and onto the back of the wagons. The sarcophagus the last item to be removed from the cold tomb. By now they were confident that they had covered everything inside, and after a lot of grit and heft, the large sarcophagus was removed from its earth, slowly, carefully moved up and out into Ra's hot embrace. The gold shone new, and the colours gave the appearance of life in the face of the sarcophagus.

Professor Argus surveyed the now empty tomb, unbeknownst to him, for the last time. He would return to England with the artefacts to study them further. Find out the identity of this priest of his. In the meantime, the tomb would be sealed shut and left to wait for his return the following year where he would set about removing the art from the walls. He smiled at the thought of the hieroglyphs on display in the British museum. What a sight it would be! In the meantime, the photographs they had taken would have to suffice. He turned and made his way up the stairs, back out into the heat of the day. The wagon with the sarcophagus was waiting. It would be a convoy to the Nile, taking skiffs up to Port Said where they would transfer their haul into their ship, making their way back to London. As the tomb was sealed shut, the last fingers of golden light being cut off one by one, the darkness filled the void, covering the name plate that they had missed.

It was carved into the foundation that the sarcophagus had rested upon.

"Ammit. Devourer of the Dead."

London, England, 01 April 2020.

The team of curators worked carefully and quickly to open the sarcophagus of the unknown priest. Discovered in 1911 by Professor Argus and his team from the Egypt Exploration Society, it had remained sealed and on display in the British Museum.

Until now.

Professor Argus never did return to the tomb as he had planned. Shortly after returning to London, while working on identifying his priest, he had been found dead in his office the day after he had opened the sarcophagus. It was rumoured that in his right hand he clutched the tooth of a crocodile that he had taken from the inside of the sarcophagus. The autopsy report listed the Professors' cause of death to be from a heart attack, but there were those who let superstition take hold, and the sarcophagus was sealed shut, never to be opened again. But that was back then, and this is 2020 – we know such beliefs about the tombs and the mummies are all just scary stories to tell in the dark. Numerous mummies have been taken from their coffins and are now propped up in hermetically sealed, temperature-controlled glass coffins for all to gawk at. The public love it. There has always been a fascination with the burial practices of Ancient Egypt, and thanks to modern science and technology, we can now peer through the shrouds to get up close and personal to the body within.

Professor Argus' Priest was about to finally have their big reveal. Analysis of the treasures and furnishings in the tomb told of their standing in life, and in death.

Marked as a faithful servant of Osiris on the ceiling of the tomb, and with extraordinarily little else to go off for all the other hieroglyphs in the tomb had told only stories of Egypt at that time. Of the Book of the Dead and of their Gods and Goddess, but the identity of this priest was not mentioned once. Following Professor Argus' death, a team from the Egypt Exploration Society returned to the site of the tomb only to find that the entrance was no longer there – it was solid rock. It was as if the tomb never existed. They detonated dynamite in the spot in the mountain side, exactly as marked on the map that was taken from Professor's papers, but when the smoke cleared, all that was revealed was more solid rock. There was no way of retrieving the writings on the walls. All they had to work from now were the photographs the Professor and his team had taken while they were in the tomb.

There was no way of knowing who this person had been back then, so now they were going to put the mummy through a CT scan in the hopes of glimpsing the face of this enigma.

Professor Argus' supposed Priest.

The crack and grind of the lid of the sarcophagus shifting caused the curators to pause momentarily. The silence in the room lingered, they seemed to be waiting for… for what? A spirit to seep out from the gap and curse them all? Or the mummy, flinging off the heavy lid and sitting up – with its arms rigid, held out in front of its body, bandages trailing off to expose its old, mummified flesh – just like you see in the movies. Seriously? With the years of combined experience and knowledge there

120

that surrounded the sarcophagus, these little bits of fancy still appear and excite and terrify. No spirit appeared, no curse of scarabs to swarm and devour them. No mummy was moving within. Hamish Jarvis, one of the senior curators and Egyptologist currently working at the British Museum, stepped forward and pushed the lid further askew. The others helping him, they now worked quickly to remove the lid, setting its gilded body down on the blankets set out on the floor. Its dark eyes cast upwards, searching for the Scales of Justice. For Ma'at…

They gathered around to look at the small, mummified corpse within, shocked at what they saw for the bandages were pristine, time nor decomposition had stained a single piece of cloth that swaddled the corpse in its eternal slumber. A gold mask had been placed over the face; its serene expression was a thing of beauty. Adorning the mummy were gems carved into animals – hippopotamus, crocodile, and lion. Little obsidian scarab beetles and animal teeth were also scattered around the body, and clasped in its hands, crossed over the chest was a gold ankh encrusted with emeralds and rubies. The symbol of life. The team gently lifted the mummy out of the coffin, placing it now on a gurney lined with a sheet, ready to whisk it up to radiography. One of the curators removed the gold mask and the ankh, setting them down back inside the sarcophagus. Hamish noticed that in the sarcophagus, at the mummy's feet, was a set of bronze scales. In his time studying mummies and their sarcophagi, he had not encountered such an item placed with a mummy. Now was not the time to worry about it. They sealed the sarcophagus shut and transported the body quickly to where the radiographer and his assistants were waiting.

***

The CT scan was set up and ready for the patient. The team of museum curators, directed by Hamish, moved the gurney alongside the padded slab of the CT table. The mummy was gently lifted across from the gurney to the table, using the sheet to hoist its featherweight form, careful not to touch the body for fear of contamination. The team stood back now to discuss with the radiographer what was to take place. Hamish remained by the mummy to get a proper look at it under the fluorescent clinical lights. The bandages were intact, but the corpse had obviously shrunk and withered. Poking out from the bandages that were wrapped around the right hand was the tip of the mummy's forefinger. The skin was blackish green, and the bone protruded slightly out above the gnarled fingernail. He leaned down to get a better look at it for he thought he saw the fingertip twitch. Surely a trick of the light? No! It had moved ever so slightly! Hamish blinked once, twice and a third time for good measure. The finger was still slightly twitching. Looking at the others in the room to see that they were preoccupied with starting the scan, Hamish reached out and touched the mummy's finger.

"Mr Jarvis we are ready now to start the CT. I am going to need you and the others to come and wait in the room behind us."

Hamish startled and pulled his hand back quickly.

Looking at the radiographer who motioned to him with his clipboard to go into the small room with the large glass windows, lit up by the soft glow of computer screens.

"Of course. Yes." Hamish stammered, looking down at the mummy to find the twitching finger was now detached from its hand, and laying on the bed next to the mummy. In a lapse of poor judgement, Hamish quickly snatched up the digit and put it in his shirt pocket. Telling himself that it could fall off and get lost inside the scanner, and he would reunite the mummy with its digit once it was safely back inside its sarcophagus. He retreated to the small room to watch with the others as the mummified corpse slowly entered the scanner. He soon forgot about the finger in his shirt pocket.

***

It had been a long day when Hamish walked into his apartment. Kicking his shoes off, he dropped the keys on the side table and headed down the hall towards the living room. He slung his jacket over the back of one of the dining chairs and stopped by the sink to grab a glass of water. The CT scans were unreal, the mummy was beautifully preserved, but despite this they were still no closer to working out their mummy's identity. The abdominal cavity was filled with lots of sharp teeth, teeth from the Nile crocodiles. The face, despite the leathered skin, was serene, almost looking like it was smiling, Hamish thought to himself. Taking a swig of water, he then remembered the finger in his shirt pocket. He forgot to slip it back into the sarcophagus before they sealed the mummy back in! Crap!

Taking out the finger, he examined it. Blackened, the skin all leathery, the finger was slightly curled. The tip of the finger bone had pierced the skin. How on earth could he have thought this rotted old finger had been moving back there in the CT room? A trick of the lights in the room perhaps. Now he was standing at his kitchen sink, holding an incredibly old fore finger from the right hand of an unknown mummy.

"Bite it!"

The thought flashed into his mind from nowhere. Rotating the digit around, something within him was urging him to just bite it.

"No! Urgh!"

Hamish repulsed for entertaining such a thought set the finger down on the kitchen bench and backed away from it. It had been a long and exciting day for him, and now he was tired. Maybe it would be best for a quick dinner, shower, and early night. He would work out how he was going to return the finger to its owner in the morning. He moved the finger from the kitchen bench to the empty fruit bowl on the edge of the bench, and then set about fixing himself some dinner. In the fruit bowl the tip of the finger twitched, the protruding bone scratched at the base of the bowl before the finger extended out, stretching after thousands of years bound in place.

It felt so good to be free again…

After dinner Hamish dropped his dishes into the sink and went off to have a shower.

Washed and ready for bed, he stopped by the sink to

grab himself another glass of water. He glanced into the fruit bowl, the glass slipping from his hand and shattering in the sink. The finger was plump. The finger was now not black and leathery, it was mottled. Patches of fresh flesh appearing before his eyes. No! How is this possible? He rubbed at his eyes, but it was no use. The finger was filling out and moving more and more now, trying to drag itself from out of the fruit bowl. Hamish moved quickly, snatching up the pair of tongs from the second drawer and grabbing the empty plastic food container that had once held the left-over fried rice that had been reheated for his dinner. As the tongs gently grasped the wriggly finger, Hamish heaved; a little bit of goo dribbled out of the end of the finger that had been attached to its owner's hand. The finger made a soft "plop" as it landed on the dregs of oil and rice. The sound of the lid clicking in place seemed to make Hamish feel a little bit better.

Holding the container up so he could look at the finger, he struggled to process what it was doing. By now most of the decay had gone, and the finger was nice and plump. The bone protruding from its tip was no longer visible. Flesh now covered it. Its fingertip tapped about, dragging itself around and stopping to dip into a small slick of oil as if it were tasting it. No. Imagination was getting the better of him, it was time for bed. Convinced there was no way the finger was going to go anywhere, he set the container on a shelf in the fridge and headed for bed. The finger tipped-tapped about until it brushed against a grain of fried rice. Quivering in excitement, the tip of the finger pressed down upon the grain, a small mouth appearing filled with rows of tiny sharp teeth it devoured the grain of rice, its first meal in what had been an eternity. The finger pulsated. Digesting. More! It needed more!

A change was coming.

***

She rested back on the sofa cushions, surrounded by empty packets and containers. Scraps of fruit and vegetables, empty bottles of the strangest beer she had ever tasted-called "Worcestershire Sauce". Not as good as the sweet honey beer brewed by the Priests of the Temple. That cold, dark space she had been put into the night before was now wide open and completely stripped of all its contents. Every cupboard open, every shelf left bare of anything that was edible. The hunger was intense, and despite eating everything in this strange tomb – what possessed the priests to entomb her in such an ugly space? Where were her treasures? Her stomach grumbled and gurgled, crying for her real food. By now she was fully flesh and bone, but not yet complete. She wondered where all the cloth she was supposed to have been wrapped in had gone. Naked save for crumbs and dregs of her Underworld provisions, she sighed and let herself relax.

***

Hamish rolled out of bed and proceeded to get ready for work. He was still half-asleep as he pulled on his shirt and slacks, searching in the sock drawer for his lucky socks. He was going to need all the luck he could get today to return that finger without being caught. A loud burp from outside his bedroom stopped his search for luck, and he strained his ears to work out if he had indeed heard a belch coming from the living room. Another long-winded burp had Hamish reaching for a weapon (in this case all he had was a ten-kilogram barbel) and heading out to confront the intruder.

Sneaking out and peering around the corner he saw a figure leaning back on his couch. He hesitated as he studied the shape in front of him. Human, but not human. Unusually large, it was eating a raw potato like it was an apple! It was oblivious to his presence.

And then it wasn't.

Mid-chew, it sniffed the air and its eyes, the colour of amber tracked across the room, stopping at a human who was now agape and visibly shaking at having been seen. It was now or never as Hamish rushed at this stranger sitting on his couch. Before the barbel was raised, he was snatched up and thrown onto the ground, landing on a pile of apple cores and crisp packets. The face of this creature was inches from his, the eyes now flashed a hot red, nose rankled, lips drawn back revealing sharp teeth. Odour of raw potato filled Hamish's nostrils as the full weight of the creature was now crushing him. Tongue with sandpaper texture ran across his face, his skin stung at the roughness of it, and a feminine voice purred,

"Finally! A priest! Where is everyone? What has happened to my Egypt? Where is my feast? I am so hungry it hurts!"

Hamish gasped and struggled to free himself, but

the creature was quicker and was back on the couch and watching him as he sucked in air and pushed himself back against the coffee table for support. He surveyed the chaos before him, this thing had eaten everything. But where had it come from? The creature shifted slightly to get comfortable. It was large, bigger than a normal human and despite a humanoid shape, its features were definitely not human. The amber eyes focused on this strange priest. Eyebrow arched; lip curled up on one end, a snaggle-toothed fang protruded over the bottom lip. There was something inherently dangerous about its presence. Black mane of hair crowned its head. The torso and arms were covered in a course golden coat of fur. The lower half of its body was a grey colour, a swollen, grey belly pulled at its lower back. It was the belly of a… Hamish felt numb… like the belly of a hippopotamus. The belly was quite distended now, and it churned and gurgled as it continued to digest the entire contents of the fridge and pantry. It burped again.

"Who are you and why are you in my house?" he stammered. Blood flow had reached his limbs again and his muscles tightened, ready to spring him up and out the room. The strange creature on the couch slowly lifted its right hand up and wriggled its forefinger before pointing at the now empty takeaway container that the night before had held the reheated fried rice, and the mummy's finger. Then it spoke:

"Don't you recognise me? Afterall I am in the Book of the Dead. I am the one who is always hungry. I am the one who sits by Ma'at, the Scales of Justice."

"I am "Ammit."

"Devourer of the Dead." Hamish struggled to get the words out.

"I don't think I am going to have much luck getting this into the sarcophagus" he thought to himself.

The room suddenly became a cold and sinister space that he needed to escape. Ammit slid off the couch and crawled on all fours towards him. Her tail flicked and twitched. Her full belly hung down and swayed as it moved towards him.

"I'm hungry." She purred.

***

The sarcophagus sat in the cold storage room down in the bowels of the museum. Surrounding it were other specimens of animals and curated curiosities for an upcoming exhibit. The gold glittered in the soft light, the lapis lazuli and garnets shone, and the carved figure seemed to be alive as Hamish approached it. He was going to open the sarcophagus and confirm that the lion, crocodile, hippopotamus, humanoid creature that called itself Ammit who he had left sitting on his couch eating a bag of unwashed potatoes was nothing more than a figment of his imagination. As a kid he would get so engrossed in Egyptian mythology, that is how he came to be working now as an Egyptologist for the British Museum. Maybe the excitement of this unknown figure in the coffin got the better of him?

Checking to make sure no one had followed him, placing his hands on the lip of the sarcophagus lid, Hamish carefully and quietly pried it up, sliding it over to glance at the mummy within. Only when he looked, there was nothing save for jewels, carved animals, teeth, and the bronze set of scales. Where was the body? He let the lid rest offside, spinning around and scanning the room for any evidence of the body being moved. He was certain there were no more scans booked. Amber eyes now appeared from out of the dark as Ammit moved slowly towards him. Her glare dropping to the sarcophagus. Her sarcophagus. How did she get here? He left her in the apartment. He looked over at the entry, expecting security to come running in, but the door remained sealed shut. Ammit was kneeling now beside the open coffin. In her hands she held the little carved animals and jewels. Her mane quivered, shoulders tense. The fur down her back bristled. Such a strange demon, Ammit, the Devourer of Death. She was a terrifying presence to behold, and for the Ancient Egyptians she was the last thing they would see before either crossing over to the Underworld or being torn asunder by a mouth full of sharp crocodilian teeth, thus suffering the greatly feared "Second Death".

"How did you get in here?" Hamish whispered, still waiting, no hoping, for security to come in and save him.

"I move through another realm. I make myself visible to those I choose." Ammit moved the lid further back, picking up the scales. When she turned back to Hamish her eyes were now dark red. When she spoke again her voice was demonic, setting Hamish's nerves on fire.

"Anubis. Where is he? Where is my King?" Her face started to stretch. Her nose and jaw became elongated.

130

Her eyes now shifted apart on either side of her face. Scales, the colour of moss now covered her face, and as her body contorted and shifted form, Ma'at fell from her grasp, the brass scales clanging onto the floor. Now on all fours, face of a crocodile, the torso of a lioness, the belly and lower half of the hippopotamus, her size grew to that of an elephant. She bore down on Hamish, pressing her snout against his chest, pinning him against the compactus.

"Anubis!" She snarled.

"Long gone. He went with the Ancients."

A long, mournful bellow escaped her. Surely everyone in the museum would hear her. Her chest heaving, her crocodile head swayed from side to side, she moaned again.

"I'm so HUNGRY! I need my KING!"

Hamish slid down the compactus that he had been pinned against and rolled away from her mouth full of sharp teeth. Ammit swiped at him, her paw missing him by centimetres. She stopped moaning and moving about. A cracking and snapping of bones and ligaments erupted from her body. Tendons and muscles contracting, changing to bring her back to the humanoid form. She took up the scales and gave the storeroom a final glance before marching across the room to Hamish. The force of her hand striking his chest knocked the air out of his lungs and he folded, but before he could steady himself, she was moving him backwards, his shirt clenched in her large hand. She was heading for the shadows of the storeroom and Hamish believed he was heading for the Underworld in the clutches of Ammit. Doomed to a

Second Death.

He closed his eyes and felt his body move through space. A blow to the back of his head knocked him out cold. He woke when she had finally released him, and he fell to the ground in a crumpled heap. Her amber eyes glowed with anger, her sharp teeth visible, reminding him he was in the presence of a demon. They were still in the storage room of the museum. His head throbbed and he gingerly sat up, wincing as pain, like darts, pierced his brain.

"I have had time to think." Said Ammit. "What is this place that my treasure and coffin are held? Where is my tomb?"

She looked angry.

"Your tomb is a long way away from here. You were discovered a long time ago. Your Egypt is gone. But, but…" he struggled to talk, the fuzziness was laying on thick.

"Why did you take me away? Where are my treasures now?" Ammit's eyes blazed in the shadows. "Who am I now without my King?"

"Your treasures? They are upstairs. On display. Here, I can show you."

Ammit lunged forward, dropping to all fours "yes! Show me. I need my treasures back."

She pulled Hamish up and landed him on his feet, his legs still shaking. Looking at his watch, it was midnight. No chance of being found, security would be all snuggled up in their office with pizza and playing cards. He swayed and staggered, eventually regaining his composure and gait, leading Ammit out of the storeroom and up through the museum to her exhibit. Her bare feet padded along the marble floors, she towered over him, keeping close by him with her focus on where they were going and not what was around them. In her right hand she clutched Ma'at tight. Occasionally her big belly would bump into his shoulder, sending him stumbling forward.

Ammit, it seemed, was oblivious to the space she took up.

Now stopping, Hamish threw his arms open dramatically at the entrance of the Egyptian exhibit. On either side of the door stood two Egyptian statues, their staffs held out as if ready to strike trespassers. Within the room, glass cabinets were lit with the soft glow of lights. Artefacts, sarcophagi, and bodies out for all to see. Tablets with stories about those who lived long ago. Of Gods and Goddesses. Of rulers, and of the ebbs and flows of Egyptian existence. Ammit bowed her head to avoid striking it on the entryway. Hamish followed. She moved from each display, hands and face pressed against the glass, moving along until she found her belongings marked under "The Unknown Mummy, discovered Abydos, Egypt, May 1911 by Professor Harrold E. Argus."

He heard her gasp at the recognition of her past life laid out for the public's pleasure. Her fingers tensed; claws scratched the glass. Hamish instinctively reached out to stop her, but she ignored him. Her eyes could only see the empty space where the canopic jars should be. She needed them. Now.

"Where are my jars? WHERE ARE MY JARS?" Ammit's voice rolling from a low growl to a chest rattling rumble.

"Jars? Jars, they are in the room out back." Hamish sidestepped Ammit and the display case. "We were going to open them-" He heard her body popping and cracking and knew he needed to diffuse her and fast. "Follow me." He ran around the display cases, reaching for the access card attached to his belt, slapping the card against the reader, red light turned green, and the pneumonic seal broke as the door swung open. Ammit barged in over him, sending Hamish sprawling on the floor. There on a stainless-steel table the jars were set out ready to be opened. That was what he was meant to have done yesterday instead of being knocked out cold by a Death Eater. Before he was upright, Ammit had snatched up the jars and vanished into thin air, leaving Hamish on his own. First the mummy's body and now the canopic jars-how was he going to explain this to the museum board of directors?

A knot was starting to appear on the back of his head where he had been struck by the paw of the giant, she-demon. The throbbing in his head was increasing, he needed to get back home. He would call in sick in the morning and hope that until he had a plan, no one would discover he had summoned Ammit, the Devourer of Death.

***

The pain in his head vanished when opening the door to his apartment revealed an assault of aromas to his senses. There was also a lot of smoke filling the place. His home was on fire! Rushing in, phone in his hand ready to call nine-nine-nine, he found Ammit in the kitchen, her belly hanging down, pressed against the kitchen bench. She had made a makeshift fire pit in the middle of the dining room, the smoke rising from the ashes-the dining setting had served as the kindling. Fuck! Ammit looked up from the cast iron pot on the bench in front of her. "The loud birds hurt my head" was all she said as she took up a ladle and stirred the contents of the pot. Birds? It was then he realised the smoke detectors had been yanked out of their attachments in the ceiling. Smoked furniture and carpet aside, he was struck by the strong smells of garlic, onion, chilli. His stomach growled.

Without looking at him, Ammit took up a large bowl and ladled the mixture from the pot into the bowl. Steam rising from the rust-coloured concoction.

"You are hungry, yes?" She asked. Hamish slowly nodded.

The bowl was thrust at his chest, the tip of her big, fat thumb was dipped into the food. "I must eat. But I need you to eat first."

This made Hamish to back up. "No. No Ammit. No, I am not going to die!' Ammit moved towards him, bowl extended. She bared her crocodile teeth, her eyes, quick to anger. He instinctively took the bowl. Whatever it was smelled so good. "What is this?" he asked.

"A dish made by my beloved people. We call it Foule Medammes. It is fava beans, red lentils, garlic, onion, cumin, chilli, lemon, olive oil and salt. It is good. Now eat for I am hungry."

Following him to the couch (the dinner table long gone up in smoke), Ammit sat down at his feet and watched as he began to eat. It was the most amazing thing he had ever eaten, and he was scooping it up, soaking the pieces of cut up flat bread she had given him, in the thick rust-coloured mash. He stopped short of licking the bowl clean. Falling back on the couch, Hamish now waited for his inevitable death by Ammit, but Ammit did not move from Hamish's feet. She was waiting. For what?

It started at the base of his skull. A gentle vibration at first that soon ran down the length of his spine. Popping as his neck twitched and tweaked. Spasms paralysed him from the chest down. He struggled to scream as his body jerked about, joints snapping and muscles feeling like they were on fire. A sharp contortion seized his whole being and his vision was becoming sharper than normal. Colours vibrant. Atmosphere changing. When he looked down at his body, he was long, lean and the colour of obsidian! His whole physical being seemed to be taking up more space, even Ammit now moved back onto her haunches. Her gaze never leaving Hamish's. A disembodied scream tore through the living and the dead.

And then there was nothing.

***

Eyes opened to the light of soft glow of sunlight. No concept of date or time, everything within him hurt so. He was overcome with a heavy tiredness of someone who had slept for too long. Eons, it felt like. A dream, no, a nightmare, that he was now free from. The thought short-lived as the face of a crocodile entered his vision. He felt different. Something was living in his body with him, he could feel the presence there.

"My King." a soft whisper, slipping from the mouth of the crocodile-faced demon.

"No, I am not." Hamish protested, but then he heard another voice within him say "I have returned!" He rolled now over onto his side, and there she sat, Ammit, in her true form-the crocodile head, lioness torso and belly and rump of the hippopotamus. On the coffee table sat Ma'at.

"What did you do Ammit? Tell me!" he demanded. His lips were parched, and his throat was sore. He watched as Ammit set the canopic jars out before him, all save for one, had been unsealed.

"I brought back my King. These are not of my body, but of Anubis'. I took his lungs, his stomach, his liver, and intestines and ground them into powder to mix within the Foule Medammes that you ate. I needed a vessel to bring back my King because I am hungry. So very, very, hungry."

Bile burned his throat as he pushed himself upright. He was bigger now, much more than a normal human, and his body was hard as marble and glistened like the finest obsidian gem. Hamish the human was gone. Sitting there before a prostrate Ammit, was Anubis. Ammit slid the sealed canopic jar over for Anubis to open. The clay lid crumbled in his hand, and within the jar was a single, white, feather. He carefully held it now between his thumb and forefinger. Ammit watched him patiently.

"Ah my faithful Ammit! At last, we are reunited, but what a strange tomb the priests buried you in!" Anubis gestured around Hamish's apartment. "You must be famished!" Ammit nodded. "Indeed, I am my King. I need the souls to feed on."

Anubis smiled, baring his white canines. "Praise Osiris! Let us now go forth and find the hearts for judgement. I have a feeling Ammit that here in this realm you will be feasting for a long time to come on heavy hearts and damned souls."

FOULE MEDAMMES (EGYPTIAN FAVA BEAN DIP)

CONTRIBUTED BY JASMINE JARVIS

Serves 4.
Ingredients:
500 grams fava beans *(wash and soak for ten hours prior to cooking or use a bit of "modern magic" and use canned fava beans – Anubis will not judge you; I promise!)*
½ cup red lentils
2 cloves of garlic
½ white onion, finely diced
Good dash of cumin powder
Hearty pinch of chili powder/flakes
Squeeze of lemon juice to flavour
Olive oil
Pinch of salt

Method:
Wash the fava beans (see option for canned).
In a pot pour the fava beans, red lentils, and enough water to cover and bring to the boil.
Cover and let the beans simmer until they are soft.
Remove from heat and mash the beans.
In a pan, bring the oil to heat and throw in the onion, garlic and sauté until translucent. Add the good dash of cumin, hearty pinch of chili, and pinch of salt and cook through – enjoy the aromas, my mouth is watering just

thinking about it.

Pour the contents of the pan into the pot of bean mash and mix through.

Serve the dip with a squeeze of lemon and a swirl of olive oil. Enjoy with flat or crusty bread, and a platter of figs, cheese, dates, vegetables of your choice, boiled eggs, cold meats, and your favourite beer (Egyptians apparently enjoyed a beer or two with their meals – beer was more appealing than drinking the Nile water). Ready? Good. Now it is time to proceed with the story.

Bon Appetit!

Jasmine Jarvis is an Australian Author of Speculative Fiction. After joining a local writing group in May 2019, she was encouraged to try her hand at writing fiction - sending off her first pieces of fiction into Black Hare Press' call out for Beyond. Realizing how much fun this writing gig is, and how much she loves to tell stories, Jasmine has continued to shape her writing and is drawn to the absurd, the creepy and the downright terrifying.

Since landing her spot in Beyond, she has had 23 drabbles and 4 short stories published. Jasmine hopes her readers enjoy her stories as much as she enjoys writing them.

LONG MAY SHE REIGN

RHIANNON LOTZE

Ribbons of smoke twined into the sky, bruising the blue canvas. Below the grey shroud, a sleepy village became a graveyard. The dead and dying pocked the ground. They cradled savagely parted limbs, pressed organs into rightful places, and scared the birds silent with wails of agony.

Torn wings and sawed-off horns, carelessly tossed in a heap, burned in the heart of the town.

A cadre of knights sped away from the village, whooping with delight atop steeds splashed crimson. Congratulating themselves on a job well done.

An hour later, the final wails collapsed into silence.

The birds resumed their song.

***

"Brothers!" A booming voice echoed in the immense throne room, welcoming the conquering knights home. Arthur, Son of Uther, King of Camelot, stood from his famed Round Table with such vigour the heavy oak chair behind him tipped over backwards.

A servant quickly righted it, but Arthur paid him no heed. He strode to the returned knights, his muscular legs eating up the ground between them.

"Welcome home!" he bellowed enthusiastically. "Congratulations on your triumph over evil!"

Every one of the hundred revellers crammed into the throne room heard him as clearly as the thunder that roared beyond the stone walls of Castell y Brenin.

Arthur clasped each knight by the arm and clapped them on the shoulder, greeting them each by name. Lancelot, and his son Galahad. Then Bedivere, Gawain, and Percival.

Each of the knights had changed out of their gore-spattered armour and into attire fit for a feast, which was precisely the reason the members of Arthur's court were gathered during the most barbaric storm in living memory.

When the greetings ended, Arthur returned to his seat at the table. His customary throne sat empty on a raised dais behind him. The five knights sat as well, filling out the empty spaces left for them.

Once settled, Arthur lifted a chalice. Wine slopped over its rim and splashed the table. A servant ran forward to sop it with a rag, but Arthur waved him off, grinning at the servant who blushed.

"To my Knights of the Round Table," Arthur declared, raising the chalice high above his head. "For the services you render in protecting the realm of Camelot from the evil that threatens our way of life."

Raucous cheers soared to the ceiling, then bounced off the stone in a sonorous echo.

Everyone drank deeply.

Numerous calls for more wine followed and a fleet of servants scurried obligingly through the hall.

"To Arthur, the king legends are written about!" Lancelot declared when cups brimmed once more. He stood from his chair, raising his own chalice. "Long may he reign!"

"Long may he reign!" the gathering echoed.

A series of toasts followed, each praising a different member of the Round Table, and ending with a toast for Merlin. The magical wards he erected around Castell y Brenin kept its inhabitants safe from the dark, evil magic of faerie-kind.

The sorcerer was the only honoured member of the Round Table without a knighthood.

He raised his cup and drank the barest sip of wine from it in honour of the toast. Most of the sip missed his lips and trickled in thin rivulets down his long, grey beard. He swiped a drop from his chin, skin unnaturally ashen.

When it became clear Merlin wasn't going to continue the train of toasts, the list of knights having been exhausted, Arthur slapped his palms down on the table before him and called for the feast to begin.

Another wave of servants flooded the throne room, threading through the gaps between the crowded banquet tables. Hundreds of covered dishes were laid upon the tables, just waiting to be revealed.

A sharp whistle pierced the anticipatory quiet of the

hall and dozens of hands lifted silver cloches in unison.

No one watched the servants leave the room as efficiently as they had entered it. All eyes eagerly devoured the tableau of food fit for a god, much less a king.

There were entire roast boars, their mouths stuffed with aromatic vegetables, trussed pheasants, thick venison steaks smothered in rich gravy, dishes of potatoes blanketed in melted cheese, pots of stew and kasha, steaming pies a foot high, piles of fresh crusty bread, platters heaped with mountains of fresh fruit, and towers of desserts—plum puddings, raspberry and cherry tarts, pan-fried flat cakes, custard-filled pastries, honey-sweetened oats, tiered cakes, candied fruits, and more.

The decadence of the display vanished in a waft of steam when the starved feast-goers fell upon the dishes like ravenous beasts, occasionally deigning to use cutlery, more often digging in with bare hands. Plates became mountains and grease, gravy, and cheese painted fingers and chins.

Swears peppered the clamour when some unlucky fellow got a fistful of the most freshly cooked fare and burned their flesh.

A band of minstrels struck up a lively tune when the feasting began in earnest, drowning out the obnoxious cacophony of chewing followed by noisy belches that signified one reveller or another had just made room in their belly for another helping of venison.

The Knights of the Round Table ate with the same level of decorum—which is to say, none—despite their elevated status in Arthur's throne room. In fact, only Merlin showed any restraint at all, slicing tiny morsels off the dishes with his cutlery and placing them neatly on his plate. He hardly ate a bite.

"What's the matter, Merlin?" Arthur asked, keen eyes noticing the sorcerer's hesitance. "Is the food not to your dainty standards?"

Gawain and Galahad laughed as though Arthur rivalled the court jester. The other knights were too distracted by their plates to pay attention to any conversation.

"The food is excellent, m'lord," Merlin answered calmly. He folded his hands in his lap, however, not even feigning enjoyment. "I just don't feel myself."

Arthur studied the sorcerer with some amount of trepidation. The old man truly looked unwell. His skin—what was visible around his grey beard—was waxen. The beard itself hung limply off Merlin's chin, devoid of some of its natural fullness. Sweat pearled on Merlin's brow, and deep shadows purpled his eyes.

His study concluded, Arthur shrugged and returned to the depths of his chalice.

The old man was smart enough to call for a healer if one was needed.

Or to heal himself. He was a magician, after all.

The king fervently hoped the old man didn't kick the bucket, though. Finding another sorcerer to maintain the wards around Castell y Brenin was nearly impossible.

Merlin was one of only two known magic-wielders who used their magic in the fight against evil rather than for evil, the other being Nimue, the Lady of the Lake.

Unfortunately, Nimue could only imbue objects—like Excalibur, the sword that gave Arthur divine right to rule—with her magic. She didn't cast warding spells, or any other type of spell for that matter.

Perhaps she could imbue the stones of the castle with warding magic? Or suits of armour, to defend its walls against the army of evil rising against their king?

Arthur's musings were interrupted by a wild boom of thunder. It clapped so hard, the king's teeth slammed together and the dinnerware on the tables rattled.

A rush of gasps and giggles rose skyward, and then the wooden shutters, closed tightly against the raging storm, blew inwards, flying clean off their hinges.

Arthur ducked reflexively, as did the other knights around his table.

Howling wind rushed into the room, screaming with the same vehemence as the terrified revellers. It snuffed the torches and candles that bathed the hall in their warm glow. Even the fires burning in two monstrous fireplaces banked to flickering embers.

The throne room plunged into darkness and chaos, scattered bolts of lightning the only illumination.

Between flashes, carnage reigned.

The half-dozen heavy shutters that blew into the room, followed by a hailstorm of glass, had obliterated the servants edging the walls of the hall and battered several tables of feasters.

Those still alive were wreathed in agonized moans that sparred with the thunder and wind for dominance.

Pools of blood, slick and black in the vibrance of the lightning, spread across the flagstone floors.

One roast boar, flesh mostly uneaten, was swathed in a suit of knife-like glass.

An eager reveller, his hand still outstretched for the boar, was riddled with glass as well. A large shard pierced his eye, and another sliced clean through his cheek. Arthur could see flickers of glass shine when the courtier opened and closed his mouth, still frantically chewing on a shred of boar meat. He slowly keeled over sideways and splayed on the floor, motionless.

The howling gales whipped a whirlwind of odours at Arthur. Savoury meat and vegetables, yeasty bread, sweat, the unmistakable dampness of a storm...and a bittersweet aroma, like burnt hazelnuts, that Arthur recognized immediately.

The scent of magic.

He gingerly stood from where he crouched on the floor, half sheltered by the legendary Round Table, and faced Merlin. The magician remained calmly upright in his seat.

"Merlin, explain this!" Arthur ordered. Castell y Brenin was warded against all magic but Merlin's. If the king could smell magic, it had to have come from the old sorcerer.

Merlin remained silent, stoic.

"Merlin!" Arthur demanded again, drawing Excalibur from the sheath he had slung across the back of his chair before the feast began. The silver blade flashed in the lightning.

But Merlin still said nothing.

"I'm afraid he can't answer you," a husky female voice replied in his stead.

Arthur spun around, lifting Excalibur defensively.

At the same time, the torches sprang back to life. Flames roared three feet in the air before settling into sleepy, romantic flickers.

Though the storm continued raging, thunder trying to shake down the castle walls, the wind swept from the room.

The air suddenly felt thin, but oppressive at the same time.

An unexpected sight greeted Arthur when he rooted his feet again.

An unfamiliar woman—she wasn't in attendance at the feast a moment ago; Arthur certainly would have noticed if she was—draped languorously over his throne.

She wore a rich, black gown, threaded with silver that glimmered in the torchlight. It was fine enough for the grandest of queens. In fact, his own Queen Guinevere didn't wear anything so luxurious.

The woman's lips were painted bright scarlet and black kohl swept along lashes that curtained piercing grey-blue eyes. Her dark hair, a chestnut brown so deep it bordered on black, was unbound and spilled over her shoulders. A single swatch of grey shot it through, where it parted to the right of her forehead.

Despite the grey strands, the woman otherwise looked as though she was in her early twenties. And a gorgeous decade those twenties were.

"My dear, Arthur, I won't have a conversation with you if you're going to gawp like that," the woman chided. Though her tone teased, her gaze cut.

Aware he looked like a buffoon, Arthur snapped his

mouth shut and straightened, readjusting his grasp on Excalibur.

"Explain yourself," he ordered, hoping for an answer from her if Merlin wouldn't give one. The scent of magic thickly perfumed the air around her. "How did you get in here?"

"With help from your pet, of course." She waved towards Merlin. The king half turned, waiting for the sorcerer to deny the outrageous claims.

But instead of an outraged old man—or even one trembling with guilt—a corpse sat in Merlin's place... and not a fresh one.

Where Merlin drank and ate mere moments ago, a rotting, thickly juicy cadaver slouched in the wooden chair. Flesh, slowly liquefying on lifeless bones, hung loose from the body's face.

As Arthur watched, a slab of it slipped off the skull—grimy from the juices of putrefaction—and caught in the limp, grey strands of hair that remained attached to the remnants of Merlin's chin. A dull, shrivelled eye followed in due course, bringing a rainfall of maggots with it.

The stench hit Arthur a moment later and he keeled over and vomited a torrent onto the flagstone floor.

"How?" he rasped, straightening as soon as he was able, willing away the embarrassed blush that clawed up his cheeks.

The woman arched off Arthur's throne, sinuously easing to her feet. She didn't answer right away.

Instead she prowled, catlike, to one of the banquet tables nearby.

The lords and ladies gathered around it flinched as she drew near. A few scampered away, and one lord, too drunk to make a clean escape, merely pushed himself backwards off the bench he perched on, his back slamming painfully against the stone floor. He yelped, then clamped his mouth shut, trying to avoid the woman's attention.

She daintily picked up a decadent cherry tart and bit into it.

"Oh, Arthur," the woman crooned. "My compliments to the chef; this is absolutely delicious."

As her teeth sank through the soft fruit, it disintegrated. The crimson filling liquefied and turned to blood. The crisp pastry shell collapsed into itself and became muddy sludge. Hellish stains marred her alabaster chin and a fresh waft of magic flooded the room.

Everyone gathered cringed in terror at the display of dark magic.

"Did you think that your sorcerer was celibate?" the woman finally asked the room at large. She directed her attention back at Arthur, flinging the rest of the tart aside. It exploded wetly on the floor in a heap of mud and blood.

Her pale eyes were expectant, the question not rhetorical.

"I—"

She immediately cut him off.

"No, you didn't think about your sorcerer at all, unless you were considering how he could benefit you. But one crook of my finger and he came running, so eager for a taste of pleasure with one of his own kind, now that your crusade against magical beings ensures no human will come near us. I lifted my hem to my knees and the promise of more to come was enough for him to sing out the warding spells used on your lovely castle here."

Her voice took on a lilting, sing-song tone.

"And then I slipped a dagger between his ribs, used a simple reanimation spell—a temporary one, mind you—and shipped him off back here to unknit your wards from the inside."

She clapped between her sentences, punctuating each statement.

"Merlin would never—" Arthur began.

"Once a traitor, always a traitor," the woman cut him off again, glacial. "He betrayed his own kind, faerie-kind, my kind. It's not a stretch to imagine he'd betray you, now that you've revealed your genocidal intent for us."

Arthur finally managed to squeeze out a full sentence.

"It's not a betrayal to fight for goodness against evil and the extermination of black magic." Despite his quaking knees, Arthur's tone was righteous, heroic even. Fit for the king of Camelot.

"There is no such thing as black magic," the woman hissed. "There is only magic. But I suppose you would consider it evil if not used directly to your benefit. The only evil I recognize is that in the hearts of you and your knights, who just today slaughtered an entire village of innocent faerie-kind and rewarded yourselves with a feast."

"Is that why you're here?" Arthur demanded. "Deluded vengeance for a single village of demons?"

A laugh danced from the woman's lips. The sound skittered unpleasantly along Arthur's spine.

"You mistake my intentions if you think I'm here because of a single village, my dear Arthur. I'm here for your head and your sword, so that I might rule Camelot and due to your people what you are doing to mine."

Arthur battled her laugh with one of his own, a deep chuckle that shook him heartily.

"You are one woman against a room of one hundred people, and the entirety of my Round Table. Even with your foul magic, you will never take this sword from me."

As if his words were a call to action, the knights gathered behind him unsheathed their own swords, bristling at the witch.

She pouted.

"'One woman?'" she parroted. "Don't tell me you don't recognize me."

"I'm not in the habit of keeping company with witches," Arthur retorted, but suddenly a sinking feeling yawned open in the pit of his stomach.

"In that case, allow me to introduce myself. I'm Morgan Le Fay."

Multiple gasps breathed through the room and no fewer than three nobles fainted at the name, renowned through Camelot for the horrors lacing every syllable uttered.

The general evil of faerie-kind paled in comparison

to the acts of Morgan Le Fay. She ripped unborn babes from the wombs of women, roamed the forests with monsters, worshipped the devil at Black Masses and, worse, she rivalled the power of Merlin, now dead and reeking.

The facts did not faze Arthur. Though she wielded magic, he wielded a sword and could still draw her blood, take her head.

Which he intended to do.

She was now only six feet from him, having wandered closer as she spoke. Well within the reach of Excalibur.

Arthur kept his expression carefully neutral so she couldn't read his face.

But before he so much as twitched, whatever shield she held over the room to keep out the wind and rain vanished.

Brutal gales rushed back into the hall, shattering Arthur's concentration.

Oozing, inky shadows slithered in on the heels of the wind. They poured over the flagstone floor with the speed of a rushing river, thick and knee high. Terrified screams punctuated the howls of the wind and the shadows exploded, solidifying into monsters with hands tipped in six-inch razor-like claws.

Dozens of veins opened in unison, waterfalls of hot blood splashing the remnants of the feast. Heads slammed against the tables and other corpses slumped backwards, tangling on the floor and disappearing into the swirling murk of shadows which devoured the flesh from their bones.

Their savage blood stolen, the monsters—the demons—melted back into the black lake on the flagstones.

Arthur whirled in shock and bellowed with fury when he noticed every knight of the Round Table was dead, aside from the five whom he had sent to erase the stain of the faerie village that very day. Lancelot, Galahad, Bedivere, Gawain, and Percival.

Each knight, though their swords were drawn, quivered like saplings, jaws agape with shock, eyes glassy with terror. Percival had wet himself.

Enraged, Arthur spun back around, lunging blindly for Morgan. His blade sliced empty air. When he regained his bearings, she was strolling casually alongside a banquet table, surveying the offerings.

She popped a fat blackberry into her mouth before biting into another cherry tart which she cradled in her milk-white palm. Her chin was still stained with mud and blood.

She returned to his throne, lounging irreverently atop it, legs draped over the armrest.

When Arthur advanced, five shapes loomed from the shadowy pool, solidifying before his eyes. Each monster he recognized. They were the stuff of legends made real. And they halted him in his tracks.

His anguished, infuriated gaze landed on Morgan, who grinned brashly.

She uttered only one word, a lover's whisper, as her monsters advanced one menacing step.

"Run."

And Arthur, goddamn him, did.

***

Percival was alone.

The remaining Knights of the Round Table scattered at that witch's one word, a band of brothers leaving each other to die.

Percival cursed their names in turn as he ran.

Never mind that he had been the first to flee, the stench of urine following him.

His brothers-in-arms soundly cursed, Percival turned his attention to his only objective: escape.

Slowing his frantic pace, he finally regained his wits and looked around him.

Then laughed.

Though he would have sworn it a moment ago, nothing was following him. The halls of Castell y Brenin were completely empty, devoid of anyone but him.

He was running for no reason, off his head with panic, and not even heading for an exit.

Well, that could be remedied.

Still wary of heading back the way he had come— back towards the monster in a woman's skin—he took the next left...and froze.

Was that a footstep behind him?

He poked his head around the corner he had just turned.

Nothing was there. But he could have sworn he heard a footstep.

Peering deep into the murk hardly touched by the flickering torches, Percival finally caught a glimpse of something prowling through the dark.

His knees knocked together and he couldn't bring himself to move, to run again. His chest burned from the furor of his frantic marathon.

A moment later, a small, hungry-looking cat emerged from the gloom, and Percival wheezed with relief.

The wheeze morphed into a yelp, however, when the cat grew with every step, until it was twice his height.

Razor sharp teeth gleamed in its mouth, dripping venom when it peeled its lips back and roared with enough might to drop a weaker man dead.

Percival jumped clean around and broke into a dead sprint, running from the monster—the cath palug, a demon from legend—for dear life.

As Percival ran, he shot continuous glances behind him, hoping to outrun the beast. But though it never moved faster than a lazy prowl, and Percival kept pouring on the speed, it always remained at his back.

Even when he vaulted down a flight of stairs and slammed a door shut behind him, his next glance back revealed the demon still there, with eyes flashing fire.

He charged down three more hallways, ducked into empty chambers, slipped through hidden alcoves built into the castle, but never once was the beast out of his view.

A set of doors leading outside the castle finally came into sight. If he could only get outside, he could find a horse and outpace the beast, or find help.

Percival desperately flung himself at the latch, yanking the door open hard enough that he wrenched his shoulder.

He threw himself bodily through the opening, expecting the punishing storm to pummel him the moment he was through it.

But he remained dry. No rain cut his skin, no wind whipped his face and clothes.

Instead, the door, which should have led outside—he would have staked his knighthood on that fact—led him right back into the banquet hall he had fled.

Morgan Le Fay, beautiful but utterly terrifying, remained lounging on the throne, snacking on another luscious cherry tart.

She grinned wickedly at him.

"Oh, I'm sorry. Did you think that door led somewhere else?" she asked. Sickly sweet pity spilled from her tongue.

A sudden force threw Percival onto his stomach. His lungs squeezed tight, all the air in them whooshing away.

When he tried to push to his knees, a heavy weight pressed him back to the floor, which was slick with gore.

The weight vibrated, shaking Percival's body. He realized, belatedly, that it was the cath palug, purring atop him and eagerly awaiting Morgan's instructions.

She finally seeped off the throne, the very movement of her limbs sensuous yet oily. She lifted the pastry in her hand towards him.

"Tart?" When Percival didn't answer, she blew him a kiss and he wept.

"Please," he begged through ugly sobs. Tears and snot painted his face.

"Tell me, Percival. Do you like cats?" Morgan

asked. He didn't answer; she didn't care. "My cat likes you. In fact, she wants to play. What do you say?"

"Please!" Percival wailed again, trying desperately to twist, to reach the sword he had sheathed while running.

He abruptly found himself on his back, flipped deftly by the immense paw of the cath palug.

"Go on, my sweet," Morgan crooned. "His entrails will make the perfect ribbon for you to play with."

One razor claw hovered daintily over Percival's abdomen.

He screamed and screamed, begged and begged, until a savage rip silenced him.

***

The stairs of Castell y Brenin spiralled upwards forever.

Lancelot and Galahad were dizzy and nauseous from their climb.

When they escaped the throne room, they raced for the nearest doors out, only to find them locked. Likewise, with the shuttered windows.

Now, their only hope lay in reaching the castle's towers, coils of rope in tow. If they could scale the walls, they could escape with their lives.

"Keep going," Galahad urged his father.

"Shut up," Lancelot growled. Though he was older, he was in better shape than his son and was several steps above.

"I think we lost whatever was following us,"

Galahad wheezed, lowering his sword slightly.

Indeed, the thunderous footsteps that hounded them from the shadows, all the way to the bottom of the tower, had finally receded. The beast, a monstrous cat, had been distracted by something else.

But that didn't mean it was the only demon tailing them.

Lancelot's keen eyes constantly searched the shadows that swallowed them deeper as they ascended the dim tower stairs.

The torch in his free hand barely beat the darkness back and Lancelot jumped at every slither in the murk.

So far, only his own shadow threatened him.

"I see the door," he finally gasped, elation lacing his oxygen-deprived voice.

He all but collapsed against the heavy wooden door that led to the open-air tower roof, praying that it was unlocked.

Galahad whooped with joy when the door slammed open, dragged by the wind and tugging Lancelot with it.

Even the older knight chuckled when he let go of the handle and dropped the torch.

He began unspooling rope from the coil around his shoulder, striding across the flat roof and tying three sturdy loops to one of the merlons jutting up from the castle wall.

Galahad followed suit. In moments, father and son were ready to climb.

They sheathed their swords and simply gave one another a quiet nod for good luck.

Fear quivered in their guts, but not from the extreme

height they had to conquer. Rather, something deep below their feet, in the belly of the castle, roared with horrifying ferocity.

"Stop standing about," Lancelot ordered, unnecessarily, with a growl.

Percival snatched his length of rope, the end of which beat against the side of the castle, caught in the wind. The noise sounded like wings in the night.

Percival wished he had his own wings.

The fanciful thought kept him company as he and Lancelot eased themselves over the tower wall and lowered their heavy bodies slowly down the rope.

Sweat beaded on their palms within moments, and bits of rope fibre stuck in the ruts ripped into their flesh every time they slipped.

But father and son steadily worked their way down the castle wall, well on their way to escape.

The bottoms of the ropes still slapped against the stone, so like the beating of wings.

Galahad let the sound beat out a rhythm to move to.

With each slap against the wall, he lowered himself a little further, then a little more, until he began to outpace his father.

He made it so far away that he couldn't hear Lancelot's bellowed warning over the raging of the storm or the slapping of the rope.

The barest second later, something sharp dug into both of his shoulders and wrenched him from the wall. Instead of climbing *down*, he was suddenly being lifted *up*, high into the air.

Galahad roared with pain, glancing at his shoulders.

Two curved blades skewered them both, buried so tight in his skin that the wounds barely bled. His muscles stretched and tore under his own weight.

The sound of the rope slapping against the castle stone followed him, even as whatever lifted him skywards took him further from the castle. Though the pain in his shoulders forced the muscles of his neck to clench and petrify, Galahad willed himself to look up.

The sound of the slapping rope really did belong to a pair of wings, after all.

An enormous bird, its feathers writhing like oily shadows, flew above him. The blades in his skin weren't blades at all, but talons.

Galahad whimpered, recognizing the bird as one of the demons of legend, the adar llwch gwin.

At the pitiful sound, the bird suddenly looked down, craning its neck to pierce its burden with blood red eyes.

It banked abruptly, flying back towards the castle, soaring over its walls.

"Please, no!" Galahad begged, willing to do anything to avoid a return to the castle and the witch in its heart.

Naturally, the creature didn't obey. Instead, it angled its wings, and flew in ever tightening circles over the tower with two fluttering ropes beating against its side.

The knight's eyes caught on the gleaming pikes, kept atop the tower for anyone in need of a weapon with which to defend the castle.

He didn't have time to cry out before the enormous bird dashed him atop a cluster of pikes, impaling him.

He yelped and whimpered in agony then, feeling

every spot where the razor-sharp blades threaded through him.

Galahad's back bowed uncontrollably around the pikes, drawing them further into his body. His limbs hung askance, no longer in his power.

He dimly noticed the adar llwch gwin alight beside him. Lancelot's own body, treated to the same fate by a second giant bird, thumped wetly into a second cluster of pikes. Blood sprayed.

Galahad looked away, trying not to see his father, trying to ignore the feathered beasts. But he was all too aware of the sharp beak that plucked out his eyes, then pulled out his tongue.

***

The infernal howling just wouldn't end.

Gawain's hands clamped painfully around his ears as he staggered through the abandoned halls of Castell y Brenin.

The moment he left the throne room, an incessant, eerie howl filled his head.

No matter how tightly he squeezed his hands against his ears, or how loudly he screamed, trying to drown out the noise, he couldn't escape it.

It was simultaneously haunting and grating. Spastic shivers ran down his spine, joined by wrenching tears of unbridled sorrow from his eyes.

Gawain sobbed as he stumbled down another flight of stairs, trying to escape the pervasive noise.

He was heedless of the creeping things writhing in

the shadows, no longer aware of them.

Even if he saw them, his sword had been abandoned ages ago, dropped to the floor when he couldn't stand the ethereal howls any longer and needed his hands free to shut his ears in vain against them.

And now, they were getting louder.

Every new hallway he passed was blocked by a shadowy monster, barring his way. He was being funnelled, herded like sheep, made to go dead ahead, to an end he couldn't even imagine. Yet, he walked willingly towards it, so long as it was the end. So long as the noise didn't follow him in death.

The next right turn opened up, the path ahead and to Gawain's left blocked by demons.

He swayed unsteadily as he rounded the corner, the noise growing still worse.

His feet stopped of their own accord when Gawain saw what waited up ahead.

A skeletal, moon-white woman floated two feet in the air, shrouded in a gown that wept thick blood. Drops of it spattered on the floor beneath her in a growing pool that washed towards Gawain and wetted the toes of his boots.

She was a cyhyraeth, a nightmare made flesh.

The woman's eyes were jet black and fixed directly on Gawain. Her mouth was open.

The horrific sound, screams of the tortured and nails scraped down stone walls, spilled from lips almost as white as her flesh.

As Gawain stared, the sound intensified further. He dropped to his knees; the cloth of his pants soaked through immediately.

His own blood dripped into the pool, fluttering in small ripples. It dribbled from his eyes and nose and gushed from his ears.

Gawain screamed again, but he couldn't hear the sound. Beating too frantically, keeping pace with the screams of the wraith, his heart exploded inside and through his chest, rending a gaping hole through flesh and bone.

Gawain fell down dead, and the wraith shut her mouth. Silence reigned.

***

The black dog's eyes blazed with hellfire.

Bedivere found himself paralyzed by them.

The dog had stalked him through the castle, seeping through every door and wall Bedivere put between it and him.

In a last-ditch attempt, the knight had thrown his sword javelin-style at the dog. It caught the blade in its powerful jaws and shook it like a bone, before sending the sword flying across the room.

Whimpering with fear, Bedivere's legs had collapsed beneath him.

Now, he was backed against a wall, the black dog's snout an inch from his own nose.

Its hot breath reeked of rot and the promise of death.

But Bedivere couldn't wrench his attention from the infernal fires blazing in the dog's eyes.

As he watched, a stray spark landed on his tunic. He

frantically slapped at it, trying to brush it off. The spark caught instead.

It ate its way up the fabric, then down the fabric, before digging into Bedivere's skin, blistering and melting his flesh.

The flames swallowed him whole, ignorant of his horrific screams, which didn't stop until the roasted husk of his body fell sideways, unrecognizable.

***

Castell y Brenin sprawled for more than a mile, an endless morass of halls and chambers.

Despite its gargantuan size, the screams of every one of his brothers-in-arms rattled Arthur's bones as they died.

Bedivere's bellows of agony were the last.

Arthur was alone now. He knew he couldn't escape. But escape was no longer on his mind.

With Lancelot's death came the pervasive knowledge that Morgan would win Arthur's head. It iced the blood in his veins.

He'd be damned if he let her claim Excalibur, though. With the sword in her possession, she'd become queen of Camelot. The very thought was as vile and repulsive as the witch herself.

If he could just get it to Nimue, the Lady of the Lake could protect it until a worthy ruler could be found.

That was precisely why Castell y Brenin was built on the shores of the lake.

And Arthur was finally near the castle doors.

Every turn he took in the labyrinthine halls of the castle had been blocked by monsters hewn of inky shadows. Excalibur dribbled with blood black as pitch.

But none of the demons managed to land so much as a scratch on the king. Now, the way out of the castle was clear.

Arthur broke into a run, no longer trying to conserve his energy to smite his foes.

Speed was of the essence, now.

The heavy front door of Castell y Brenin swung open easily under the force of the shoulder he dug into it. He pitched himself into the raging storm outside.

Two thick forests hemmed the castle in on the left and right. Arthur aimed for the right one. The lake was just through the trees.

As soon as he crossed into the border of the forest, a sword swung at his head. Arthur ducked on reflex, dropping to his knees and rolling under the blade.

He bounced back to his feet, lifting Excalibur to parry and dispatch his enemy.

His jaw dropped at the sight.

The sword's wielder was none other than Percival.

"Percival, stand down!" Arthur commanded, baffled. How had the knight survived, after screams as horrific as that? Why was he attacking his king?

It quickly became apparent that, though Percival moved of his own accord, he was far from alive.

Intestines dragged over the wet forest floor from a brutal wound in the knight's abdomen. Blood dirtied his chin and stained his teeth. His eyes were glassy, unseeing.

Percival's corpse didn't raise its sword again, as though he had heeded Arthur's order. But that wasn't right. Instead, it looked up at something above Arthur's head.

Against his better judgement, he turned his back on the knight and spotted Morgan Le Fay, standing on the thick bough of an oak tree ten feet in the air.

Her hair was plastered to her head, the voluminous black dress drooping under the weight of the rain. Black kohl bled down her face.

Despite the havoc wreaked by the rain, she was no less beautiful or terrifying for it.

"You really never considered that your escape from the castle was a ruse, did you, Arthur dear?" she asked. Arthur didn't answer and Morgan grinned. She held her hand out imperiously. "Hand over Excalibur and I'll grant you a dignified death."

"No," Arthur spat. Morgan grinned wider.

"I was hoping you'd say that. Boys, have at him."

Arthur whirled back to Percival, who was no longer alone. Lancelot and Galahad flanked him on either side, each with holes in their chests large enough that Arthur could see clear through them. Their eyes were gone, only bloody abysses remaining in their skulls. Red stained their chins from tongues also plucked out.

Gawain, his rib cage torn right open, brought up the rear, along with an unrecognizable hunk of immolated flesh that Arthur assumed was Bedivere.

They held up swords studded with diamonds of rainwater.

Swearing viciously, Arthur raised Excalibur against

them.

Though Arther was outnumbered, only Percival advanced.

Arthur cursed again. Morgan was toying with him.

With a single, fluid swipe of his sword, Arthur severed Percival's hands. The sword in them fell aside. Another swipe at his neck sent Percival's head tumbling after it.

Lancelot and Galahad stepped forward together, displaying intricate sword work that wasn't meant to kill, but to push Arthur back.

A root pricked his heels and he fell over backwards, none too soon. Lancelot's next swing went for his head, which was no longer there.

Instead, with no resistance, the sword continued its arc and embedded itself in Galahad's neck, where it stuck. Any knight worth his salt could have corrected such an error, which gave Arthur hope.

Either these husks of knights were being puppeted directly by Morgan, who didn't know enough about swordplay to stand against Arthur, or they were simply clumsy in death.

As Galahad fell, his spine severed, he took Lancelot's sword with him. Arthur pressed this advantage, jumping to his feet and decapitating the eyeless warrior. Lancelot collapsed atop the body of his son.

Gawain and Bedivere advanced side by side, but sluggishly.

Arthur didn't stick around to discover why they were so slow.

Instead, he turned tail and ran, hoping he was faster

than them. He only needed to make it to the shore of the lake for Nimue to emerge and collect the sword, protecting it against Morgan. The evil witch's magic couldn't touch Nimue within her enchanted waters.

A slice of silver peeked through the trees ahead and Arthur whooped with delight. He charged from the shelter of the trees and onto the rocky shore of the lake, eating up ground faster and faster.

The rocks shifted beneath him and Arthur's ankle twisted sharply. He careened to the ground, landing hard on his chin. Blood welled in his mouth when his teeth clamped around his tongue.

But his arm, the one carrying Excalibur, was outstretched when he landed. The very tips of his fingers sank into the surprisingly warm waters of the lake.

Nimue had received his summons.

The centre of the small lake boiled and began to glow gold.

A head of golden hair, bone-dry, emerged, followed by the elegantly beautiful faerie who lived in the lake. Nimue looked around serenely, her calm eyes alighting on Arthur.

"Nimue!" he choked out, winded by his run and the fall. "Help me! Take Excalibur. Protect Excalibur!"

Despite his frantic commands and wild expression, Nimue's calm demeanor never faltered. Her feet, bare beneath the golden drapes of her gown, stepped onto the glassy surface of the lake. Ripples spread with every step as she drew closer to Arthur.

Finally, she was right before him and Arthur raised the sword in his grip, shoving Excalibur directly into her waiting arms.

"Go!" he ordered, collapsing back against the wet rocks. "Morgan Le Fay is here. Go before she gets the sword!"

Beneath the water, Nimue was safe, but she remained vulnerable while above the surface.

Instead of turning and walking back to the centre of the lake, to the arms of safety, Nimue straightened her shoulders and stepped onto the shore.

She walked past Arthur, who twisted on the ground.

"Nimue, wha—"

Morgan Le Fay cut him off with a click of the tongue. She stood regally in the centre of the beach. Nimue walked right to her.

Arthur, utterly horrified, could only watch as Nimue kneeled before Morgan, her golden gown the perfect foil to Morgan's midnight one. Morgan followed suit, kneeling and bowing her head.

"Morgan Le Fay," Nimue intoned, enchantment rippling beneath her words. "I present to you the sword of Excalibur and bestow upon you the divine right to rule. Rise, Queen of Camelot."

Nimue settled Excalibur delicately into Morgan's hands.

As Morgan regained her feet, a slash appeared in the roiling storm clouds above. A bolt of moonlight struck the ground, bathing Morgan in its light. Conjured by magic, a silver crown capped Morgan's dark hair.

She was queen.

Nimue remained on her knees before her, bowing her head in reverence.

Morgan turned to Arthur, who felt the keen stab of betrayal as vividly as a dagger through the heart.

"When you lead a crusade against magical beings, Arthur, you lead a crusade against all of us, even those you favour. Merlin and Nimue were never going to wait idly by for you to turn on them too. Your reign is over."

Morgan clicked her tongue one last time and jerked her head towards Arthur, prone on the ground.

The bodies of Gawain and Bedivere shuffled out of the trees, swords raised.

Arthur's head rolled into the lake a moment later, staining the water red.

Morgan examined the carnage ruefully, Excalibur cradled in her hands. It didn't have to be this way.

A moment later, she turned back to the castle, eager to return to her throne, and the platter of cherry tarts.

Long may she reign.

CHOCOLATE TART WITH CHERRY COMPOTE

CONTRIBUTED BY RHIANNON LOTZE

Makes One 9-Inch Tart or Ten 4-Inch Tarts

<u>Chocolate Tart Shell</u>

1 large egg yolk
1 tbsp heavy cream + extra as needed (15ml)
½ tsp vanilla extract (2.5ml)
1 c flour (160g/5.5 oz)
¼ c cocoa powder (30g/10oz)
⅔ c confectioner's sugar (85g/3oz)
¼ tsp salt (1.25ml)
8 tbsp unsalted butter, cut into ¼ inch pieces and chilled (110g/4oz)

Whisk the liquid ingredients (egg yolk, heavy cream, and vanilla) in a small bowl.
In a food processor, process the flour, cocoa powder, sugar, and salt until combined.
Sprinkle the butter over top and pulse until the texture resembles coarse cornmeal.
With the machine running, slowly add the liquid mixture and continue mixing until the dough just comes together. If the dough is too dry, slowly dribble in more cream, a teaspoon at a time.

Turn the dough onto a sheet of cling film and flatten it into a 6-inch disc. Wrap with the cling film and refrigerate for 1 hour.

Once chilled, roll the dough onto a work surface lightly dusted with cocoa powder (if it's too hard to work with, allow it to soften on the counter for about 10 minutes).

For a 9-inch tart:

Roll the dough into an 11-inch circle, about 2-3mm thick.

Gently lift the dough, using a rolling pin or steady hands, onto a 9-inch tart pan with a removable bottom. Press the dough into the edges of the pan then trim the excess using a knife, or by running the rolling pin over the top of the pan.

If there are any holes or weak spots, use the excess dough to patch them tightly.

Freeze the tart shell for 30 minutes before baking to prevent shrinking.

While the tart is freezing, preheat an oven to 375F/ Gas 5/190C. Line the frozen tart shell with a layer of parchment paper and fill with pie weights.

Bake for 30 minutes, turning halfway through, until the parchment paper no longer sticks to the dough. Remove the paper and pie weights and bake for another 5-10 minutes until fully baked and slightly crisp at the edges. Allow to cool completely before filling.

Note: The dough can be made ahead and refrigerated for two days (or frozen for up to 1 month).

For 4-inch tarts:
Roll the dough into a circle, about 2-3mm thick. Cut it into 5-inch rounds.
Gently lift the dough circles, using a rolling pin or steady hands, onto each 4-inch, removable bottom tart pan.
Press the dough into the edges of the pans then trim the excess using a knife, or by running the rolling pin over the top of the pans.
If there are any holes or weak spots, use the excess dough to patch them tightly.
Freeze the tart shells for 30 minutes before baking to prevent shrinking. Note: We recommend freezing each tart immediately after lining with dough.
While the tarts are freezing, preheat an oven to 375F/ Gas 5/190C. Line the frozen tart shells with a layer of parchment paper and fill with pie weights.
Bake for 10-15 minutes, turning halfway through, until the parchment paper no longer sticks to the dough.
Remove the paper and pie weights and bake for another 5-10 minutes until fully baked and slightly crisp at the edges.
Allow to cool completely before filling.

Note: The dough can be made ahead and refrigerated for two days (or frozen for up to 1 month).

Chocolate Ganache Filling
1 c heavy cream (250ml)
12 oz semisweet chocolate (340g)
6 tbsp butter, softened (85g)

Bring the cream to a simmer over medium-low heat.
Once simmering, remove from heat and add the
chocolate and butter. Cover and let stand for two
minutes.
Using a whisk, stir until the mixture is thoroughly
combined and smooth.
Pour into the cooled tart shell(s).
Refrigerate until set, 1-2 hours.

<u>Cherry Compote</u>
½ c dry red wine (125ml)
⅓ c granulated sugar (60g/2oz)
1 tsp lemon juice (5ml)
2 c jarred sour cherries, pitted (400g/14oz)
1 ½ tsp cornstarch (7.5ml)
1 ½ tsp water (7.5ml)
½ tsp almond extract (2.5ml)

Add the wine, sugar, and lemon juice to a medium
saucepan. Bring to a boil over high heat, stirring to
dissolve the sugar.
Add the cherries and return to a boil. Reduce heat
and boil gently, uncovered, for 15 minutes, stirring
occasionally.
Remove cherries with a slotted spoon.
Stir together cornstarch and water and whisk into the
cherry syrup. Bring to a boil and boil for 30 seconds to
one minute, stirring constantly.
Remove the cherry syrup from the pan and stir in
almond extract. Pour over the cherries.

Allow to cool completely before using.

For a sweeter tart, top with whipped cream and the blood of your enemies.

Rhiannon Lotze is a Canadian author from Windsor, Ontario, which means she's 97% maple syrup and 3% Timbit. Her published works include the short stories "Barrens and Brine," "Non-Prophet," and "Ratten-fänger," as well as the short story collection "Of Gods and Myth." Rhiannon is also an avid reader and camper, and her favourite place to do both is on the shores of Lake Huron

ITADAKIMASU

LYNDSEY ELLIS HOLLOWAY

Foreign food had never really had a place in Chatham, Louisiana. For those of the younger generation that had escaped the Southern town, it was a place stuck very much in the past, and to see a Confederate flag adorned in the window of a house was a fairly normal occurrence.

Chatham was not a large town. It consisted of a gas station, a post office, one Southern, and one Cajun diner, a hardware store, a dollar store, and of course a Church, not to mention the Mason's lodge. The town boasted a population of 543 people, and not one amongst them could have said with any confidence that they could pronounce the bizarre names listed on the menu, located just outside it's double doors.

'The Oni's Feast' Japanese Restaurant appeared in Chatham overnight. One minute the building on the outskirts of town had been the degraded remnants of a failed diner, the next... The walls were painted white, a brightly painted Torii gate arching over the doorway to greet the restaurant patrons, the red columns stark against the white walls. Above the Torii, in black letters framed in red, lay the restaurant's name - large, bold letters that were visible from the other end of the street.

When the townsfolk woke the next day, and ventured into the town about their business, the building had immediately grabbed their attention, quietly shouting its presence from the far end of the main street, Intriguing and far too mysterious to ignore. Murmurs and whispers had spread like wildfire amongst the population. They were all sure that the building had not looked like that the day before. In fact, not one citizen amongst their number could remember anyone even near the abandoned diner the previous day, so how in God's name had this new restaurant appeared like this? Pristine and ready to open its doors to its patrons in less than 24 hours.

Chatham attempted to go about its business as it always had, but it was difficult for its citizens to concentrate with a mystery sitting at the end of the street. It was all any of them could talk about. By midday they had erected an enormous banner across the Torii gate, fluttering in the light breeze, as it announced, 'Grand Opening, All Welcome!' in bold black letters flecked with gold. Underneath, in smaller lettering, the banner proclaimed, '1st Meal Free!' Though no one could recall seeing someone putting the banner up to begin with.

First meal free? You bet your ass they would take the restaurant owners up on that offer! It might not be American food, but who in their right mind would say no to a free meal?

***

Harold--Harry--Oldham was one of the few people who might pass up a free meal, especially if it was that foreign muck. Harry was a patriot, through and through, if it wasn't made in America he didn't want to know, and he didn't have time to tolerate the stupid bloody foreigners finding their way into his beloved country. He was the epitome of everything toxic, and the Confederate flags that adorned every surface he could fit them on, screamed his views for all to hear. Loud and clear.

"Harry? Hon, you in the den?" The lilting tones of Harry's second wife, Martha, carried through the house, a slightly uncertain tone, stinging words that would otherwise have been melodic.

Harry grunted loudly, a guttural, irritable sound like a water hog snuffling in the undergrowth. He was an extremely unpleasant man, and he was well aware of it. In fact, Harry took great pride in how the town perceived him. Harry Oldham had a grand sense of self-importance, he was the big cheese, the grand poohbah. Harold Oldham was hot shit, and anyone that was lucky enough to be given an audience with him should feel honoured. Or so Harry believed. This included his poor, suffering, second wife.

Now, it may seem trivial to emphasise the point that Martha was his second marriage, but in Harry's eyes it was a way of reminding Martha of just how good she had it. After all, he could have picked anyone to replace his first wife, couldn't he?

As Martha came into the den, shuffling into the room

as quietly as possible, so as not to disturb her husband's shows anymore than she already had, the man did not even deem her worthy of a glance. Hardly a surprise really, Harry was too busy watching the TV to look at a woman like Martha, it wasn't like it was anything he hadn't seen before.

"Harry, how do you feel about eating out tonight?" Martha asked, placing a hand on the back of his chair slowly, keeping herself positioned slightly behind it.

"Where?" Harry replied gruffly, almost spitting the word at the television as he continued to slouch in the armchair, wispy grey and white hair laying upon his sweaty brow. His bulging stomach peeked out from beneath his mucky white shirt, hanging over the faded blue sweatpants he wore, the TV remote held loosely in one hand, sausage-like fingers clutching it like it was his lifeline.

"There's a new place just opened in town, everyone's talking about it. Just appeared overnight!" Martha continued, her enthusiasm rising a little now as she let the town's excitement infect her as it had when she'd been at the store.

Harry turned off the TV and turned to face his wife, narrowing his watery blue eyes at her. While Harry held himself in high estimation, and thought himself the bee's knees, it had to be said that he wasn't the brightest bulb in the box. Hardly an academic, it was a wonder how the man had made a minor success of himself, let alone why he thought he was so highly regarded in Chatham, but that was how he held himself, regardless. That said, no one could deny that Harry was sharp in some respects, and people deflecting from the truth was one of the few things he could spot from a mile away, and he knew Martha was pussyfooting around something.

"What type of place is it?" He asked the words hissed through his yellowing teeth.

"Well," Martha hesitated, hand removed from the armchair as she flinched and habitually took a step back from her husband, "it's a Japanese place, I think, or that's what the girls said it was, while I was down at the store."

Harry spat, literally, onto the floor, at the very mention of another country, spinning back around in the armchair and aggressively turning the TV back on, the power button of the remote threatening to disintegrate under the ham-fisted attention.

"I know, Harry, I know, but they're giving away the first meal for free." Martha added swiftly, ringing her hands together in front of her skirt.

The TV was muted, but not turned off, and for a minute that lasted a lifetime, the pair remained in silence as this additional information whirled about in Harry's head. It was foreign food, cooked by a race one step away from being like those Gooks he'd fought during the war. In fact, as far as Harry was concerned, they were the same Gooks he'd fought during the war.

As loathe as Harry was to agree to going out for dinner, the idea of a free meal (that he could kick up a good old-fashioned stink about when it tasted like piss-soaked cats, which was probably what it consisted of), rather than suffering another of Martha's clumsily made, burnt meals was appealing.

"Fine," Harry grunted, unmuting the TV again,

"we'll go out. It'll be shit but can't be any worse than whatever slop you were planning on giving me."

***

A crowd had formed outside the covered double doors that led into the restaurant, as what seemed like the whole of Chatham waited to be let into this new marvel that had appeared within their little homestead.

Harry scowled at the Chathamites who stood in his way; as reluctant as he might have been about coming to the place, he was loath to wait for it as well, but he was not about to turn around and go back home. That wouldn't do his reputation any favours either. Holding his head high, Harry grabbed hold of his belt and gave his trousers a wiggle, pulling them up as best he could when his gut refused to budge, grunting at Martha as he barged his way to the front.

There were cries of indignation, and irritation, as Harry forced his way through the waiting diners, though most of the scorn thrown his way from the residents of Chatham soon dissipated when faced with the apologetic, and dejected, expression of Harold's long suffering second wife. Harry was more than aware of the insults and mutterings that followed in his wake, he just didn't care. Sadly, Chatham expected this kind of behaviour from Harold Oldham, and arguing about it was a fairly pointless endeavour.

"Evening Harry, didn't expect to see you and the little lady here."

Harry nodded to the squat; crimson faced toad of a

man that had addressed him as he reached the front of the queue.

"Jameson," Harry replied with a nod, putting a hand on the man's shoulder in greeting as he looked at the restaurant with disdain. "Martha said the entire town has a bee in its bonnet about this place, wouldn't be right if I didn't come down to see what all the fuss was about now, would it?"

"True, true. Did ya know they were building this place?" Jameson continued, pointing over his shoulder with a fat thumb.

"No, did the lodge not know?"

"Sounds like no one did. I don't remember anyone even showing an interest in that old diner, but here we are." Jameson snorted, sniffing loudly before he wiped his bulbous nose on the back of his hand.

"Won't last, Gook food like this has no place in Chatham, and I'll make sure it goes as quick as it appeared." Harry growled, crossing his arms over his chest as he glared at the audacious red Torii gate.

The crowd was getting restless as 6:00 came and went, and the doors remained closed, the black fabric covers still hanging on the inside of the glass, blocking the view of whatever lay within. Harry and Jameson shared an amused look that said they had suspected these foreigners couldn't deliver on their free meal promise; clearly the proprietor had chickened out.

Just as Harry was about to suggest to Martha that they leave, they tied the black fabric back, and the staff members opened the glass doors, hurrying in uniform fashion to line up on either side of the entrance, in front of the Torii gate. Ten members of staff, in identical black uniforms with a red and gold logo emblazoned over their hearts (Harry couldn't quite see what the logo was) stood in a perfect line, their heads bowed low to their customers.

Another staff member strode confidently through the doors, head held high, black hair swept neatly out of his handsome face, his almond-shaped eyes oddly enchanting as he beamed at the crowd. As he stepped in front of the others, Harry could to see that the logo, intricately embroidered onto the pristine black uniform, looked to be some strange demon-like face.

"Ladies and Gentleman, my profuse apologies for our tardiness, in my culture we do not accept things not working to the time they are expected, however we wanted to ensure that everything was perfect before we received you this evening. My name is Kai," the man spoke in perfect English, his Japanese accent thick but the words easily intelligible compared to what Harry had expected, "I am the head waiter, and host of this fine establishment, and I welcome you all to 'The Oni's Feast' where we will serve you traditional dishes from all over Japan." Kai continued to smile warmly as he bowed with a flourish, almost bending entirely in two, before he was upright once more. "Please, allow me to welcome you all, and may you enjoy what we offer."

"Unlikely," Harry hissed through his teeth, not exactly careful about who heard him, "not if this debacle is anything to go by. I bet the food is as sloppy as their timing."

Kai's sharp eyes seemed to flash like molten gold

for the briefest moment, and while Harry was taking no notice, Martha had seen the dark expression on the handsome man's face as he heard her husband's words. It had been there for only a second, but the look had been unmistakable.

"Sir, please accept my most humble apologies for our delay. If you follow me inside, then I shall offer you our very best table for yourself and your lovely lady wife, and complimentary champagne. Please follow me and I shall ensure you are well looked after as our most honoured guests." Kai offered, bowing low again and motioning with an arm for Harry and Martha to enter the much-anticipated establishment.

"That's more like it." Harry snapped, grasping Martha by the elbow as he all but propelled her through the Torii gate, passed the doors into the restaurant proper.

Harry remembered the diner that had occupied the building previously, but there was not even one remnant of that dingy, greasy spoon left in the place. The entrance opened up to a white path of fine gravel that crunched underfoot, with a reception desk in the corner to the left. A small flowing stream separated the entrance/waiting area, winding its way across the room with a gentile, calming trickle, fed by a magnificent fake waterfall that took up the entire left half of the t-shaped entrance of the building. A fine mist coated the air as the water splashed into the pool below, crashing into the rocks and showering the stunning koi that called the pool home. Ordinarily Harry would have been irritated at the wetness in the air, especially as it settled onto his clothes and skin; yet it was almost warm, soothing somehow, and scented like flowers in spring, fresh and clean and calming.

Kai directed Harry and Martha over a wooden bridge that led over the stream to the main part of the restaurant. They had fashioned the walls to show off the beams that made them, painted a glossy black to ensure they stood out against the deep read of the walls themselves. The ceiling reflected the same, but they had edged the black beams in gold that gleamed in the hanging lights. The walls were adorned with a variety of traditional paintings, all of which seemed to depict strange creatures, or long banners of elaborate calligraphy that meant nothing to Harry. Close to the ceiling, casting strange shadows from the lights, were a variety of masks, the strangest of which was a red faced demon-like creature with an extremely phallic nose that caused Harry to scoff in disgust.

The path from the entrance split into three, the right path led off to a door that led to the toilets and the kitchen, the left led to an area adorned with gently swaying bamboo plants, elaborate red parasols and blossoming Sakura trees - which Kai explained was the family area. Harry pushed Martha down the middle path, continuing to follow their host. As his own footsteps crunched upon the gravel, Harry was struck by the fact that he could not hear Kai's, even as he concentrated on the man's quick, nimble feet, he could only make out his own footsteps, and the smaller shuffling ones of his wife.

The middle path led around the bar that lay in the very centre of the restaurant, a huge square counter that appeared to have been constructed from one solid piece of perfectly polished, jet black wood. As Harry and Martha passed it, the bar staff all stopped what they were doing to bow to their arriving guests. As reluctant as Harry was to admit it, he was somewhat impressed, and he could definitely get used to being bowed at as he passed.

Finally, Kai stopped at another Torii gate that led to an indoor, covered structure at the very back of the restaurant. Had the building always been this big? Or had these Japs extended it somehow?

Kai slid open the wooden doors, bowing as he motioned for his guests to enter the walled structure. Once they were inside, Kai followed them, closing the doors behind him. "Welcome to the adult only side of the restaurant, if you follow me to the end Sir there is a private booth, with its own bathroom, where you and your lady wife can eat undisturbed. It's reserved for only our most honoured guests."

Harry snorted his approval, waving a dismissive hand at his host to lead the way. They strode past several tables and booths, all made of similar black wood to the bar they had seen before, ivory tablecloths draped over them with the cutlery set out perfectly. Kai slid open the door to the private room, bowing as Harry and Martha moved inside.

"I will return promptly with your champagne, please look at the menu, I will be back for your order shortly."

"Bring me a beer, I can't stand that fruity shite, the wife will drink it though, call it a treat hey Martha?" Harry grunted, elbowing his wife hard in the ribs.

Martha flinched, and gave Kai a weak smile, noticing the darkening of the man's eerie eyes that disappeared as he smiled and nodded his acknowledgement of her husband's request.

"Could get used to being treated like this." Harry chuckled, sitting back heavily in his seat, a step away from resting his feet on the table entirely.

For all of Harry's bluster and distaste of foreigners, being treated like royalty was one sure-fire way of ensuring the deplorable, bloated, buffoon was half-way to agreeable. He'd believed himself to be important, and finally someone in this backwater town was giving him the proper respect a man of his position deserved. Even the lodge didn't favour him half as much as they should do, but no matter, he knew plenty about the foolish members of the Mason lodge that they knew to tread carefully with him. It was never wise to drink too heavily around Harold Oldham, not if you wanted to remain squeaky clean and free of owing him a 'favour'.

The Oldham's browsed the menu as they waited for Kai to return with their drinks, Harry (in true Harry fashion) making snide comments about every dish, with Martha offering suggestions (most of which were spat back at her) for dishes Harry might at least find tolerable.

Just as Harry had turned to snarl at his second wife again, the door slid open, and Kai came into the room with their drinks balanced gracefully on a tray, although he was moving while bowing. Harry's beer didn't even wobble as Kai moved to their table with eerie agility, depositing the drinks with one fluid motion before he stood up and smiled at the couple.

"Have you made a decision about what you might like to eat?" Kai asked.

"We'll both have the soup-noodle thing, the, what

is it, the pork ramen. I'll also have er, what's it now, the chicken kara, chicken karag - karaaadge." Harry grumbled.

"The chicken ka-ra-ah-gay," Kai smiled with a bow of his head, "a very good choice Sir, I will order it for you promptly."

As Kai opened the door to leave the room, the cacophony from the restaurant beyond struck the couple. It appeared the entire town was now settled in for their first Japanese dining experience, and despite the Southern scepticism there was some genuine excitement amongst the townsfolk at this new dining experience.

Harry listened to his wife blabber on about whatever unimportant nonsense she needed to get off her chest, finishing his first beer swiftly. As soon as he had finished the last drop, Kai appeared unexpectedly in their room to remove the empty bottle and replace it with a new one, without Harry even having to get up.

"I'll say one thing for them, they're attentive fuckers ain't they?" He observed to his wife with a smirk, taking a sip from the fresh bottle.

It wasn't long before Kai opened the door to their room, letting in two other uniformed servers who brought in the Oldham's food in a similarly elegant fashion, their heads down as they moved on silent feet just as their host had. Harry wondered how they all managed not to make a sound on the gravel path.

Without even asking, the waiters placed the correct bowls of ramen down in front of Harry and Martha, along with the karaage that Harry also ordered. The aroma wafting from the dishes enticed a hungry grumble from Harry's bulging belly, his mouth salivating as the smells filled his nose.

"Enjoy your meals, if you need anything please call for me." Kai's eyes seemed to dance wickedly, but again only Martha noticed the sudden shift in the man's demeanour, her husband too caught up in himself as usual.

Harry hadn't even waited for Kai to leave their private room before he had grabbed a fork and a spoon, dismissing the option of chopsticks entirely, and shovelling the first mouthful of noodles into his mouth with a sickening slurp, soup flicking all over the pristine table cloth and flecking his face.

"Hey! Martha, it's good!" Harry managed between mouthfuls, as he took a literal handful of karaage and stuffed them into his open maw, chewing on them with a loud smacking sound that was enough to set even the strongest stomach on edge. "Here, try one."

Martha blinked in surprise at this offering, Harry had never offered her his food, not in all of their married lives. Even at their wedding he'd given her a slice of her own from their wedding cake, rather than offering her a bite of his. Not willing to turn down this minor miracle, Martha took the breaded chicken bite from her husband's saliva-slick fingers, swallowing hard as she tried not to think too hard on how wet his hand was, before she put the karaage in her mouth.

Now Martha rarely disagreed with her husband at the best of times, not because Harry was never wrong (as he claimed) but because she knew better than to poke the angry, sweaty bear she had married. For once, however,

Harry was both right and wrong - the chicken wasn't just good, it was amazing! In fact, there were no words to describe the myriad of delectable flavours flowing over her tongue.

Eyes widening, Martha reached out and snatched another piece for herself in an uncharacteristically bold move, and for once Harry did not grab her wrist and silently threaten to snap her bones for daring to eat his food, in fact he encouraged it by pushing the bowl into the middle of the table, making it easier for his wife to share.

The couple remained silent as they ate their meals, barely taking breaths between each mouthful, stopping only to take a swig of their drinks, which Kai continued to replace as soon as they were empty. The whole restaurant had followed suit, silence filling the building as every resident enjoyed their meals. The only sound that could be discerned was that of chewing, and cutlery clinking against crockery.

In less than twenty minutes, Harry and Martha had devoured their gargantuan bowls of ramen, lifting the bowls to their faces to slurp the last remnants of broth down their gullets, before licking their fingers and gathering the karaage crumbs, not willing to waste a morsel.

Harry sat back in his chair, hands laced over his bloated stomach as he licked his lips, burping as he wiped his face with the back of his hand, reaching a hand out for his beer and grunting as he struggled to lift himself forward.

"Allow me, Sir." Kai offered, appearing as if from

nowhere, and handing Harry the bottle with a smile. "Did you enjoy your meal?"

"Very much so! I was surprised by how tasty it was, I don't much like foreign food, can't trust anything that ain't American, but that wasn't bad by any means."

"Well, I am very glad to hear that, Sir. I shall inform our chefs; they will be delighted to know it was to your satisfaction. Would you like to see the dessert menu?"

"Ya know what, normally I would, but that has filled me right up."

"Well then, it has been a pleasure, Sir. Will we be seeing you again soon?" Kai asked, helping Martha stand up from her chair.

"Oh, you can count on it!" Harry replied, shuffling his seat back slowly, before he waddled out of the room, wife in tow, Kai bowing as the couple left.

***

In the three weeks since 'The Oni's Feast' had opened, it had never once been empty during a mealtime. Once neighbouring towns had heard of the place, and its phenomenal feasts, everyone had rushed to book tables as soon as the restaurant could accommodate them. In such a short time they were booked up at least two months in advance, with a few tables kept open for the locals of Chatham at all times.

One such local, despite all the odds, was in fact Harold Oldham. Every day, at least once, Harry made the trip to the restaurant, and in fact he knew most, if not all, of the staff by name. Whenever he arrived, despite the queue formed in front of the Torii gate, Kai would wave Harry to the front, escorting Harry straight to the private room he had shared with Martha the first time they had gone.

The trip was made a little more difficult these days, considering the pounds Harry had put on eating at the restaurant every day. not that he cared in the slightest. He wasn't about to turn down a good meal! Especially not when Kai had offered him a VIP discount for being such a loyal customer. For a Jap, Kai wasn't too bad, though that was mostly because Kai treated Harry like some sort of Lord, which perfectly fed Harry's ego.

Harry waddled down the street, watery-blue, piggy eyes fixed on his destination, rolling his hips as he swung his gargantuan belly along, his mouth already salivating at the thought of the ramen, with a side of karaage. Harry's thick, bulbous tongue flickered over his fat lips, his lungs straining with each wheezing breath, sweat pouring down his back as he raised a chubby hand to motion to Kai above the crowd blocking his path.

"Excuse me, excuse me ladies and gentlemen, would you mind stepping aside so that my esteemed guest can come through, please? Arigatou gozaimasu, thank you." Kai bowed to the crowd as he ushered them aside to allow Harry passage.

"Thank you - Kai - always - happy to - see - you - on - the door." Harry heaved, his chest rising and falling heavily with exertion. "You always know how to treat a - man." He grunted, patting his belly as he got his breath back.

"Always a pleasure to see you Mr. Oldham. I have

your usual table free for you, I take it you'd like your regular order?"

"That's right, with extra pork today I think, then I don't have to suffer Martha's cooking this evening. You should have seen the shit she gave me last night, slop. I wouldn't even feed to the pigs, wouldn't even feed it to the Gooks!" Harry laughed, his belly jiggling as he waddled after Kai. "Should have just come back here again, rather spend the money here rather than force myself to swallow her crap cooking."

"Well, we're always happy to serve you Mr. Oldham." Kai replied, though he offered no opinion on Mrs. Oldham's cooking.

A family of four made their way towards them, waddling merrily in Harry's direction, cheeks flushed red from full, bulging bellies. The two children giggled and tottered as quickly as they could along the gravel path, cheeks puffing as they struggled for breath, their chubby thighs rubbing together as they 'chased' one another. As they were about to cross Harry's path, a server came from the left, forced to jump aside in an almost cat-like fashion that caused even Harry to be impressed, at least until the waiter jumped into Harry.

"You fucking Jap imbecile!" Harry snarled, lashing out at the waiter, backhanding him hard across the face with a chubby hand, propelling the unsuspecting waiter across the floor.

"Are you alright Mr. Oldham?" Kai asked, placing a gentle hand on the man's shoulder.

"No, thanks to this idiot. You should fire him, Kai, useless piece of shit." Harry snarled. "Get out of my way." He snapped, barging his way through the family who stood there, stunned, their eyes fixed on a spot just behind Harry's shoulder. As always, all that mattered to Harold Oldham, was Harry. Had he thought to see what the family was looking at maybe, just maybe, he'd have seen what had them so stunned.

He would have seen the molten gold gaze of Kai boring into his back as the head waiter helped his colleague off the floor, and muttered something swiftly in Japanese before sending the young man off into the kitchens. But of course, Harry was too busy with Harry.

While Kai lingered behind, Harry made his way to the private room he always used, greeting a few of the Mason Lodge members on his journey, stopping to shake hands with a few along the way.

"Ah! Harry! Good to see ya ol' man." Jameson called out, waving from the booth he had somehow managed to shuffle his bloated, toad-like frame into, his stomach pressed up against the table in a way that threatened to cut him in two, not that he seemed to mind, or notice.

"Jameson, how are ya?" Harry replied, shaking the man's meaty fist with his own.

"Not too bad, not too bad. Ya heard about Iris an' that old miser Ford?"

"No? What about 'em?"

"Gone missing."

"What do you mean missing?"

"I mean what I said. They've gone missing, Sheriff Peters says they're the sixth ones this week, apparently there's twenty missing altogether in the last three weeks!"

"From Chatham?!"

"Yup! Couple of tourists too, but Peters says he's not sure about them, 'cos they could have gone home or onto another town anyhow."

"Mr. Oldham? Would you like to take your seat, and I will bring your meal?" Kai interjected, making Harry jump since he'd forgotten all about the man.

"Yeah, yeah good point Kai. See ya later, Jameson." Harry muttered, scowling as Jameson's words went round and round in his head.

Twenty people were missing. Even as Harry heaved his portly form into his seat those words turned over in his mind. Ordinarily such details wouldn't have bothered a man like Harry, after all it had nothing to do with him personally, however even Harry felt that this was strange, especially for such a quiet place like Chatham.

Whatever worries Harry's narcissistic brain was about to consider were soon pushed aside when the enchanting smell of his lunch arrived, causing him to salivate and think of nothing other than the meal he had come to enjoy daily. Kai opened the door, head bowed as usual, waiting for two other waiters to hurry into the private room, plates balanced atop their fingertips.

"I brought you a complimentary plate of gyoza for you to try as well Mr. Oldham, to make up for the trouble with my colleague. They are like meat dumplings; I know you will enjoy them." Kai smiled, nodding to Harry as he put the plate down on the table alongside Harry's other dishes.

"I should think so too." Harry grumbled, reaching over with a dumpy hand and snatching up one of the hot dumplings, shoving it inelegantly into his mouth.

Kai smiled and bowed his way out of the door under the watchful eye of Harry. Even looking the head waiter in the eyes, Harry seemed utterly oblivious of the subtle, and brief, shift in Kai's usually cheerful demeanour. The dancing brown eyes, and warm smile swiftly replaced with a dark, wicked smile, and turbulent molten gold irises. But none of this registered with Harry, not with his food in front of his face.

It didn't take long for Harry to devour his meal, the memory of the tender pork that almost melted like butter, already becoming a distant pleasure that he couldn't wait to revisit. Sitting back in his chair, ignoring the groan of the wood under his enormous load, Harry sighed happily, smacking his fat lips together as his head grew thick and fuzzy. It had been an extremely filling meal, but he rarely got drowsy until he was at home in his armchair, given these restaurant ones were hard and barely accommodated his rather large backside. Maybe the gyoza had been a little much, or the extra pork.

Harry sighed, pushing his chair away from the table with a grunt, using the table to pry his carcass from the chair, albeit with some reluctance. Once he got himself upright, Harry stood still, catching his breath, his lungs on fire from the effort, his head swimming. Placing his palms flat on the table, Harry groaned as he closed his eyes, unable to properly focus as his head seemed to fill with cotton candy.

Panic set in as Harry lifted a shaking hand from the table to rub against his clammy face, sweat pouring from his furrowed brow as he gasped for air, his lungs feeling as though they were on fire with every breath he attempted to take. Blinking through the sweat, Harry squinted at the door, reaching out with a pudgy hand, trying to call out to Kai to no avail, a mere squeak wiggling past his swollen tongue, moments before everything went black, and Harold Oldham met the floor with a large bang.

***

"He's a good size Kaibyo, well done, I knew we could rely on you to bring us a decent one."

"Always happy to provide for the Feast, Sensei, especially with humans like *this* on the menu." Kai's voice had lost its usual warmth, or at least, the warmth and respect that Harry expected from the Jap. It was sharp, and full of malice, and Harry wondered who the waiter was referring to.

"He's certainly gorged himself on our food, hasn't he?" The other voice continued, a deep, vibrating bass that sounded like it came from deep within a mountain.

"He's one of the viler ones, Sensei, and that's saying something with their kind. *This* one, however, is quite foul at heart. Racist, abusive, self-important. Thankfully, he has eaten here every day since we opened, so his meat should still be succulent regardless, I believe our dishes will have counteracted the sourness of his soul." Kai snorted.

Poor Harry. Kai was right of course. If one were to look at Harry's soul it could have been coloured a sickly green, vomit yellow, or pitch black - depending on who was looking at it. Had Harry been a better person, maybe karma wouldn't have come around to bite his fat arse as hard as she intended to now, unfortunately, since he had been deplorable for the majority of his existence, karma was coming for him hard.

Harry was vaguely aware of being on something cold, hard, and metal, though how he had come to be lying on it he wasn't sure. He was *also* aware that he felt a bit like a turtle turned over on its shell, unable to move, his fat pressing down uncomfortably on his lungs.

"K-Kai? What the fuck is - going on?!" Harry demanded through laboured breaths, pressure building in his head, his face beet-red.

"Ah! Mr. Oldham, you've woken up, how marvellous." Kai grinned, spinning about on the spot to lean over Harry.

There was no ignoring the change in Kai's appearance this time, no matter how much Harry might want to. The flowing golden irises sported a slitted pupil, each that widened almost hungrily as Kai looked down into Harry's puffy face. No longer was he the handsome, jovial man that had served Harry since the restaurant had opened, now his face had contorted into that of a cat, with sleek black fur and long whiskers. Out of the corner of his eye, Harry could see something flickering in and out of his vision. As he concentrated on it, he realised it was two twin-black tails, the tips of which were on fire.

"One moment Mr. Oldham, let's get you upright, it must be terribly uncomfortable lying on your back, prostrate like this." Kai purred, one clawed hand reaching under the table Harry was lying on.

There was a metallic 'clink' and suddenly Harry was being propelled upright. For a minute he expected to slide straight off the table, until he felt the restraints (that he hadn't noticed before) strain against his body, holding him in place.

"There we are! Now we can speak properly." Kai continued, his tone soft and full of malice as he smiled, lips pulling back to reveal the sharp fangs in his mouth.

"What the fuck is happening, what in the *fuck* are you?!" Harry demanded, holding onto what little control (which was none, though he was never going to admit that) he had left.

"I wouldn't expect an ignorant, racist, *foul* creature such as yourself, to have the faintest *clue* about who, nor *what*, I am. But don't worry Mr. Oldham, I'll educate you!" Kai growled gently, tapping Harry on the end of his nose with the point of a claw. "I'm known as a Nekomata, a specific type of Yokai, my race, you might say. There are hundreds, thousands of us, most have been forgotten, but some of us are harder for people to forget."

Kai moved away from Harry gracefully, picking up a finished dish from the countertop, and handing it effortlessly to one of the waiters. Harry shuddered as he watched the exchange, the waiter looking him dead in the eye, his feline-face similar to Kai's, the cat-like features melting away until he looked human. Harry realised it was the waiter he had struck earlier, and he swallowed a hard lump that had formed in his throat at the hatred in the man's eyes.

"The citizens of Japan have more respect for our kind, they're more wary and not as trusting as you Westerners, they knew to avoid the restaurants we set up, so we relied on moronic tourists instead, whose instincts for danger had been dulled by their ignorance. So, we decided to come *here*, to the source, so that we could feed our numbers easily, and how simple you made it for us! Even here, in this backwards town where you judge your own species based on the colour of their *skin* rather than their value, you lapped it up, you came in *droves*, it was better than we could ever have expected." Kai smiled that wicked smile again, looking over his shoulder at the chefs who had continued to work without once looking back.

Kai danced away from Harry, his twin tails still alight at the tips, coming dangerously close to Harry's face as the Nekomata sprang nimbly onto a countertop, crouching and tilting his head to one side, ears twitching atop his head.

"So easy to entice you in with free meals, you couldn't get enough once you'd had that first taste, yet not one of you ever questioned what you were eating. Too eager to stuff your faces and get fatter and lazier than you were before, not *one* of you looked too closely at *what* you were shovelling into your mouths, did you?"

Kai raised a hand above his head and clicked his claws together. Two of the chefs, backs still to Harry so that he could not see their faces, just their hunched, hulking frames as they lumbered away, heads kept low as they almost brushed the ceiling. Harry watched as they opened a huge metal door that hissed as they yanked on the handle, cold mist swirling from the seal as they pulled it wide enough for them to slip into the icy, dark interior out of sight.

Before Harry could gather his thoughts, the hulking pair had returned, and this time he could see *everything*. Their faces reflected the embroidered logo on the shirts of the staff; bright red with shocking black hair and beards, a jutting lower jaw sporting fangs or tusks that could not be contained within their mouths. Their horn jutted out from beneath their chef's hats, and between their muscled, clawed hands, they carried a large, frozen carcass covered in frost. They heaved the frozen meat onto the countertop that Kai was crouched upon, the Nekomata deftly jumping out of their way, landing beside Harry gracefully.

"You see, Mr. Oldham?" Kai purred, pointing at the meat with a claw.

Harry blinked, staring at the frozen lump, swallowing hard as a shiver ran down his spine, followed by several beads of sweat. A face stared back at him from out of the freezer-frost, eyes blank, white spheres of ice, and Harry realised it was Tom Ford, who Jameson had mentioned being missing only a little while before.

A wave of fire rushed from his stomach, into his gullet, until it propelled itself violently from his mouth, spattering on the floor as he ejected half his lunch onto the tiles. People. They had all been eating people.

Kai laughed, the sound sharp, reminding Harry of cats fighting in the alleyway. "*Now* you understand, don't you?! All this time Mr. Oldham, you've been happily stuffing your friends and neighbours down your throats, licking your fingers so you don't miss a morsel! The more you eat, the better your flesh tastes for us, and given how you gorge yourselves there's always plenty for us to feast on, without us having to worry about running out of ingredients for all of you." Kai clicked a claw against the tabletop Harry was bound to. "It was my Sensei's idea, he's the wisest of us here you see, it's why we named the restaurant after him, in a way. '*The Oni's Feast*', clever, isn't it?"

"W-what are you going to do with me?" Harry stammered, the stale taste of vomit and bile lingering on his tongue, his throat raw, his voice hoarse.

"Well Mr. Oldham, ordinarily we would kill you quickly, a slice across the throat and you don't even know what's happened, but for a specimen such as yourself, one as *deplorable* as you, we have something special in store. My Sensei is going to carve you himself, it's an honour you don't really deserve, but since he is the most skilled with a knife, and you think so highly of yourself, we thought we'd allow it." Kai spun out of sight behind the table, the tell-tale 'click,' of the lever warning Harry that he was on the move again.

The table tilted backwards, but Kai stopped it so that it was still angled, allowing Harry full view of the kitchen. The Nekomata had vanished from Harry's line of sight, leaving the man to watch the twitching muscles of the Oni-Chefs as they continued to make dinner for the other restaurant patrons, all of whom were utterly unaware of the horrors going on in the kitchen.

A clatter brought Harry back to his current predicament, and he turned his head, eyes widening at the sight of an Oni far larger than the others, which was saying something. The creature was bent almost double, his arched back touching the ceiling as he crouched as low as he could, moving in a perpetual squat. His slick black hair fell in natural waves over his deep red back, his long beard tied into a neater 'ponytail' with a golden ribbon, jet-black eyes glinting at Harry as the thing looked over its shoulder, smiling wickedly at the man.

"Greetings Mr. Oldham and thank you for joining us for dinner. Kaibyo has told me all about you, I cannot wait to test your flesh. Don't worry, I'll talk you through my plans, you might be interested to know which dishes you'll be making for our feast tonight." The Oni rumbled in its deep bass tones, a mirthless, oily chuckle escaping between his fangs.

"No! No! Let me go!" Harry squealed, struggling against his restraints as the glint of a knife caught his eye, and the reality of what was about to happen finally struck him.

Kai's feline cackle filled Harry's ears, and he flinched as something sharp dug into his shoulders. Looking up, Harry met Kai's eyes, the Nekomata looming over him from behind, digging his claws into Harry's shoulders to keep him still as the Oni turned to face him, jet black claws outstretched over Harry's bulging stomach.

"First, Mr. Oldham, I shall slice you open at the belly, we'll use all this excess fat and meat to make our karaage that you so enjoyed shoving into your piggy face, your rump meat will be tenderised to make our 'pork' tonkatsu steaks, your intestines will be washed and shredded to make our *delicious* noodles," the Oni described softly, one claw gently tracing its way over Harry's body as the creature's jet black eyes glinted menacingly. "I will use every inch of you Mr. Oldham,

I'll even boil down all your bones to make stock for our miso soup. Nothing will go to waste; it'll be the only time you've been worth a damned thing." The Oni smiled, large, yellowing fangs close to Harry's face, its warm, fetid breath filling his nose and bringing on another wave of nausea.

"Shall we begin Sensei?" Kai purred excitedly from beside Harry's ear.

"Hai, Kaibyo, remove his clothing for me and we shall get started."

No matter how much Harry screamed and writhed, there was no give in the restraints, nor did it seem that anyone in the restaurant could hear him to come and help. All Harry could do was watch in abject horror as Kai used his claws to strip away Harry's clothes, exposing his bulging, naked flesh to the world. Harry's bottom lip quivered, his eyes transfixed on the glint of the knife in the Oni's hand as Kai's Sensei shuffled to the table, smiling wickedly as he drew the knife across Harry's belly.

The blade was so sharp, that for a moment Harry didn't realise they had cut him until he felt the hot, sticky, wetness flow over his lap. Looking down he screamed, his mouth almost as wide as the gaping gash now staring back at him, wiggling wormy intestines spilling from the wound into a bowl held underneath him by Kai. Harry's eyes rolled back in his head, but a sharp flick in his temple swiftly brought him back.

"No, Mr. Oldham, you need to be awake for this. It's something rather special." The Oni smiled, waggling a clawed finger in Harry's face.

It seemed Harry's whimpering, or his moans, or the screams of pain elicited from his throat perturbed none of the creatures the Oni touched the open wound. The knife was swift, and Harry never felt the cuts as the Oni sliced great swathes of his skin back from his bones, the first he knew of what had been done was when his nerve endings were exposed to the air, or what he could bear to watch with his own eyes. Had he not already emptied his stomach onto the floor, he would have done now, but he had nothing left to give.

The steady drip of his blood onto the kitchen floor was almost soporific, and Harry's head was feeling fluffy, his vision clouding as the blood loss finally took him. His tongue lolled from his mouth, and Harry's last image was that of a knife flashing through the air, his intestines freed from his innards, the bowl handed to one of the other Oni shuffled away to start making them into noodle, before his vision faded and his head slumped backwards.

****

A satisfying sound of meat sizzling on a pan filled the air, mixing with the delectable aroma of soup bubbling away on a stove. They had closed the restaurant for the night, and now it was time for the staff to eat. The various Yokai had cleaned the restaurant and set out the long table they always used when they shared a meal together. Down the centre lay a variety of dishes - all of which had been set out purposefully.

At the top of the table, Harry's head took pride of

place. His dead eyes stared emptily at the ceiling, his gaping mouth stuff with ice, cut from ear to ear to help widen his jaw so that a bottle of sake could rest within it. Each dish that followed had been set out in the location where the ingredients had been taken from Harry, a vast bowl of ramen noodles settled where his intestines had once resided.

The staff hurriedly took their seats, each in their true forms, unrecognisable from the human staff members that Chatham knew and greeted whenever they came to eat at the restaurant. Kai took up a seat next to Harry's head, the Nekomata grinning at the blank look on the man's grey face, before turning his sharp gaze onto his Sensei, the Oni able to stand at his full eight feet now he was out of the kitchens.

"My friends, we have a mighty feast in front of us tonight, courtesy of the deplorable Mr. Harold Oldham, may he serve us better in death than he served anyone in life. Please, eat." The Oni rumbled, opening his arms to the room and smiling.

In unison the staff clapped their hands together, bowed their heads, and roared, "Itadakimasu!"

CHICKEN KARAAGE & MISO RAMEN

CONTRIBUTED BY LYNDSEY ELLIS HOLLOWAY

Chicken Karaage
Serves 4

For the marinade
100ml cooking sake
3 tablespoons mirin
3 tablespoons rice wine vinegar
3 tablespoons lime juice
2 tablespoons sriracha (or other hot sauce)
3 tablespoons soy sauce
1 tablespoon sesame oil
10 garlic cloves, peeled (hope you like garlic as much as I do!)
4 echalion (banana) shallots
30g pureed or grated ginger
½ teaspoon black pepper

For the flour
400g cornflour (cornstarch)
1 teaspoon ground black pepper
1 teaspoon salt
2 teaspoons sesame seeds
1 teaspoon dashi powder

2 teaspoons Shichimi (or chill) powder
1 teaspoon ground ginger

500g chicken thighs - diced
Oil for deep frying
Karaage is often bought as a side dish with ramen, or during a drinking session with friends at a bar. A convenient food often found in convenience stores as well as bars, street stalls and generally anywhere else in Japan that does fried chicken, it's a quick and easy, tasty meal. You can also do a tofu version for your vegetarian friends, but there's something particularly good about a juicy piece of fried chicken...

Method
Throw all the marinade ingredients into a food blender (or bowl with a hand blender) and blitz until the marinade is nice and smooth. Put in the diced chicken thigh and leave to marinade - the longer the better to allow the meat to take in the flavours. You can marinade the meat for as little as 2 hours, but I'd recommend 24-48 hours for *really* juicy, tasty karaage. When you're ready to make the karaage - set aside a deep pan filled with oil (vegetable is best if you can't get a large amount of sesame, add a little sesame oil to the pan if that's the case) and turn on the hob to heat it up while you prepare the chicken.
With another bowl add the flour ingredients together and mix until they're combined. Take one piece of marinated chicken at a time and cover in the flour mixture, placing carefully into the oil once it's hot.

Rinse and repeat until the pan is full and sizzling away merrily. With a slotted spoon, take out the chicken when the outside is nicely browned and put to one side. If you still have some chicken left to cook, put them through.

If you have an air fryer, take your cooked chicken and give it a quick ten minute cook on a hot setting, if not, back in the oil for ten minutes to make the skin really crispy!

Remove the chicken once it's ready and put into a bowl. Enjoy on its own or with a dip, mayonnaise, sriracha, ponzu or soy sauce with a little lime juice go perfectly with this dish!

Miso Ramen

Serves 4 & then some (depends on how hungry you all are!)

For the soup

200ml chicken stock

1ltr water

100g Dashi (if you can't get this, just add some extra miso paste!)

100g miso paste (brown or white)

30ml fish sauce

50ml soy sauce (preferably light salt)

50ml mirin

50ml rice wine vinegar

60ml cooking sake

Tablespoon pureed ginger

Tablespoon pureed garlic

For the rest (this is where you get to be creative, throw in whatever you like!)
Pork belly - thinly sliced
Beansprouts
Bamboo shoots
Water chestnuts
Boiled egg
Spring onion
Soba or ramen noodles
Chilli flakes or chilli oil
Sesame oil
Shichimi spices
Ramen is a staple in Japan; after a long day at work, or a good session of drinking, you can find a small ramen restaurant open at all hours for a bowl of restorative yumminess. It's a comfort food you can adjust to your own tastes as much as you like, and every bowl can be different depending on what you put into it. Filling and tasty, ramen is one of those foods that gets better if you leave it a day or two before you eat - allowing the broth to mature so that all the flavours come together.

Method
You're going to need a large pot to make this dish. Start by adding the chicken stock (homemade is great for this dish, because homemade stock always changes from batch to batch, changing the taste of the miso broth). Mix in the dashi and the miso paste along with the water and bring to the boil - stirring to ensure the pastes have broken down into the liquid properly.
Once the soup is boiling and the paste has dissolved,

bring it down to a simmer. Add in the fish sauce, soy sauce, mirin, vinegar and sake along with the garlic and ginger and leave the broth to cook for another five - ten mins and taste. Miso is a personal preference type dish, if you're not happy with it, add in some of the ingredients again until you're happy! If you're happy you can either use it right away or store it for the next day when the broth will have stewed and become richer.

Once you're happy with your broth it's time to start adding in the other ingredients. Quick fry the pork belly slices (chicken, tofu, beef, whatever your main of choice is!) in a pan with a dash of sesame oil. Once they've been cooked, add them to the broth along with the beansprouts, bamboo shoots and water chestnuts, and any other veg you may want to eat.

While the ingredients simmer in the soup and take on some of the flavours, cook your noodles in a separate pan. If you cook them in the miso, chances are your noodles are going to eat up all your soup and you're going to be left with no broth.

When the noodles are done, put them into a deep bowl, layer up your pork and veg with a slotted spoon and then ladle in the soup. Cut a boiled egg in half and place on top where it can warm in the soup, along with some freshly cut spring onions. If you want a little spice - add in some chilli flakes, chilli oil or Japanese Shichimi spices.

Congratulations! You're ready to enjoy!

Lyndsey Ellis-Holloway is a writer from a mysterious little town in the UK famous for having its own witch. She spends most of her time in the dark recesses of her mind. Specializing in fantasy, sci-fi, horror, and dystopian stories, she focuses on compelling characters and layering in myth and legend at every opportunity.

Her mind is dark and twisted, and she lives in perpetual hope of owning her own Dragon someday, but for now, she writes about them to fill the void… and to stop her from murdering people who annoy her.

When she's not writing she spends time with her husband, her dogs, and her friends enjoying activities such as walking, movies, conventions, and of course writing for fun as well!

https://theprose.com/LyndseyEH
Twitter: @LEllisHolloway
https://www.facebook.com/groups/199284024728104
https://www.facebook.com/Lyndsey-Ellis-Holloway-Author-102383921610775

THE ICE STORM

REBECCA ROWLAND

The man in the wool fedora shut his car door tightly but not forcefully. He was focusing all of his energy on staying upright and didn't need the additional obstacle of reaction force sending him sprawling onto the ground. Ass over teakettle, he thought to himself as he made his way across the slippery parking lot, his feet shuffling in small, careful steps like an old man's trapped in a potato sack.

The building was only a few yards away, but the short walk felt like an onerous journey as he inched toward the bright neon entrance sign announcing My Brother's Place. Everything in sight—the asphalt, the handful of plastic patio chairs askew near the doorway alongside a rusting stand with an ashtray, even the two other cars in the lot—was covered with a glittering sheen of fresh ice. Thin droplets of frozen mist drifted continuously from the sky, landing on the man's face in a thin glaze. He was used to the cold: it was Massachusetts, after all, but an ice storm in mid-October was unusual even for these parts. The maple trees hadn't yet lost their leaves, and in the evening dark, he could glimpse the foliage trapped like fossils in ancient amber glittering under the streetlights.

He felt the ice on his face dissolve into dampness as he stepped into the extreme heat of the room. The only other individual, a tall, bearded man dressed in a black dress shirt, stood behind the bar, wiping glasses with a rag. He nodded at the man in the fedora.

"Are you open this evening?" the man asked the bartender hopefully. He took off his wool hat and drops of water sailed from it onto the floor. "I sure hope so: 'electricity went out in my house. I was just about to make myself a late dinner when poof! off it went. Ain't it just like fate to wait until it's complete dark to cut off the lights?"

The bartender stopped his wiping and tucked the towel into a belt loop on his pants. "I'll stay open for as long as the power stays on. 'Helps that we're down the street from the plant, on a main line, I suppose. I don't have electricity at my place either, so I figured I'd get some upkeep done while the place is quiet." He scratched his beard thoughtfully. "I didn't think I'd get much business tonight, but I suppose if people are out looking for a warm place to hide out while the lines are fixed, I may see more than a face or two after all."

The visitor peeled the brown trench coat from his body and slid onto a nearby stool, draping the wet coat gingerly over the seat next to his. "Well, the roads are a mess. Damn ice rink out there. It's a good thing your lot is almost empty, or I may have slid right into another car." He paused, fished a crumpled tissue from his pants pocket, and wiped the bottom of his nose. "You wouldn't have a kitchen back there, would ya? I'm damn near starving, and none of the fast-food joints were open on Main. I'd settle for a bag of pretzels, even." He shoved the dirty rag back into his pocket.

The bartender glanced about the shelves under the bar top, squatted, then re-emerged with a small bag of potato chips. He offered the bag to the visitor; where his fingers had touched the plastic there were clean streaks in the layer of dust. "Let me fire up the oven in the back: I think I saw a few boxes of frozen apps in the freezer. In the meantime, these are on the house…" he paused, then added, "I can't speak to their freshness."

The man snatched the bag from his hand greedily and tore it open. As he shovelled the greasy bits into his mouth, he nodded. "Thanks, my friend. Yeah, that would be real nice." When the bag was empty, he brushed the crumbs from his fingers on his dark sweater and offered his hand to his host. "James. James Shawcross," he offered. "From Granby."

The bartender shook his hand warmly. "Todd."

Shawcross withdrew his hand. "Well, much obliged, like I said." He leaned his body sideways in an attempt to look around Todd's torso at the display of liquor bottles. "Would ya pour me a Maker's Mark when you get a sec? Jeez, it's cold out there. Gotta warm up the ol' blood."

At that, the door opened, and a gust of wind shot into the room, pelting the sodden doormat with icy droplets. A figure scurried inside and pulled the door shut. It was dressed in a bright pink hooded jacket, the trim a fuzzy leopard print yellowed with tobacco stains. The woman climbed onto a stool on the corner of the bar and unzipped her parka at the same time.

James brought the bourbon to his mouth, let it caress his lips, but didn't drink. Not yet. He lowered the rocks glass and nodded at the new visitor. "You here to escape the storm, too, I take it?"

The woman's mouth was tight; a smattering of deep lines spiderwebbed from her mouth and out to her cheeks. She glanced quickly at Shawcross and nodded at Todd. "Chardonnay, please," she said, then shifted on the stool as if to get more comfortable. The glass barely grazed the bartop before she brought it to her lips, and Todd disappeared into the curtained doorway to the backroom.

"I'm James," the man continued. The woman ignored him and stared blankly at the television set hanging on above the liquor bottles. The volume had been muted and a rerun of a 1970s sitcom shimmered fuzzily on the screen.

Todd returned, wiping his hands on his thighs. "Oven's warming," he reported dutifully.

The woman swallowed the last of the wine and pushed the empty glass toward him. "You new?" she asked. "Haven't seen you behind the bar before." She coughed, a dry, hacking sound that made James' own throat tickle.

Todd smiled and glanced at her coat. "You sure? You're usually out by the ashtrays when I'm leaving, right?"

The woman coughed again. "Ah, day shift. Yeah, that explains it." She touched the bottom of her glass again. "No need to give me a clean one. Just use the same glass."

As Todd poured more wine, James turned sideways to face her. "I'm James," he repeated. "Figure we might as well get acquainted if we're the only ones here."

The woman rolled her eyes and pushed her parka from her shoulders. "Tina," she said reluctantly, then stood slightly on the rungs of the barstool and shoved her coat beneath her before sitting down again. "And I don't know what you're thinking, James, but I'm just here for a drink and some heat while my landlord changes some fuses. Damn lights went off as soon as I got home."

"They're out over most of the city," Todd said, running a towel over a beer stein. "Ice on the lines."

The door blew open again; this time, a gangly, baby-faced young man held it wide open, glancing back into the darkness outside.

"Jesus, hurry up and shut the door," called Tina, her voice gravelly. "What's the point of being inside if you're just gonna bring the cold with you?"

From behind him, a short, grey-haired man in his 50s shuffled inside, pointing a thick cane in front of his left leg. "Thanks," he said, nodding to the kid. "Appreciate it." He shook his head slightly and made a slow beeline to the stool next to Tina. When he saw her lean slightly away, he shook his head again and pulled out another stool further down. He nodded at James and then at the bartender, then with some effort, climbed onto the chair.

The boy removed his jacket, a bright yellow and black parka with a Bruins hockey insignia displayed prominently on the back and hung it on the rack near the entrance. He was carrying a long, rectangular parcel and had to juggle it between his hands as the garment was removed. He strolled over to the bar and hopped onto the stool next to his companion, laying the box on the bar in front of him.

James swallowed the sip of bourbon resting in his mouth. "Out for a little father-son adventure?" he offered, smiling at the two new visitors.

The gray-haired man glanced at the boy, then looked at James. "Him? I don't know him. He just happened to be going inside as I made my way across the lot and was kind enough to hold the door for an old man." He looked at Todd, who was standing in front of him, expectantly. "Gin and tonic, please. Bombay Sapphire if you have it," he said. "And extra lime. Please."

Todd nodded and looked at the boy next to him. "Don't suppose you have an ID, do you?"

The boy pushed the box to the side and leaned forward, his hand fumbling in his back jeans pocket. He nervously presented a slim black wallet to the bartender.

"I'm not robbing you, kid," said Todd. "I just want to see your driver's license. Can't have high school kids sitting at a bar, no matter what the weather outside is like."

The boy opened the wallet, pulled out a small card, and showed it to the man. "I'm twenty-two."

Todd scanned the license. "Your name is Wayne Gretzky?" Todd said, laughing.

James raised his eyebrow. "Seems a little disloyal to be sporting a Boston jacket, don't you think, Wayne?"

The kid snatched his card back. "That's my real

name. Wayne Gretzky Miller." He closed his wallet and replaced it in his pants. "My parents are from Edmonton and were big hockey fans, okay?" His face was pink with embarrassment, but he added, "Got any IPAs on tap? That, or in the bottle is good for me."

"Americans," called a Slavic-accented voice from the far end of the room. "Such control-freaks. In Poland, you can drink at 18." The man sat down a few chairs away from Wayne and rested his elbows on the bar. "Stoli rocks when you get a moment, my friend."

Todd busied himself behind the bar as James eyed the stranger with interest. "Isn't Poland in the top ten countries for rates of alcoholism?"

"That's Russia," barked the man immediately. "Russia, Poland, very different." He accepted the short glass of clear liquid and ice cubes and brought it to his lips, then paused, as if remembering something suddenly. He tipped the glass slightly at the other four customers and mumbled, "Na Zdrowie," then drank a healthy swallow.

James took another sip of his bourbon. "Well, my name is James. This young lady," he raised his elbow toward the woman, "is Tina, and that's Wayne, and...I didn't get your name, sir." He looked expectantly at the gray-haired man.

"What is this, a group session at a weekend retreat?" Tina grunted and raised her eyebrow.

The gray-haired man smiled patronizingly at James. "Doug. Douglas Coffin."

The gruff looking stranger down the bar laughed heartily. "Coffin, eh?"

Douglas smirked. "Yeah, like the box. That's funny?"

The man laughed again. "Lukasz Zabojca," he said, waiting for a reaction. When none came, he asked, "None of you speak Polish?"

"Again, America. Land of the control freaks, monolinguals, and…" Tina glanced at James. "Irritating party hostesses."

James ignored her and gestured to the bartender. "And this is Todd, everyone." He lowered his voice. "I feel a bit foolish saying that. Just because I'm from out of town doesn't mean everyone else doesn't know you already."

"I'm not from here," volunteered Wayne. "I was supposed to go to my grandma's birthday dinner over in Ludlow, but the turnpike just got too crazy. Cars skidding all over the place. Damn near slid off the exit." He sipped his beer. "I'm giving the crews an hour or so to salt and sand, then I'll try again."

"You have way too much faith in the Department of Public Works, kid," said Douglas. "Those roads ain't gonna clear up until the temp rises in the morning." He unzipped his coat and draped it over the stool between Tina and him but did not loosen the heavy scarf around his neck. "I'm about ten minutes away, and I was glad to see your lights on. I don't expect to drive much further than this tonight."

"Zabojca means killer," Lukasz continued as if the others hadn't spoken. He nodded at Douglas. "I am a killer, and you are the coffin." He laughed again.

Tina pointed to the silent television. "Looks like

at least one of you has a busy week planned." On the screen, the local news was beginning. An anchor-woman with a blonde pageboy hairdo stared grimly into the camera, her curls bobbing slightly against her neck as her mouth moved.

"Turn it up," instructed Douglas, and Todd, after looking around for a remote without luck, balanced on his toes to reach the volume button. The sound screamed to life, jarring the relative silence.

"…initially attributed to a faulty space heater, but officials state that preliminary tests show no unusual carbon monoxide levels in the home…"

The screen changed to a wide shot of a team of coroner's office workers carting two stretchers with long black body bags out of a white-shingled home's front door. On the edge of the frame, a large German Shepherd sat patiently panting in front of an ice-covered evergreen bush.

"…apparent visitor, as of yet unidentified, is wanted for questioning regarding the…"

Lukasz slammed his glass down onto the bar top. "Smart murderer. Suffocate your family during a weather emergency. No one the wiser." He laughed and lifted the glass to signal for a refill. As he did, the camera panned onto the dog. The side of the animal's head was splashed with a reddish-brown substance, nearly black.

"Looks like the dog didn't go hungry," quipped Tina.

"That's not blood," protested Wayne. "Besides, it's on the side of his head. If he was eating dead people, it would be all over his mouth."

James pressed his lips together. "I'm not sure I like where this conversation is going."

"I think that's a crime scene dog," said Douglas.

"No, if it were a police dog, it would have the collar: you know, the coat-thing with the insignia on the side," said Wayne.

"You think the crime scene dog was chewing on the evidence?" asked Douglas.

"Smart killer. Disguise your work, cover your tracks," said Lukasz.

James' voice rose in volume. "You're not listening. I said—"

"Shut up, all of you!" yelled Tina. "I'm trying to hear." As she said this, the screen dissolved into a scene of a pig-tailed girl cleaning her room. Nancy Sinatra's "These Boots Were Made for Walking" chimed in the background. A fast-food burger chain commercial. "Change the channel," Tina commanded the bartender. "It's probably on one of the other stations."

"Piqued your interest, did it?" said James. "You one of those true crime junkies?"

Tina kept her eyes on the screen as Todd stretched again to hit the buttons. "I think—wait, there! Back one." Todd did as she instructed, and another local news reporter's voice called out to them from the speakers. The same shot, from a slightly different angle, of the white-shingled house ejecting its plastic-wrapped residents ran as a male voice-over narrated.

"…officials have ruled the deaths of the four family members suspicious and are asking for help from anyone with information about this brutal tragedy who…"

Douglas snorted. "Brutal tragedy seems like a bit of editorial hysteria, don't ya think? I mean, if the family died of CO2 poisoning—"

"News said the police originally thought that, but something—apparently—changed their minds," said Tina.

"But brutal… I mean, if you're going to die, CO2 seems like the best way, yeah? You just fall asleep, right?"

"My dad killed himself in the car in the garage," Lukasz announced suddenly, too loudly. Everyone turned to look at him. "Not when I was a boy, but much later, when I was in my twenties." He stared up at the television screen. "My mum died years earlier, mmm... and I moved into my own place before that. Dropped in to say hello one Saturday and found him."

Tina put her hand over her mouth. "Oh, god…I—"

Lukasz continued as if he hadn't heard. "Doctor said later that he was probably there for almost a week. Skin was bright pink, like a raspberry, it was. But stripes of flesh color here and there, maybe where the skin was folded over. His mouth—" he touched his index finger to the space above his top lip, "under his nose, was black. Like soot. This bloody…spit dried on his chin. Crusty." He removed his finger and looked down at his drink. "The smell. Never forgot the smell…"

Tina drew an audible breath in, looked back at the screen, and covered her mouth again. "I knew it," she said. "That house is right down the street from here. I knew it looked familiar."

The screen's image changed to one with a handsome,

dark-skinned man behind a news desk. "Again, we want to repeat anyone with information about this incident is asked to call the sheriff's department immediately at the number at the bottom of the screen."

Wayne removed his cell phone from his front pocket and began poking at the screen. Douglas looked at him. "What are you doing?" he asked. "What information do you have? You said you aren't even from this area."

Wayne's fingers continued to tap. "I am looking it up on the web. We didn't hear the whole story. I want to know what we missed."

Todd, his arms crossed along his chest, looked around the bar at the patrons. "Anyone need anything?"

James pushed his empty glass forward. "I could use another one. And how are those freezer apps coming?"

Todd hit his forehead gently with his palm. "Right. Completely slipped my mind. Let me take a look." He disappeared behind the heavy curtain.

"Here it is, I found it," said Wayne. He scrolled through the screen and began to read to himself. "Family of five, four dead…They suspect poisoning." He looked at Tina. "Poisoning? How can a whole family be poisoned?"

Tina frowned. "Food poisoning doesn't kill people that quickly. It doesn't kill at all, most times."

Wayne scrolled further down. "No…I think like, outside substance poisoning. Purposeful, you know."

"Who uses poison to kill people these days?" Douglas asked. "What is this, Game of Thrones?"

Lukasz tipped his head backwards and swallowed the rest of his vodka. "Now that's a good show." He held his hands in front of his chest like he was balancing oranges there.

"Yes, I was just thinking, there aren't enough naked women on television these days," Tina said, then coughed violently. She snatched her wine glass and gulped, trying to quell the irritation.

Todd reappeared. "Sorry, my friends. The apps in the freezer are way past their prime. There's more freezer burn than food there."

Wayne set his phone face down on the bar. "If everyone's hungry, you could throw this in the oven." He pushed the rectangular box toward the bartender. "I was bringing it for my gram. Bread pudding. It's the only thing I know how to make, but it's ready to eat. Just toss it in the oven for a few minutes to warm it through."

"I haven't had bread pudding since," James thought for a moment. "My goodness, since my own grandmother made it."

"It's better with rum sauce," Tina suggested.

"Maybe we just dip it in rum?" Lukasz said.

Todd picked up the box. "That's kind of you to donate," he said. "You sure?"

Wayne nodded. "I don't think I'll make it to Ludlow this time around."

As Todd returned to the back room with the package, Douglas said, "My grandmother made it, too, come to think of it."

"A fellow Brit?" James inquired.

"Argentinian," said Douglas.

Wayne had returned to pawing at his phone. "Aluminium phosphide would do the job pretty quickly," he volunteered. "But it would have to be in the food. Any contact with water and it emits a poisonous gas."

Douglas reached over and grabbed the boy's arm. "Wait: didn't you just tell us you made the pudding?"

Wayne smiled. "I work for a landscaping company in the summer. They use it to kill off rodents." He put his phone face down on the bar top again. "Nasty shit, but it works pretty fast. The poisons they use today usually do." He glanced around the room. "Where's the bathroom in this joint?"

Lukasz jerked his thumb to indicate the entrance to a short hallway behind him. "Down there. The light switch is on the right, just inside." As Wayne wandered out of sight in the direction of his motion, Todd reappeared behind the bar. Lukasz raised his glass and said loudly, "Refills for all, on me."

James lifted his empty glass and tipped it in the air at him. "Thank you, my friend."

Todd set the drinks on the bar and looked at Wayne's empty stool. "Where did he go?"

"Little boys' room," Tina said.

"Did he find any further information about the family?" Todd asked, nodding at the phone on the bar.

"Nothing in particular," said Douglas. "But I think our growling stomachs distracted us." He glanced at the entrance to the hallway, then picked up the phone. "Let's take a look."

"I'll check on the pudding," Todd said, and ducked behind the doorway curtain again.

"Probably password protected," said Tina. She pointed to herself. "Mom of a teenaged boy. Trust me on this one. They don't want people to see the twisted porn they have bookmarked."

Douglas furrowed his brow as he ran his finger across the screen. "No…no password." He continued to frown.

Todd re-emerged, clutching the sides of a glass dish with bar rags. He placed it hurriedly on the bar in front of Wayne's empty chair, then squatted to search the lower shelves for utensils. "I don't see any plates; I'm sorry," he said, dumping a handful of plastic forks next to the dish.

Lukasz slid off of his stool and hovered over the steaming dessert, inhaling deeply. "Cinnamon. Smells good." He grabbed a fork.

Douglas put his hand on the man's arm. "Hold on," he said. He looked up and watched Wayne wander back to the bar. "I thought you were researching the local news," Douglas said to him. "What in Christ is this?" He held up the screen for the other patrons to see. On it was a photograph of a bloated male body, naked from the waist up. The chest was grey-green in places, a rotting bruise that was spreading along his left shoulder and onto his face. The man's eyes were partially closed, but between the lids peeked wet marbles of black. Wayne reached out to snatch the phone from him, but Douglas pulled his hand back.

"I was looking at—" Wayne began.

"Maybe the kid was researching poisoning," James offered. "We were just talking about the possibility—"

"This photo isn't on his web browser," said Douglas. He slid his finger sideways along the screen and another photo appeared, this one of a woman with short wavy hair and closed eyes. The woman's lower face was covered in a sticky, reddish-black substance that appeared to have come from her partially opened mouth. Douglas ran his finger along the screen again and a photo of a silvery-white body face-down in a pool of bloody vomit filled the space. In the corner of the shot, a handful of small insects—roaches or large beetles—seemed to be scurrying toward the corpse and sick. "These are in his photos."

Lukasz looked at the young man, amused. "You a sick fuck, huh?" He chuckled and stabbed his fork into the bread pudding, pulling out a large piece and stuffing it into his mouth.

"He could have poisoned it," James said, his mouth slightly agape in disbelief.

Lukasz shrugged and picked up another mouthful. "If I was concerned about safety of food, I could stay home." He laughed. "I make pierogis fresh every few months, enough to freeze. I ask my wife one night; can you cook some pierogi for us? You know what she did? She tossed the frozen pierogi right into the pan, no thaw, no boil." He stabbed the pudding again and pulled out another chunk. "She's a terrible cook. This, this is very good." He patted Wayne on the shoulder with his free hand. "Even if you are a sick fuck."

Tina grabbed a fork.

"What are you doing?" James said. "It could be poisoned."

"He brought it with him," she said, digging the fork into an untouched corner of the dish. "What do you think? He drove around with poison, just looking for potential victims?"

Wayne grabbed a fork and began to chew a heaping portion. "It's fine, see?" he said, his mouth still full.

James leaned over and examined the dessert. "What are those dark red things?" he said, wrinkling his nose.

"Dried cranberries," Wayne said, his voice slightly muffled with dough.

Douglas reluctantly handed the phone back to Wayne. "Still doesn't explain why the hell you have those photos. Where did you get them?"

Wayne swallowed. "I—"

"Hey, turn it up: there's an alert," Tina said, pointing her fork in the direction of the television.

Todd stretched his arm and tapped the volume button. The handsome news anchor returned to the screen. A red bar with the words Alert: Update on Suspicious Deaths screamed below his image.

"Police are asking residents in the neighbourhood of Grove and Front Streets to be on the lookout for anyone suspicious but warn that under no circumstance should anyone approach that individual…"

"Who the hell voluntarily approaches creepy-looking strangers?" Wayne said. "Why do—"

"Shhh," hissed Tina.

"…what appears to be intentional poisoning…"

"They aren't saying anything we didn't already know," Douglas said, putting down his fork. He rubbed his eyes. Beads of sweat had begun to dot his forehead.

"…police believe this may be tied to the discovery of another gruesome crime scene police are currently processing in the neighbourhood of Madison and Huntington Avenues. We go live to our crew who have just arrived at the residence…"

"Holy shit," Wayne said, putting down his fork. The six stared at the screen in silence as the camera panned to the front of a two-family home with a wide front porch. Along the margin of the stairs, a spray of reddish-brown liquid was visible in the glare of the camera crew's lights. Just beyond it, the body of a middle-aged woman was sprawled on the sidewalk, her red wavy hair a tangled clump at the back of her neck. Although she lay on her stomach, her head was turned to the side, facing the camera, her dark eyes lazily open and still and her mouth gaping open in a stifled cry. Maroon bile was visible on her chin and neck.

"Fucking Jesus," Lukasz called, slamming his fork down. "They put this on television?"

"What the hell did they eat?" Tina said.

The five glanced down at the dish of bread pudding, nearly empty.

Douglas ran his hands over his face. His face and neck were flushed with angry splotches of dark pink.

"You okay?" James asked, sliding down from his stool.

Douglas pulled at the scarf around his neck. "Yes, just…hot." His hands jerked at the wool and with some effort, pulled his scarf from his throat. On his exposed skin was a splatter of two days beard growth as well as a wide, dark red stain.

"Oh," Tina leaned closer, holding her hand up toward Douglas' face. "You nicked yourself: there's a

232

bit of—"

Douglas slapped her hand away. "Don't touch me," he said sharply. He dabbed the scarf against his neck. "I'm sure it's nothing."

Wayne leaned closer. "You have blood on your neck," he said.

Douglas rubbed at his cheeks and along his neck, his dry hands making a scratching sound against the unkempt darkness of hair. "I cut myself shaving. I take blood thinners. It can get messy."

Wayne frowned. "That's not a dribble, guy. That's like a big splotch of—"

"I think I see scratch from here." Lukasz had moved back to his seat a few stools down and was emptying the rest of his drink into his mouth. The ice cube knocked against his teeth, and he brought the glass back down to the bar and pushed it forward. "Either good sex or someone not so happy with you." He nodded to Todd for a refill. "Someone with claws," he laughed.

Tina looked down at her own hand: the short, bitten nails and chewed cuticles.

"…if you have any information regarding this incident, police are asking that…"

Todd stretched upward to tap the volume button down to mute.

Wayne squinted at Douglas's neck. "I don't see a scratch."

Lukasz shrugged. "Maybe I'm wrong." He nodded toward the television screen. "Maybe it's splatter from when he left his family to haemorrhage to death from… what did you say it was? Phosphorus?"

"Aluminium phosphide," corrected Wayne. "You could use zinc phosphide, too. But it doesn't cause bleeding until you're, like, vomiting so violently that your stomach or throat rupture. The primary signs are similar to a heart attack: shortness of breath, nausea, collapse. You're much better off with arsenic: it's quicker and quite lethal in small doses. Or ethylene glycol." He looked around at the group. "Anti-freeze." He leaned closer to Douglas and continued to examine the splatter. "Get it without the sweetener and you can add it to just about anything. Your victim will just seem a little drunk…until they collapse into seizures or—"

Douglas pushed him away. "You want to take a picture? Add it to your little portfolio, you little freak?"

"I tell you: he is a sick fuck," confirmed Lukasz. "Watch that one."

"How do we know it's not you, running about, poisoning strangers?" James said. "None of us saw you come in."

Lukasz slipped from his chair and walked closer to him. "I was here before you. I was in the washroom." He leaned in, nearly touching Shawcross's nose with his own. "I live just across the bridge. Stopped into the Windsor first, but no power there, so I walk three blocks to here."

"You walked? In an ice storm?" Wayne said. "No one is walking in this weather."

"I walked here," Tina piped in.

James ducked away from Lukasz and looked at her. "You walked here?"

"Yes, I told you: the house with the dead family is

right down the road."

"You didn't say it was your neighbours that were killed."

"Well…" Tina stopped to take a gulp of wine. "Yes, they were my neighbours."

"And you just happened to walk down to the bar right after they are found dead," Wayne said.

Tina held her hand up. "I don't think the boy with the corpse photos gets a vote on what constitutes proper behaviour."

"Wait a minute," James said. He turned to Douglas. "You drove here, right?"

Douglas nodded, mopping sweat from his brow and running the scarf over his neck.

"And you did too, right?" James asked Wayne.

"Yeah, why?"

James looked at the door. "How many cars were in the lot when you walked in?"

Wayne thought for a moment. "Three, no, four. I think?" He got down from his stool and walked over to the exit. Before anyone could protest, he opened the door wide and looked around. A frigid wind blew grains of ice into the bar like a handful of spilled salt over a shoulder. Wayne ducked back inside and shut the door. "Five. Mine, his, and three others."

"Mine's the black Subaru," offered James.

"One of them is mine," Todd offered. "The other was there when I pulled in." He pulled his silver shaker from below the bar and dumped a handful of ice inside. "Always happens: a customer drinks a little too much and gets a ride home from a friend, or maybe a car service."

He surveyed the bottles of schnapps on the shelf behind him.

"Bet he's pissed he has to come scrape his car out now," Lukasz chuckled, then clapped Shawcross on the back in a friendly manner. "I say a round of shots for everyone, yes?"

Todd wiped his hands on the rag hanging at his waist. "What did you have in mind? Whiskey? Vodka?"

Lukasz scanned his fellow patrons' glasses quickly. "Surprise us," he said. "But make it a double."

"Triple," said Douglas, laying his scarf on the bar. He jutted his head sideways toward the door. "By that quick preview, I don't think the storm has let up. We won't be leaving for quite some time."

Todd carefully dumped the contents of an assortment of bottles into the large shaker and gracefully agitated the contents with a few careful movements. He bent down to pull something from under the bar and re-emerged, lining five rocks glasses in front of him. One by one, he poured a healthy amount of light brown liquid from the shaker into each glass.

Lukasz grabbed the glass nearest to him. "One for you, my friend?"

Todd shook his head. "I have a long night of cleaning ahead of me and an hour of scraping ice from a windshield after that. But I appreciate the thought."

James selected a glass and held it in front of his face to examine the contents. "This is my last one for the night," he announced. "I can give you a ride home, if you'd like." He glanced cautiously at Tina, who rolled her eyes. "Either of you," he added, reluctantly glancing at Lukasz.

The remaining patrons each took a glass. Lukasz tipped his glass slightly toward James. "Na Zdrowie."

James lowered his glass and tilted it toward the others. "What he said." Each swallowed their glass of liquor and set the empty back onto the bar.

"Ooof," Lukasz pounded his chest with a fist. "Heartburn." He struck himself twice more, then rested his hand on the bar, appearing to steady himself. A look of confusion washed across his face. "Not…" he began. His cheeks blushed bright pink and he doubled forward in a forceful cough. "Not…not…" His comment was silenced by a terrible hacking bark.

Todd quickly filled a glass with water and offered it to the man, who continued to sputter and wheeze.

Tina rubbed her forehead as the terrible sound continued. "I'm not feeling so hot myself," she said, turning her head slightly to look at Wayne. "What did you say was in that dessert?"

But instead of responding, Wayne stood up from his stool and tried, unsuccessfully, to walk toward the hall to the washroom. After only two steps, his legs folded beneath him, and he collapsed onto the floor and began to convulse. Above him, Lukasz stopped coughing and lay forward onto the bar, his eyes open and eerily still.

Douglas pushed his stool backwards, his eyes wide. "What the hell is happening? I—" He, too, began to cough painfully, his face flushing a bright purplish-red, just as Tina leaned sideways and vomited onto the floor between them, a watery mixture of Chardonnay and bile dotted here and there with masticated bits of deep red cranberries. She shuddered violently and fell sideways, knocking the empty stool next to her onto the floor in a cacophonous clatter, her writhing body falling after it as she coughed and sputtered, trying to call out.

James' face blanched white as a sheet. He reached forward to wave at Todd for assistance, his mouth bobbing open and closed, a fish gasping for oxygen helplessly tossed out of its tank. Finally, a wet sucking sound coursed forward from his throat, and James began to cough as his fellow bar mates had, his final choking seizure spraying a fine mist of bright red along the bar top and nearby liquor bottles.

When the patrons had stopped moving at last, Todd pulled the black rag from his belt and tossed it toward the floor. It landed squarely on the half-empty thermos hidden below. He surveyed the five bodies lounging languidly about the room. "My goodness, that storm outside really is dreadful, isn't it?" he said, as if continuing a pleasant conversation from hours earlier, his voice strangely hollow in the stillness of the room.

Above him, the silent television broke from commercial to showcase a quick update on the earlier report. Todd, in an antiquated government ID photograph taken long before he'd let the beard grow thick and heavy, glared angrily from the screen.

A thin red stream of saliva leaked from the side of James Shawcross's open mouth. "Why, yes, James, I do take you up on the offer of a ride. Black Subaru, did you say?" Todd said, leaning forward to rest his stomach on the bar. He stretched his arm to pat the pockets of the brown trench coat on the stool next to Shawcross. His hand returned clutching a set of keys and a thin, worn wallet.

Todd shoved both pieces into his back pockets and before turning to walk toward the heavy curtain shrouding the back office, reached over to grab James' fedora. He placed it onto his own head and pulled his stowed jacket and gloves from the small space behind the insulated travel container. Linking his index finger around the thermos handle, he stepped gingerly behind the heavy curtain and over the thick corpse of the sandy-haired bartender sprawled across the floor of the back room.

Once he retrieved the building keys, zipped up his coat, and pulled his heavy winter gloves onto his hands, Todd returned to look a final time at the five visitors draped in lackadaisical poses around the bar. Before turning off the lights, locking the door, and driving away, he snatched an unused plastic fork and scooped the last bit of bread pudding into his mouth.

It had cooled significantly, but it was still delicious.

THE ICE STORM'S BREAD PUDDING WITH RUM SAUCE

CONTRIBUTED BY REBECCA ROWLAND

Ingredients:
6 cups challah or dinner roll bread
Cooking spray
3 Granny Smith (or any other sweet-sour variety) apples
½ cup dried cranberries
1/2 cup butter, divided into ¼ and ¼
1 tablespoon cinnamon
5 large eggs
2 cups whole milk or half & half (half whole milk, half cooking cream)
1 tablespoon vanilla extract
1 cup sugar
½ teaspoon salt
1/3 cup brown sugar

The day before baking, leave bread out to stale slightly.

On the day of baking, break bread into small pieces.
Preheat oven to 350 degrees (F)
Coat (1) 9x13 inch glass baking dish or (2) 8x8 inch glass baking dishes with non-stick cooking spray
Arrange bread evenly in dish
Cord and peel apples, then cut into ½ inch pieces

On stovetop on medium heat, melt ¼ cup butter and
add apples, cranberries, and cinnamon
Stir and cook until heated through and evenly coated,
approximately 5 minutes. Set aside
Melt remaining butter
In a large bowl, combine eggs, milk, vanilla, white
sugar, salt, and butter until well blended (if using 2 8x8
pans, increase milk by 1/3 cup)
Fold in apple-cranberry mixture
Pour over bread, mixing slightly to ensure all of the
bread is coated and fruit is evenly distributed
Let set for 30-60 minutes
Preheat oven to 350 degrees (F)
Sprinkle brown sugar over the top of the bread mixture
Bake for 40 minutes or until toothpick or butter knife
inserted in middle comes out clean
Serve warm, cut into squares, topped with rum sauce
and/or whipped cream

To reheat, cover and place in 350-degree (F) oven for
five to ten minutes

Rum Sauce (optional)
2 tablespoons butter
1 tablespoon corn-starch
½ cup white or brown sugar
1 cup half & half (or ½ milk and ½ cooking cream)
3 tablespoons light or spiced rum

Combine sugar and corn-starch
In a small saucepan, melt butter, then stir in sugar

mixture
Keeping stovetop at medium heat, add half & half
slowly, stirring constantly
Continue to stir and heat until mixture thickens
Remove from heat and stir in rum
Pour over squares of pudding to serve.

Rebecca Rowland grew up in Western Massachusetts but spent much of her early adult life in the Boston area. She has taught high school English, worked as an obituary writer and a librarian, and freelanced as a ghostwriter and editor for publishing houses, a celebrity's blog, and a large city union. Her writing genres of choice are psychological, transgressive, and satirical horror heavily influenced by Flannery O'Connor, Joyce Carol Oates, A.M. Homes, and Chuck Palahniuk. Despite her infatuation with the ocean and unwavering distaste for icy weather, she has made a home in a landlocked city of New England.
Visit RowlandBooks.com for more information!

Inside the Dollhouse

Elizabeth Nettleton

"Alright class, get your ingredients out," Mrs. Williams commanded. She went to push a strand of frizzy brown hair away from her face, but it coiled around her finger and sprung straight back, hitting her square in the forehead. She let out a loud huff. "I said get your ingredients out!" she barked.

The class scrambled to the line of refrigerators at the back of the home economics classroom. Mattie trailed behind them, standing on his tiptoes as he looked for an empty space between the jostling students. At last, the sea of bodies parted. He thrust his arm out to grab his eggs, but just as his fingers grazed the carton, a thick arm pushed in front of him. Mattie watched, speechless, as the carton sailed through the air and landed on the floor with a loud thud. Yolk and goo oozed through the cardboard and puddled around Mattie's shoes.

"Hey! What did ya do that for?" he cried.

His classmate Tom grinned, revealing two rows of teeth that resembled soggy baked beans. "Felt like it, didn't I?"

Mattie raised his hand to tell Mrs. Williams, but when her narrowed eyes fell on him, he lowered it again. Sighing, he picked up a couple of sheets of paper towel.

"Whatcha making today, Mattie?" Tom sneered, leaning against the bench.

Mattie mumbled something under his breath. Despite his best attempts, the egg white brushed against his fingertips and seeped under his nails. He tried not to gag.

"Didn't hear you there, bud."

"I said I'm making fairy bread lamingtons. We have them back home in Australia."

"You're making what?" Tom's eyes widened in glee.

"Alright boys, get to your stations and start baking!" Mrs. Williams snapped.

Mattie placed the sodden mass of paper towels into the bin and hurried to wash his hands.

"Miss, my eggs broke," he said over his shoulder.

"And how did that happen?"

"Um." Mattie glanced at Tom, who drew a line across his throat with his finger. "They fell," he muttered.

"Borrow some of Lily's then."

"Is that alright Lily?" Mattie asked his booth partner. Lily sighed and pushed her eggs towards him.

"Don't use them all," she snapped.

Mattie took six of the eggs and placed them next to the rest of his ingredients.

"I'm making fairy bread lamingtons," he told Lily.

"What? I can't understand a word of what you're

saying," she replied. A girl behind them giggled.

"I'm...making...fairy...bread...lamingtons," Mattie repeated, emphasising each syllable. He smiled. "What are you making?"

"Can you not talk to me? I'm trying to concentrate."

"Oh. Okay."

The next forty minutes passed in a blur of spilled flour and burnt fingers. Yasmine, a petite girl who received a penalty slip each morning for her nose stud, accidentally dropped her tray of cupcakes as she took them out of the oven. She stared at the mess for a moment, sighed, then walked out of the classroom. Mrs. Williams didn't seem to notice.

"We call these hundreds and thousands back home," Mattie said as he dipped his lamingtons into a bowl of sprinkles. "Do you call them that here?"

Lily rolled her eyes.

Satisfied with his work, Mattie placed his lamingtons onto a tray. The colourful cakes seemed to glisten beneath the fluorescent lights, and Mattie felt a sudden pang for home.

He'd had these treats at so many parties back in Australia. It all started with Olivia's birthday, when her mum decided to put a twist on the classic lamington. The children had shoved them into their mouths with a fervour ordinarily reserved for Red Frogs, and after that, everyone in the class had to have fairy bread lamingtons at their party as well. It was the unspoken social law of the school.

Then over Christmas break, Mattie's dad had informed the family that they were moving to England.

And with that, Mattie said goodbye to his friends, fairy bread lamingtons, and social laws he could understand.

Mattie arranged the lamingtons on a plate for Mrs. Williams' inspection, his mouth watering in anticipation. He couldn't change much about his life, but at least he had one of those three things back now.

"Hey fairy boy," Tom said as he sauntered back over to the booth.

Mattie's stomach clenched. "Hey, Tom," he replied warily.

"How did your fairy cakes turn out?"

"Um, okay I think."

"Um, okay I think," Tom mocked. "Listening to you talk is always emu-sing."

"Huh. That's funny. I bet you 'roo the day I came to this school," Mattie said with a tight smile.

"What?"

"Oh. Nothing."

"You being smart?"

Tom took a step forward and Mattie shrank back a little bit.

"No, I'm really not. I was just trying to make a joke. You know, make you laugh."

"Am I laughing?"

Mattie's back curved around the edge of the plastic bench. He glanced at Mrs. Williams, but her attention was on a cookbook Lily was holding in front of her. Lily looked over at him and winked.

Tom leaned in closer until his nose was pressed against Mattie's. Mattie tried to turn his head, but Tom grabbed onto his cheeks with his thick, stubby fingers.

246

"You'll watch your mouth around me. Got that?"

Mattie nodded, tears burning his eyes.

"Good," Tom said. Then before Mattie could register what was happening, Tom grabbed the plate of lamingtons and threw it onto the floor.

"No!" Mattie cried, dropping to his knees. He reached out to save a piece that hadn't touched the scuffed linoleum, and a heavy black shoe stamped down upon his fingers. Mattie shrieked.

"What's going on over there?" Mrs. Williams snapped.

"Mattie's acting up again," Lily yelled.

Tom moved his shoe, and Mattie held his injured fingers to his mouth.

"Tell her you dropped your plate," Tom ordered under his breath.

Their teacher strode over to the booth, and Mattie felt a tear slip down his cheek. Tom laughed behind his hand.

"What happened?" Mrs. Williams asked, eyeing the broken plate. Tom elbowed Mattie in the ribs.

"I dropped my plate," Mattie answered.

"Then you'll spend your break cleaning it up," she replied.

She stalked back to the front of the classroom, and Mattie's shoulders drooped. Tom laughed as he headed back to his own station, making sure to step on as many lamingtons as he could along the way. Mattie watched him leave, then grabbed a fistful of paper towel. He bent down and started to pick up the crumbs and clumps of icing, his stomach growling the whole time.

***

"Did you have a good day today?" Mattie asked Polly as he reached the primary school gates.

"Same old, same old," she replied, echoing their father's favourite phrase. Mattie laughed, and Polly slipped her arm through the crook of his, pleased with herself.

"Did you have a good day?" she asked as they began the five-minute walk home. A car drove by, and Tom stuck his head out the window.

"Fairy!" he shouted. The car sped off, and Mattie's cheeks flushed.

"Why did he call you a fairy?" Polly asked.

"Um, I made fairy bread lamingtons today, and he really liked them."

"Ooh, can I have some?"

Mattie felt a pang in his stomach. "Sorry, kiddo. I, um, ate them all."

"You ate them all?" Polly asked, her mouth agape.

"Yeah."

"You didn't leave any for me?"

"Just leave it, alright? I was hungry."

Another car sped past. A water bottle flew out the window and struck Mattie's face. He stumbled backwards, too surprised to even cry out.

"Hey!" Polly screamed.

The car drove away, its screeching tyres drowning out the passengers' roars of laughter. Further down the road, an elderly man yelled at them to slow down.

Polly turned to Mattie, eyeing the purple bruise that

was now blossoming along his cheekbone.

"You didn't eat all those lamingtons, did you?" she asked softly.

Mattie shook his head, and they walked the rest of the way home in silence.

***

"Is there anything to eat?" Polly asked.

Mattie pulled a half-filled sleeve of crackers out of the cupboard. Empty cereal boxes sat in unruly piles around his feet, next to a bottle of milk that had long-since expired and begged to be poured away. He bit his lip. "When does Dad get back home?" he asked over his shoulder.

Polly shrugged. "Dunno."

Mattie exhaled loudly, then perked back up again. "Hey, we bought all the ingredients for the lamingtons. There'll be enough left to make another batch."

Polly cheered, and Mattie went to collect everything they needed. He pulled the heavy iron baking tray from the drawer, a gift their father had given their mother after some fight, but Polly shook her head.

"No, no! Fairies hate iron. We can't make fairy bread lamingtons with something fairies hate. We have to use…that one!" she said, pointing at a battered non-stick tray.

"You're thinking of cold iron, Polly. Like swords and stuff. Weapons."

"Let's use this one anyway," Polly said. "Even if the fairies wouldn't be mad, Mum would be."

Mattie laughed as he got the other tray out, and together he and Polly followed the recipe until they'd made six fresh lamingtons.

"You want to do the honours?" Mattie asked, handing Polly the jar of hundreds and thousands. She poured the sprinkles into a bowl and rolled the first lamington around in it.

"Why do they call this fairy bread?"

"'cause they look like little fairies, I guess. All colourful and stuff."

"Is that what fairies look like?"

Mattie chuckled. "I've never seen a fairy. What do you think fairies look like?"

"They're probably colourful," Polly decided. "And small. With big wings that are kind of see through."

"Do you reckon they sparkle?" Mattie took a bite of his lamington and almost sighed as it settled in his stomach. He'd been hungrier than he was willing to admit.

"Definitely," Polly said with an emphatic nod. She shoved half of a lamington into her mouth.

"What do y'think fairies eat?"

Polly thought for a moment. She finished chewing, then gestured at the remaining lamingtons. "What about those?"

"That would make sense!"

"I'm being serious, Mattie. How 'bout we give one to the fairies?"

"Um," Mattie said. He finished his lamington and glanced at the ones that were left. His stomach growled again, eager for as many as he could get his hands on. "I mean…"

A loud snore slipped under their mother's bedroom door. Polly turned to look up the stairs, and Mattie hurried to touch her arm. She stared at him; her dark eyes wide.

"That's a great idea, Poll," he said with a gentle smile. "How do we give it to them?"

"We'll have to make a fairy garden!" Polly said, her face brightening with excitement. "Let's paint some rocks and, um, oh! We can get my old dollhouse and put it outside, with all the furniture and stuff."

"What if it rains?"

"We can put an umbrella over the top!"

"Well, I can't argue with that." Mattie laughed.

He placed one of the lamingtons on a plastic plate while Polly went to grab the paints. They ran to the garden, then settled in the corner and painted as many rocks as they could find. Once they'd finished, they arranged the stones around the dollhouse and dug the pink umbrella into the ground next to it.

"Now for the final touch!" Polly declared. She placed the lamington in front of the dollhouse and clasped her hands together. "Here you go little ones," she whispered.

Mattie put his arm around his sister's shoulder. "It looks great Polly. Now how about we go back inside and have the rest for ourselves? It'll be a very special dinner tonight."

***

"Mattie! Mattie, get up quick!"

Mattie cracked an eye open. The first rays of

morning sunlight filtered through his curtains, painting rainbows across his wall. He smiled, then turned over. A pair of brown eyes hovered inches away from him face.

"The lamington is gone!" Polly squealed.

"What?" Mattie gasped, his heart hammering in his chest.

"The lamington is gone!"

Mattie went to rub his eyes, but Polly grabbed his arm and pulled him towards the window instead. She pointed at the dollhouse in the garden.

"See! The plate is still there but the lamington is gone. The fairies ate it!"

Mattie forced himself to smile. "That's awesome, Poll. I'm glad the…the fairies liked them."

"Let's make some more!"

"Aw, Polly." Mattie's heart sank. "We used up all the ingredients yesterday."

"They left us some more!"

"What?"

"Yeah, I found them sitting by the back door."

"What are you talking about?"

"Come look!"

She pushed Mattie out of the room and ushered him towards the back door. Mattie shook his head, then started to laugh, certain she was playing a joke on him.

With one last grin in his direction, Polly wrenched the door open and pointed at the doormat. Sitting on large green leaves that didn't match any of the trees in their small yard were: six eggs; a slab of butter; a dollop of cream; piles of flour, sugar, and cornflour; and at the very back, a handful of hundreds and thousands.

Mattie glanced at the window above them. Was this their mother's way of saying sorry? It seemed unlikely, but he supposed it wasn't impossible.

Their dad? His father wasn't home when Mattie went to bed last night, and if Mattie were to guess, he was probably still out. "I have deadlines to meet, son," he imagined his father saying when he eventually returned. "I stayed in the Travelodge to save some time."

It was a line that was all-too familiar now. Mattie was old enough to assume, as he knew his mother did, that 'deadlines' was codename for Madison, his dad's receptionist. The family had met her a few times and Mattie had picked up on a vibe. He couldn't put into words what that vibe was, or why he'd felt it, but he'd been right before.

No, it must have been their mother. She'd probably stumbled downstairs in the early hours of the morning, searching for a way to numb the guilt before she reached for another bottle of merlot.

"Can we make some now before school?" Polly asked eagerly, pulling Mattie from his thoughts.

"Huh?"

"Some fairy bread lamingtons. Can we make some now?"

"Oh. Right. Um, sure, I guess. It's early enough," he said with a wry grin.

They picked up the leaves, being as careful as they could to avoid spilling anything and carried them into the kitchen. The next hour was spent mixing, baking, and decorating, until they had six fresh lamingtons lined up in front of them.

"We'll save some for the fairies though, won't we?" Polly asked as she took a bite of her treat.

"Of course, Poll. They gave us the ingredients, after all."

Mattie picked up a pencil and some paper. "Thanks Mum. Hope you like it," he scribbled, before sticking the note next to one of the lamingtons. He took two for his and Polly's lunchboxes, then placed the rest on a clean plate and carried them outside to the dollhouse.

"Perfect!" Polly said with a smile.

"It looks good, Polly," Mattie said. He squinted at his glowing Spiderman watch. "But we'd better get ready for school. It's getting late."

Ten minutes later they were back at the door, their bags over their shoulders and the front door key in Mattie's pocket. He didn't like taking the key, not without telling their mother first, but he couldn't leave her alone in an unlocked house. She wouldn't need it, he tried to reassure himself. She never went anywhere.

Mattie glanced in the direction of her bedroom again. If he was honest with himself, he doubted she'd even notice they were gone.

***

Every eye in the classroom followed the long, thin second hand as it made its way around the clock.

Five, four.

The class leaned forward.

Three, two.

Fingers curled around notebooks.

One.

The bell rang, and the class sprang out of their seats, ignoring the teacher's feeble suggestions to complete the rest of their sheet as homework. Shoulders knocked together as everyone raced towards the door, but Mattie held back, taking as much time as he dared to place his work into his backpack. When the last footsteps receded from the building, and his teacher started hovering by the door, a defeated look on her face, Mattie lowered his head and finally left the classroom.

He made his way through the empty corridor, his heels clicking against the linoleum. Through the window he could see students trudging through the school gates, waving at each other as they parted ways. Just beyond the gates, out of reach of the principal's roving eyes, a group of boys decked one of their friends. While Mattie had every bit of sympathy for the poor boy who was now struggling to pull his trousers back up, he also felt a pang of loneliness as the waves of laughter rolled towards him.

A door slammed shut, and Mattie jumped. He glanced over his shoulder, his heart in his throat, but found the corridor just as empty as it was before. Shaking his head at himself, he made his way down the staircase.

He went to skip the last step, a habit he'd carried with him from Australia, when something struck him from behind. Mattie flailed his arms but missed the banister. He fell forward and felt his nose crunch as it smacked against the cold floor.

Laughter roared behind him. Mattie pushed himself onto his elbows and a heavy black shoe drove itself into his ribs. He gasped.

"Come on fairy boy, get up," a voice taunted.

"Use your wings," a second voice added.

Mattie raised his head and found Tom staring down at him. A smile stretched across Tom's face, but his eyes remained cold.

"Get him up boys," he commanded.

Droplets of blood splattered on the floor as three of Mattie's classmates hoisted him up by his armpits.

"Guys, please, I'm sorry," Mattie whispered. "I don't know what I did to annoy you, but I'm sorry."

"Shut up." Tom jerked his head back, and the boys carried Mattie up the stairs. Mattie tried to wriggle free, but his classmates only tightened their grip on him.

"Where are you taking me?" he panted.

"We're gonna have a cooking class," one of the boys taunted. Mattie didn't even recognise him. He was tall and gangly, with a long, hooked nose and steel grey eyes. What could this stranger have against him?

The boys hauled him back to the other side of the building, and Mattie's stomach clenched. Cooking class? Images of knives and burning stoves flashed in his mind, and he began to thrash against his captors.

"Let me go!" he started to scream, but one of the boys clamped his sweaty hand over Mattie's mouth before any of his frightened words could reach a teacher. The boys pushed Mattie into the home economics room, and Mattie fell down upon his knees.

"Please don't hurt me," he begged as he scrambled to his feet.

"Stand against the wall," Tom ordered.

Mattie hesitated. He glanced at the door, and one

of the boys, a classmate named Will, moved in front of it, his arms folded across his chest. Swallowing hard, Mattie stepped backwards until he was pressed against the wall.

Tom rustled around in one of the cupboards before placing a carton of eggs, a bag of flour, and a bag of sugar on the countertop beside him. He picked up one of the eggs and inspected it, turning it this way and that under the light, then spun around on the ball of his foot and threw it as hard as he could. The egg exploded against Mattie's forehead, sending shell and yolk sliding down his face onto his shirt. Mattie opened his mouth into an involuntary gasp.

"Stay still!" the boy Mattie didn't know shouted.

"Alright men," Tom said with a smile. "Arm yourselves."

The gang of boys grabbed whatever items they could find. Tom held the bag of flour, another boy grabbed the sugar, and Will held a pair of scissors between his fingers.

"Ready?" Tom asked.

"Ready boss," a boy replied.

"Now Mattie, you've gotta stay still. If you duck, we're just gonna keep going until you don't move. Got it?"

"Please don't do this," Mattie begged.

"That's not what I asked. You're getting one last chance to answer my question."

"I've got it," Mattie whispered.

The boys raised their arms. Mattie tried not to look at the gleaming scissors. Tears soaked into the collar of his uniform.

"Alright, on the count of three. One…"

Mattie squeezed his eyes shut.

"Two…"

His heart thundered in his chest. The sound reverberated inside his mind, so loudly that he was sure the other boys could hear it too. Did his fear repulse them, or did it encourage them?

Just say it, he wanted to scream at them. Just say three already!

Another second passed.

Just say three!

When the word still didn't come, he cracked his eyes open.

The boys' arms were still above their heads, but their cheeks were no longer painted with an excited flush. They stared at Mattie as if they didn't even recognise him; their mouths were relaxed, their brows straight, and their eyes seemed to look straight through him.

"Alright men. See you tomorrow, yeah?" Tom said monotonously. He put the ingredients back into the cupboard, and his friends did the same. One walked over to Mattie, and he flinched, but the boy only began to clean the egg up from the floor.

"Need any paper towel?" he asked, gesturing at the egg on Mattie's face.

"Um, yes please. Thank you," Mattie said cautiously. The boy held out the towel and Mattie looked it, his eyes narrowed.

The boy waited for a moment, then stepped forward and pressed the paper towel to Mattie's cheek. He wiped across Mattie's face, taking care to avoid his eyes and mouth. "You're a bit of a mucky pup, aren't you?" He laughed. "That's what my nan would say. 'You're a mucky pup'."

The boys laughed together. Mattie's eyes darted between them, trying to crack whatever trick they were playing on him now.

Tom finished chuckling and slapped his hand down upon the counter. "Okay, well, I'd better be off. We got tons of homework from Mr. Mathers, didn't we?"

The boys murmured in agreement. "Too much," the boy wiping Mattie's face agreed.

"See you around Mattie," Tom said.

The boys walked out of the home economics room, leaving Mattie standing, dumbfounded, against the wall. He forced himself to wait a few minutes, then staggered towards the door, poking his head outside before sprinting down the staircase and out of the building. He didn't stop running until he reached Polly at the school entrance.

"What happened to you?" Polly exclaimed, eyeing the new bruise on his forehead.

"I'll explain later," Mattie said between gasps for breath. He nudged his sister forward, and they began to walk home in silence.

As they rounded the first corner, Mattie glanced over his shoulder at the school. A crisp breeze brushed against its dark windows, and Mattie shivered. He had no idea what the heck had just happened, but whatever it was, he hoped it happened again.

***

"Mattie, it happened again!"

A hand gripped Mattie's shoulder and shook him hard.

"Polly, I'm sleeping," Mattie grumbled, his voice muffled through the pillow.

Polly ripped the covers from the bed and shook him again. Mattie pulled himself away from her clawed hands and frowned, his eyes still heavy with sleep.

"Polly! What is it?" he exclaimed.

"You have to come outside; the fairies have eaten the lamingtons again!" Polly said, her eyes bright with excitement. She reached out to shake him once more, and Mattie raised his hands in surrender.

"I'm awake, I'm awake! I can't get any more awake!" he tried to joke, but his fatigue added an edge to his tone that he hadn't quite intended. He offered a slight smile to lighten the tension. "I'm glad the fairies have eaten the lamingtons. Can I go back to sleep now?"

"No, we have to bake some more!"

"Poll," Mattie groaned.

Polly clasped her hands together in front of her chest, and Mattie's exasperation softened. "We can't make lamingtons every single day," he explained gently. "We don't have the ingredients or the time. It was fun to do a couple of times, but…"

"But they want us to do it!"

"What?"

"The fairies asked us to make more!"

"What are you talking about?"

"They wrote us a note!" Polly thrust something towards Mattie, and he accepted it with a frown.

Pinched between his fingers was a small piece of bark from one of the trees in the backyard. And there, written in what looked like mud, were two tiny words. Mattie leaned forward and squinted.

"More pleez," he read aloud. He glanced up at his sister. "Very funny, Polly. Did you write this?"

"No, I told you. It was the fairies!"

"Okay, this is getting weird now," Mattie said. He passed the bark back to Polly, and her shoulders drooped.

"I'm not making it up," she protested softly. "It was on the mat outside, where we found the eggs and stuff."

"Where Mum put the eggs and stuff." Mattie sighed. "Polly, fairies aren't really…well, real."

"Who wrote this then?" Polly asked.

Mattie shrugged. "I don't know. I guess it was Mum again."

"Mum wouldn't do anything like this, and you know it."

"Then Dad. Or the neighbour. I don't know! But fai—" The words died on Mattie's tongue. A strange sense of calm descended upon his body, and he felt his gaze shift from Polly to the window. You believe her, a voice whispered in his mind. It didn't sound like his voice, not exactly, but it was familiar in a way Mattie couldn't quite put his finger on.

No, fairies aren't real, he tried to correct himself, but the thought melted behind his eyes until he could barely remember it. You believe her, the voice said again, firm yet kind.

"It was the fairies," Mattie heard himself say through a broad smile. "They loved the lamingtons, and think it was really nice of us to bake them some. We should make more!"

Polly narrowed her eyes. "Are you making fun of me now?"

Warmth spread through Mattie's body. "No, I really mean it. You were right."

"Why do you look so funny?" Polly's voice caught in her throat, and a jolt ran through Mattie. His mind cleared for a second, and he stared at his little sister, his brow furrowed.

"What did I just say?"

"You said that fairies are real."

"I guess I did."

But why? Thoughts flitted from one side of Mattie's mind to the other. He could feel himself thinking them, but the words disappeared as quickly as they formed. Panic seared a crimson flush onto his cheeks.

Don't be afraid, the voice whispered.

Who are you? Mattie tried to stretch his eyes wider, but his face remained set in the same serene smile.

Don't be afraid, the voice repeated. You showed us great kindness when you built us a house and fed us. We are very grateful.

Grateful?

Thankful.

I know what grateful means, I'm not ten! Mattie's thoughts felt sharper now, but still seemed to fizzle out whenever he focused on them too much. The second voice pulled towards the front of his skull.

262

You know many things, and so do we. You can do many things, and so can we. If you help us, we'll help you.

Help you how? Mattie's mouth felt dry behind his placid smile.

We'd like some more lamingtons, please.

The fog inside Mattie's mind cleared. Beads of sweat pricked across his forehead and slid down the sides of his face.

"Mattie?" Polly asked in a small voice.

"I'm okay, Poll," Mattie said, his voice cracking. "Really, I'm okay."

"Why did you look so funny?"

"Um," Mattie stammered. He licked his lips. "I'm just tired, Polly. You woke me up, remember? Listen, I've changed my mind." He glanced at the garden. The umbrella shielded half of the wooden roof from sight, but even from here he could see that something had changed overnight. A ring of mushrooms had grown around the dollhouse, and daisies now lined the painted rock path. The flowers' brilliant white petals shimmered in the early morning sunlight.

Just like magic.

"Changed your mind about what?" Polly asked.

Mattie's lips tugged into a nervous smile. "I've changed my mind about those lamingtons. Come on, we have just enough time to make a batch."

***

Mist descended upon the school, creating curtains

of clouds across the classroom windows. Mattie tried to find the trees he knew were outside, but all he could see were fingers of white and grey, knitted together against the glass. Not even the fierce wind could move it.

"Alright," Mrs. Williams said. "Has everyone finished?" She ran her bloodshot eyes across the class.

Mattie stared down at the plate of cookies in front of him. He'd completely forgotten to bring any ingredients to school, so had to make do with whatever he could find in the cupboards. The result was sugar-free and egg-free cookies that had half the butter they needed and sultanas instead of chocolate chips. The cookies looked, unsurprisingly, like…

Crap, he thought miserably.

A screech roared through his mind, and he covered his ears in surprise.

We don't like foul language, the voice chided.

Rubbish then, he thought. The screech quietened, and he lowered his hands.

They're nothing compared to your lamingtons, the voice purred.

Mattie swallowed hard. He glanced out the window again and tried not to let his panic twist into decipherable words.

Stay calm, stay calm, he thought instead.

Yes, stay calm. We won't hurt you if you keep helping us.

The air inside Mattie's lungs escaped through his mouth in a loud hiss. Lily tossed him an annoyed glance.

If I keep making lamingtons for you, will you stay out of my head?

There was a pause.

No.

I'll stop making them then! Mattie gripped the edge of the counter, and his knuckles turned a pearly white.

No, you won't.

And Mattie immediately knew it was true. As long as they controlled his thoughts, they controlled his body. If he didn't make the lamingtons himself, they would force him to do it. And who knew what else? His eyes filled with tears, and he hurried to brush them away. The last thing he needed was to be caught crying in class. Again.

Something shifted to his left, and Mattie glanced over his shoulder. Tom stood about a foot behind him, his eyes focused on the other side of the room. Yellowing teeth peered through his slack lips, and a lock of hair had fallen down his forehead. In his hand was a large container of salt.

Mattie drew his brows together. He went to ask if Tom was okay, but his tongue wouldn't form the words. He stepped backwards in fright.

Don't be scared, the voice cooed. He wanted to pour salt over you.

Tom's eyes flicked over to Mattie.

What are you doing to him? Mattie screamed inside his mind. Let him go!

He wants to hurt you. Every day he tries. We've seen his thoughts, and we don't like them.

A flush crept into Tom's cheeks. His eyes darted around the room, landing on Mrs. Williams, Lily, his friends and even Mattie, but the rest of his body didn't move. Threads of purple and blue began to creep up his neck, and a scream rattled inside his throat.

Mattie's face paled. He tried to speak again, but the only sound he could make was a loud shriek.

From the front of the room, Mrs. Williams lifted her chin. She glared at Mattie and Tom, an admonishment dancing upon her tongue, then raised her brows.

"Somebody call 999!" she barked.

She raced forward and skidded to a stop in front of Tom. The pair stood frozen, blinking in unison at one another. Tom gasped for air, his face now mottled black and red, and slapped his hand down on the counter beside him. Mrs. Williams opened the drawer and pulled out a familiar pair of glistening silver scissors.

Stop! No! Mattie went to take a step but couldn't lift his foot. Spittle slid through his paralyzed lips, and he strained until the veins in his neck stood taut. Finally, he was able to shift his gaze to the side. His classmates stood in silent lines, observing Tom and Mrs. Williams with unseeing eyes.

Stop this, Mattie begged. You can keep them frozen, and I'll slip away. They won't hurt me. They won't!

If not today, tomorrow. If not tomorrow, the day after that. We let him go yesterday, and he did not change his ways. No harm can come to you, so it must come to him.

You can't do this, Mattie thought desperately.

We can do whatever we like.

Mrs. Williams raised the scissors and plunged them into Tom's stomach. A scream seared itself through Mattie's head, but Tom's face remained blank. He wrapped his fingers around the silver handles and pulled the blade from his flesh. Blood clung to his hands as he turned the scissors around and thrust them forward.

Don't make me watch this, Mattie begged. The pressure in his face relaxed, and he squeezed his eyes shut just as Tom and Mrs. Williams fell with two dull thuds.

Let me go. Please, please let me go.

You may go.

Mattie spun on his heel. His classmates watched him, unmoving, as he ran.

***

Each step Mattie took sent a jolt through his body. The mist followed him home, draping beads of water across his shoulders until his uniform was soaked through. He quickened his step the last part of the way, and after clearing his front yard, swung the front door open.

Silence greeted him. He tiptoed through the living room and was almost at the back door when he heard a soft snore. Mattie's heart sunk. He shouldn't have expected otherwise, but if there was a day, he needed his mother to pull herself together and be somewhere else, anywhere else, this was it.

Taking a deep breath, he eased the back door open. The ring of mushrooms around the dollhouse had grown even taller in the few hours he'd been away. Their long, thin stems now bowed toward their masters' home, tipping their caps in reverence.

Aren't they magnificent? the voice cooed. Aren't they beautiful?

Yes, they are, Mattie thought in reply. He scanned the garden, trying to keep his mind as clear as possible, but found nothing that inspired any sort of idea.

Idea for what? the voice purred.

It's hopeless. Mattie sunk to his knees. They'll always be one step ahead of me. There's no way to defeat them. I can't even see them!

It's true, it's true, it's true, the voice sang.

Mushrooms burst through the soft ground, drawing Mattie into the ring around the dollhouse. He ran his hand across their rubbery caps, and they recoiled slightly. Mattie paused.

One. Two. Three. Four. Five.

The muddy ground squelched as he rose. Mattie repeated the chant in his mind, forming the numbers so carefully that they glowed red behind his eyes. He filled his head with as much noise as he could, pushing and pulling the numbers until they echoed inside him, overpowering any other thought that might seep into his consciousness.

He meandered towards the small, wooden shed on the other side of the yard. His fingers trembled as he undid the hook lock, but somehow, he managed to keep his count steady.

Forty. Forty-one. Forty-two.

Mattie glanced around the shed. In the far corner, his dad's garden tools poked out of a peeling wicker basket. He strode over and picked up a pair of thick gloves, the rake, and after the briefest hesitation, the iron trowel.

A dull pain slithered through his skull.

Fifty-seven. Fifty-eight. Fifty-nine.

He carried the equipment to the edge of the garden and placed them on the grass. A bead of sweat rolled down the side of his face.

Sixty-five. Sixty-six. Sixty-seven.

Mattie wrapped his fingers around the trowel's wooden handle. The pain in his head intensified momentarily, but Mattie's steady counting kept it at the back of his mind. He bit his lip.

Here goes nothing.

He raised his arm and brought it down over the dollhouse. The air beside his wrist parted with a soft whoosh, and for a moment, Mattie was sure that his plan was going to work.

Then the muscles in his body tightened. Mattie let out a small cry, and the trowel clattered upon the rocks that he and Polly had painted so carefully only a few days before.

Did you really think you could trick us? the voice hissed. Did you think you could disguise your intention behind childish incantations?

I just want you to go away!

Fire burned behind Mattie's eyes, bringing him to tears. His hand jerked forward and grabbed the trowel.

Foolish child. You cannot destroy us with tools your father bought from some dreary supermarket in town. Maybe at one point in history we would have succumbed to such, but we are more powerful now. Oh yes, our magic is far more powerful now. The voice paused. Nevertheless, you must be punished. You intended to hurt us with iron, so you must be hurt with iron.

Without another word of warning, Mattie's hand raised the trowel and sliced it down his left forearm. The pointed end dug into his flesh, mixing mud and rust into his blood.

"I'm sorry, I'm sorry," he cried. His right arm rose again and slashed his left shoulder. Rivulets of blood slid down his arm and sank into the soft ground. "I won't do it again!"

No. You won't.

The trowel collided with his face. The bones in Mattie's nose crunched together again, and his lip split open. Sweat and tears streamed down his face, and his mouth filled with sharp metallic blood.

Mattie raised his eyes to the dollhouse. He wasn't a smart boy; the Lord knew he'd been told that enough in his lifetime. Maybe he should have known that any plan of his would never work. Maybe he had been foolish to try.

It didn't matter now. The fairies had won. They'd proven they could do anything to him and the people around him; the ones he cared about and the ones he didn't. Nothing he did would stop them.

But maybe, just maybe, he could hurt them a little bit too.

A shudder ran through Mattie's body. He tightened his grip around the trowel and sliced the cap off one of the mushrooms. The voice inside his mind shrieked, but it was softer now, panting between each strained word.

No, you shan't! it cried.

Mattie crushed a second mushroom. The voice

shrieked again, but it sounded further away, as if the fairies were cowering in the back of his mind.

He painted the trowel with more of his blood before slicing through the remaining mushrooms. A golden mist rose above the blade. It shimmered slightly, pulsating around the blood, then disappeared into the thick air. The fairies tried to pull themselves across his mind again, but they lost their grip.

Cold, cold, they whimpered.

"It's not just the material; it's what you do with it," Mattie realised. "You used the trowel as a weapon. The magic protecting you against the iron is broken!"

He stumbled towards the dollhouse.

"And you thought I wouldn't fight back. You thought…you thought you knew me because you lived with me for a couple of…a couple of days?" Mattie's breath came fast and hard. He pointed the trowel at the house and narrowed his eyes. "No. You're going to leave this place. You're going to leave this place, and me, right now."

He brought the trowel down upon the dollhouse. The roof cracked beneath the blade, sending shards of wood flying onto the muddy ground. Mattie raised his arm over his head again.

Something hissed, then his arm yanked itself back down. His shoulder burned from the sudden, rough movement, and Mattie gritted his teeth. He wrestled with his muscles, both he and the fairies panting, then wrenched his arm back over his head. He smashed the trowel against the tiny front door with all the strength he could muster.

High-pitched screams echoed through his skull, but they became dimmer and dimmer as he rained his fury upon the dollhouse. The noise in his mind became a whisper, then finally, mercifully, dissolved into silence.

The fairies were gone.

Mattie pressed his hands against his face and cried. His arm throbbed in pain, and his nose whistled every time he exhaled, but he forced himself to his knees and dug out every trace of the mushrooms in the garden.

Once he'd finished, he placed the trowel in front of the dollhouse. He wasn't sure how long it would repel the fairies; there were already patches of rust on its blade, and the umbrella wasn't going to protect it much from the ever-drizzling rain. However, that was a question for another day. For now, it would do.

Mattie pulled off his jumper and filled it with the broken mushrooms. Twisting the sleeves together, he carried it through the house to the bin outside.

"Mattie!" a shrill voice shouted.

Mattie glanced up and found Polly running towards him, her face grey.

"Mattie, are you okay? They sent us home! You'll never guess what happened at your school!"

He grimaced. "Polly," he said, not quite sure how to finish the sentence. Polly jogged the rest of the way, and her eyes widened as she took in his bloodied nose and arm.

"Polly," he repeated. Tears pricked his eyes, and another stab of pain ran through his body. "Let's have some lunch. I have a lot to tell you."

"Lunch? Are you serious? I want to know what's

happened to you!" Polly cried.

"I know, and I'll tell you everything. I just…I just want to sit down and have something to eat." Mattie leaned against the bricks, and Polly pressed her lips together.

"Fine. I've got that lamington in my lunchbox."

"No!" Mattie shouted. Polly looked at him in surprise, and his shoulders dropped. "No," he repeated in a softer tone. "I'll tell you everything you want to know, as long as I don't have to see another lamington as long as I live."

FAIRY BREAD LAMINGTONS

CONTRIBUTED BY ELIZABETH NETTLETON

<u>Ingredients</u>

For the Lamingtons:
6 eggs
1 cup caster sugar
1 1/2 cups self-rising flour
1/2 cup corn flour
2 tbsp butter
1/3 cup hot water
Approx. ¾ cup whipped cream
For the Icing:
2 ¼ cups icing sugar mixture
3 ½ tbsp butter
1/2 cup hot water
Hundreds and Thousands sprinkles

<u>Method</u>
1. Preheat the oven to 180°C.
2. Beat the eggs until they are smooth. Add the sugar slowly and continue to beat the mixture.
3. In a second bowl, mix the self-rising flour and corn flour together.
4. In a third bowl, stir the butter into the hot water until it has melted.

5. Add the flours to the egg mixture, then add the butter and hot water.

6. Divide the mixture evenly between two lamington tins. Bake for 30 minutes, or until a skewer comes out clean.

7. Place the cakes on a wire rack to cool. Once cooled, cut each cake into six pieces, making twelve in total. Trim the pieces so that they are flat and even.

8. Spread as much whipped cream as desired on six of the cakes, then place the other six pieces on top.

9. Place the lamingtons into the refrigerator.

10. To make the icing, mix the hot water and butter together, then add the icing sugar. Stir until the mixture is smooth.

11. Using two forks, roll the lamingtons in the icing mixture, and then in the hundreds and thousands.

12. Place the lamingtons on a wire rack to set.

Elizabeth Nettleton grew up in Queensland, Australia, and now lives in Oxfordshire, England, with her family. Her short stories and drabbles have been included in The Sirens Call eZine, Trembling with Fear, Short Fiction Break, and several anthologies by Eerie River Publishing. Her horror novel, "The Price of Gold," and middle-grade fantasy novel, "Solum's Landing," are available now.

Something Shitty About That Chap

Drew Starling

Drip.

Drip.

Drip.

Drops slowly fill the steel sink basin in the kitchen of the Hotel Monaco. The weight of the water presses hard against the trap of arugula blanketed over its drain, leaves bending firmly around the drain's cylindrical contours, but not breaking. The leaves are strong because the Hotel Monaco only orders the finest arugula, and they always, always serve the same day. But the Hotel Monaco will not be serving arugula tomorrow. They won't be serving anything.

Drip.

Drip.

Drip.

The hours drag as the basin fills. The water rises, tranquil save for the bobbing of bloated grains of risotto stippled upon its surface. The water's inches from the tip of the U-shaped tap, and mere millimeters from the curved bevel of the sink's edge. The arugula holds firm, the leaves united in their defense.

Plop.

Plop.

Plop.

The first drops land squarely on the underside of the gold wedding band bulging from the flesh of Martin Schlosser's dead ring finger. Martin had been manning the sink at the Monaco Hotel just as he had been each Saturday (except for one two-week vacation) for the last fourteen years. It wasn't glamorous work, as Martin would be the first to admit, but it was steady and it paid well. Everyone at the Hotel Monaco was paid well because the Hotel Monaco always had money. Even in the off-season.

Plop.

Plop.

Plop.

Tap water runs down his finger and pools in his palm, eventually spilling onto the linoleum floor and mixing with another liquid already soaking his white Hotel Monaco uniform – his blood. Martin's other dead hand still hopelessly clutches the gaping gash in his stomach, an awkwardly ripped fissure running the entire width of his waist.

The tap water is no longer itself. It's red, it's somehow more alive than it was before, and it's spreading its tentacles throughout the kitchen towards three other pools of blood, three other dead bodies.

It first reaches Jessica Hopwell, line cook fresh out

of culinary school, bursting with pride at the beginning of her rags to riches tale, but now dead. The only part of Jessica that was bursting tonight was her stomach, from the inside, and now she lay face down in a pool of her (and now Martin's) blood.

Rodrigo Domingo, the bus boy, lay face down because first he fell to his knees. Kneeling next to a still standing head chef Janet Tresch, he wrapped his hands over his waist, and when he felt something bulging, squirming, writhing in his stomach with such force his fingers could trace it, he knew he was going to die.

Janet took the necessary deep inhale to unleash a scream loud rip through glass, but the muscles in her diaphragm exploded in pain before she could release it. By the grace of God, or Satan, or some other entity, or by absolutely nothing at all, Janet passed out from the excruciating pain before she even knew what was happening. It was the smack of her skull against the marble countertop that killed her before her stomach, too, burst open. She now lay next to Rodrigo in a puddle of pooling blood and the dull silence of the kitchen.

Gush.

Gush.

Gush.

The silence evaporates as tap water laps over the sink's edge and spills onto the floor, into the growing puddle that's already there, injecting it with the power it needs to jump the threshold of the boxy batwing doors that lead to the ballroom. One of those two doors is held open by corpse of Jeremy Grim, manager of the Hotel Monaco, a portly, balding man stuffed into a silk three-piece who just about wished for death to find him as he barged into the kitchen to demand, "What the hell did you put in the food?!"

Blood water now flows past his lifeless body, gently blowing past the scraps of flesh still hanging from his open stomach. Because of the angle at which he fell, Jeremy's intestines have also spilled out of his stomach. They are hardly a deterrent as the water creeps forward.

Seep.

Seep.

Seep.

The ball room's beige wall-to-wall carpet sucks up the blood water, as if the nylon fibers themselves are somehow thirsty, but the water is too much and flows on. It basks at the sheer size of the room. The height of the ceilings, the elegance of the wall sconces, the immaculately ornate table clothes draped over all three dozen round tables – and the hundreds of bodies lying in various states of suspended panic, which if the blood water has its way (and it will) will turn red, too.

A woman's scream from miles away penetrates the walls of the Hotel Monaco and reverberates off the ball room walls. The blood water hears it as it flows into the tightly bound auburn hair of Corbitt Goemert, a 17-year-old girl laying in a sticky puddle of her own insides. Gooey white clumps of partially digested lobster are spilling out of her open stomach cavity.

"Goddammit, Margaret, I simply cannot understand what you see in Broadmoor. I just cannot." Bennett Goemert – Mister Bennett Goemert, Thank You – had said hours earlier, fish fork in hand and pointed at his wife. The starched white collar around Mr. Goemert's neck didn't budge as he swallowed another bite of lobster and chewed loudly. His hair was black. His neck and his face were beet red.

Mr. Goemert liked (not likes, he's dead now) his collars tight for the same reason he liked handmade leather shoes from London that squeezed his toes into a single, mashed appendage. Because the tolerance of great physical discomfort, especially in formal settings such as this one, was a noble trait earned by the very rich and the very egotistical. It was a constant reminder of the pain and struggle it took a man like Mr. Goemert to get to places like the 93rd Annual Spotted American Mink Benefit Dinner at the Hotel Monaco in Haasport, Maine. Surely, he didn't get here simply by being the heir to the second largest box spring company in the United States. Surely.

"You'd really rather send her to Oakdale? To that absolute brothel?" said Margaret Goemert – Doctor Goemert, Thank You Very Much. "She's liable to just spread her juices around and shoot up cocaine all day. She'll never be in a position to focus and finish three semesters worth of pre-med credits in her first year." She patted her daughter's lap but didn't look at her. "Like we talked about, remember, dear?"

Mr. Goemert turned to Corbitt. "You don't shoot up cocaine, do you, angel cupcake?"

Corbitt sighed.

"Anyway," Dr. Goemert continued, "this is not your decision. It's her decision. She will decide where she wants to go, and she certainly will not want to go to

Oakdale."

Mr. Goemert closed his eyes, shook his head, and placed both palms on the table. He spoke with his mouth full, again. "Did the pinot grigio running through your veins make you somehow magically forget the U.S. News and World Report rankings? Do you actually want your daughter to attend a shit pre-med program? Because lest I remind you Oakdale is ranked second in the nation. Okay? Broadmoor is thirteenth. Okay? You got that? Okay?"

Jeremy Grim suddenly shuffled so hastily past Mr. Goemert that his gut bumped the back of the red-faced man's chair hard enough to knock the fish fork from his hand. Corbitt snorted with laughter, and Mr. Goemert screwed his neck around to watch Jeremy Grim charge towards an angry customer in the back corner of the ballroom.

"There's something shitty about that chap," Mr. Goemert said.

"Oh, for Christ's sake, Bennett. There's something shitty about you!" Dr. Goemert vice gripped her utensils and sliced off a succulent piece of lobster tail. The fluffy, white layers rippled as she placed it in her mouth. "And who in God's name says the word chap?"

Mr. Goemert coughed, and three specks of white chum flew across the table. "Not to mention, the tuition costs—" More of a hack than a cough this time, and the bolus of mostly chewed lobster and risotto projected forth and globbed on Dr. Goemert's water glass.

"Egh! Jesus Christ, Bennett!" she cried.

Bennett's red face devolved into a maroon-ish

territory before turning downright purple. His lips stiffened, his eyes bulged, and the great vein in his forehead stood out like a weather-hardened rope. He hacked again, this time clutching his stomach.

"Bennett? Bennett!" Dr. Goemert said, rushing around her husband.

Corbitt didn't say a word, she didn't even look up, but the patrons behind Bennett Goemert did. They gawked at the struggling man, whispering in hushed tones, wondering if they should be the one to call for help. No, no, someone else will do that. Don't want to be part of the scene.

But they would be part of the scene. All of them.

Mr. Goemert launched up from his chair, smacking the edge of the table with his knees and clattering the glassware. Corbitt shot an annoyed glare at her father while he stood clutching himself and moaning.

"Bennett! Bennett! What's wrong? Do you need the Heimlich?" Dr. Goemert said.

He didn't answer. He just kept coughing, kept clutching. Dr. Goemert wrapped her arms around her husband's waist and jerked inward.

Mr. Goemert howled in pain. "Ahhh!! S-stop!"

Dr. Goemert jerked again. Mr. Goemert howled again.

Corbitt stood up. "Dad, are you—"

A slow stream of blood began to trickle from the four hands gridlocked over Mr. Goemert's midsection.

"What—What is that?" Dr Goemert said.

Every single pair of eyes in the ballroom swung towards Mr. Goemert, none projecting more visceral worry than Jeremy Grim's. The Hotel Monaco's manager had in an instant forgotten about the argument he was trying not to have with 87-year-old Beverly Einhorn over the arugula being too tough to chew.

Because the room was now silent and watching Mr. Goemert with bated breath, everyone heard the wet rip that emanated forth and Dr Goemert's subsequent shriek as she flew from her husband's back, as if repelled, onto the beige carpet. Dr Goemert whipped her arms into the air and screamed again, and the room gasped as they tried to make basic sense of the blood streaming down her two now handless forearms.

Mr. Goemert, somehow still standing, turned slowly around to face his dilapidated and hysterical wife, and as he did, dark abdominal blood poured out of him and into his wife's face and hair. She screamed again. He was too weak to scream and simply wilted over his chair.

The ballroom buzzed frantically like an army of bees defending their besieged queen. Two men got up to assist the Goemert family, but both jumped back out of some apparent fear of an unbelievable and otherwise unseen thing.

"Oh God!" one of them yelled.

Back in the corner, Beverly Einhorn wrapped a withered hand around Jeremy Grim's pudgy wrist. The strength of her grip caused him to peer down at her in wonder, but the thought was suddenly replaced by a morbid curiosity when he saw odd movements taking place under the blue satin waist section of her dress. It bulged and caved and twisted like a bedsheet rippling in the wind, and then it tore, and the midnight blue fabric instantly turned blood red. Another wet rip identical to the one heard across the room came from her expanding pool of blood. The fabric began to tear, and two blood-soaked tentacles emerged from the hole they had just cut – in not only the dress, but Beverly Einhorn's stomach.

Like two needles passing through cloth, the tentacles pushed their way an inch out through Beverly's stomach, then two inches, then six. Another rip, and the tiny island of intact flesh between the two tentacles – or antennae, or blades, or whatever they were – gave way to a domed, head-like object punctuated by eight, obsidian-coloured eyes and a tiny, fanged mouth that emitted a chittering sound resembling a robotic radio signal. Two more tentacles – no, legs – emerged and sliced the hole in Beverly Einhorn's stomach wider, allowing a bulbous black body to yank itself through. The creature fell into Beverly Einhorn's dead lap, stopped for a moment, and scuttled under the table, chittering the whole time.

Jeremy Grim was too preoccupied with the demise of Beverly Einhorn to notice all the other screams and wet cracks and chitters behind him. When he turned around, he beheld a Gothic era war painting of carnage. Dozens of patrons had collapsed into pools of their own blood. Some onto the beige carpet, some onto the tables, some still slumped in their chairs. Dozens more stood or kneeled, yelling and moaning with their arms folded hopelessly over their stomachs. A few ran like headless chickens around the room, not yet impacted but knowing they would be, until the spider-like creatures inside them grew large enough to escape.

Jeremy Grim hurdled over bodies, dodged woozy

patrons, and stumbled to the boxy batwing doors that adjoined the Hotel Monaco's kitchen. He leaned against one to keep it open while he clutched his stomach and glared at head chef Janet Tresch.

"What the hell did you put in the food?!"

But Janet wasn't looking at Jeremy Grim. She was looking at Rodrigo Santoro, who had just fallen to his knees.

Lurch.

Lurch.

Lurch.

The water mixed with blood has made some progress now. It spreads into the corners of the ballroom, eddies around corpses, and stains every inch of the beige carpet red. A handful of side-lying bodies become blood-gorged fountains, as the current fills their butchered stomach cavities, climbs their throats, and spills from their gaping mouths. The blood of all 322 patrons, all of whom had paid top dollar for their tickets to the 93rd Annual Spotted American Mink Benefit Dinner, coagulates into one stream churning with a new momentum towards the door.

The halls of the Hotel Monaco are silent as the blood passes over millions of tiny red dots littering the halls. Spider tracks cover every inch of the mosaic-tiled floors and paisley-wallpapered walls. Some of the room doors are open, but many lay strewn about the halls with ripped hinges and splintered jambs. Streams of blood jut off from the mainstream and flow into each room, each closet, each hall, each floor, every single nook and cranny of the utterly dead Hotel Monaco until there is no more hotel to fill. It flows down the stairs to the lobby, around the legs of heavy furniture pieces of great expense, and through the broken revolving door. No one sees because no one is alive.

Because just a few hours ago, an avalanche of spiders surged through the Hotel Monaco, driven by some twisted collective consciousness.

"What the hell is that?" Tommy Podesta, the concierge, said in response to a faint chittering that seemed to rise out of nowhere. Jane Ramsey, the bellhop, cupped her ear and leaned into the sound. A handful of guests in the lobby twisted their heads as the whisper grew into a calamitous shriek, and a black sea of eight-eyed monsters rumbled down the stairs. They moved as a single unit, a phalanx of death, and so great in number were they that all colour in the hallway evaporated under their charging darkness.

They poured into the lobby, spilling over themselves, and they crashed over a distinguished couple at the base of the stairs like a tsunami. Tommy watched in disbelief as the couple became two bulges beneath a carpet of these heinous things, and seconds later, were flattened out and simply gone. A handful of spiders broke off from the pack and leapt through the air at the patrons in the lobby. If their foot speed was fast, their airspeed was somehow faster, audibly whooshing through the air as they sunk their razor-sharp legs into human bodies.

Tommy had seen enough when a spider struck the chest of Jane Ramsey and drove two legs clean through the back of her neck. Two more hit her, one in the face, instantly slicing off her left ear and half her jaw, and another that kept flying after it ripped clean through her ankle. Tommy sprinted for the revolving door. He had just set his hands on the bar and began to push when a spider rocketed over his shoulder and shattered the glass. Tiny daggers rained down upon him, but he pushed on, even as two more spiders shattered the windows on either side of the door and clattered into the great stone patio separating the Hotel Monaco from Connecticut's deep, dark wilderness. Wave after wave of spiders crashed into the revolving door, some squirming through it's the broken windowpanes, others filling all four quadrants of the well. The frame released a screech of metallic agony before buckling and completely dislodging from the wall. It took an awkward tumble onto the patio and rolled, stripped and defeated, into a wall of azaleas that had just begun to bloom.

Tommy ran but he didn't get far. The spiders that hurdled out the windows had reversed course and were now charging back towards him, while the larger company cleared the lobby and poured through the gaping hole in the Hotel Monaco's front wall where the door used to be. Three spiders in front of him leapt, four spiders behind him caught up, and the two units collided with a force that ripped off Tommy's head, tore a cannonball-sized hold in his torso, and slashed his right thigh to ribbons. The rest of the spiders crusaded onward, stampeding towards… something… and leaving the diced remains of Tommy Podesta marinating his still-warm blood.

Flow.

Flow.

Flow.

The silent summer night welcomes the current of blood just as it welcomed the spiders. It washes over the remains of Tommy Podesta, now cooled on the patio from the crisp forest air. It follows not the road out from the Monaco hotel, but the tracks, the millions upon millions of spider tracks that cut into the thick pine forests of the Connecticut wilderness. The earth's richness makes the journey difficult, slowing the current down to a trickle. It flows for several miles in this manner, inching through moss and grass and soil until its supply is nearly depleted. Only when it reaches the surface of a flat wooden board – a stair – does it find the will to flow in earnest again. It does not climb the stairs, but seeps under the porch where fresh blood pours from the floorboards.

Marcella Stapleton, who'd lived in the cabin for 26 years with her husband, Mort, heard them coming miles away. When the chittering began, she rose from the couch and grabbed the .22-gauge shotgun in the closet.

"What in the red hell is that?" she said.

"Huh?" Mort said, glued to the recliner in front of a droning television.

"That chippy, chirpy sound."

"I ain't hear nothin'."

"Mute that sumbitch!" she said, gesturing crudely at her husband.

He obeyed but showed no intention of moving.

A long moment passed between them as chittering continued to rise around the cabin.

"You hear it now?" Marcella said.

"Yes'm. Have no idea what that is. Squirrel?"

Marcella loaded a cartridge into the barrel and took

quick steps across the tiny cabin to the porch. She stood in the doorway, peering out into the night, shotgun raised to the vast blackness around her.

A small white dot appeared in the distance. Another appeared, then another, then dozens, until an ocean of tiny white specks covered the dark forest floor. The specks lurched towards her as a one globular mass, but each jerked crazily in its immediate vicinity. The chittering sound rose into a high-pitched drone as the mass of mad, white specks engulfed the black space that separated it from Marcella Stapleton.

"Ain't no squirrel, Mort!" Marcella swung the shotgun to her left, to her right, and back to centre. Her heart slammed in her chest as this unseen army of white-speckled raiders approached the warm ring of porch light that extended just a handful of feet in front of her. She kept her eyes glued to the edge of the blackness just outside the light and tilted the shotgun down.

"Mort! MORT!!"

A mess of stick-like limbs and horrid eyes raced into the porchlight. The tiny white specks revealed themselves to not be specks at all, but reflections of moonlight bouncing off tightly clustered groups of eight obsidian eyeballs. Marcella released a scream that could be heard all the way back at the Monaco Hotel, just as the river of blood seeped into Corbitt Goemert's auburn hair.

She fired into the anonymous mob of black monsters, and a sharp explosion of neon-green liquid burst up from the pile. One down, millions still scuttling, still chittering, the spiders ripped through Marcella's flesh before she had time to scream again, or even before Mort had realized what was happening. Two spiders leapt into the air and fixed themselves onto either of her shoulders, while nearly a dozen sliced through her feet and ankles as they blanketed the ground. Her armless and footless body teetered back and fell on a pack of spiders already surging into the cabin, and a second wave washed over the top of her so that she lay sandwiched between them. She was gone in seconds. They made quick work of Mort, still prone in his chair, as good a place to die as any, and charged onward.

They're close now. So close to home.

Run.

Run.

Run.

The blood of Marcella and Mort Stapleton injects the current with enough life to roll forward through the remainder of forest and down the slope of a granite rock face butting the wonder that brings so many, rich and poor, to Haasport, in the first place: the Atlantic Ocean, glistening in a midnight blue repose under the paling light of a crescent moon. But there's a disturbance in the water, a vague patch of lime green light miles from the rock face and the wake of carnage up above in Haasport. Like grains of risotto bobbing in the sink basin at the hotel Monaco, there are a dozen or so objects floating in the phosphorescent glow, one markedly larger than the rest.

The army of spiders had hours earlier plunged from the rocks and into the ocean. Each dipped down before floating back to the surface, and, defying the laws of buoyancy, scuttled on. They danced over the calm ocean current towards the only impediment left.

The entire crew of the Two-Oh-Seven, the vessel that caught and sold top dollar Maine lobster to the Hotel Monaco and dozens of other regional establishments, was asleep when the spiders scuttled up the sides of the boat. None woke, all died, and within seconds, the glowing water became a graveyard of limbs and torsos of men.

It was only then, with no man or creature left to see them or know of their power, that the spiders retracted their limbs, curled into balls, and drifted slowly downward. The sank like drops of black rain in a teal green sky, and one by one, struck the hard surface of a massive, triangular, glowing object lodged in the murky shoreline mud. The glow came from a thin green line of light stencilled along the edge of all three sides of the object. The spiders unfurled themselves after landing on the object, and raced over the edges, bathing themselves in a temporary neon glow as they scuttled over the sides and underneath the object where several small openings awaited them. They paid no mind to lobsters, who in some twisted sense of reality looked not so unlike them but appeared to be receiving some kind of microscopic insemination of particles from the glowing, triangular object.

Back on the surface, the motor of a U.S. Coast Guard rescue boat hummed in the distance. It was on its way to investigate the claim of a resident reporting a black and green triangular object hurtling through the sky and crashing into the water early that morning.

292

The boat hadn't noticed the hordes of spiders pouring over the rocks, the thousands more sprinting across the water from various places across Haasport, nor the ones dropping through the water and clanking on the surface of the object, smacking it like drops of Hotel Monaco sink water smacking Martin Schlosser's ring finger. It didn't yet know what hell awaited it, but it would soon.

Lobster Risotto

Contributed by Drew Starling

Lobster Stock

2 Whole Lobsters 1.25-1.5 pounds each

5 cups Water

1 cup White Wine

1 Large Onion (quartered)

2 Sticks Celery (washed and cut into large pieces)

2 Carrots (washed and cut into large pieces)

1 tbsp Tomato puree

2 Bay Leaf

15 Black Peppercorns (whole)

2 tsp Sea Salt

Lobster Risotto

2 tbsp Butter

1 tbsp Olive Oil

½ cup Shallots (finely diced)

1 ½ cups Risotto Rice

¾ cup White Wine

¼ cup Dry Sherry

4-6 cups Lobster Stock

Lobster Meat chopped

2 tbsp Mascarpone Cheese

Sea Salt & Cracked Black Pepper (To Taste)

1 - Add the stock ingredients to a large pan and bring
to a rolling boil. Quickly add the lobsters to the boiling

water, cover and set a timer for 4 minutes. Fill a bowl with ice water while the lobster is cooking. As soon as the 4 minutes is up get those lobsters out using tongs and plunge them into the ice water. You want to stop the cooking process as quickly as possible. Leave the stock pot on to simmer.

2 - After a few minutes, remove the lobsters from the cold water and disassemble. To remove the tail, hold the body in one hand and the tail in the other. Holding the lobster over the stockpot, twist the lobster to pop the tail off. Doing it over the pot ensures that you save all the juices. Now, twist off the large claws and legs. Set the tails, legs, and claws to the side then put the bodies back into the stockpot, pushing everything down. Bring the pot back to a simmer and cook for 20 minutes. Strain and keep warm over a low heat.

3 – Remove the claw, leg, and tail meat. This can be tricky. Don't be shy about getting the tools out. A pair of pliers and a hammer work wonders.

4 – Sautee the shallots in the butter and oil until they have softened.

5 – Add the stock, wine, sherry, and seasoning and bring to the boil.

6 – Add the rice and simmer until the liquid is reduced and the rice is al dente.

7 – Stir through the butter and Mascarpone cheese.

8 – Reheat the lobster meat in a little stock and butter. Bring it to the boil for one minute.

8 – Serve the risotto on a plate with the fresh lobster meat draped over the top.

A bestselling author of horror and dark fiction, **Drew Starling** is a husband and dog dad who loves strong female leads, martial arts, and long walks in the woods with canine companions. He would like to think his plots are better than his prose but strives to make his words sound both beautiful and terrifying at the same time. He listens to Beethoven, Megadeth, and Enya when he writes, and all of his work can be found at drewstarling.com. His only rule of writing: the dog never dies.

(Fake) Meat is Murder

Chisto Healy

Jackson D'Amico smoothed his trench coat and sat down on the bench across from the restaurant. He lowered the brim of his hat some to obscure his face and he just watched. He watched the patrons go in and out. He was waiting to see if anyone did the former and not the latter.

Jackson took notes, jotting down quick descriptions of everyone who entered. He crossed them out when they came back through the door. He knew that something was amiss at Where It All Vegan. The chef that founded and still personally ran the five-star small town restaurant, Abigail Boston, was a shady character to say the least. Jackson didn't trust her as far as he could throw her and after a perp threw him off the roof of a building onto the hood of his own car three years ago, wrecking his back, that wasn't very far.

He was taking it hard at first, not being able to remain on the force after working so hard to earn Detective and follow in his father's footsteps, but the

P.I. business was treating him well and it allowed him to come out here and investigate where it would have been out of his jurisdiction before. Sometimes it did seem like everything happened for a reason, even if it was hard to believe in the moment.

After hours of watching people go into the restaurant and come out safely, Jackson felt frustrated. He frowned when the lights went out and the employees started to exit the building. He bit his lip. Surely, one of them had to know what was going on behind the scenes in that place since they were there every day, but which one. He couldn't just go up to all of them and start asking questions. It would draw too much attention and could put his own life in danger. In his mind he envisioned Abigail's ruthless grin, the off-putting gleam in her eyes, even as she smiled to end her own television commercials. You ate him, didn't you, he thought.

Maybe the best bet would be to let the employees go and follow the queen herself when she left. Jackson scratched at his beard. He didn't have to rush it. He didn't have to solve this thing today, but he sure as hell wanted to, now that his own brother had made the list of possible victims. There's no possible about it, he thought, his lip curling. I know she had something to do with his disappearance. Today, tomorrow, whenever, I will nail you to the wall, Ms. Boston.

Then she was there, back to him, locking the door. It crossed his mind to let them all leave and just break in and search the place. He wasn't above it. He'd done it before for other cases, but he knew that a woman like Abigail Boston would have an alarm system. She had too much to hide, and he didn't want to have to contend with the local police. That would complicate things a lot. He'd already spoken to them on the phone, and they all but laughed at him. People just associate vegan places with hippies and hippies with pacifism. No one thinks they're capable of evil. People were people, no matter what they ate, Jackson discovered the hard way, and people were definitely capable of evil.

That was if they were even truly vegan. Jackson didn't buy it. Vegan restaurants had some good food and big fan bases within that community, but the craze over Where It All Vegan was something else, something bigger. It was where it all began, he just didn't know what it was. He suspected cannibalism. It sounded crazy, but there was something about the food on Abigail's menu that captured the minds and hearts of carnivorous people and wouldn't let them eat anywhere else. Jackson felt like it was definitely possible that the master chef was feeding people to people and leading them to believe that they weren't even eating meat. It was Asheville Chainsaw Massacre.

Asheville was a small city, maybe 80,000 people total, and it was a progressive place in the middle of the Bible belt, blue state, North Carolina, which was strange in itself. Jackson stood from the bench when he saw Abigail head towards her car. He found that curious.

Asheville was a tourist town, but the locals had a lot of pride in it regardless. Most of the city dwellers lived nearby and walked everywhere. When he arrived, he walked the entire city in a matter of a couple of hours. There wasn't much to it; some old buildings that had never been renovated that all came with their own ghost stories, a few museums, several parks with street kids involved in drum circles as their dogs looked on from the ground, and a whole shitload of bars and restaurants.

As Jackson walked to his own car, a beat up old Bonneville that he couldn't bear to part with, he thought about how much he hated tourist towns. He always had, because the whole town was suspect. The town itself was a business and they had a reputation to uphold in order to maintain that business. Therefore, many things were hidden, swept under the rug, kept from the general public. People heard about how beautiful the leaves were on the Blue ridge Parkway in the fall. They didn't hear about the overwhelming heroin problem and how many people, young people, overdosed daily. People heard about how there were only two official homicides so far this year. They didn't hear about how there were a hundred people stabbed or shot, and most of them just happened to live. Jackson preferred cities like Chicago and his home state of New York where they wore their ugliness like a flag and put it on display, despite the tourists. Everyone wanted to go to New York and see the Empire State building, and they all knew that New York was dangerous. In a strange way, that felt safer to Jackson D'Amico.

Jackson's brother Joey had come here and never returned and no one seemed to know anything. Someone stabbed Joey in the back, quite possibly literally, and Jackson's heart was set on Abigail Boston. If she didn't do something to Joey, she had someone else do it. His gut screamed it. Jackson was determined to get answers from this small progressive little hippie town, even if it killed him. Unlike his brother though, Jackson was aware of the danger, so he planned to face it head on. Joey had been stabbed in the back, but they would have to stab Jackson in the front and then he could at least have the satisfaction of giving them the finger while they did it.

Jackson had a 9mm strapped to his side and a conceal and carry permit for it. If it came down to it, he wasn't afraid to use it. Of course the last time he fired a weapon it led to him being thrown off a building which in turn led to the end of his career, but life or death, he would choose life every time, something he felt in his heart his brother wasn't given the option to do.

Jackson followed Abigail's BMW from a distance in the Bonneville. Bonnie certainly didn't scream law enforcement to people and that was a plus in some situations. In others it made people feel like they were going to be robbed or killed and pushed them to call the police. Jackson learned that lesson the hard way too. Now he made sure to stay far enough back and make the following seem like coincidence.

Chef Boston didn't drive too far from the city. There were a lot of little towns surrounding Asheville and compiling Buncombe County. That part wasn't strange. Seeing that her home was in Biltmore Forest didn't surprise him either. It was the rich neighbourhood and she had made a small fortune off of that damned restaurant. Jackson drove right past her house as if he was just passing by behind her, but he could swear that Abigail looked his way as she got out of her car. What was even stranger was the way she looked at him. She hadn't glanced at him like she just felt a car or a presence and turned to see who it was. She looked right at him like she knew him. There was something in her eyes, something sinister. He had seen it every time he had seen her and now in person, even in a split second, as he drove right by her, it wormed its way under his skin and completely unnerved him. A chill scurried up his spine like the tiny legs of a dozen insects that had been dropped down the back of his shirt. Jackson squirmed.

He had intended on waiting until she went inside and then going to do a little spy work, but now that he felt that he had been made, it didn't feel like a truly viable option. It was too dangerous. He couldn't afford to screw this up. He owed it to Joey not to.

Jackson thought about driving back to his hotel, but he decided against it. He had learned a whole lot of nothing in his first day here and it would just drive him crazy. He wouldn't be able to stop thinking about all of it. It would tumble around in his head like a drier until the accumulating lint caught fire and he finally burned out. Even now as he drove back towards the city, Joey was in his mind. Sure, Jackson's little brother was a loud-mouthed opinionated asshole, but he was actually a really good guy at heart if anyone took the time to get to know him. He fostered dogs and gave to charity every year. He was just a true New Yorker and it rubbed a lot of people the wrong way. No matter what anyone thought of Joey, he didn't deserve whatever happened to him on his trip into this little town. Whatever it was certainly didn't make the news either. Couldn't have people thinking tourists went missing. Bastards.

Jackson decided to park in one of the garages and take a gander at the Asheville nightlife. It wouldn't hurt to find out what the locals thought of Abigail's overpriced restaurant and he definitely felt like he could use a drink or twelve.

To his surprise, Jackson found out that Asheville was hopping after dark. There were so many clubs and bars and invite-only parties, things that required memberships. There were fetish gatherings and goth dance parties and industrial parties and everything New York had to offer, just on a smaller scale. Asheville was an odd and interesting place to say the least. Jackson tried to find out how to get into one of the private clubs, but he got shut down pretty quickly. "You need a membership."

"Alright. How do I get a membership?"

"I'm sorry, but we're not taking new members right now."

"When are you taking new members?"

"I don't know."

Jackson stood there and looked into the young man's drug laced eyes for a moment. Then he walked on. He thought he heard someone calling him, but it was a city at night, and they could have been calling anyone, even God, depending on what they had taken.

He walked to the end of the block and heard it again. Looking that direction, a girl with green dreadlocks in a corset with low rise leather pants and paisley Dr. Marten boots was waving him over. Jackson took a deep breath. Why the fuck not?

Jackson crossed the street and waved at her as he

approached. She had a nice smile under a sparkling nose ring. Both shined at him. "What's up?" she said cheerily as he got close. "You looking for somewhere private to kick it? What's your poison?"

Jackson just shrugged. "I'm interested in all this city has to offer I guess."

"You looking for calm or exciting? Sex or no sex? Music? Liquor or just drugs? I know where everything is at man. I've lived here all my life."

Jackson smiled at the strange girl. "So, you're like my magical fairy tour guide huh?"

"Sure, if that's what you're into." She laughed. It was a pleasant sound. "I'm Chasey. Chasey the fairy tour guide at your service."

"Jackson. Tell you what, Chasey. You pick. I'll go wherever you take me. Surprise me."

Chasey's smile returned. He found it contagious. She nodded. "Now we're talking. Follow me." As she led him through the streets she asked, "So what brought you here? You got family here or something? You look like Dick Tracy or something. It's kinda hot in a funky way and that's totally Asheville."

"You were right," he told her. "It was family that brought me here, but I'm staying in a hotel and flying solo mostly. Trying to figure this place out."

That melodic laughter came from her painted and pierced lips. "Don't try to figure Asheville out, bro. You'll break your brain."

Chasey led him down a flight of stone steps to a big steel door that she wrapped on to a specific rhythm. It was a song, Jackson was pretty sure, something he'd heard before. "Closer by Nine Inch Nails!" he shouted as he realized, right when the door was coming open. The man on the other side just shot him a peculiar look. He looked him over his eyes scanning him and obviously assessing him. "It's alright. He's with me," Chasey said.

The big man just shrugged and stepped aside. The hallway was lit by a red light and loud bass and crunching guitars bellowed from speakers above the doors that lined the walls. "Okay. Not what I was expecting," Jackson said as he followed his guide further into the space.

"That's Asheville," she said back. She retrieved a key from beside a door and unlocked it, ushering him inside. He thought he heard someone scream from somewhere, but he wasn't sure. Jackson entered into a room with a single chair and two tables full of S&M toys as well as chains and ropes that dangled from the ceiling. "Sit."

Jackson's heart started to thunder in his chest. He didn't know this girl at all, but he did know that something was going on in this town, something that made his brother disappear. She was the first real lead that he had though, and he knew if he didn't trust her and he fled, he would lose her entirely. With a shaky deep breath, he sat in the chair. Chasey flashed her glinting diamond smile before she wrapped a blindfold around his face, tying it tightly behind him. She helped him shrug out of his coat. "Be careful with that," he said. "It was my dad's."

"I wouldn't dream of hurting it," she said playfully. Then she unbuttoned his shirt.

Jackson decided that he needed to take his mind off of whatever was coming. His brain was reminding him of the scream he heard and the blasting music and the thick steel door. He decided it was best to ask some questions regarding the case, to get his mind on Joey and off of his own possible murder. "You ever eat at Where It All Vegan?"

There was a sudden quiet in the room, a heavy silence. Jackson had been a detective a long time. He knew how to listen. Chasey wasn't moving. She wasn't breathing. Had it been his question that froze her?

"What are you, an angry carnivore who hates veggie places?" He said in an attempt to lighten things, but his words were so shaky with nerves it probably hadn't helped the situation at all.

"No. I don't eat there," Chasey said at last. "Abby is a weird one, and not Asheville weird, the bad kind of weird. I steer clear."

Jackson felt his hands getting chained and the idea of being restrained by a stranger in a place no one would ever find him, scared him, but he didn't voice it. Instead, he said, "How so?"

He flexed his wrists against the chains and found them to be quite tight, not tight enough to hurt if he didn't fight, but tight enough for him to never escape without assistance. "I don't know. It's crazy. There's just something about her that feels wrong, and people eat there and then get all weird. Not me, baby."

Jackson felt the tip of something sharp drag over his chest and his breath caught in his chest. He could hear Chasey giggle quietly at his shock. "Since I'm obviously trusting you with my life," he said, his breaths shallow, "I'm going to go full disclosure. She's the real reason

I'm here."

Jackson found himself not breathing as the sharp tip of whatever instrument she had danced delicately around his nipple. When it lifted and his breath returned, he said, "My brother Joey was a food critic. He had a column in the New York Daily Gazette. He travelled all over the country to do write ups on big restaurants, and his words were never too kind. He knew how to get ratings, readers. The last place he came was here to review that woman's food and no one has seen or heard from him again."

The sharp edge dragged its way up his stomach, and he trembled. "How long has he been missing?"

"Several months. I let the police work first. They found nothing. He just vanished."

The knife returned to his throat and took his breath away. "He could have just liked it here, the underground, the places like this literally hidden beneath the surface of the city."

Jackson didn't speak, couldn't speak until the knife dragged gently away from his jugular. When it did, he shuddered and sighed with relief. He was sweating despite the chill in the room. "Not his style," he said when he could. "Joey was the type to give you two minutes of missionary and say you're welcome."

"So why are you saving this creep?"

Jackson slumped his shoulders with visible relief when he felt the chains coming off his wrists. "He's my brother," he said.

As Chasey untied his blind fold se said, "You think she killed him? Wouldn't the police have found some evidence? They had to go to her if they investigated right, since it was the last place he'd been?"

"Yeah," Jackson said as he stood and stretched his muscles, fumbling to button his shirt with quivering fingers. Chasey giggled and moved over to help him. He could see over her shoulder that his coat had been folded neatly and placed onto one of the tables. This strange girl had definitely earned his trust. "That's why I think that place isn't vegan at all. I think she put him in the food and fed him to the customers, disposing of the evidence."

Chasey leaned her head back and gave a hearty laugh. "And what about the bones and the blood? Wouldn't that stand out in a vegan restaurant?" She laughed again. "I believe you that she's the culprit, but cannibalism is a cockamamie theory, bud."

"Then what?"

"I have no idea," she said with a playful shrug. "Time for you to play with me."

Jackson met the girl's eye and felt a surge of hunger he hadn't felt in a long time. "I'd rather skip that and go to the sex if that's okay with you."

Chasey's eyes widened with surprise, but her pierced lips curled up. "I'm trans, Mister Jackson. I was born biologically a man."

"You're all woman now," he said, leaning in and kissing her hard. She jumped up and wrapped her slender legs around his waist. They crashed into the wall. Outside of the room, no one could hear their moans over the sounds of the blaring heavy metal booming from the speaker above the door.

When the door reopened, they stumbled out panting

and laughing, holding hands. Jackson tucked a card with Chasey's number on it into his pants pocket. "You're fun," she said to him as they headed out of the place. "I hope playing detective doesn't get you killed."

"I'm not playing," he told her. "I'm a for real detective."

"Better be careful saying that around here," she said with a wink and a grin. Then she opened the door and the cool night breeze felt so refreshing.

"Noted." Jackson looked around. He wasn't sure what to do now. He hadn't really learned anything from Chasey outside of the fact that the locals felt the same way about Abigail Boston.

Chasey seemed to see the wheels turning in his head, the heaviness of his heart. "Tell you what," she said to him. "Meet me at Pritchett Park tomorrow around six, and we'll go to the restaurant together. We'll call it a date and see if we can't learn what happened to your brother in the process."

"Best tour guide ever," Jackson said with a smile before kissing her on the lips. "See you tomorrow."

Jackson headed back towards his hotel, but he still didn't feel he could go there yet. He was invigorated by the fact that he met a woman, by what he allowed her to do, by the prospect of going to the restaurant tomorrow and not having to go it alone, by everything. He saw a place with people dancing to traditional Irish music. There was a clover on the sign. Why not?

Inside, he went to the counter and ordered himself a drink. To go with the theme, he had a double shot of Jameson. An obviously drunken red faced stranger clinked glasses with him. "Cheers," Jackson said.

He headed through the dancers, surprised by how many were going full in on Irish culture with their outfits. As he moved towards the back of the place he wondered if they were truly Irish or if Asheville was a place that went full in on cultural appropriation.

At the back of the bar, a guy with a green top hat said to him, "Bloody brilliant, aren't they?" in reference to the live band on the stage in the corner belting age old celtic songs.

"Was that supposed to be an Irish brogue because it sounded British?" Jackson said back with a shrug.

"Aye. Feck ya, with your judgment, ya cunt."

"Bad Scottish now, like a Shrek impersonation. Just sad."

"Man, fuck you for real," the guy said with a southern twang.

Jackson just laughed and shook his head. He decided to move along and not get this guy fired up any more than he had already. "I mean it. Fuck you," the guy called from behind him.

Jackson bit back his laughter and went to sit at a table that had an open seat. A guy at the table, wearing a tye dye Grateful Dead shirt with his beard braided nodded at him. "I come here because they make the best old fashioned in town," he said.

"Cool," Jackson said back. "You know if they serve drinks at Where It All Vegan?"

"At a fancy shmancy place like that? Probably just wine I couldn't afford, brother."

"You ever eat there?"

"Hell no. I want burgers and chicken. My brother went there, and he swears by it, but it's not for me, man."

"I hear ya." Jackson fingered his own beard. "I don't think it's for me either. My brother went there too. Seemed like something in that food made him strange. I don't know what they put in it, but I don't want it."

The man eyed him thoughtfully for a moment, but then he took the bite. "Yeah, I know what you mean, brother. My guy, Pat went there with a girl because it was what she wanted and he was not the vegan type of guy at all, you know? Now he can't stop going there. I mean I get that that happens if a place is really good, but ol' Pat acts like a damn drug addict man, trying to come up with the money to afford the place. It's just plain weird."

"Hell, maybe they do put some kind of drug in the food," Jackson said with a shrug.

"Maybe," the man said with an agreeable nod. "Ya ask me, I think they put the devil in it."

Jackson found the man's perception more interesting than farfetched and that was curious to him. Something about this little city was changing him. He patted the man on the shoulder and downed his drink on his way back to the front. He placed the empty glass on the bar top with a wave to the bartender and then he was back outside. He imagined his brother hanging upside down in the kitchen of the vegan restaurant, dangling above a giant bloody pentagram while a knife wielding Abigail shined her creepy smile and slit his throat.

Jackson shuddered at the thought. He decided that this was his cue that it was finally time to head back to the hotel and try to sleep. He didn't feel confident that his dreams wouldn't be twisted, but he didn't want to see what else Asheville had to offer him tonight. Now that he was having satanic visions of his brother's grisly murder playing out like a horror movie in hsi mind, he felt that was enough for one day.

When he got back to the hotel, he gave a shy smile and a wave in passing in response to the overly bubbly greeting from the woman behind the desk. Then he went straight to his room where he made sure to lock the door and plopped down onto the bed, burying his face in the pillow. He didn't realize how exhausted he was, how much this strange little city drained out of him, until he hit the bed. Then it became painfully clear as he seemed to melt into the comforter. It wasn't until he arrived here that he discovered the city was full of rustic bed and breakfasts, some that came with in room massages. He would keep that in mind if he decided to ever come back and visit. His gut was leaning towards never returning to the place where his brother went missing but his mind's picture of Chasey's contagious smile said otherwise. He would have to wait and see what happened. As he thought about it, he drifted off into dreams that were thankfully full of Chasey and not Abigail.

When he woke up in the morning, Jackson rubbed at his face and looked towards the digital clock on the nightstand. He was surprised to see that it was almost noon already. With a groan he climbed out of the bed and stumbled into the bathroom for a shower. By the time he was cleaned up and ready to go, it was the afternoon and his stomach was screaming for lunch. He'd already missed breakfast and wanted to be full when he went to Abigail's place for dinner, so he decided to go get something to eat. He still had a few hours to kill before he was supposed to meet Chasey anyway, which was good because he had no idea where Pritchett Park was.

Jackson stepped outside and found an entirely different but still interesting Asheville during the daylight hours. There were buskers everywhere, too close to each other in fact, as their music often clashed creating a chaotic cacophony. There were street performers all around as well, by the giant modern art sculptures, many of which Jackson wasn't even sure what they were. There were giant mimes on giant unicycles and human statues, jugglers, and the like. The tourists were eating it up, throwing their dollars at everyone.

Jackson knew enough about Asheville though, to know that many of these street performers were trust fund babies from the rich folk in Biltmore Forest who didn't need to work and needed something to do with their time. He just snorted and walked through the ever-growing crowd. He was looking for a restaurant, but he didn't want to be near all this commotion, so he decided to check the other side of town. It would take him closer to Abigail's place anyway, and curiosity was still tugging at him.

He found a cosy little Asian noodle shop and had a bowl of ramen with a bottle of plum wine. It was divine and really hit the spot. He left feeling a lot better, until he saw Abigail Boston coming his way. Maybe she was headed into work. Many of the big restaurants didn't open until the afternoon. At this point, being a famous chef as she was, she probably just oversaw everything and didn't need to do any actual cooking herself.

Jackson didn't want to waste an opportunity, so he quickened his step, and ended up almost colliding with her. "Sorry," he said with a smile.

"No harm, no foul," she said, giving him a smile of her own that didn't make it to her eyes.

"Do you know any good places to get lunch around here? I'm from out of town," he said, hoping that she hadn't just seen him come out of the restaurant.

"What kind of food are you looking for? I'll bet you I have something at my restaurant." Somehow her smile grew even more sinister.

"Oh wow. You have a restaurant," Jackson beamed, trying his best to seem authentically excited. "That's fantastic. I always wanted to open one."

"So, what kind of food? Name it."

"Oh." Jackson thought to himself. He knew he didn't have time to ponder so he just thought of the bar from the night before. It was the first thing that came to mind. "Irish."

"Hmm," she said, as if his choice was unexpected. "I have a vegan shepherd's pie that is to die for. You should definitely come grab a slice."

Jackson smiled and thanked her before walking past her, but in his head, he was thinking, to die for. I bet. Jackson wanted to just grab the woman and shake her and demand to know what she did to his brother but he knew in his heart that it wouldn't gain him any answers but it would attract a lot of unwanted attention on the crowded Asheville city streets.

After he heard her walking in the opposite direction

for a bit, he stopped walking himself and turned back to follow her. After three blocks she came to a complete stop and just stood there with her back to him. Jackson studied her, waiting to see what she was going to do.

She started walking again, so he did the same. Then she stopped and whirled around. "Can I help you with anything else?" she said harshly. How did she know I was there? It was the same when I was in my car. It's like she can sense me.

Jackson gave his best friendly smile, added a chuckle for good measure and waved. "Yes. I'm sorry. I can't eat at your restaurant. I don't know where it is."

Abigail pointed upwards towards the sign above her. It read Where It All Vegan. Jackson clapped his hands and laughed. "Right here apparently. Fantastic. Maybe I'll come back for dinner. Do you know where Pritchett Park is? I'm supposed to meet someone there."

Jackson listened with feigned interest as Abigail rattled off directions. "Do I know you?" she asked him then, her eyes scrutinizing him like she was combing through a catalogue. "You look strangely familiar."

Jackson gave a genuine smile this time. "Oh, you probably just know my brother. He's kind of famous."

A blood red fingernail brushed over her equally red lips. "Oh, you don't say. Who is your famous brother, may I ask?"

Jackson's smile returned. He felt a bizarre sense of pride in this moment. "His name is Joey D'Amico. He has a column in the New York Daily Gazette. He does nationwide and sometimes worldwide, restaurant reviews. I'm sure you know who he is."

"I can't say I do," she said, but her eyes told a different story. "Have a good day. Come back for dinner later. Try that Shepherd's Pie." With that, she spun on her stiletto heel and marched into the restaurant.

"I will!" Jackson called out behind her, almost laughing, but without any humour. Guilty, he thought. You're going down Ms. Boston. Tonight.

Jackson found out that Abigail's directions were actually quite good as he found the park easily. He also frowned when he found the type of people that frequented it. The place was full of some of the seediest characters he had come across since arriving in Asheville. He had felt safer in the Dominatrix Dungeon. The characters that surrounded him now were either on drugs or selling drugs. Some of them were yelling at passers-by or even lunging at them. Several fights came a hair's width from breaking out right there in front of him. He checked the time and it was almost six. He didn't want to leave and miss Chasey. Why did she have to pick this place of all places?

A thin man in a deerstalker with a rap t-shirt, dirty jeans and galoshes approached him. Jackson sighed and tried not to make eye contact. "You driving? I need a ride," the man said.

"No," Jackson said back plainly. "Not driving."

"You're a fucking liar!" the man screamed, spittle showering Jackson's face and sticking in his beard. Fucking disgusting!

Jackson snarled and turned back to him. "Your shirt is cool but spitting in my face isn't. Walk away now or swallow your last remaining teeth."

The stranger snarled back and jammed an index finger into Jackson's chest. It was quickly grabbed and bent backwards until there was a loud crack. The crying man grabbed his hand and fell to the ground and then Jackson walked to the other side of the park to avoid attention. When he got there, he found himself facing Chasey and said, "Oh thank God."

"Aww. That's sweet," she told him. "You ready?"

"More than you could possibly know."

Jackson followed her out of the park, and they began to walk towards the restaurant. "Why would you pick that park? That's the worst of the worst," he asked, as they strolled along, hand in hand.

"I don't know. They don't bother me. I guess you get used to them after a while. It's just a big easy landmark."

"I kinda hate this town."

Chasey shrugged her shoulders. "We all do, and we also love it. Fucked up, isn't it?"

"Very."

He told Chasey about his run in with Abigail and how she reacted at the mention of his brother. Chasey found that really interesting if her hugely widened eyes were any indication. When they arrived, the restaurant was completely packed and there was a line that went outside and around the building. It hadn't been like that earlier and Jackson frowned. "Maybe we should have made reservations."

"Maybe. We can at least make them for tomorrow while we're here," Chasey told him. She pushed through the crowd to the hostess at the podium, and asked, "How long is the wait?"

"Are you with him?" the hostess asked, pointing a thumb at Jackson. Chasey nodded and looked back at Jackson with another shrug. He put his arms up as if to say, I have no idea.

"There's no wait for you," the hostess said to Jackson, looking past Chasey as if she didn't even exist. "Chef Boston reserved a table for you when you spoke earlier. She has been waiting for you to arrive."

Jackson raised his brows at her and locked eyes with his date. "Oh, well isn't that nice," he said. He looked back at the woman behind the podium. "Please do tell her thank you for us."

"Tell her yourself," the woman said back, almost robotically. "Come this way." She grabbed two menus and then turned around and started walking through the crowded restaurant that was exceptionally loud with the clanking of silverware and the clinking of glasses and plates being stacked. The strange zombie of a hostess led through the entire restaurant through a doorway and into a separate room. The carpets and drapes were blood red and the tables and chairs were polished black wood. Before Jackson could ask, the hostess said, "This room is for the esteemed guests. Chef Boston will be with you shortly."

Neither Jackson nor Chasey said anything as they took their seats at a table in the room's centre. As soon as they sat, a man in a tux came in and lit two candles, placing them on the table. He hurried away without speaking and another man came and sat at a big grand piano in the corner. He immediately started to play some romantic Italian sounding music.

"The royal treatment is a little creepy," Jackson said in a hushed tone.

Chasey smiled and it lifted some of his tension. "Yeah. Maybe they really are going to eat us. By the looks of the decor, maybe they're vampires."

Jackson gave a forced laugh, but he didn't sell it. For all he knew, she could be right. She sighed then and reached across the table to take his hand in her own. "Thanks," he told her. "For being here with me, for everything. I hope playing detective doesn't get you killed."

"Me too," she said, squeezing his hand.

They felt someone's presence and when they looked up, Abigail was standing beside their table. Neither of them had heard anyone enter or seen anyone move and they both jumped at the sight of her, gasping out loud. Abigail gave a small, composed laugh and said, "I didn't mean to startle you. My apologies."

"No, it's fine," Jackson told her, selling the forced smile a little better this time. "I feel bad. Why are we getting special treatment over everyone else?"

Abigail grinned and Jackson fought the shiver it brought him. Something about her just made his skin crawl. "Why, you said your brother is a famous restaurant critic, did you not? I can't have you running back to him with a bad review now, can I?"

"I see," Jackson said with a nod. "Well, in that case, let's start off with one of your finest wines, something you recommend." He winked at her.

"Of course." With that, Abigail was gone. Neither he nor Chasey saw her move. It was like she just vanished.

"Well, that's gonna make it hard to sneak around," Chasey said with a chuckle.

"You're not kidding," Jackson said, sighing his frustration.

"I mean I was actually."

Jackson gave a genuine laugh then. He looked across the table at the beautiful yet exotic woman that was seated there. This fine creature had an almost magical way of lifting his spirits and calming him. His heart rate went back to normal and his breathing came back to him, his anxiety subsiding. Then a bottle of wine came down in between them and they both jumped again, but this time they found themselves laughing. Abigail didn't seem to understand the humour and was rather stoic in pouring the wine into their glasses.

"This is a house wine," she said through her lips that matched the decor. "It's a red blend. I am confident you will find it to your liking. Take some time to enjoy it before I return for your order."

Jackson and Chasey both thanked her. Then she was gone. Jackson snapped his fingers, knowing she was going to up and disappear, but Chasey was looking over his shoulder at the doorway to the room. "She actually did exit properly," she said to him. "I saw her go out, but I don't know how she got from here to there so fast."

"And so quietly," he added.

"Yeah." Chasey picked up her menu and started to leaf through it, looking over the options. "Are we actually eating? I kinda feel like we have to now."

"Well, we're definitely ordering," Jackson said, looking at his own menu. Then he set it down and sipped the wine. "Damn. It actually is really good."

Chasey was holding her glass but looking sceptical. "Like magical, turn you into a zombie, good?"

"I guess we'll find out," Jackson said, taking another sip. His date gave a reluctant sigh and joined him, following her own sip with an "Mmmm."

A minute later, Chasey asked, "Now what?"

Jackson sighed. "I need to find the restroom and wash the junkie spit out of my beard. Will you be okay by yourself?"

"Of course, but I'm feeling relieved that I hadn't kissed you yet."

"Yeah. Sorry. I'll get it good and clean before I find your lips, don't worry."

Chasey laughed. She said, "In the meantime," and kissed his cheek. Then he got up from his seat. It didn't make even the slightest sound on the plush red carpeting. This room was a complete contrast to the main dining hall. Jackson waved at his date and then hurried out, wanting to get the bathroom and back as quickly as possible.

When he reached the hall, things were tiled, and drab and it felt like stepping into a different world. The hallway was long and there were several doors that he didn't notice before. He decided to investigate and walked along checking the doors while watching for anyone that could find his behaviour suspect. The first door was a simple supply closet. The second was locked and that piqued his interest. He reminded himself to come back to it. The third was the women's room which he didn't need to or feel comfortable with opening. The third was his own bathroom. He went inside and found it was lavish marble that shined, and he went right to washing up.

A stall door opened behind him. Jackson raised his eyes to watch in the mirror. He didn't truly trust anyone in this place. A burly middle-aged balding man stepped out with a groan, tugging on his pants and patting his belly. He laughed for Jackson's sake and waddled to the sink beside the one Jackson was using. "This place is great, but the food gets ya, doesn't it?"

"Maybe. It's my first time," Jackson said, cutting off the sink and selecting a towel to dry his hands on. Real towels. It's nice but is it sanitary?

The man chortled as he began to wash his hands. "Oh, get ready. You'll be back every day after this."

Looking at the manmade Jackson think. He was trying to remember the other patrons when they walked through the dining area. If his memory served him correctly, many of them were overweight, which seemed unusual for a vegan place. How fattening could it be? If they were eating here every day, there was a direct correlation between the weight and health of the patrons and the food. Something about that felt significant to him.

"Well, enjoy," he said with a friendly smile before hurrying out of the room. He felt like he had left Chasey alone in this creepy place for too long. His heart was beating quickly with the tension of it. He expected to get back and find her missing, knowing he didn't pass her in the hall where she would have to have gone to go to the bathroom. He imagined her being dragged away to a slaughterhouse, screaming, only to realize she was next to his brother's dead body, limbless and hanging on a meat hook.

When he reached the fancy secluded room they had been put in, he pushed the door open in a hurry and all but jumped into the room. Chasey was sitting at the table just as he had left her but with an empty wine glass. She shot him a peculiar look for barging in the way he did. "Something happen in the restroom I should know about?" she asked as he came back to the table.

"No, sorry," he said. "I'm just really on edge."

"I can see that. Try this corn beef hash. It's actually amazing. Abigail returned while you were gone. She said you were looking to eat Irish, so she brought it as a free appetizer."

"I'll pass," he said, looking at the dish like it was full of live bugs.

"Suit yourself," Chasey said, digging in for more.

"Between the supply closet and the bathrooms is a locked door. I wish I could see what was behind it."

"I can pick the lock and get in before anyone sees me," Chasey told him casually, shoving a forkful of corned beef in her mouth.

Jackson shook his head. "What can't you do?"

"I'll let you know when I find out."

"I adore you."

"I know."

"Alright, so wait until we actually order our meals and then you can go to the bathroom. Be careful. Make sure no one sees you and then find out what's in that room and come right back. Don't get yourself into trouble. If you're gone more than eight or nine minutes, I'm coming looking, and I swear I will shoot anyone that so much as thinks about doing you harm."

"Okay, but maybe you can hurt me in a good way later."

"I can, and I will. Let's just survive this vegan horror story first."

Chasey nodded.

The door flew open with a bang like there was a great wind. Jackson and Chasey both turned to look that way. There didn't seem to be anything to see but the door was wide open, leaning against the wall. They stayed looking for a moment, waiting to see if anyone came through. There was no movement, no shadows, no sound, just the open door.

When they turned back to face each other, Abigail was standing beside the table. "Damn it!" Jackson yelled, pounding his palm down on the table. "You've got to stop doing that! I don't know how you're doing it, but I don't care. Just stop before you give us both a heart attack. That won't make for a good review at all."

The chef stood there stoically beside their table. She blinked, her only reaction to being yelled at. "I'm sorry but I'm unsure what you're referring to. Are you not pleased with the corned beef hash?"

Jackson glared at her, but Chasey smiled. "It's wonderful," she said. "I can't believe it's vegan. I think we're ready to order our meals now."

"Excellent. What will you have? I know Mr. D'Amico wants the Shepherd's Pie. What sides with that? It comes with mashed potatoes and gravy."

324

"I don't know. How about some mac and cheese?" Jackson said.

Chef Boston's brows raised when she looked at him. "That doesn't truly fit the meal and it's all heavy then, not a great pairing."

"It's what I want," Jackson sneered. "Thank you for your hospitality, Abigail."

"I'll take the tempeh steak and roasted red potatoes with garlic butter sauce, side of broccoli and cheddar," Chasey said, handing the host her menu.

"Vegan cheddar?" Jackson questioned.

"There's vegan everything these days," Chef Boston said with an ominous smile. "Isn't it wonderful?"

"Truly," Jackson said back with a roll of his eyes. He waved his hand, knowing she would be disappearing.

Chasey frowned and patted his hand. "Being high strung isn't going to find your brother. I'm going to check that door, err, I mean, go to the bathroom." She got up from her seat with a small chuckle and stopped at his to lean down and kiss his lips. "Thanks for washing that nasty beard," she said with another laugh before exiting.

Jackson turned in his seat to watch her leave. "Be careful," he said.

Chasey gave him a thumbs up and made her way out, gently closing the door behind her. Jackson immediately felt nervous. Was I wrong to ask her to do that? Did I just put her in danger? I shouldn't have even brought her here.

As the minutes passed by, his anxiety got worse. He was staring at the clock on his phone, his eyes rolling over to glance at the gun strapped to his side. He wondered when he was going to have to use it. He was drumming on the tabletop with his fingers, and glancing back at the door, trying to will Chasey to walk through it.

It was Abigail Boston that did walk through it though, carrying a tray of food. She practically floated to the table and laid the plates down gently before him, her eyes going to Chasey's empty seat. "She had to go to the bathroom," Jackson said. "Seems that wine went right through her."

"Hmm," was all Abigail said. She held the empty tray and stood there statuesque at the tableside. Jackson looked at her nervously, wondering what she was waiting on.

"Thank you," he said, almost impatiently.

"I must insist upon staying for your first bite," she said with her finest attempt at a genuine smile. It still made him shiver.

Jackson nodded. He swallowed the invisible bite that felt like it was already lodged in his throat and then he picked up his fork and pushed it down into the truly beautiful looking pie. The lentils and sauce oozed out as he did. He looked up at her and saw her staring at him with a fiery intensity. He felt wholly uncomfortable, but he knew that he wouldn't get her to leave if he didn't take the bite, so he shoved it into his mouth, chewed quickly and swallowed. He hadn't chewed enough, and he choked some and coughed. Then he patted his mouth with his napkin and sipped at his glass of wine. After which he looked up at the chef and gave her a thumbs up.

"Good?" she asked.

"Quite," he told her. "It really is. You're an

impressive chef Ms. Boston."

For the first time since he'd met the woman, or even seen her on television, her smile seemed real. She nodded and left with the empty tray. Jackson turned to watch and saw Chasey come in as she was going out. They had to move around each other. He almost sighed with relief, but he didn't want Abigail to hear that kind of reaction and think they were up to something. Once she left, he did stand to hug his date and kiss her before she sat back down.

"You were worried about me," she said with a grin and a gleam in her eye.

"Yeah, a little."

"A lot."

"Fine. So, what did you find?"

Chasey hesitated a moment, her eyes hanging on the door. When she judged it safe, she said, "It was an office. I went in and snooped around a bit. Everything was normal. There are files with the companies she gets ingredients from and a ledger on her finances, but everything looked fairly normal to me. I mean, I'm no expert, but there was no poison or eye of newt mentioned anywhere. There was a certification on the wall for her schooling. A ficus by the window. It was exactly what you would expect to find in a restaurant office, almost too normal honestly. There was the framed first dollar on the desk and a photo of the grand opening framed on the wall. There was no computer. Maybe she uses a laptop and carries it with her or she's old fashioned and really does just write everything on paper by hand."

Jackson sighed. He was really hoping that door

would lead to answers. "But you agree that something strange is going on here?"

"Definitely, but whatever it is, it isn't out in the open."

"Maybe I should get lost," he said using finger quotes. "And then find my way to the kitchen. That's where Leatherface or the cauldron would be right?"

Chasey laughed. "That's the spirit. Now you sound like me. Though, the police would have discovered those things already and this place wouldn't be open and booming with business if that were the case."

"You're right. So, what is it?"

"I don't know, Jackson, but this food really is amazing." Chasey shoved bite after bite into her mouth. Jackson just cast his eyes downward at his plate and stared at the contents like they were evil, like the pie itself had murdered his brother.

"Slow down," he told her. "We don't know what's in that stuff."

He jumped when he saw that Abigail was once again beside the table. "Would you like an ingredient list?" she inquired.

Jackson growled and pushed his seat back, standing up. "No. I'd like you to cut the shit," he said, pulling the gun from its holster and pointing it in her direction. Chasey's eyes went wide but she continued to eat like she was starving. "I know you know my brother and I knew you did something to him. You're doing something to everyone. Did he know? Is that why you felt like you had to get rid of him? Tell me what you did."

"Whatever are you saying? If you don't like the pie,

I can get you something else, but there is no need for all these senseless accusations," Abigail said, calm as ever.

"I said cut the shit." Jackson was angry now. His face was red with the rush of his boiling blood. "Don't make me put a bullet in you. I will. Start telling me the truth."

Chasey looked up at him, but she continued to clear all the food on her plate and then went for his meal afterwards.

Abigail looked at his gun as if it was a gnat that was annoyingly buzzing around her face. She sighed with irritation. "Fine. I guess this is the moment we've all been waiting for isn't it," she said. Then she clapped her hands and the floor opened under him and his chair. Jackson didn't have the chance to scream or fire his weapon. In a blink there was open air below him and he was falling into the darkness. As he fell, face displaying the horror he felt, he looked up and saw Chasey still seated and eating. Then he saw the floor close again and there was nothing but darkness. It was all around him, thick, tangible darkness. It was then that he found his scream.

"Oh dear. Don't be so dramatic," Abigail said as there was a buzzing sound and lights flickered and then blazed almost too brightly before dying back down to a normal bearable level. Jackson had landed on his bad back and even though his mouth had stopped screaming, his body had not. He was laying on concrete, tears in the corners of his eyes. His gun had come loose from his hand and scattered across the room when he felt the impact of the cement on his already damaged spine and pelvis. He did his best to look around, groaning with the effort it took to try to sit up.

Abigail was standing before him. She was no longer dressed in her chef's uniform. Instead she was wearing a long black flowing robe. Her hair flowed about just as wildly under the large brim of a tall pointed black hat. Behind and around her, everything was stone, spattered with the reddish-brown stain of old dried blood. There were large piles of human bones in the corners of the room, skulls that seemed to be staring at him. *Is one of those my brother?*

"What is this?" he groaned, his eyes darting over to the gun laying on the cold stone across the way. "What is going on here? Where is Joey?"

Abigail laughed. It was a loud, hearty, genuine laugh now that came from the pit of her. It was deep and bellowed through the room, reverberating off of the stone walls. "You're as terrible of a detective as your brother was a food critic," she said, stepping closer to him.

When she moved, Jackson was able to see behind her and spotted the oven for the first time. It was a huge old-fashioned gated oven, a waterfall of ashes and bones cascading out of the doorway onto the stones before it. Jackson's eyes grew with the horror of what he was seeing. It even took precedence over the pain in his back. "Did I just fall into Hansel and Gretel?"

Abigail gave her booming laugh again. "You think so small, Jackson. Yes, yes. It started there, a million years ago now, or at least it feels that way. But I couldn't just sit around in the woods waiting for people to stumble

330

into my cottage. I would starve to death. I needed to take my act on the road."

Jackson remembered what the patrons like the guy in the bathroom. "You're fattening them up, all of them, eating them one by one. Why a vegan restaurant? Why not a burger joint or something more fattening?" He started to crawl on his belly across the floor towards his gun.

Abigail groaned this time and shook her head. "Number one, Jackson, is its business. You have to judge the area and go by demand. Number two is it's a better disguise. No one is going to suspect the vegan place of fattening everyone or cannibalism. Just the idea is absurd."

"I thought of it, and someone else will too," Jackson said. He was almost to the gun and reached his arm out, stretching for it.

"Oh please," Abigail sighed. She held her hand out and the gun slid away from him across the floor to her. She kicked it across the room towards the oven, far from him. Jackson just collapsed onto the ground, defeated. "I spellbind all the food, to make people crave more. I get tons of plump juicy morsels to still my hunger and I get rich in the process. It's really ingenious, wouldn't you say, Mr. D'Amico?"

Jackson used the wall to pull himself up into a sitting position. He was sweating from the pain and the exertion. "So, I was right. You did eat Joey."

The witch threw her hands up and shrugged her shoulders. "I did. And I didn't even have to fatten him up. He came to me fat already. I don't usually eat high profile people. Too much attention, but your arrogant brother didn't know a damned thing about good cooking, I'm afraid. I couldn't let him print that awful review and ruin what I have going."

"Asheville is a small city, Abigail. If people keep disappearing, it will lead to you eventually. You can't get away with this forever."

The witch bellowed her bassy cackle again. "Oh, my dear Jackson. This is a tourist town. Fresh meat comes here all the time. I almost never pull from the local population. Plus, the city itself gives me cover. They don't want to discourage tourism because it funds the town. They cover up the overdoses and shootings, the stabbings and kidnappings, keeping as much as possible out of the public eye. This progressive little hippie city is the best place ever for my operation. I can do this for a long time, until I can't. Then I will move on again and find a new way, as I always have. I've enjoyed this talk though. It gets a little lonely at times."

"So, what now?"

"Now it becomes a pity that you didn't eat your last meal. I really did make it delicious for you. Believe it or not, I did go to school and I am quite the chef, although I prefer my own food, burnt and crispy, full of fat and gristle." She laughed again and lifted her hand. Jackson felt himself being pulled away from the wall the same way the gun had been drawn to her. He panicked, his breaths coming in quick sharp bursts. He slid loudly across the stone floor, the ridges between stones bumping his pained back and adding to the soreness.

Abigail walked towards the oven and Jackson

dragged across the floor behind her, tethered to her palm by an invisible strand. He tried to grab at it but there was nothing there to grab. He gasped and fought but to no avail.

With her other hand Abigail lit the flames in the oven which immediately rose several feet, crackling and whipping with a fierce intensity. "Thank you for coming to Where It All Vegan," she said to him. "I hope you enjoyed your time here. Now this is where it all ends."

She dragged Jackson up to the edge of the oven. He couldn't fight the pull no matter how hard he tried. His sweating intensified as the flames licked at his face. Silently, he apologized to his brother and to Chasey for failing them. Then he started to lift off the ground towards the opening of the oven. He looked away from the flames and stared up into the witch's face. His eyes locked on hers and they held each other's gaze for a moment.

Then something his Abigail in the back. She lost her hold on Jackson who fell back to the ground and she stumbled forward. A cry on her foul lips, she fell into her own fire. Then Chasey ran up and closed the gate. Jackson looked up at her in shock and she graced him with one of her contagious smiles. The burning witch screamed from within the oven.

Jackson shook his head. "How?"

Chasey shrugged. "I watched you fall away, and I still couldn't stop eating. I knew something was wrong, that you were right, and she had done something to the food. So, the moment my plate was empty and I had nothing left to hypnotically gorge myself with, I went to the lady's room and stuck my fingers down my throat. It was admittedly not my finest moment. It still burns and I never want to do that again. Gross. Then I went back to the room and tried to figure out how the hell to get the floor open. It wasn't easy because there was no handle. She just opened and closed it with magic I guess, so I'm glad you kept her talking. Gave me a minute to use some of my pins to pry the damn thing up enough that I could get a hold of it. Then I saw her dragging you to the oven and I slipped down as quietly as I could while she was distracted. The rest you know."

"You are the most amazing magical creature I have ever encountered," he said to her as Abigail's screams died down and faded away, leaving only the screams of the fire.

"Says the guy laying on the floor in a witch's dungeon."

"Still true."

They both agreed that it was better not to call the police. The witch was gone. The town was safe, and chances were the police wouldn't believe a word of it. Chasey found a hidden door in the back wall behind a pile of human remains that led to a tunnel. She helped him up and together they limped down that dark tunnel until they came out under Helen's bridge which was supposed to be one of Asheville's most haunted attractions. "Makes sense to me," Chasey said.

Jackson just shook his head. Chasey called for an Uber and then sat beside him in the grass to wait for it. The car took them to Mission Hospital so Jackson could have his back checked out and make sure that nothing was actually broken. The ER doctor wanted x-rays, so they took him back. Jackson made up a story about falling off of a ladder. He told them about his previous injury. When he was in his room, he said to Chasey, "Any chance I can convince you to leave this city?"

She shook her head and flashed the smile that made him fall in love with her. "Nope. Asheville's a part of me. Asheville is what gives me the magic you so adore, you know."

Jackson sighed and winced at the pain in his back. "How can one place be so terrible and so great at the same time?"

"That's life isn't it? How about you just stay?"

Jackson frowned. "I can't. New York is a part of me just the same. It's where I belong."

"I had a feeling you'd say that. Well, you have my number. Maybe we'll get to go on another adventure sometime."

"I hope so," Jackson said, smiling through the pain. Then Chasey bent over him and kissed him hard on the lips, they said their goodbyes and he watched her walk out the room, his heart heavy. At least he got closure on what happened to his brother and with Chasey's help the witch paid for it too. He knew that he couldn't have done this without her, any of it. He would be dead right now instead of in a hospital bed, if it wasn't for her. Am I wrong to let her go?

A nurse came in the room then, with her head down, looking at a clipboard. "I just need to get your food order," she said. "Any dietary restrictions?"

When she looked up, Jackson was staring at Abigail's

twisted smile and his face paled. He pressed the button to call for help on his bed with nervous trembling fingers and Abigail started to cackle her deep bellowing wicked laughter.

The End...for now...

WHERE IT ALL VEGAN'S VEGAN MAC AND CHEESE AND SHEPHERD'S PIE

CREATED BY CHEF ABIGAIL BOSTON AND BROUGHT TO YOU BY CHISTO HEALY

Hi. If you're someone who wants to cut out meat, and dairy because you are dieting, you find it to be your moral responsibility, or you're trying to steer people away from what's really in your basement, these recipes are for you. Maybe you never want to quit eating meat and you just have friends that don't or a girlfriend you're trying to impress or a private detective that is onto the fact that you're eating people. No matter what the reason is that you're looking for delicious vegan food, I'm going to help you cook it.

Let's start with the Mac and Cheese because it's fast and easy, and has a lot less steps, though when you're making both, it's better to make the pie first because it will need time to bake and cool down and that will give you the time to make the mac and cheese and serve both hot and ready. Of course, you're your own person so you do it in whatever order makes you happy. I'm telling you how I would do it cund have done it, but I've never once read a recipe that I didn't change or tweak in some way to make it my own so I expect no less from you. Unless we're talking about people. When they're fat and ready, I just throw them in the oven. But we're not talking about people. We're talking about a nice Irish dinner plate of Shepherd's Pie and Mac and Cheese. So let's get started. Here's what you'll need:

A blender, a large (usually 8 qt) pot, and these…

Ingredient List
1 level cup of finely chopped cashews (small pieces)
1 cup of nutritional yeast
1 cup of sauerkraut (if you're vegetarian and not vegan - the saverne craft beer flavored kraut adds flavor - but for the vegan bunch I usually just stick with the jar of Silver Floss Kraut because it is fresher)
1 13oz can of unsweetened coconut milk
8oz (or half a container) of Follow Your Heart Dairy Free Sour Cream (this stuff is great!)
¼ tsp of Mustard Seed
¼ tsp of chili powder
¼ tsp of paprika (preferably smoked)
½ tsp curry powder
½ tsp turmeric
½ tsp onion powder
½ tsp granulated garlic
¼ tsp cumin
¼ tsp black pepper
¼ tsp coarse salt
1 tsp of fresh chopped basil
Then of course 1lb of your favorite vegan pasta. I prefer shells but many go for the traditional elbow noodles. It's mac and cheese. We're not talking spaghetti here. I have to say it because one person will do it and say I

didn't specify and just said their favorite pasta. I will eat that person.

Step one: Put all the ingredients (except the pasta!) into a blender starting with the cashews and going on down the list. Then blend it on a milkshake or similar setting if your blender doesn't have that. Also, buy a new blender. Yours sucks.
Blend it for a while, let it thicken and make sure the cashews get liquified. Sometimes I stop it and stir it up just to make sure it's all getting mixed well. Be the judge. I believe in you.
Step two: While your blender is going, boil a pot of water.
Step three: put pasta, a pinch or dash if you're feeling frisky of salt in the water and a splash of olive oil. This will prevent sticking. (but that wasn't on the ingredient list! - Fine. Don't do it. You do you. I need to show you my really cool basement)
Step four: Cook the pasta for 12 to 13 minutes until it's tender, stirring occasionally
Step five: Drain the pasta. DO NOT run cold water over it. Just pour it into the colander and let the excess water out and then pour it back into the pot.
Step six: Add a few pats of country crock plant-based butter w/avocado oil (absolutely necessary for survival if you're a vegan) and mix it up
Step seven: pour the blended vegan cheese sauce over the still-hot pasta and stir it up. Voila. There ya go. Delicious vegan mac and cheese. Though I'd prefer if you came to my restaurant and ate it there.

When you're done, I'll give you a tour and show you my basement. It's really cool down there. There's a cauldron. You don't want to miss it.

Moving along. Now that we've gotten the side made, let's delve into the main course: human flesh. No. Wait. This is vegan. Scratch that. Shepherd's Pie. There's no meat. Seriously. I don't eat the people til afterwards. They're much healthier and more tender then. Anyway…
Here's what you'll need for this one: another large pot, an even larger bowl, a potato masher, and a large skillet or wok…. oh, and these of course…

Ingredients
Your favourite frozen pie crusts (check to make sure there's no butter or animal biproducts used if you're vegan) My favourite is the Marie Callender Deep Dish. You get two per package and this recipe yields 3 pies so get two packages or halve the recipe. These are restaurant portions. It'll get you through most of the day or at least a huge lunch rush.
6 - 10 golden potatoes (sizes vary - however many you can fit in your 8qt pot)
8oz (the other half of the container) of your Follow Your Heart Dairy Free Sour Cream
16oz of early peas
1 ½ cups of sweet corn (drained)
1lb Beyond chopped meat (or your preference of vegan meat substitute. If you don't like any of that stuff a 1lb bag of lentils substitutes nicely)

1 cup of finely diced celery
1 cup of diced carrots
1 medium sized onion finely chopped into little bits
1 cup of diced shiitake and portobello mushrooms cut
into small chunks
½ cup of minced garlic
1 full stick of Country Crock plant-based butter with
Avocado oil
6oz of tomato paste
2 cups of vegetable broth
¼ cup of Orrington farms vegan beef base powder
½ cup of flour
½ tsp black pepper
½ tsp coarse salt
1 tsp of olive oil
1 tsp fresh thyme diced
1 tsp sage
½ tsp of fresh basil chopped
1 tbsp of fresh chives (this is a guesstimate because
I just chop the chives with scissors over the food -
usually about 8 stalks)
Parsley to garnish.

Step one: Boil the potatoes - skins on. It adds so much
flavour and they're not thick like russet skins or that
detective that won't quit
Step two: When the potatoes are good and soft, drain
them and put them into the large bowl and mash them.
Step three: Add the stick of faux butter and the sour
cream and whip until smooth and creamy. Then let sit
for now.

Step four: put the pie crusts in the oven to bake and be ready to fill. Make sure to stab the bottom and sides with a fork first or it will rise, and you don't want that, unless you're thick like a russet skin.

Step five: while all that is happening, throw a tsp of olive oil in the skillet and add the onions and minced garlic. Cook until onions are transparent.

Step six: add the (fake) meat and fry it on medium heat until its brown sauteing it with the onions and garlic

Step seven: add the other vegetables in one at a time, stirring as you go.

Step eight: add the tomato paste and spice and continue to stir

Step nine: add the vegetable broth and the (vegan) beef base and continue to stir it all together

Step ten: add the flour and then stir it again so the broth thickens, and the food becomes more like a paste with meat and vegetable chunks.

Step eleven: Add the human flesh. No. Sorry. Wrong recipe. Umm...for this step, just preheat your oven at 400 degrees

Step twelve: take the mix and pour it into the cooled down pie crusts. It should net three pies. Fill the crusts most of the way, maybe a centimetre from the top.

Step thirteen: Take your mashed potatoes from earlier and spread it on top like you would icing on a cake. It should come a bit above the top of the crust. If done correctly, it should look similar to a lemon meringue pie.

Step fourteen: Take your chives and chop them over the top of the pie onto the spread mashed potatoes or just sprinkle them if they're already chopped. Add the parsley as well.

Step fifteen: Put the pies in the oven and bake for roughly 40 minutes, checking them every few minutes after 20 (the potatoes will lightly brown on their whipped edges when done.)

Step sixteen: Pies will be hot and if you cut them immediately, the mashed potatoes will run like a witch is trying to eat them. Let it cool down some before you dig in. The great thing is once it is cooled, it will reheat perfectly and cut into nice looking pie slices. Add your side of mac and cheese we cooked earlier and you're good to go.

Step seventeen: if you're feeling fancy, or trying to impress a date, I like to add a drizzle of balsamic glaze on the plate before I put the pie slice on it and then throw a bay leaf in on the open space away from the pie and mac. This is completely optional and simply for presentation sake. Don't overdo it because you don't want the food tasting like a ton of balsamic.

Step eighteen: Lure the people who ate your vegan masterpiece to the basement and throw them in the oven

That's it. I hope you had as much fun as I did and you made and enjoyed this food, even if you're a carnivorous witch, or her next meal. See you soon. Happy eating!

No humans or animals were harmed in the making of this recipe or meal. That happened afterwards.

Lunch Break

Callum Pearce

'Pick your bag up, Faggot!"

Lee stumbled forward reaching out to pick up his school bag from where his main tormentor Craig Perkins had thrown it. As he got close to the bag, Craig kicked it hard toward his younger brother, Johnathan. The third bully, Ian Leach just stood back and laughed, for the moment. He only ever joined in when the punches started flying. Ian was the muscle of this group of fifteen and fourteen-year-old bullies. Craig, the ringleader, was a fairly good fighter himself but he found it always helped to have a bit of extra muscle hanging around. Just in case one of their victims got it into their heads to fight back. Fights were over quickly once Ian joined in; the big dumb idiot would just swing one of his big meaty fists. Usually, the person previously standing up to them would suddenly be lying down for them.

"What's up faggot, you going to cry?" Craig was laughing as he and Johnathan kicked the bag between them. Lee ran from one to the other trying to scoop his belongings up and make his escape. He stumbled forward and fell to the floor in front of Craig.

"Oh look, Little queer wants to give me a nosh," he grabbed Lee's head and shoved it into his crotch. "Loving that aren't you gay boy? you can't get enough."

They had cornered him behind the school, where the bikes were locked up during the day. He tried every day to get his bike and get away before his three regular harrassers had met up and made their way there. They were always looking for trouble. This had become a daily occurrence every lunch break or after school. He had never got on with Craig and his group of thugs. They had largely managed to stay out of each other's way, until this year. Craig had one day decided that Lee was the new target. The gay taunts had nothing to do with his actual sexuality. Craig just used those words as a way to justify his actions to himself. This is surprisingly easy to do when you're a young man of very few brain cells. Lee had promised himself that the next time they tried to corner him he would boot Craig hard in the balls and get away. This never happened. Lee didn't really have it in him to deliberately hurt someone, so instead every day he was shoved around, pushed, punched and beaten. Eventually, they would get bored and he could go home and fantasize about the revenge he would take next time.

"Stand up Faggot," Craig shouted.

"Fight back you fucking Fairy."

Lee stood up and closed his eyes waiting for the first punch to hit him, any minute now they would close in, throwing punches and kicks.

"What's going on here?"

Lee opened his eyes to see the staff entrance for the canteen was open and one of the dinner ladies, Mrs Williams was standing there. She was angrily staring at the boys.

"We're teaching this faggot a lesson," Craig shouted "What are you going to do about it?"

"You're Craig Perkins, aren't you? Is that Ian Leach? I'll be giving your names to the headmaster."

"And fucking what?" Craig picked up the bag and threw it at Mrs Williams. "Here fag, the old bag's got your old bag,"

Lee was almost impressed; he had never seen anybody stand up to Mrs Williams before. Dinner ladies were like royalty in English schools. Mrs. Williams especially, she could be very strict with most people, she had always been nice to Lee, but he was very well behaved. Her grey hair was always pulled back against her head with a small bun on top. Her face was gaunt and stern looking. Most normal people would crumble with the just right look from Mrs Williams. Not Craig, he stared at her, daring her to say anything. She stared back refusing to break eye contact until eventually, even Craig had to give up. He turned and walked toward Ian and his brother.

"See you tomorrow faggot," he turned back to Mrs Williams.

"Hey, I may even come and try some of that fucking slop you serve in the canteen tomorrow. Maybe I'll show you how to spell my name for the headmaster you old bitch," with that, they walked away and it was all over for Lee again until tomorrow.

"Are you okay?" Mrs Williams stretched out a bony hand to help him up from the floor.

"I'm starting to get used to it," Lee said, standing and taking his bag from her.

"He's a very unpleasant young man that Craig. You just stay away from boys like that."

"Believe me, I try to stay out of his way every day, but he always seems to find me at some point," Lee moaned. "I'm not even gay."

"That doesn't matter, people like that will always find something to pick on people for. They think it masks their inadequacies."

"It doesn't," Lee smiled.

"Well you get yourself home, I'll have a word with your year head and the headmaster tomorrow," with that, Lee jumped onto his bike and set off home. Mrs Williams went back to cleaning the school kitchens.

When Lee got home, he went straight to his room. He had ridden home in fear that Craig and his friends would catch up with him at some point and start the shite up again. Luckily, this hadn't happened. Now, alone in his room, that fear turned to anger. He threw his bag across the floor. He was picturing their taunting faces and wishing he knew what to do to stop this being his life, every single day. He imagined fighting back. In his head, he had all the best moves, legs sweeping, fists flying. In his mind, he gracefully brought all of them down and stood over their crumpled, bruised, bodies smiling as they writhed in agony. If only he was so swift and powerful in real life.

He hadn't made many friends in school. This meant

that most evenings were spent in his room playing games or dwelling on the events of each day. Lee barely spoke to his parents when he was called down for dinner. He just ate quickly still thinking about Craig and his friends, knowing that they would be waiting for him again tomorrow. After dinner, he made some excuse about homework and went back up to his room for the rest of the night. Putting on his headphones, he lay on the bed hoping the music would drown out thoughts of today and anticipation of tomorrow. Eventually, he fell asleep with the music still pumping in his ears.

He felt wet leaves beneath his bare feet as he walked through the local park on a dark, foggy night. Ahead of him, he saw somebody else walking slowly. Appearing and disappearing as they passed under the scattered lampposts dotted along the main path. He felt taller than usual as he closed the distance between him and the person in front of him. Striding closer on legs longer than his own, he saw that the person walking slowly in front of him was Craig. His first instinct was to turn and run but he didn't feel like he had any control over this body. Instead of turning and running he grabbed Craig's shoulder and turned him around. As Craig opened his mouth to speak Lee shoved his bony fist hard into his face. There was a loud cracking noise as Blood poured from his victim's nose. Without any signal going from his brain to his body, the fist swung again, slamming into his already broken, bleeding beak. Craig slumped to the floor. Lee jumped onto him and punched again several times. He had no idea where this strength was coming from. It felt as though he was occupying a far bigger, stronger body than his own and he had trouble controlling it. Even though it worried him that he had no control over this body, the feeling of satisfaction was far more overpowering than fear or confusion. Seeing Craig lying there half-conscious in pain made him much happier than he was comfortable with.

The hands were moving again now, Lee watched in horror as hands like claws ripped open Craig's shirt and started tearing at his chest. One hand pulled a knife from somewhere and sliced down the middle and then the claw-like hands dug in and ripped the chest open. He wanted to scream as the old, clawed hands scraped chunks of flesh from the boy lying on the floor and forced them into his own face. He could feel all of the hot, wet flesh filling his mouth. He could taste the coppery, salty flavour of the blood. Strands of raw flesh slithered between his teeth, making him want to throw up. Lee turned to gag and spit out the disgusting flesh that filled his mouth. Instead of seeing the leaves on the floor that he had expected, he saw that he was now kneeling on the carpet in his bedroom alone.

No vomit came, so he climbed back into bed. He still felt the disgusting texture of the raw, slimy flesh in his mouth. He still experienced the pain and the sensation of warm, sticky blood on those larger, older hands. It took him a while to shake off the feelings from the dream. Hardest to shake off was his guilt at the satisfaction he had felt whilst hurting the helpless victim. It gave him no small amount of pleasure to see Craig lying on the floor, taking the punches that he had so richly deserved. Even when the dream had taken a gorier turn, he couldn't get away from the idea that the little shit had deserved it. It made him feel good to imagine living in a world where bullying little bastards got their just desserts.

Lee got ready for school slowly the next day. Flashes from the dream kept forcing themselves to the front of his mind until he pushed them back down. When not dwelling on the dream, his body was filling with dread. His heartbeat faster, his stomach rolled. He couldn't stop thinking about running into his enemies again. He rode his bike slowly past the park on his way to school. He was almost expecting to see the scene from last night's nightmare. Blood, police tape, anything. There was nothing, everything seemed calm and normal. He knew it had been a dream obviously, but a small part of him had held on to a tiny bit of hope that it was actually some sort of premonition. Everything had felt so real at the time and for long after he had woken up.

Somehow, he managed to get to his first lesson without running into Craig and his friends. Now, as he waited for the register to be called, he could see that Craig's chair was empty. He thought for a moment again of the mutilated corpse lying on the ground in the park. In his mind, Craig stared up at him from the path, his chest sliced open and face smashed. Shaking those images out of his head, he allowed himself to feel a bit of relief. If Craig was sick, Lee may have a couple of days without being harassed. The other two would be unlikely to start anything without being goaded by that little prick. The day dragged but he was enjoying the fact that he hadn't seen Craig or his ratty little brother all day. He had seen Ian at the lunch break, but he just looked lost and vacant standing around on his own. He was nothing without the other two winding him up and shoving him in the direction of some poor kid whose turn it was to be picked on.

He breathed a long sigh of relief when getting his bike at the end of the day to go home. A whole day without seeing that evil smirking face. After just one day without him, Lee already felt a massive weight had been lifted from his shoulders. He rode home quickly and chatted happily through dinner with his parents. After his homework was done, he played on his games console in his room for a while, eventually he got into bed with a film playing on the TV.

A Picture of Johnathan, Craig's brother, flashed up on the TV. Lee sat up Rubbing his eyes and stared at the flickering screen. The scene changed and he was watching somebody roughly his age, they were sat in a bedroom at a desk. Behind them, a tall, hooded figure slowly crept up towards them. He stood up to look closer at the screen but as he did, he found himself standing in the room he had just been viewing. There was a rope in his hands, and he was walking slowly towards the seated figure. When he was close enough that he was sure the boy in front of him would be able to hear him breathing. The rope went quickly around the boy's neck. Lee crossed the bony clawed hands of the body he occupied over, pulling the rope tightly. The boy tried to stand up. The lamplight showed it to be Johnathan as Lee already suspected. The hands he had no control of were pulling the rope hard. Johnathan was clawing at it weakly and kicking against the wall behind the desk trying to push the attacker away. This body was strong. There was no way the young man was going to be able to escape.

Eventually, the legs stopped kicking, his hands fell to his sides and his body slumped further into his chair. Lee in the body he was occupying dragged the boy from the room and down the stairs, his head banged loudly on every step. Somehow, Lee knew that nobody was home to be disturbed by the noise. Johnathan was dragged from the house and thrown into the boot of an old car. The boot slammed shut and Lee woke sitting up straight in bed. He dropped the game controller he had still been holding. His hands ached as he still felt the pain of pulling the rope so tightly and struggling with Johnathan. He was ashamed to admit even to himself that again he felt satisfied. He hadn't even fought against what was happening. This time, he had passively accepted all of it. Enjoyed every minute of it was probably closer to the truth. He really hated those brothers. The idea of some monster picking them off was frankly delicious. He even wondered if somehow his own hatred of them had conjured some kind of terrible creature. A monster stalking the nights wiping out his enemies. It was a ridiculous thought of course but when he thought of Craig's empty chair in school, he was a little excited.

Arriving at school the next day, Lee was thrilled to see that Craig's chair was empty again. He thought about the dreams and wondered if there could possibly be something more to it. He knew that had to be highly unlikely. It could only really be a strange coincidence. Imagining never seeing either of them again was quite pleasant though. The day was going along quite nicely until after lunch when an announcement came out of the speakers around the school that there would be an emergency assembly in the main hall for his year. His heart jumped. This was highly unusual. Lee couldn't remember this ever having happened before. By the time he got to the assembly hall, everybody was mumbling and gossiping. Everyone trying to guess what this strange announcement could mean. Nobody was without a theory, but they were devoid of any useful information until the headmaster walked out in front of them with a policeman.

"Everybody settle down please," the headteacher shouted above the mumbling, gossiping crowd. After a few attempts, people started to face forward to watch the two men standing nervously in front of them.

"I know this is a little unusual, but I need you all to pay attention. We've had some very unsettling news about two young men who attend this school," The mumbling started up again.

"Please everybody, please calm down. There will likely be a reasonable explanation to all this, but it seems the Perkins brothers have gone missing."

Lee's heart was banging in his chest. He could barely hear what was being said as his hearing was being dulled by his rising blood pressure. The headteacher was saying that Craig had not returned home yesterday and then the next night his brother had disappeared. They assumed Johnathan had gone off somewhere with his brother and hoped that they would turn up soon. The school children were told that if anybody knew anything they would need to stay behind and speak to the policeman. No matter

354

how small the detail anything that could give a clue as to the boys' whereabouts. After they had finished speaking, the crowd of children started excitedly chattering until the headteacher told them all to go back to their usual lessons.

For the rest of the day, Lee couldn't think of anything much, other than his nightmares. He kept seeing the killer closing in on the boys and wondered if it was really possible to be seeing things through the killer's eyes. He even wondered if it was possible that he was committing the murders himself and somehow blocking it from his waking brain. There was never any evidence when he woke. No blood on his clothes or hands, no sign that he had left the room. The killer in the dream didn't feel like him either. The body he occupied was taller and the hands were nothing like his. He knew of course logically that it was unlikely that his dreams were anything more than a strange coincidence. The brothers had probably just run away from home. Craig probably left first, then his brother found out where he was and joined him. That seemed to be the theory the police had so far. It made a lot of sense. There had to be a reason that both the brothers had turned out the way they had. Usually, people who behaved as they did had problems at home.

Assuming that to be true, running away was the likeliest scenario. The rest of the day went quickly as he dwelt on the thoughts of the boys and wondered about what could have happened to them. It couldn't be denied that even with the strange things that were happening, the atmosphere at school was far better without the

Perkins brothers.

At home that night, Lee struggled to fully work out how he felt about everything. He was happy not spend the whole day in fear, waiting for Craig to appear shouting abuse. His day was far better without either of the brothers harassing him or encouraging their friend to. If he was truly honest with himself, he wasn't sure that he would feel too bad about it if he found out they were actually dead. As much as he hated to admit it to himself, their deaths wouldn't be a bad thing for a lot of people in his school. They made so many people's lives a misery for their own entertainment. In fact, there were probably several people, just in his school, quite capable of killing them both. After dinner, he played on his games late into the night. The idea of sleeping and dreaming again made him nervous so he tried as hard as he could to stay awake. Eventually, his eyes started to get heavy, his limbs seemed to sink into his bed.

Lee felt as though he was being pulled into the dream tonight against his will. One moment he was in his room, the next he was standing in a garden at night looking at a small shed with a warm light glowing from inside. Walking slowly to the side of the shed, he peered into the window. Ian Leach was inside, he was carefully poking a hole into either end of an egg and blowing the contents into a bowl. Looking around the shed, Lee could see cases around Ian of many different types of eggshells. They were all carefully arranged in display boxes, each one labelled with the type of bird it came from. The bony claw-like hands of the killer reached into the deep pocket in their coat and pulled out a hammer.

Lee could feel the weight of it as though the hands were his. He was walking against his will around to the side of the shed with the door on it. Even though Lee knew what was going to happen, he had no way of stopping it. He didn't really have very strong feelings about Ian either way. If he wasn't encouraged by Craig and his nasty little brother, he would probably never have any involvement with him at all. Surely killing those two was enough. He knew that it didn't matter how he felt about it. This was happening and he would have to witness it all.

He threw the door open in this stranger's body and swung the hammer quickly into the back of Ian's head. He half expected it to crack open like one of his collected eggshells, but it was a dull heavy thud. The hammer raised and fell again and again until Ian slid off his chair and onto the floor. His eyes were still open, but Lee knew he was gone. As he leaned over the body, he tried to see his reflection in the eyes. The body he was inside didn't look at Ian long enough for him to get a good glimpse. It was already busying itself pulling Ian out of the shed by his arms. The killer glanced a couple of times towards the house to see if anybody was peering out and then dragged the body towards the gate at the back of the garden.

Lee's alarm woke him before he could see any more. Images of all three boys filled his head. The violence of their deaths repeated on a loop. He needed to get to school and see if Ian turned up.

Lee dressed quickly, skipped breakfast and ended up arriving at school half an hour early. He waited at the front of the school, watching to see if any of the three boys turned up. He didn't see any of them until it was time to go to his form room for the register to be called. Craig's seat was empty again but nobody, so far, was talking about Ian. Minutes seemed to take hours as he attended his morning lessons until about 11am. Suddenly, a girl at the back of his class jumped up and ran out of the classroom crying. Everyone was baffled until her friend looked at the phone she had been fiddling with before her outburst. The teacher saw the girl's face turn white as she read, he rushed over to take the phone from her hand. Now it was his face the colour drained from and he quickly left the classroom, possibly following the girl who had rushed out. Lee turned to see the girl at the back of the class excitedly telling those around her what she had seen on the phone screen.

"The police have found three bodies in the park, kids! It's got to be the Perkins boys and somebody else," she was both horrified and thoroughly enjoying being the centre of attention at the same time. She licked her lips as eager eyes stared at her from around the classroom. "Ritual murder suspected it said, could be devil worshipers or witches or something."

"Witches! Come off it," someone said from behind him.

"Yeah really, it says that they all had organs removed, and a circle cut out of their stomachs."

Lee's head was swimming now, he felt as though at any minute he could slump forward into unconsciousness. That relief didn't come, instead, his head filled with images from his nightmares. When he felt less dizzy, he stood and walked quickly out of the classroom and headed outside for fresh air. His heart was pounding, and his stomach was turning over as though it were full of worms. He gulped deep breaths of air and bent forward trying to fight against his spinning head and stomach. When it didn't go away, he sat on the floor and carried on taking slow, deep breaths. There was no point going back to his lesson now. Everybody would be excitable and gossiping or upset and crying. He decided to stay where he was until nearly dinner time, then he slowly walked towards the school canteen. He got there early and could see Mrs Williams setting out the food on the counters in anticipation of the hungry students arriving. He realized he hadn't thanked her yet for the other day so went over before the canteen would start filling up.

"Excuse me miss," Mrs Williams turned and smiled happily at him. "I wanted to say thank you for the other day."

"No need at all, I can't stand bullies."

"Have you heard the news about the bodies being found in the park, I think it might be them," Lee blurted out more than he had intended to say.

"And what makes you think that?" Mrs Williams asked.

"Well first, the brothers went missing and then Ian didn't turn up for school today."

"Could be a coincidence." Mrs Williams looked worried as it was clear Lee was starting to panic again.

"I think I may have dreamed the murders," he had said it without thinking as though, like in the dreams, he had no control over his own body. "I dreamed of all of them being killed and then they weren't in school the next day, Now their bodies have been found and everybody is talking about witches or devil worshipers," his voice was shaking as his mouth ran on in autopilot.

"A strong Witch could certainly make you see through their eyes. Perhaps they felt it was something you should witness." her straightforward, matter-of-fact tone cut through any doubt and uncertainty even before they could form in his mind. She was talking about witches as though they were just an everyday problem around these parts, and he didn't even question it.

"They had all had body parts removed."

"Yes I heard on the radio earlier," he glanced at her bony, claw-like hands as she started to put out the trays of hot food. People were starting to file into the canteen waiting to get their dinner, so he stepped out of the way a bit.

"Liver, heart and a chunk of their stomachs I heard," she said.

For a moment, he thought he saw bruises on her knuckles, but they faded before his eyes. His imagination was clearly playing tricks on him.

"Sounds like somebody turned them into the thing they hate the most," she grinned.

"What? Gay?" Lee asked bemused.

"Not quite,"

"Eww miss what's that?" a girl at the front of the newly formed queue pointed to a tray with meatballs and gravy in it.

"Faggots dear, an old English dish… Now don't be childish, don't snigger. It was a dish long before it was a Diss," Mrs williams explained.

360

Lee looked in horror at the tray of food and back at Mrs Williams smiling face.

"They're just meatballs made with offal. Very tasty and very good for you."

"What do you mean offal? " the girl asked. She was already sure she wasn't going to like the answer.

"In these? Heart, Liver and a little bit of fatty stomach meat. It tastes much better than it sounds."

"Ooh no thanks, I'll just have the chicken," the girl shuddered dramatically as Lee stared at Mrs Williams. She was happily carrying on with her work as the pieces of the puzzle slowly fitted together in Lee's head. She looked over at him and smiled.

"Must be a relief, hey, knowing you've seen the last of them?"she asked.

"But they're dead," Lee mumbled.

"Probably for the best,"

He remembered the strength he had felt occupying her body. It was hard to believe the old woman stood in front of him was capable of such violence. Now people were queuing up to take a plate full of his tormentors. Unknowingly munching into the people who had made his life a misery. He needed to warn them, to say something. No way could he watch them tucking into their dinner knowing what he knew. All of those people that in all his time in school had never really bothered to get to know him. All of those who had walked past him when he was being pushed around by the bullies. He felt relieved every time somebody chose the chicken dish but horrified to watch the tray of faggots emptying quickly. Lee did nothing to stop them.

"Are you doing okay there young man?" Mrs Williams asked. Lee hadn't moved from the counter he was just watching in horror as people on different tables tucked into the awful dish in front of them. When he saw somebody taking a bite of the large disgusting looking meatballs, he remembered the feel and taste of Craig's raw flesh in his mouth.

"Aren't you worried you'll get caught?" Lee asked when Mrs Williams had finished serving people and stood next to him on the other side of the counter.

"Witches don't get caught. Besides whatever they are looking for, it certainly isn't going to be a frail old dinner lady, is it? You wouldn't say anything, would you?"

"No of course not, no. Who would believe me anyway?"

"Precisely." She picked up a chip and ran it through the gravy left at the bottom of the faggot tray. "I don't know about hot or cold, but I find revenge is a dish best served with chips."

Lee was surprised to find himself laughing along with her as she chuckled at her own terrible joke. They both smiled as they watched the school kids happily scoffing down gravy covered lumps of the group of bullies.

TRADITIONAL BLACK COUNTRY FAGGOTS

CONTRIBUTED BY TIM MENDEES

500g Minced pork liver
1kg Minced pork
1 bunch of sage
1 bunch of Thyme
3 Cloves of Garlic
Salt & Pepper (to taste)
300g Caul fat (soaked in water)

Peel and chop the garlic.
Finely chop the herbs
Pre-heat the oven to 150c
Put the liver, mince, herbs, garlic and seasoning into
a large mixing bowl and mix until it goes sticky. I
find it easiest to use your hands for this. If you are
squeamish, you can use gloves or a spoon if necessary.
It's important that the mixture is sticky and even or they
can fall apart while cooking.
Drain the caul fat. Spread it out on your work surface
and place some of the mixture in the centre. I like them
quite fat and juicy so about 200g, but this is entirely up
to you. Small ones work too. Wrap the mixture in the
caul fat and allow to relax for 5-10 minutes.
Place the faggots in a roasting tin and cook in the centre
of the oven for one hour.
Once they are cooked, serve with mash and peas in the

traditional Black Country style.
Onion gravy is a nice addition, but the juices poured
over the faggot and mash will suffice.

FEATHERS OF FEAR

TIM MENDEES

"If yer after my birds, asshole... I'll put a bullet in yer melon head!"

The clattering, banging and muttering of hushed voices had abruptly stopped as Bob neared the barn that housed his eighty-plus plump turkeys. He was sure that the disturbance was something to do with Vince. He should have fired that creepy bastard months ago; leaving it until November was just asking for trouble. The other hands had warned him that he was up to something, with his weird old books and candlelight chanting in his rusty trailer. Bob should have expected him to come back tonight. After all, it was slaughter day tomorrow.

Bob broke open his trusty shotgun and inserted two shells loaded with rock-salt and buckshot. If someone was after his livelihood, he was damn sure that their death would hurt and hurt bad. "Damn you, Vince, I'll fix you good." Snapping the barrel shut, he marched with purpose towards the barn.

Vince had found himself on Bob's personal shitlist

after the discovery of two of his prized Bourbon Red's with their throats cut in the woods behind his home. Suspicion quickly fell on the gangly youth due to the ritual nature of the cull.

Feathers and blood had been daubed and placed on a cinder-block in a strangely overlapping star design. Yellowish wax from foul tallow candles had been mixed and blended with the poor bird's innards into a glistening paste then painted on the ground in a circle around the stars with a bundle of bound feathers. Bob had flown into an incandescent rage and threatened to beat the name of the perpetrator from the assembled hands. It didn't take long for each one of them to point their grimy fingers in Vince's direction.

Storming up to Vince's trailer with his fists balled and his teeth clenched, he thundered on the door and demanded Vince show his face. As soon as the door opened, his fate was sealed.

Stinking of moonshine and festering blood, Vince staggered into the light with bloodshot eyes. Bob looked him up and down and practically exploded at the sight of bloodstains and ginger feathers engrained in the man's tatty dungarees. In the next second, Vince was on his backside with a bloody nose and told to have his trailer gone by sundown or it would be set on fire... Vince did as he was told.

Vince's actions had confused more than one of his fellow hands, he had always professed a love for the unfortunate creatures that had bordered on the paternal. Bob hadn't given his motivations a moment's thought, he just wanted him gone.

In the week following the incident, Bob had deeply regretted not going further than flattening Vince's nose, now he was fixing to right that regret. Yanking the weathered wooden doors to the barn wide, he stepped into the darkness with his finger on the trigger.

"Show yerself... I'll make it quick!"

The interior of the barn was still, preternaturally so. His heart skipped as his eyes adjusted to the gloom, and he didn't see a single turkey in the shallow cone of vision afforded by his low-power flashlight. There should have been pandemonium, startled turkeys usually erupted into a frenzy of mad gobbling and flapping feathers, but not tonight.

"Nobody messes with my goddamn birds, asshole... Show yerself.

The only sound was the gentle clanking of the feeding apparatus. Grumbling obscenities, he stalked towards the inner gate, opened the mesh door and stepped into the run. Peering ahead, he became suddenly aware of a huge black mass at the back of the room. It was his precious turkeys, every one of them was huddled at the rear of the run staring at him with their glistening black eyes.

"They aren't yer birds any more, Bob." A hollow-sounding voice announced from the rafters.

Shining his flashlight upwards, he revealed Vince's grinning face, leering down at him. "Get yer ass down here!

Vince chuckled and took cover behind a stout wooden beam. "I don't think so, Bob... You'll have to get yer fat ass up here and bring me down."

Bob snarled and rushed forward before coming to a sudden stop as an icy chill gripped his heart and gave it a good squeeze. Fighting for breath, he flashed the light around him and was aghast to see that he was standing in the dead centre of another circle of wax and giblets. A dizzying cyclone of straw, corn and turkey droppings rose around him, pelting and scratching his ruddy features.

Stepping out of the shadows, Vince stood above Bob, laughing manically, with a mason jar of hot sticky blood in his hands. "Mankind has said thanks for far too long, doncha think?"

"Wh... What are you... talkin' about, you crazy bastard?"

Bob's ire was cut short as Vince upturned the jar and covered his head in turkey blood. "It's time for the turkeys to give thanks! … Iä! Iä! Gobbuth'akka!

Bob screamed as two swirling purple eyes appeared above the horde of turkeys at the back of the room. They glowed and shimmered, casting the barn in oddly unnatural shadows. Trying desperately to move, Bob looked in horror as an enormous hooked beak appeared under the eyes. It would have been a mercy if that had been the true extent of the horror, but sadly, it wasn't. In place of a turkey's wattle was a writhing mass of slippery tentacles that whipped and coiled in the air just above the turkey army.

On the point of fear-induced apoplexy, Bill could only stare in terror as the turkey god, Gobbuth'akka, unleashed a hellish din and sent its kin on the attack.

Feathers flew, and blood splattered as the turkeys

fell on their prey. They pecked and scrabbled at the farmer's neck until his blood had joined the circle, and his head was severed. One slender tentacle lashed across the barn and snagged Bob's noggin. With a crunch and a splat, Gobbuth'akka enjoyed his feast and gave thanks for his release...

* * *

The assembled guests at the annual Arkham County Farming Society thanksgiving feast were mildly perplexed when they sat down in the Miskatonic University canteen and glanced at the menu. For a start, there was no turkey; not a wing, not a drumstick. Burley men in pilgrim hats grumbled amongst themselves at the break in tradition. The other thing that ruffled their feathers was the inexplicable absence of Bob Whateley, Dunwich's premiere turkey farmer. Their displeasure was quickly quietened by the arrival of the mayor.

After the mayor's droning speech and the rasping parp of the military band, the students from the catering college across town appeared with trays of steaming hot food. All gripes were quickly forgotten as the head chef unveiled the turkey substitute... a massive joint of roast pork.

As the chef set about divvying out the generous portions, nobody questioned the general length of the porker, nor the strange 'brand' on the skin. Sure it may have looked like a tattoo of a turkey in a gun's cross-hairs, but it was obviously some kind of student prank.

In the end, the guests went away happy with full

bellies and a rosy glow. The meal had been superb.

From the corner of the canteen, masquerading as a waiter, Vince chuckled as his foe was devoured... His god would be very thankful indeed.

THE PERFECT THANKSGIVING OR CHRISTMAS TURKEY

CONTRIBUTED BY TIM MENDEES

Rapeseed or Sunflower oil for cooking
1 x 5kg/11lb free-range turkey. Ask your butcher to
remove the wings and neck and chop them into 1 inch
pieces.
40g/1½oz unsalted butter, softened to room temperature
2 pinches flaked sea salt
2 pinches freshly cracked black pepper
200ml/7fl oz water
salt and freshly ground black pepper (to taste)
1-2 tsp cornflour (depending on how thick you like
your gravy), dissolved in 1 tbsp cold water
Balsamic Vinegar (to taste)
Roast Potatoes, seasonal vegetables and trimmings, to
serve

Method

Remove the turkey from the fridge and leave to rest for
an hour until it is room temperature.
Preheat the oven to 220C/Gas 8.
Heat some oil in a large, heavy-based roasting tray on
the stove top. Add the wings and neck and fry for 8-10
minutes, turning the pieces over every 2-3 minutes, or

until evenly browned all over.

Use a small bowl to season the softened butter with the salt and cracked black pepper. Using a pastry brush, or your hands if you are feeling brave, smear the seasoned butter all over the turkey. Add any remaining butter to the roasting tray.

Place the turkey on top of the wing and neck pieces, then roast in the oven for 30 minutes.

Remove the turkey from the oven and baste with the juices.

Reduce the oven temperature to 150C/Gas 3.

Pour the water into the roasting tray, then return the turkey to the oven and continue to cook for a further 1 hour, basting the bird with the cooking juices every 20 minutes.

At the end of the cooking time, test that the turkey is cooked through by pricking the thick part of the thigh with a fork or skewer. If the juices are clear, the meat is cooked. Alternatively, use a meat thermometer; if cooked, the temperature should be 65C for 10 minutes, or up to 74C for 2 minutes. If the turkey is not fully cooked, return it to the oven until the juices run clear.

Remove the turkey from the oven and transfer it to a large, deep-sided tray. Set the tray it was roasted in along with all its lovely juices aside for later. Let the turkey aside to rest for preferably 1 hour. This is a relly important part of the process which allows the meat to become tender and succulent as the juices inside the meat become more evenly distributed throughout the bird. Make sure you do this step, you will thank me for it.

While the turkey is resting, get your spuds, trimmings and veggies on the go.

When you're almost ready to serve the meal, return the roasting tray used to cook the turkey to the stove top. Bring the cooking juices to the boil over a medium heat, scraping up any burned bits from the bottom of the tray using a wooden spoon.

Tip the juices released by the turkey as it was resting into the gravy. Season, to taste, with salt and freshly ground black pepper. Add a few drops of Balsamic Vinegar to the mixture. This will lift the meaty flavour and is an old chef's trick.

Reduce the heat and simmer the gravy for five minutes then stir in the dissolved cornflour and cook until the gravy has thickened. I tend to use a balloon whisk on this bit to avoid clumps.

Strain the gravy into a jug and keep warm.

Carve the turkey and serve with the spuds, trimmings and vegetables. Pour over the gravy.

Now would be a good time to say thanks to Gobbuth'akka. After all, you don't want to end up on his table, do you?

MORE FROM BREAKING RULES PUBLISHING EUROPE

Novels/Novellas

Face of Fear by C. Marry Hultman
9789198671001

Dawson Junior G3 by Brian Wagstaff
9789198671049

Boy in the Wardrobe by Esther Jacoby
9789198684018

New Life Cottage by Esther Jacoby
9789198671056

The Wait by Esther Jacoby
e-book:https://books2read.com/u/4Dgz8Q

Liebe ist Warten by Esther Jacoby
9789198671070

Das Cottage by Ester Jacoby
9789198684070

Musing on Death & Dying by Esther Jacoby
9789198671063

Earth Door by Cye Thomas
9789198671025

An Odd Collection of Tales By Cye Thomes
9789198684124

Graffiti Stories by Nick Gerrard
9789198671018

Punk Novelette by Nick Gerrard
9789198671087

Struggle and Strife by Nick Gerrard
9789198684049

Fake Escape by Natalie Hughes
e-book:https://books2read.com/u/bMXL5X

Murder Planet by Adam Carpenter
9789198671032

Generation Ship by Adam Carpenter
9789198684063

Cold as Hell by Neen Cohen
9789198684094

Six Days to Hell by E.L. Giles
9789198684087

Anthologies

Just 13
9789198684025

Lost Lore & Legends
9789198671094

Adventure Awaits

Volume 1
9789198684124

Volume 2
978-9198684155

Volume 3
9789198684179

Mortem Cycle

Death House
9789198684117

Death Ship
9789198684148

Death Beyond
9789198684162

Coming Soon

Hell Hath No Fury by Chisto Healy

True Mates by E.F. Vogel

Soldier's Song by C. Marry Hultman

Wicked West Anthology

Rise and Fall Anthology

Find us at:
http://www.breakingrulespublishingeuro.com

www.ingramcontent.com/pod-product-compliance
Lightning Source LLC
LaVergne TN
LVHW031428170726
843492LV00010B/2900